SHADOWS OF DIVINITY

BOOK ONE OF THE ENOCHIAN WAR

LUKE MITCHELL

To the lost ones, and to the ones not yet found.

CHAPTER I
APOSTATE'S FOLLY

For ours is not to ask, but to serve.

That's what they'd always told us, at least. Which is why I didn't ask when I once again found myself hunkered down behind a slug-riddled skimmer, gritting my teeth as another barrage of shots smashed into the vehicle's rigid plating. I just squinted against the sunlight, gauging distances and angles, counting rough numbers in my head.

Then I spun from cover and dropped two of the rebel bastards in the space of one breath.

Crack-crack. Crack-crack.

The rifle kicked in my hands. Two red-garbed forms dropped.

The rest opened fire.

I was already back behind the skimmer, adjusting my grip on the rifle, wondering if I could shift forward and manage a clear shot from the hood. The clang of a slug ricocheting from that direction said no.

For now, they had me pinned. So I dropped back down to sit out another wave of hostile softsteel, studying the patterns of brilliant sunlight pouring through the cracks between the sprawling towers of the city.

Notwithstanding the half-dozen men trying to kill us, it was actually quite the beautiful day. And besides, it wasn't like these particular apostates were much of a real threat. Still, no excuse to be anything less than perfect.

Through discipline, divinity, after all.

No sooner had the mantra run through my head than a throat cleared

"

beside me, and I looked over to find Johnny closing down the mint green message display of his palmlight with a quick curl of his fingers. He sighed and scooped his own rifle up from the ground—the very antithesis of discipline. When he spoke, his tone was nonchalant, as if we weren't sitting there amidst a hail of apostate gunfire.

"But seriously, man, he's definitely up to something. And can you blame him? Kublich's servitor is stupid hot. I mean, have you seen the swells she's packing underneath—"

"Johnny."

He paused, mouth still hanging open, side-eyeing the tiny debris explosions kicked up by the slugs pelting into the permacrete wall we sat facing.

"Underneath Kublich's… files?" Johnny shot a sidelong glance at me and cleared his throat again. "I mean, uh, lovely lady. Great servitor, I'm sure."

"My father is not—"

Something crashed just over our heads, and what little glass remained of the skimmer's last window rained down between us. For a second, we both tensed. But the incoming fire was slowing down. Another few shots, and it died completely.

They were waiting.

And so was Johnny, who was watching me expectantly with those blue-green eyes that only made his blatantly red hair stand out that much more, even trimmed to Legion regulations as it was.

"My father is not running around with the High General's servitor," I hissed. "He… He wouldn't do that to my mom."

The skeptical arch of Johnny's fiery-red eyebrow let me know just how naive I sounded. But it was true, dammit. It had to be. And besides, we had more pressing issues.

Except now Johnny was laying his rifle in his lap. Holding my gaze all the while, he pointedly raised his hands up in front of his chest and made a series of emphatic squeezing motions, as if cupping handfuls of imaginary —and bountiful—bosoms. He cocked his head, his expression warring between an apology and a juvenile, *Right? Riiiiight?!*

"You're an idiot," I sighed, shaking my head. "And you're gonna get us killed."

Johnny affected his best offended face. "C'mon, broto."

He turned to peek around the rear of the skimmer. The storm of gunfire renewed almost immediately, and Johnny quickly scooted back into place beside me.

He shrugged it off.

I fixed him with a glare.

"Okay," he sighed, "but don't say I didn't warn you, buddy. Now let's go bag us some blasphemers!"

"Johnny, wait!" I cried. But he was already in motion.

He bounced to his feet and made for the next skimmer down the walkway with a sloppy diving roll. Rough as the landing looked, though, Johnny was back up in no time, shooting me a grinning thumbs-up from behind his new cover as a fresh blaze of gunfire kicked up dust and debris all around him.

"Such an idiot," I muttered.

But that idiot was my friend, and my friend needed some cover.

With the apostates focused on Johnny, I was clear to pop over the slug-riddled skimmer hood and drop two more of them. The rest quickly turned their fire back on me, and I ducked for cover. Before I even had time to give him the sign, Johnny capitalized on the opening, leaning out to take down another apostate while they were focused on me.

He could be a lot for some people to handle, but Johnny was damn reliable in his own way. And a crack shot to boot—there was no arguing that.

I skirted away from Johnny's position and around the front end of my skimmer, trying to get a clear angle at the remaining hostiles. The sound of Johnny's taunts and jeers followed me all the way as he applied liberal blindfire to keep our enemies' attention fixed on him.

I got in position and leaned out long enough to take down another man.

Two more left.

Off to the right, Johnny emerged from cover with a cocky assuredness that made my stomach fall.

"Johnny!" I snapped.

He wasn't listening.

His first burst cut our enemies down to one. The second burst never came.

Instead, Johnny jerked back, the gray fabric over his left shoulder staining dark with blood. He tried to raise his rifle one-handed, but two more shots punched into his chest. He fell to his knees, clutching at his belly, dark blood running from his mouth.

"Dammit," I growled.

Every damn time.

I stowed my anger and gunned down the last apostate with cold precision, then I strode back around the skimmer toward Johnny and his slowly growing patch of bloody permacrete. Nothing moved along the sun-soaked street. Nothing but the smoke winding up from the piles of burning debris our grenades had birthed at the beginning of the engagement.

They'd been twelve at the start. The magic number. Now they were zero—the other magic number. In the wake of the cacophonous gunfire of the past few minutes, the silence that hung in the air now was particularly somber and profound, broken only by the sounds of my boots on the pavement and the crunch of shattered glass underfoot.

I came to the spot where Johnny lay unmoving on the sidewalk and stopped, staring down at the bloody exit wounds on his back. "You're still an idiot," I finally said. "Just for the record."

The sound of Johnny's laughter rolled into my ears, though the body on the ground remained perfectly still. The effect was rather unsettling.

I straightened the fingers of my left hand to wake my palmlight and keyed a command on the azure holodisplay that appeared across my palm. The world of the sunny street momentarily flickered then rapidly disintegrated into the dark, empty space of the sim's default state. Johnny—or his projection, rather—stood a few paces from where his simulated death throes had occurred, shaking his head.

"Man," he said, "those death animations are just too creepy… Gets me every time!"

"That's only because you get yourself killed every time," I pointed out.

Johnny shrugged. "We can't all be as good as the mighty Haldin Raish, can we?" He extended his hands toward me in a gesture of mock reverence. "Ladies and goodfellows, the shining new star of Sanctuary. The son of the honorable Captain Martin Raish and—"

"All right, all right." I cut him off with a raised hand, resisting the urge to remind him that, even in our personal hours, these stunts of his still cost him points in the eyes of the Legion. "Just don't pull that crap at drills or they're gonna give you the boot and hand you over to the Sanctum. Then it'll be nothing but mops, candles, and praise be to Alpha for you."

Johnny made a face of mock horror, then reconsidered. "Still beats getting brigged, I suppose."

I smiled, but it faltered quickly enough when his expression sobered to that serious look he brought out only on rare, grave occasions.

"Seriously, Hal. I know you don't wanna hear it, but this thing with your dad… it doesn't look good." He dropped my gaze. "I'm sorry, broto. I'm just trying to be a good friend, here."

"I know that, man. It's just…" I consciously unclenched my jaw and relaxed the toes that had flexed tight against the soles of my combat boots. "He's just busy. He's always busy. You know that."

"Busy sneaking around with Servitor Swells?"

"We saw them one time and—"

"Twice."

"Fine. *I* saw them one time, you saw them twice, and neither one of us saw any reason to think it was anything other than routine Legion business we were looking at."

Johnny hesitated—which wasn't really something I got to say very often. "Did that really look routine to you the other day?"

I looked away into the empty darkness of the sim, clenching and unclenching my fists, trying not to think about the sight we'd so unluckily stumbled upon. My father speaking with the High General's admittedly gorgeous servitor as the two of them shuffled through the foot traffic outside central command. Both of them looking tense. Him taking her by the elbow. The two of them slipping off into a quiet dead-end nook. Together.

"Hal, all I'm saying is—"

"You know what? You're right. I don't wanna hear it. Don't even wanna think about it. He wouldn't do that to my mom."

"Yeah. You're probably right," Johnny said, though I could tell he couldn't quite convince himself. He glanced at his palmlight and wrinkled his nose. "Anyway, guess we'd better call it quits for now. Show's starting soon."

"Yeah, praise be to Alpha," I muttered with a grimace. Just what I needed right then—more grim thoughts. "Guess I'll see you tomorrow."

"That you will, my friend," Johnny said, pausing with his finger poised over his palmlight. "Try not to suffocate under all those heavy thoughts of yours before then, huh? It's gonna be okay, buddy. One way or another."

I thudded my chest in a sarcastic salute. He killed the connection and vanished from sight, leaving me alone in the open, plain gray space of the sim room.

For a minute, I stood there, awash in a rushing current of unsettling possibilities.

The rendezvous with the General's servitor had hardly looked routine, I couldn't argue with Johnny there. But there could've been a thousand reasons for them to whisk off for privacy—some urgent order from the General or an operational update that required immediate attention. Plenty of legitimate explanations, I told myself. But not so many that also explained why my father had been behaving so oddly for the past several cycles—because there was no denying something had been off with him lately.

He'd always been a busy man, of course. Being a Captain and an Alpha-blessed hero of the Legion came with a full schedule. But lately, it'd been excessive. The hours he put in were never-ending. When he did manage to make it home for supper, he looked disgruntled, his eyes bloodshot, his boots unpolished. Worse, I'd stumbled onto more than one whispered argument between him and my mom of late—which, while not completely unheard of, was absolutely not the norm.

Something was up. But an affair?

The thought made me queasy. I wasn't ready to buy it. Not until I had damn good reason to.

For the time being, I turned my thoughts to steeling my stomach, hung my practice rifle and sim mask on the wall, and headed down the hallway for the living room, preparing myself for the evening's morose show.

I FOUND my mom nestled up in the living room with her tablet and stylus.

"Writing?" I asked, settling down on the opposite end of the couch.

She looked up from under her neat brunette bangs and favored me with a warm smile. "An optimistic use of the word," she said, frowning down at her tablet, "but I suppose so, yes."

A pang of queasiness rippled through me at her smile, and at the thought that anyone—least of all my father—could ever betray someone so loving, so caring.

I pushed the baseless thought aside. "No Dad?"

I only ever used that word when it was just me and my mom. To his face, it was always Father, or Captain. Not because he demanded it. It had always just felt right that way. But today, the word tasted bitter on my tongue.

"No Dad," she confirmed with a little shrug of her eyebrows, thankfully missing my internal consternation. "He should be home soon, though. He'll want to watch."

On that note, we both turned to the wide display on the wall, which was already tuned to one of the WAN's live feeds. The shot rotated through multiple angles of the Great Hall of the White Tower as hundreds of the citizens of Divinity filed in, preparing to dutifully witness the execution of one Andre Kovaks for his crimes against Enochia, as decreed by the Sanctum.

The poor bastard.

Not that I didn't think Kovaks was a criminal. The evidence against him didn't leave room for argument there. Amongst other things, he'd committed half a dozen different break-ins, most of them involving offices belonging to Enochia's premier biotech giant, Vantage Corp. On the last one, he'd been apprehended trying to steal something directly from Vantage's main lab facility. How in Alpha's good grace Kovaks had gotten past the place's fortress of a perimeter, I could only guess, but the fact that he'd badly injured a few of Vantage's private security force hadn't helped matters for him.

No, it wasn't that I thought Kovaks was innocent. It was just that he was clearly mad as a softsteel sipper.

The Sanctum had branded him a terrorist and sentenced him to die for his heresy. Personally, I couldn't help but wonder if it wasn't simply a room at the medica and the ear of an attentive soothsayer he needed. I hadn't had time to follow the story completely, but the base had been alive with chatter these past days, and I'd at least caught the replay of the broadcast where they'd aired the audio log they'd found during Kovaks' arrest.

From what I'd heard, the guy clearly believed some serious corruption had penetrated the ranks of the Legion, and even the Sanctum. Maybe as high up as the High Cleric himself.

It was almost certainly bullscud, of course. But at least Kovaks had sounded marginally lucid up to that point. If he'd ended it there, I might've even found his claims marginally unsettling. But instead, he'd smoothly continued on to the wild stories about malicious aliens infiltrating Enochia and how the Sanctum and the Legion were going to take over the world and trample the people underfoot.

At that point, I'd had to laugh.

Maybe Kovaks had missed the part where the Sanctum and the Legion already *had* taken over Enochia. He'd definitely missed the part where our service in the Legion—and the service of those before us—had been the very thing that kept the world peacefully spinning along for the past thousand years.

And as for the alien invasion thing… well, that part didn't really seem to merit response.

So was Kovaks crazy?

Sure. Dangerous, even.

But did any of that mean he deserved to die for being delusional?

The warmth of my mom's hand finding mine informed me my moral dilemma did not go unnoticed. I gave her a weak smile and focused back on the screen.

At the end of the day, it didn't matter what I thought. For mine was not to ask, but to serve. Even if those words did make my skin crawl at times. But that didn't matter either. Because, once the Sanctum spoke, it didn't matter what anyone thought.

Who were we to question the will of Alpha?

I shot a furtive glance at my mom and saw some shadow of my doubts mirrored on her face. She was wearing that soft frown she got sometimes when she thought I wasn't looking—the one my father always seemed to meet with a significant look or a hushed whisper.

That frown made me nervous in a way I'd never really understood.

But before I could dwell on it, she turned to me, jostling me out of my rumination, and gave my hand a reassuring pat. "Alpha is wise, sweetie."

I made a face. "I'm gonna be a legionnaire in a few cycles, Mom. I think we might have to drop the sweeties."

She cracked a smile and was about to protest when a gentle tone chirped from the entryway behind us, announcing my father's return. He strode into the living room a minute later, his eyes distant and sunken with an evident lack of sleep.

That pang of sickening doubt stirred in my stomach.

"Come," my mom said, swinging her legs off the couch and patting the vacated cushion between us. "Sit, Love. You look exhausted."

For a second, he considered the armchair to the right of the couch, but then he came, plopped down between us, and started working on the stiff muscles above his prosthetic leg with strong thumbs. My mom, as she usually did, took over for him, and he let out a contented sigh, sagging into the couch.

Something about the familiar interaction was immensely comforting to me. Maybe it was simply that I couldn't process a world in which my father could betray my mom and still accept her touch so gratefully. Maybe it was the undeniable reassurance that, whatever else might be happening, my parents still loved one another.

Maybe it was just a fleeting hope that everything really was okay.

"Easy, guys," I said, squirming further onto my side of the couch as my father gave a particularly appreciative groan. "We're about to watch a man being executed, remember?"

I'd meant the comment to be light, joking, but of course it wasn't. We *were* about to watch a man being executed. Remember?

Praise be to Alpha.

Our collective attention shifted to the screen, where the WAN's darling field reporter, Barbara Sanders, was discussing the details of Kovaks' case and the mood in the White Tower as they awaited the High Cleric's arrival in the Great Hall. It was a grim task, but she handled it with respect. Behind her, down on the main floor of the hall, hundreds of people had amassed now. Legion soldiers and officers. Sanctum clerics and acolytes. Praetors. Civilians of all vocations. Everyone come to bear witness.

"Did you try the new sim build yet?" my father asked.

I couldn't tell if he was legitimately interested or just trying to disperse the gloomy cloud I'd accidentally cast over the room.

"Yeah. Johnny and I just cleared it."

He watched me expectantly.

"Okay, Johnny went demons to the wind and I cleaned up after he got himself shot."

That put a dark frown on my mom's face.

My father tried mirroring her frown but didn't quite succeed at extinguishing the amusement in his eyes. "That sounds more believable." He sobered. "Johnny needs to be more careful, Hal. You both do. You won't be tyros much longer. Someday, maybe soon, those won't be simulated slugs flying at the two of you."

The sentiment did nothing to alleviate the shadow on my mom's face.

Much as she supported our service to the Legion, I knew there was a part of her that detested the thought of us risking our lives for peace—a part that yearned for a world where the peace of Enochia could be maintained in a manner devoid of violence. Which was fair enough, I supposed, as applause in the Great Hall drew our attention back to the screen.

But that just wasn't the world Alpha had built for us.

In the growing thunder of claps and cheers, Barbara Sanders gave her last few kind words for the peace of Andre Kovaks' spirit, her dark eyes somber and sincere beneath her dark curls. Then she signed off, and the feed switched to a view of the High Cleric emerging at the top of the Great Hall's gigantic four-tiered dais.

The ancient man looked frail in his pristine ceremonial robes of white and gold. Kind of ironic, seeing as he probably had more power at his fingertips than any other man or woman on Enochia.

Two tiers below him was an equally ancient-looking gallows—the same gallows that had been used throughout the centuries of the Sanctum's reign, or so they said. Andre Kovaks stood atop the worn wood, adorned in black ceremonial robes that were emblazoned across the chest with a great red serpent.

Beneath shaggy dark hair and a grizzled beard, he looked haggard, his eyes wild. He was shouting something, but the feed's audio must have been coming directly from up on the High Cleric's dais, because we saw nothing more than silent, frantic animations of his lips until the feed cut to a close-up of the wizened head of the Sanctum.

In a calm, thin voice, the High Cleric began.

The words, for the most part, were familiar ones. He spoke of the importance of structure and stability on Enochia. The essentialness of duty and, above all else, of faith. Familiar words, sure. Especially for a Legion family like us. But Alpha's wrinklies, did the High Cleric know how to drive them home.

My parents watched attentively beside me, my father leaning ever-so-slightly forward until the High Cleric finished his spiel and granted Kovaks leave to deliver any last words. Kovaks had a lot of them. And most of it was every bit as loopy as his alien invasion conspiracy theories had been.

I turned to exchange a look of disbelief with my father only to find him even more riveted to the screen than he'd been during the High Cleric's speech. Something about his expression struck me as odd. But, given the outlandishness of the things Kovaks was saying, maybe it shouldn't have.

The High Cleric allowed Kovaks' frenzied ramblings to continue for a minute or so before he cut the feed to himself.

"Alpha grant you peace, Andre Kovaks," he said, extending a hand toward the hangman.

Kovaks didn't die neatly. Sometimes they don't. But a minute later, he hung limply from the tight rope all the same, his sway slowly diminishing alongside whatever life was left in his unconscious body.

It didn't sit right in my stomach. It never did.

But ours was not to ask.

I turned to my father, the man who'd taken me to observe my first Sanctum execution when I was only twelve. The man who believed so completely in the Legion and his service to Alpha that I'd heard it told around Sanctuary he actually gave thanks when Alpha allowed him to sacrifice his leg to save the lives of his old fireteam. Except it wasn't that belief I saw now. It wasn't the resolute certainty that it was divine justice that had just been served.

All I saw was unease. And doubt.

"I think..." he said slowly, standing from the couch. He took a few steps toward his study before seeming to remember we were there. "I need to get some work done before supper. You two go ahead if you're hungry."

I traded a surprised look with my mom.

"All is right, Love," she replied, though her hazel eyes were full of concern as he tromped off down the hallway.

I watched him go in silence, Kovaks' limp body swaying in my mind's eye as I wondered what the hell the madman had done or said for his execution to have shaken my father's rock-steady foundations like that.

Something was most certainly up.

And, despite the immortal wisdom of Johnny Wingard, I was starting to think it couldn't be something so simple as an affair.

CHAPTER 2

HOTSHOT

The thinly-matted training floor slammed into my back at just the right angle to drive the air from my lungs in a sharp whoosh. The familiar sensation flooded in, like someone had opened my chest cavity to vacuum and shocked my diaphragm into paralysis.

"That's twice today, Tyro," a gruff voice barked. "You got something you want to share with the class, or did you just get bored with making everyone else look like a herd of softsteel-sipping goat groppers?"

I looked around the permacrete lot, taking in the glances flitting my way from indignant tyros and satisfied doceres alike. My eyes found Johnny's, and he shot me a grin. Finally, I looked up to meet the ebony-skinned drill instructor's stern gaze. Mathis' reaction to my sorry excuse for sparring this morning was understandable—and, honestly, probably kind compared to what some of the other doceres would have said.

But that didn't stop a flicker of irritation from flaming up in my oxygen-deprived chest.

"I didn't sleep well last night," I grumbled as best I could with my shocked diaphragm as I rose to my feet to face him again.

It was true. I *hadn't* slept so well last night. But he didn't need to know more than that.

He didn't need to know about my concerns for my father, or my wriggling uncertainty about whether the Kovaks execution last night could really be called justice. He definitely didn't need to know that the same thoughts that had troubled my sleep had continued tugging at me all morning.

"Apologies, Docere Mathis," I added. "It won't happen a third time."

It was only then I noticed that even some of the patrolmen walking the top of Sanctuary's massive perimeter wall had paused to look down at the spectacle of Martin Raish's boy yet again failing to live up to his father's heroic deeds.

Heat crept into my face.

The patrolmen were a fair distance away, but I knew they had zoom toggles in their helmet displays. Perks of being an officer's son. Everyone was always waiting to see you fall on your ass. Waiting to receive that overdue confirmation that you are in fact an incompetent silver spoon whose only real accomplishment was being born to the right parents.

Mathis extended his open palm to me in invitation for another bout. "Daddy's boots are going to be awfully big for those flowers you call feet if that's all you got, Tyro."

The scuddy bastard.

A part of me wanted to sucker punch him right then and there, demons to the wind with the consequences. The rest just wanted to scream that I knew I was never going to live up to my father's name and to sink straight into the permacrete and escape all those watching eyes. But neither was really an option.

So, I squared up with Mathis and tried to put my head on straight.

At just under six feet tall and an aggressively lean hundred and eighty pounds, the docere had physically outclassed me up until a few seasons ago. Now that our training was beginning to fill out some of the height I'd gained in my last growth spurt, though, Mathis' physical superiority over me had been slowly diminishing. Now, his main advantages were experience and skill, and I was fairly confident I was closing the gap on the latter of those two as well.

I was never going to be Captain Martin Raish. That much had been made abundantly clear to me pretty much since I'd learned to walk. But at least I might be able to put Mathis on his scudspout ass and regain a scrap of my wounded dignity.

I slapped my palm to his in the customary gesture.

Mathis surged forward without hesitation, eager to teach me yet another lesson in humility. I caught his jab and aimed a kick at his ribs. Mathis twisted into it and caught my knee with one arm while delivering an elbow strike with the other. I snaked an arm up, shielding my head and grabbing around the back of his neck in one motion. Mathis drove in, dropping my leg in favor of a quick gut punch, and tried to lever me into a hip throw before I could do anything more than cough for air and clutch for balance.

I fought, battling for balance like a boulder teetering on the edge. But Mathis' feet were planted in a sturdy base, and mine were caught flat and nearly in-line with my shoulders, forcing me to fight the strength of his legs with the strength of my torso.

It wasn't a fight I was going to win.

But I would've rather eaten scud than let him take me down a third time.

So I abandoned my lifeline grip on his neck to grab his chin and drive his face skyward. At the same time, I rotated in, forfeiting my balance and dropping my weight onto the leg Mathis was so insistently trying to trip me with.

The move wasn't exactly regulation, but it worked. Mathis' right leg buckled under my weight, and in his surprise, I managed to scramble into position behind him. I got his throat in the crook of my arm—the first half of a solid chokehold—before victor's pride took over and I decided a chokehold wasn't good enough.

Instead, I yanked the dull, springy polymer practice knife from the sheath at the back of my belt and planted the tip behind Mathis' clavicle, right above one of the major kill points.

Mathis stilled. I tensed, half-expecting him to hit me with a concealed stunner or something. But, finally, he reached down and tapped the mat.

I immediately released him and stood, moving around to his front to offer my hand.

"Well look who decided to wake up and come to drills." Mathis kept his expression carefully neutral as he rose to his feet without my aid. He glanced down at his palmlight then around at the several dozen pairs of combatants who hurriedly looked away from us to resume their own contests.

Mathis shook his head, a hint of irritation finally bleeding onto his ebony features. "That'll do for the sorry lot of you scud sippers," he called. "Maybe tomorrow one of you can pull your heads out of your asses long enough to give an old man a break and give Tyro Raish here a proper match."

It almost would've sounded like praise if I hadn't recognized the comment for what it was—a double-edged sword, half compliment to me, half encouragement of the festering dislike several of the tyros (and the doceres, for that matter) already harbored for me.

Oh well.

After morning drills, Johnny and I filed into our customary seats at the back of the sleek lecture hall where we studied everything from military history and small unit tactics to the more standard hard and soft sciences that every kid, Legion and civilian alike, studied through their teens.

Normally, I actually kind of enjoyed class. According to my marks, I was even a decent student to boot. Today, though, I couldn't have told the instructor what he'd been talking about over the two-hour lecture, outside of that it had something to do with communications systems. And that much I knew only because it was written in big block letters at the head of the lecture materials I'd pulled up on my tablet.

An hour later, Johnny and I sat in our usual corner of the mess hall, mechanically shoveling down highly nutritious, highly bland foodstuff before afternoon drills and lessons. That I barely remembered having arrived or left our live weapons training session just prior probably should've been more alarming, but the fact that I hadn't been yelled at by any doceres told me my years of Legion training must've carried me through the mental fog on passable autopilot.

Why was this whole thing bothering me so much?

"I mean, I get it," Johnny was saying. "The comms bunker can backdoor its way into basically every display on Enochia. That could be big if the scud really hits the turbines. Like if our dearly departed Kovaks *hadn't* been totally gropping crazy, for instance."

The mention of Kovaks snapped my attention fully back to Johnny. "What did you say?"

He studied me, clearly sensing something was up. "I'm just saying that they didn't need to spend two whole hours talking about it."

"Oh. Right."

"Alpha's wrinklies, man, where have you been off to all day?" He looked around the room, craning his neck as if looking for the source of my inattentiveness. "I didn't miss a hot new piece of tyro swell walking around, did I?"

I rested my face in my hands and couldn't help but smile.

Johnny Wingard, loyal friend and relentless—if fruitless—swell hound.

Then again, the fruitless part wasn't necessarily Johnny's fault. We didn't exactly have a plethora of available candidates to choose from in Sanctuary. As tyros, relationships with our fellow trainees were forbidden. Once we became full legionnaires, they were merely heavily frowned upon, with plenty of complicated regulations to boot. And outside of the few non-tyro girls our age in Sanctuary, it wasn't like we got out to go scope the scene in Divinity very often either.

"Huh…" Johnny's voice broke into the stream of my deliberately benign thoughts. I looked up and realized he was still glancing around the mess hall. "Hey, you ever seen that guy before?"

I followed his gaze through the throng, searching. It didn't take long to spot who he was talking about. Civilians always stood out on base, both in dress and in behavior, but this guy…

There was something odd about him, though I couldn't quite say what it was. Gray hair, though he couldn't have been more than mid-thirties. Plain clothing of dull tones, not quite ragged, but not far off. Mostly, he just looked unassuming. Almost too unassuming.

As I watched, his brow wrinkled, his pace slowing by a fraction.

Then he looked straight at me.

His eyes were pale, almost colorless. They searched my face for all of two seconds before he gave what looked like a forced smile and continued on. I watched him slide smoothly through the crowd and vanish.

"That was weird."

When I finally turned back to Johnny, he just shrugged. "Hey, you're a good-looking dude. As far as you non-gingers go, at least."

"Mmm," I grunted in non-reply, glancing back to where the gray-haired man had disappeared.

"What's up, buddy?"

I turned back to find Johnny watching me expectantly.

"Come on," he said, wiggling his fingers in a gesture of invitation. "Never mind the mysterious stranger. Tell Uncle Johnny what ails you this fine day."

"Cheeky gingers, for starters," I grumbled.

He just beamed and plopped his chin down on his bridged fingers, waiting for more.

"I dunno, man." I shook my head, my thoughts returning to the matter at hand. "It's just… What if there's more to the story?"

"Forgive me for missing the Hal Express, but which story are we talking about again?"

"Kovaks."

Johnny frowned at me, then his eyebrows slid up as understanding dawned on him. "You don't think… Andre Kovaks was a crazy person, broto. Full on lunatic. Mad. Loopy. Weapons-grade nut—"

"I know," I said, holding up a hand to stop him. "I know, I know." I blew out a breath and studied the bustling mess hall with a scowl. "But the whole thing was kind of... I dunno, off, don't you think?"

Johnny considered that for a few seconds.

He'd agree with me. He had to. Executions did happen, but they weren't overly common these days—ceremonial executions in the Great Hall of the High Cleric himself even less so. Normally, the latter were reserved for people who'd done something truly horrendous, like actively trying to sabotage the Sanctum or the Legion.

"I guess it seemed a little heavy-handed," Johnny finally said. "Guy probably could have used help, but sweet Alpha, Hal, he was spouting off against the Sanctum. He accused the High Cleric. Are you surprised they wanted to make a point with him? Let that kind of thing go, and all of a sudden we're sliding back into the dark ages, with a dozen nations spilling blood for a shot at the driver's seat. That doesn't sound like a good time to me."

I pursed my lips, considering his words. It was far from the first time we'd had this discussion, or ones very like it, at least.

It wasn't that we didn't believe in our mission. Like every other soul in Sanctuary, we were devoted to the Legion. To Alpha. To keeping the peace of Enochia. All of it.

It was just that I was a touch inept at the whole *not to ask, but to serve* thing, and Johnny was one of the few people on base willing to entertain my nonsense. Entertain as he might, though, even when we found ourselves thinking a situation like Kovaks might've been handled better, I knew Johnny tended toward the mentality of, *Hey, as long as it's better than the alternative...*

But the lesser of two evils could still be pretty damn evil, right?

Sweet Alpha, I was being paranoid. Blowing this Kovaks thing out of proportion. I had to be.

At the end of the day, the Sanctum and the Legion were doing what they thought best for Enochia. I believed that, even if I didn't always agree with their ruling on what that "best" was.

"Brighten up, man," Johnny said. "Hey, if a few seasons down the road it turns out Kovaks was right and we find ourselves fighting a bunch of invading, blood sucking aliens, you get to have the most satisfying 'I told you so' in human history. That's something, right?"

I rolled my eyes. "Yeah. Something. Totally, broto."

Johnny's recoil probably would've escaped a stranger's notice, but it was enough to tell me my words had come out harsher than I'd intended.

"I'm sorry, man," I added, dropping his gaze. "I'm just driving myself crazy thinking about the way my dad's been acting and everything."

"Hey," Johnny said, his expression serious, "if I didn't have you and your heavy thoughts around to drag me down, I'd be liable to float away on a happy cloud."

"That doesn't make me sound like the best friend."

"Ahhh," Johnny said, wrinkling his nose. "*Friend* is kind of a strong word, don't you think? Let's not get carried away, man."

"Oh, grop you," I said, smiling despite myself.

"You'd like that, wouldn't you?" he replied, waggling his eyebrows.

I shook my head and checked the time on my palmlight. When I looked back up, Johnny's expression had sobered.

"You could always ask him, you know. Old Captain Martin is a pretty reasonable guy, as far as CO fathers go."

I nodded slowly, playing out how that conversation might go for about the twenty-thousandth time in my head.

"Or," Johnny said, splaying his hands, "orrr you could run away from your problems and come move in with us. Problem solved. Or, you know, *not*. But that's kind of the point, right? Plus, Belle would probably be too flustered to speak anymore with you around, so that's a win for Johnny, right there."

I frowned a little thinking of Johnny's younger sister, Anabelle, and the peculiar habit she'd recently adopted of turning rosy red and shortly vacating any room I entered. "Yeah. Tempting, buddy, but I think I might have to wait until at least tomorrow to run away. We're having Kublich over for supper tonight."

"As in the High General of the Legion? That Kublich?"

I inclined my head. "I believe that's the one. What?" I added at Johnny's awestruck expression. "It's not like this is the first time it's ever happened."

It was Johnny's turn to shake his head at me. "What's it like, living up there in your white tower?"

I looked pointedly in the rough direction of the distant heart of Divinity. "Probably not as nice as living in *their* White Tower."

Johnny tilted his head in concession. "Fair point. So what's the occasion, then? Business? Pleasure? Are they gonna go ahead and just promote you straight to captain when we graduate next season, demons to the wind with regulations?"

I shrugged. "No idea. My mom only told me this morning. Might just be a social call."

"Well," Johnny said, leaning forward, "whatever's going on, let's just hope the good General doesn't bring that foxy little servitor of his."

The thought didn't improve my focus for the remainder of the day.

Every other tyro in Sanctuary—and most of the legionnaires, at that—would have jumped at the chance to lick the High General's boots in person for an entire evening.

I was dreading it.

Adrian Kublich was a nice enough man, I guess, but I wasn't in any mood today to play politics and dance the dance. Plus, for some reason I'd never quite been able to distinguish, Kublich had always kind of given me the creeps.

So maybe my position as a Captain's son actually *had* spoiled me.

Still, all I really wanted to do was find out what was scratching at my father's brain, because now it was scratching at mine too. So I decided I was going to listen to Johnny for once and talk to him after dinner. I'd never confronted him like that. Something told me it wouldn't be a fun conversation. But I needed to know—for my own sanity and for my mom's sake.

One way or another, I was going to find out what the hell was going on with him tonight.

CHAPTER 3

MEAT AND GRAVY

"This pie is to die for, Klara," High General Adrian Kublich said from across the dining room table as his fork descended for another bite.

I couldn't disagree. The meat and gravy pie was delicious, as usual. But something about the way Kublich looked at my mom while he said it made my stomach squirm.

My mom smiled, inclining her head at the compliment, but didn't say anything.

"How's your work coming along?" Kublich added. "I imagine you've had a productive season with Martin running around, as busy as he's been."

Was it my imagination, or did my father tense at that?

I know I did, though maybe for different reasons.

Kublich didn't seem to notice our reactions as my mom put on a thin smile and said, "It's going quite well, thank you. I'm just putting the finishing touches on a bit of an anthology."

"Hmm," Kublich said, raising his wine glass in cheers. "I look forward to reading it."

As if.

Having spent enough time watching my mom interact with people about her writing, I'd pretty much come to interpret those six words as polite-speak for, *That's great, but I don't really care.*

Then again, the High General wasn't really one for idle scudspouting, so who knew?

"And what about you, Haldin?" Kublich said, yanking my attention back to the table. "How goes the training?"

"Good, sir," I said reflexively. Then, feeling like that was a weak answer, I added, "Getting better all the time."

Great. Much better.

But it was a loaded question anyway.

If he had the slightest inclination to know how my training was going, he could have performance reports and assessments about my abilities, psyche, and a dozen other things all with a few swipes of a finger. One peek at my file, and he could probably know more about me and my training than I could tell him if I talked all night.

"Word around base is that you made a bit of a spectacle of Docere Mathis this morning," he said, his expression unreadable.

Ah. So that's where this was going.

My parents turned to me, each bearing their own brand of frown.

"I…" I swallowed. "Yes, sir. I acted… beyond what was required." He kept staring. It made me feel hollow, despite the fact that I was decidedly full of the meat pie that had seemed so delicious until only a moment ago. "I will apologize to Docere Mathis, sir. Formally. And it won't happen again."

"What did you do?" my father asked, glancing between me and Kublich.

"It was nothing," Kublich said, his mouth finally breaking into a small smile. "Haldin is simply outgrowing our ability to challenge him, I fear."

Why did that smile make me feel like I was about to be eaten?

Whatever it was, I did my best to keep my eyes on the food and avoid Kublich's gaze for the rest of the meal.

After we'd finished supping, Kublich retreated to my father's study to discuss some manner of classified business with him.

"What do you think they're talking about?" I asked my mom as we worked on the dishes together.

Under her bangs, her eyebrows shrugged as she started scrubbing the dish I'd just handed her. "You know the drill. Classified means classified."

Something about the way she said it…

She held out her hand for the next dish, then turned to look at me when it didn't come. I searched her face, the white serving dish in my hand all but forgotten.

"Are you guys…" I faltered, the words caught in my throat. "Are you, uh, okay?"

"Sweetie," she said, pulling the dish from my hands and setting it aside so she could grab my wet hands in hers. "Of course we are. Dad's just been… Well, I don't know exactly what he's been. He's worried about something. Something he can't talk about. That's why we've been… tense. But we'll get past it. He'll fix whatever it is." A small smile pulled at her lips. "He always does."

I was surprised to feel the light hint of tears not far off. I couldn't even say why. Just something about the look on her face. "Promise?"

Her smile sweetened, and she reached her wet hands to the back of my head and pulled me down to plant a warm kiss on my forehead. "Promise." She stepped back and waved her hands in a shooing motion. "Now you go relax. Watch a storyvid or something. Whatever the kids are doing for fun these days."

I smiled. "Yeah, I'm not sure you want me doing what the kids are doing these days, Mom."

Her smile grew as she shooed me again, and mine did the same as I turned to head for my room. I thought about messaging Johnny to see if he wanted to fire up a sim, but then I saw my bed and the big, inviting screen on the opposite wall and thought I might just take my mom's directions to heart.

Why not kick back and watch a vid?

Outside of Sanctuary's thick walls, in the loud, bustling city of Divinity, kids my age were playing smashball while we ran combat drills. While we practiced small unit tactics, they went on dates. While we slept, they snuck out and did all the things their parents told them not to—throwing parties and otherwise flipping the middle finger to people like me, who spent their lives in service to make sure their kids would likewise be able to flip the middle finger to ours.

But maybe I was just a touch judgmental toward the undisciplined madness that was civilian life.

Either way, taking the evening to relax was probably acceptable. I was excelling in the eyes of the Legion, and even those of the High General himself, apparently. My parents were going to be okay. And, demons to the wind, I was allowed to casually watch a vid if I damn well pleased. Plus, it'd probably help take my mind off things for a little while.

Eager energy bubbling through my chest at my little act of defiance, I waved the screen on my wall to life and began navigating through menus with little flicks of my fingers.

It took me all of two minutes to realize I had no idea what to watch.

I sighed, the excitement draining, and flicked on my palmlight, reaching for Johnny's name. "So much for—"

A pair of loud thumps sounded from elsewhere in the house, burning all thoughts of vids and leisure from my mind.

No. Not thumps. Gunshots. Distorted and dulled by thick walls.

Thick walls like the ones in my father's study.

I was already on my feet, though I didn't remember deciding to move. I tore the door open and bounded down the hall. A crash from the living room goaded my legs to move faster.

Then a horrible wail filled the air, clawing at my insides, and my step faltered.

My mom's voice. There was no mistaking it. She cried out again—a scream that ended with an abrupt, sickeningly wet noise.

I fell forward into a dazed run.

She was dead. Something about the sound told me that even before I came barreling out of the hallway. But I refused to listen. I stumbled into the dim living room, straight into a nightmare darker than anything I could have imagined.

It was odd, the way my mind took in all the inconsequential details first. The couch, uprooted and overturned. The blue ceramic vase, shattered, its pieces strewn across the neutral tones of the big soft rug in the center of the room.

The fresh spots of dark crimson staining that rug.

My knees buckled. I caught myself on the wall. I was going to be sick.

Feet thrashed next to the dark stains. Blood. It was blood. My eyes traced upward, unable to stop, my stupor too complete to do anything but stare. My mom's dress was soaked across the front with blood. A dark figure held her, arms wrapped tight around her from behind, face pressed against her throat, where a soft crimson glow illuminated her ghastly wound.

Her attacker shifted at the sound of my entry, looking up and—

My mind went blank. I couldn't move.

It wasn't possible.

Where the thing's eyes should've been, it stared back at me with twin orbs of demon fire. They pulsed crimson, lighting the dark rivulets of my mom's blood still running down the thing's chin.

I tried to scream. Tried to charge the demon. To save my mom. It was like my brain had been disconnected from my body. Like those impossible glowing eyes had cast some dark sorcery upon me.

I strained with everything I had, and I couldn't move a damn muscle.

"Haldin," it said. "I was hoping you'd join us."

Merciful Alpha. That was Kublich's voice. Deeper and rougher, maybe. But it was his. And behind those glowing crimson eyes and the bloody fangs the demon bared in a grin, that was Kublich's face.

Impossible. It was impossible. And yet it was his ruby tunic on the creature clutching my mom's bloody body. His High General's insignia.

My stupefied gaze dropped back to my mom, my mouth hanging open in a silent cry. Her body was so broken, so limp, her head dangling against the Kublich-thing's arms at an unnatural angle. Her legs kicked weakly, the last bits of her life ebbing away before me.

I met her frightened eyes just before she died.

The haze hung heavy in my mind. I couldn't move. I was trapped in that moment. It stretched, independent of time, the image of the fire-eyed demon holding my mom's broken, bloody body carving its way deep into my brain.

A thud to the left, and my father stumbled into the room, leaning heavily against the wall for support. His dark shirt hid the details of his injury, but judging from the trail of blood he left on the white wall, he was hurt, and badly. Still, his hand barely wavered as he raised his sidearm and fired three shots into Kublich's back.

In the confines of the living room, the shots were painfully loud. Kublich staggered forward as the slugs tore into him. But he handled it too well, recovered too quickly.

Armor. He was wearing armor.

Kublich turned away from me to face my father with a low, guttural growl. He tossed my mom aside as if she were no more heavy or important than a sack of potatoes. I reached out helplessly, the knots in my stomach tightening as her body tumbled over the couch and thudded to the floor in an undignified mess of slack limbs.

"Martin," Kublich said calmly, starting toward my father. "You see the price of your meddling? I—"

Another crack of thunder from my father's sidearm, and Kublich's head snapped back as if the shot had found his forehead. I waited for him to fall dead to the floor.

He didn't.

He just gave his head a little shake and reached up to rub at his forehead. I could've sworn his skin was turning green. If my eyes could even be trusted anymore. The small, dark object Kublich flicked to the rug at his feet told me they couldn't.

It was a crumpled softsteel slug. The one my father had just shot him in the head with.

"HAL, RUN!" my father roared.

I barely registered the words.

My mind couldn't work through the haze—the impossibility of everything that was happening. Adrian Kublich, the damned High General of the Legion, had just murdered my mother, survived a direct gunshot to the head, and was now stalking toward my father. My father who was screaming at me to run.

But I still couldn't move. Except... My hand. Still raised toward my mom's body.

Whatever force had been restraining me was gone.

By the time the thought fully registered, I was already charging. Not toward the entryway, but straight for Kublich's turned back.

Run? Leave my father behind with this... this monster?

Grop that. I was going to strangle the demon bastard with my own hands. But before I could close the distance and tackle him down, Kublich sprang forward, crossing the room with alarming speed, and clamped a clawed hand around my father's throat.

"NO!" I screamed, reaching helplessly out for the second time. Too late.

The demon with Kublich's face turned its fiery eyes to me and broke my father's neck.

After that, things became a blur.

I'd like to say that I threw myself at Kublich. That I gouged those burning red eyes from their sockets. But the part of my adrenaline-soaked brain that had watched him survive a gunshot to the head and break my dad's neck with one hand told me to run for my life. And I listened.

I was halfway down the entryway hall when my legs locked, that same full-body paralysis taking abrupt hold of me. I hit the floor hard, air exploding from my lungs.

"You cannot run, Haldin," he called from the living room.

I tried to fight, cold dread seeping through me.

Footsteps approached from behind. "Such a pity your father had to—"

A scream erupted from my throat, and my hands smashed into the floor as the paralysis inexplicably vanished. Behind, Kublich growled low in his throat, far too close. No time to think. I planted my hands and feet, launched halfway into a sprint for the door... and froze on wobbly feet.

Someone was striding toward me from the open front door. The strange civilian from the mess hall. Even in my panic, I recognized him. But he didn't look unassuming anymore.

The air crackled around him with some intangible energy, sweeping at his hair and clothes. He raised a hand, palm out, and a nebulous light breathed into existence there, intensifying from faint to threatening before I so much as had time to wonder what in damnation was happening.

I didn't understand. But the too-close growl at my back told me I didn't have time to understand. Kublich behind. The stranger ahead.

I was dead.

Except the stranger's eyes weren't focused on me, were they? I tensed to throw myself into a mad sprint past him. Before I could, his pale eyes caught mine, and he flicked his head almost calmly to the side, radiant palm held at the ready.

I didn't have time to ask questions. I dove out of the way and hit the floor with a hard thud. The hallway erupted like an entire crate of detonating snap flares and thumpers.

Blinding white light. A sonorous crack like thunder.

A violent rush of air smacked into me, my vision too bleached from whatever had just happened to see anything but vague outlines. I felt more than heard the enormous crash behind me—the monster, I hoped, blasted back into the living room by the stranger's... whatever.

It didn't matter.

I had to get out.

I tried for my feet, shaking my head in a futile attempt to restore my sight and clear the steady ringing in my ears. I'd made it to my knees when something grabbed my shoulder. I lashed out blindly, but a deft hand turned aside my wild defense.

There was time only to scream a wordless challenge.

Then something pressed against the side of my head, and the world went black.

CHAPTER 4
RUDE AWAKENINGS

I woke at the dinner table.

But that wasn't right. Why wasn't that right? I couldn't recall, but as I looked over at my parents, I was sure something was wrong.

Everything in the room glowed white and pristine. The walls, the table linens. Even our clothes. Kublich sat across the table, smiling amicably over his wine glass. I frowned at the sight of him. There was something there, some muffled unpleasant feeling that—

I gasped as images flashed through my awareness, too fast to comprehend. There was blood. I was sure of that. Blood and darkness. And, in the darkness, for the briefest instant, a pair of fiery red—

No, a voice said in my head. *No, everything is fine.*

Was that my voice?

It didn't matter. It was clearly right. We were all laughing and chatting at the table. Everyone seemed perfectly happy. At the sound of the doorbell, I hopped up from my chair and walked down the hall to greet our guest.

Before I reached the door, though, it burst open on a powerful gust of wind. Total, utter darkness filled the doorway, so thick it might've had physical substance. Smoky tendrils of it began to creep in past the threshold, and in their wake came a man with gray hair and pale eyes, wreathed in darkness. There was something familiar about him, but I couldn't place it.

Then his eyes came alive with red fire that blazed against the darkness, and cohesive thought fled my mind. His skin shifted sickly green as he reached for me with a clawed hand.

I turned to run.

The hallway leading back to the dining room and to the safety of my parents seemed to stretch longer as I ran, the end an ever-distant speck in my vision. A choir of growls and howling wind filled the hall around me. I ran faster—as fast as my gelatinous legs could manage, sure that every moment would be my last.

After what felt like ages of failing to draw any closer to the end, I looked up to find I'd somehow reached my destination. Something was wrong, though. The pristine white glow of the room beyond had faded, replaced by an ominously pulsing scarlet. Silence hung heavy in the air, all the thicker after the cacophony that'd filled the hall moments before. I stood there on the threshold, suddenly afraid to enter.

One step. Then another. I entered the dining room to find my parents and Kublich all slumped forward in their chairs. Horror gripped at my chest. They were covered in blood, tar black against their white clothes in the red glow of the room. The man with gray hair and a cloak of swirling shadows stood behind them, his face split in a smile full of glistening fangs. It was only then I realized that the scarlet glow pulsing through the room was coming from his eyes.

He started toward me, murder in those fiery eyes, and—

I sprang awake only to be met with a hard blow to the head.

Darkness. Complete, constricting darkness.

I pawed frantically around, head throbbing, desperate to fend off the next blow. Except one wasn't coming, I realized as my probing hands found the ceiling my head had struck. I was quite alone in a space not much larger than my huddled body. No room to extend my legs, to sit up. Only darkness, and a low, steady hum. I flicked my fingers straight. Nothing. My palmlight was gone.

Panic tried to take me then, darkness pressing in, squeezing my lungs tight. Tighter than the walls of my new prison.

I closed my eyes—not that it made a difference. I wiped cold sweat from my brow and tried to calm my rapid breathing. Control. I needed to get myself under control and figure this thing out.

At least my hands and legs weren't bound. That was something. But where in damnation was I? And how did I get there?

I focused in on the steady hum permeating the cramped darkness.

A skimmer engine?

It was the best guess I had. Which meant I was probably in a skimmer trunk, bound for Alpha knew where with Alpha knew who. The floor shifted beneath me, and my stomach informed me of an unmistakable change in velocity and direction.

Definitely a skimmer.

And if I was in a skimmer trunk... I swallowed, panic making another bid for control as I felt around in the darkness to confirm what I already knew deep down: unless I found some magical way to force the latch from the inside, I was stuck here until someone decided to let me out.

"Grop," I heard myself whisper.

My voice sounded strange in the dark space. Maybe I was just losing it. And for good reason.

Mom. Dad. The *thing* that had attacked them.

My breaths were ragged in the darkness. Quickening. A band of cold hardsteel tightening around my chest, suffocating me. Terrible sights flashing through my memory. The wrecked living room. The blood.

The demon that had killed them.

The band tightened, wrenching at my stomach, threatening to push its contents back up. I rolled over, fighting the nausea. Darkness closing in on me. My heart pounding like a wild animal, bent on escaping my chest.

My parents were dead. And I was probably about to join them.

I lost it then. Self-control fled me as I gave in to wild panic, kicking and thrashing against the darkness. I beat at the unyielding trunk hatch, anger and fear and desperation all spilling out of my throat in a strangled, word-less cry. The skimmer might have slowed at my outburst. I barely noticed. Just kept slamming my fist against the hatch, raging at that piece of scud latch holding me here to my doom, screaming like a madman for my parents, for a fighting chance, for that Alpha-cursed trunk hatch to open —*for the love of Alpha, OPEN!*

It did.

I wasn't sure how or why. Only that, one second, I was pounding and screaming against the wall of my dark prison, and the next, I was staring dumbly out past the bobbing trunk door to the lines of nighttime skimmer traffic and rushing city lights beyond, my entire body trembling with sudden and inexplicable exhaustion. I felt like I'd just been electrocuted.

But I was free.

It didn't make any sense. But that didn't matter right now. I was free, and

I needed to move my ass. The skimmer was already slowing down, apparently alert to my situation. Luckily, we were down with the street-level traffic and not up in one of the skylanes. We were still moving a good thirty or forty miles per hour, but there wasn't anything to be done about it.

I moved into a crouch, turning to face the front of the skimmer, painfully aware of how sluggish my limbs felt. But I was free, and this was my only chance.

I leapt from the trunk.

Indignant buzzers sounded from the skimmers behind. I had a brief moment to appreciate just how fast I was flying through the air toward the hard pavement. Then I hit the ground and found out in excruciating detail just how unforgiving that pavement was. I rolled as best I could, hoping to disperse the violent deceleration and clear the traffic lane at the same time. It was a sloppy roll, and only partially successful at either goal. But I lived.

If that had been that, I would've lain there on the cool permacrete for hours and allowed myself to wallow. Instead, the sight of my captor's skimmer pulling out of traffic to slow to a halt ahead had me on my feet and moving before my body even had time to fully process how much pain it was in.

I plunged into a nearby alley at a limping run, only allowing myself a glance backward as I neared the end of the narrow space. No sign of anyone following me. But I wasn't about to take that as permission to slow.

The next street over was bustling with foot traffic—civilians of Divinity, all made up in sleek, flowing garments, on their way to catch a show, or, given that it was Alphasday, probably to attend evening worship. My dark pants and green long sleeve shirt didn't exactly blend with the fashionable crowd, but at least I wasn't wearing my crisp gray tyro uniform.

I threw myself into the stream, weaving through civilians as best I could, trying to refrain from shoving people around and broadcasting my location to anyone who might be trailing me through the crowd. Two blocks later, past the flowing lanes of foot traffic, I ducked left into another alleyway, this one wider than the last and lined with several boxy blue dumpsters.

I hurried along the dim alleyway, intending to cut through and keep running until I couldn't anymore. My body had other plans.

About halfway down the stretch, it all hit without warning—the full blast of every thought and sensation the shock and adrenaline had been holding at bay since I'd stumbled into that bloody living room nightmare. I slumped down against the wall in the small space between two dumpsters, tucked my face against my knees, and tried to catch my breath against the plethora of throbbing aches I'd gained in my hasty skimmer escape.

Think. I just needed to think. Figure it out. For the moment, I was in the clear. No one would see me here, nestled between the dumpsters just like another one of Divinity's homeless.

No.

I wasn't *like* one of Divinity's homeless right now. I was one.

That Kublich creature—or demon, or whatever—had wanted me dead. Had it really been Kublich? I couldn't begin to comprehend how that was possible. Either way, I couldn't go back right now. Not while that thing was probably looking to finish the job.

So what did I do next?

I called my parents. That was the obvious, reflexive answer. I called my parents, and I asked them what to do, how to make it better. Only I couldn't. I'd never be able to do that again.

Hot tears spilled over, their wet trails warm down my cheeks one moment and cool the next in the deepening chill of the night air. It was nothing compared to the chill in my chest—the one that had nothing to do with my surroundings.

"They're gone," I whispered. It didn't sound right—couldn't be right. "Mom. Dad."

Silence pressed in around me, the low din of the distant crowds like a mocking call, only highlighting the hollow ache at my core. A shudder racked through me. I pressed my face to my knees even tighter. "Please," I whispered. "Please, please."

I wasn't sure who I was talking to—what I was even asking for—but the words came out all the same. Memories looped unbidden through my mind. The gut-wrenching crack of the Kublich demon breaking my dad's neck. The slack lifelessness of my mom's body on the living room floor.

It was too much.

I clenched my jaw, hands curling into fists, and only barely contained the wordless scream in my throat. I looked up at the building across the alleyway, tall and sturdy. A housing tower, from the look of it. There'd be dozens of families in that building, most of them supping right now, or gathering around to watch the evening worship—all of them content, completely oblivious to the tragedy sitting on their doorstep.

It was sick. It didn't feel real. A few sobbing huffs escaped me. I glared up at the high-rise, bitter rage eating at my insides. I wanted to hit something. Needed to release some of whatever it was that was building inside of me. I started pulling myself to my feet. I needed to do something. Anything. Maybe I could find a public node and get a message to Johnny.

Would that even be safe?

If by some Alpha-cursed sorcery a demon was somehow parading as the High General of the Legion—with the considerable resources that entailed —was there really anywhere I could go? Anything I could do that wouldn't be leaving a trail for him to find me?

I didn't know. I didn't know what to do.

"Gropping scudbucket of a—"

I froze, boot cocked to kick the dumpster beside me, and listened.

Voices. Low and serious. Coming closer. They were definitely detached from the din of the crowd, now. But it was probably nothing, right? Just a few civilians on their way to—

"—ust me when I say he's nearby," one of them was saying in a smooth voice as they drew closer. "And gropping be ready."

Scud.

My heart thudded straight into overdrive, fresh adrenaline lacing its electric fingers through my senses as I pressed myself flat to the wall.

Were they talking about me? Of course they were. But were they really? I didn't even know who *they* were. It could still just be a few guys looking for their hound for all I knew.

Yeah. Right.

Their boot falls were heavy, precise—uncomfortably reminiscent of those of marching soldiers. I wasn't sure if that was good or bad news. By sheer force of will, I resisted the urge to peek around the dumpster. My instincts told me I was in danger, and right now, that was all I had to go by.

I needed to move. But there was nowhere to go. Nowhere but down the alley, right in plain sight of the five or six men who may or may not be armed and looking for me. I was on the verge of bolting for it anyway when the group halted nearby. The abrupt absence of boot falls was jarring in my tense state.

I held my breath, waiting. One of them murmured something, too quiet to hear. I crouched there, cowering like a damn cornered animal, not even able to hear what my looming enemies were saying.

The anger flickered back to life, loosening the tension in my chest, fixing itself at a new target. I was trying to rein in the wild urge to round the corner and do something that would probably only worsen my situation when they finally broke the silence.

"Come on out, kid," a voice called—the same smooth voice that'd spoken a few moments earlier. "No need to hide with the garbage anymore."

That settled the question of who they were looking for. And whoever they were, something about the guy's tone told me they weren't here to give me a warm blanket and a hug.

CHAPTER 5
FALSE PRETENSES

"Come on, kid. I swear we won't bite."

Somehow, my heart managed to beat faster. They could probably hear the damn thing from twenty feet away.

Kid. They couldn't see me yet, but he'd said kid, which meant one of two things. Either some strangers had seen me running and decided to follow me into the alleyway, or these people knew exactly who they were looking for—and, somehow, had known exactly where to find me.

Either way, it wasn't good. But there wasn't really anything to be gained by trying to stay hidden behind the dumpster any longer. So I leaned cautiously out to see what I was up against.

For a second, I was terrified I'd be greeted by more glowing red eyes. Instead, I saw cream-colored armor and four disconcertingly featureless faceplates of pale gold. Sanctum Guard, I realized with a jolt. But Sanctum Guard didn't idly stroll the streets unless they were accompanying a cleric.

And the fifth man was clearly not a cleric.

He wore plain brown pants and a dull green jacket, his appearance fairly unremarkable but for the odd black circlet around his neck and the haughty smirk hanging across his mouth—a smirk that instantly identified him in my mind as the man who'd spoken.

I resisted the urge to rush out and start snapping my credentials and crying for help. In theory, the four Sanctum Guard were sworn to uphold the laws of the Sanctum and protect all its citizens. But something wasn't adding up.

"Well there he is," the guy in the green jacket said, still smirking as he splayed his hands entirely too casually. "Alpha be praised, right boys?"

Something about the guy immediately made me want to punch the smirk off his face. But that wasn't the only reason my insides were crawling. Why were the Sanctum Guard out looking for me? And, more importantly, why in demons' depths were they looking to Goodfellow Smirks like he was their commanding officer?

Could Kublich have sent him? He looked like a civilian.

Demons below, was there anyone I could trust right now?

At least none of their rifles were pointed at me. Yet.

"What do you want?" I said, stepping halfway out from the cover of the dumpster.

"Sanctuary reported a tyro abducted on base," Smirks said, taking a few steps forward, hands still held at his sides in a nonthreatening gesture. "One Haldin Raish. Some kind of home invasion."

I watched his face, searching for any hint of deception.

"You know the drill from there," he continued. "Teams were dispatched to find you and bring you home."

"I do know the drill," I said, nodding slowly. "Which is why I'm wondering who the scud you are to be leading a fireteam of Sanctum Guard."

That damn smirk didn't waver as he tapped a few commands on his palmlight and held it up for my inspection. "Undercover patrol," he said, explaining the credentials that were too far away for me to actually make out on the small display. "Called for assistance when I spotted you and it looked like you were still running from someone. Wasn't sure if we'd be needing the backup."

He took another step. I tensed to run.

"Look," he said slowly, almost gently, "I get why you'd be shaken up after getting nabbed, kid, but you're safe now."

He continued closer, moving slowly, like he was afraid each movement was liable to send me flitting for the countryside. That fear wasn't too far off the mark. Especially seeing as I didn't trust a single word coming out of his ever-smirking mouth. All I had left to trust were my own instincts. And right now, they were telling me to get away from these men.

"You know what?" I held a hand up for space and inched out from cover, away from Smirks and the four soldiers. "You're right. I'm safe. I got away from them myself, and I appreciate your, uh, concern, but I can get home myself too."

"You know we can't let you do that, kid," Smirks said. "I have superiors too. I can't just report that we found you, said all is right, and left you to fend for yourself in the streets."

"How about this?" I said, still inching backward, mind turning furiously for a plan. "How about you call my father, Captain Martin Raish, and tell him you've found me. He'll send a skimmer for me."

The words burned in my throat.

Smirks turned that over for a few seconds. If he was putting on an act, it was a good one. I actually started to think that maybe he was telling the truth—that maybe these men were simply out looking for an abducted tyro and had no idea what had really happened.

Then something shifted in Smirks' expression, and he rolled his eyes, dropping all pretenses. "Okay, kid. Let's do it the hard way, then."

I turned and ran, angling behind the second dumpster for at least a moment's cover from the four Sanctum Guard rifles at my back. Would they use them?

I didn't make it far enough to find out.

My legs went rigid as boards without warning. My momentum carried me on, toppling face-first toward the pavement. I reached out to catch myself. Or tried to, only to find my arms were likewise paralyzed. Wild panic gripped at my chest, overruled a second later by lancing pain as I crashed into the pavement like a statue of flesh and nerve endings. My arms and face took the worst of it, but there was plenty of pain to go around.

"Grab him," Smirks said somewhere behind me. "Hurry it up."

I fought to get my hands under me, to keep moving, but nothing happened. Panic returned, swirling in with the pain and yielding fearful anger as I tried again and again to move limbs that were suddenly beyond my control. Boot steps approached from behind. I tried to thrash, tried to cry out.

It was maddening.

"I know, I know," a voice whispered. But no one was there. *"Pretty disconcerting, right?"*

It almost sounded like it was coming from inside my own head.

I struggled with all my might. Not even a twitch from my cursed body. Strong hands grabbed me and began hauling me up. Was I cracking? Had they hit me with some kind of ultra-powered muscle relaxant when I'd turned to flee?

"Nothing so pedestrian," the voice said.

Again the voice was directionless, internal. And worse, I realized, it almost seemed as if it were aware of what I was thinking. As I was yanked upright, I saw it was two of the Sanctum Guard handling me. The other two were still flanking Smirks, weapons at the ready, and Smirks himself looked… vacant. Like he'd gone into some sort of standing trance.

"Well I AM a bit occupied," the voice said.

Ice crept through my insides as I realized what was happening.

"There it is," Smirks' voice said, though in front of me, his lips didn't move. Some of the awareness seemed to return to his face, and he said, out loud this time, "I've got it from here, boys."

The soldiers slowly released me. Smirks sank back into his trance, and I cried out as I felt my body take a step forward by its own free will. Or tried to cry out, at least. I couldn't make a sound. Couldn't do anything but watch as my cursed body plodded drunkenly along toward Smirks, the two Sanctum Guard flanking me all the way.

I was powerless—utterly helpless against whatever demonic sorcery Smirks was working.

So I might as well save my energy for if and when circumstances changed. I was trying to draw into myself, hoping to at least protect my thoughts, when a flicker of movement in the darkness above caught my attention. Something falling.

No. Not something. Someone.

Smirks noticed it too.

"Above!" he barked, snapping out of his trance.

Not fast enough.

The dark figure plummeted toward the pavement between Smirks and his men, moving fast enough to splatter to gelatin. Only he didn't splatter. His plunge inexplicably slowed several feet from the ground like he'd sprung a great, invisible glider. Then he hit the ground, and Smirks and the two Sanctum Guard beside him were all blasted away in some kind of explosive shock wave.

A gust of unnatural wind slapped at my face, and I staggered back, gaping at the newcomer. Something rippled through me. A subdued shock. Some flicker of familiarity. That gray hair. Those pale eyes. A stab of pain straight at my core.

Where had I seen this man?

There wasn't time for it to matter. He was already darting toward Smirks, who was spitting a curse and scrambling back to his feet, when I realized something of much more immediate importance.

I'd just moved.

I didn't wait to see if anyone had noticed. I threw a hard elbow into the right Guard's neck, drove a sidekick into his hip, and stepped to intercept as his partner turned his rifle on me. I caught the foregrip of the weapon and lunged forward to try to slam it into its owner's faceless golden mask. He staggered back, and I followed, punching, kneeing, and kicking every weak point I could until he collapsed against the alley wall. I was reaching for his gun when a pair of strong arms wrapped around me from behind and yanked.

There was no helping it. I was going down. But I caught onto the wrist of whoever had thrown me and managed to drag them down with me. I slammed too hard to the pavement. The Sanctum Guard I'd pulled landed heavily on my hip. I drove a palm into his faceplate and scrambled to untangle myself. He lunged for my throat, but I managed to get my legs up and catch him at the hips. With his rifle pinned at his side, he wordlessly drew the sidearm from his thigh holster.

Terror rolled through me at the grim determination of my faceless attacker.

He was Sanctum Guard. And he was trying to kill me.

I dropped my leg guard, threw myself forward, and caught his gun hand before he could put a shot in my gut. He cocked back with his left fist, but I was too occupied with controlling his gun hand to do anything other than tuck my chin and raise my right shoulder.

Not enough.

The world exploded into a confusing haze of sharp pain and blurry shapes and colors. I yelled, thrashing in a disoriented frenzy. My knee made a solid connection with something soft, and the Guard growled a curse. He raised his fist again… and collapsed on top of me without warning, leaving me pinned on my back.

I groaned and tried to shove him off, sure that I needed to move my ass. Before I'd budged my attacker more than a few inches, though, the gray-haired newcomer appeared above us, looking down at me with pale, calm eyes. Something clicked as I met his gaze, and my stomach lurched. Memories flashed, hazy and unfocused.

My parents. Kublich. The gray-haired man.

He'd been there.

A flash of blinding light. A monstrous roar.

What was happening to me? Why was I only remembering this now?

Grop it. Who or what this man was didn't matter. I needed to get out of here. I reached for the pistol my Sanctum Guard attacker had dropped, desperate for the advantage. Before I could find the sidearm, though, the stranger reached down and pulled the Guard's limp form off me with surprising ease.

The gun clattered to the ground.

I moved without thinking, snatching it up and rolling away from the gray-haired man. I came to my feet, planted my back to the wall, and whipped the gun up in his direction, expecting to find him bearing down on me.

He was just standing there, hands held out to his sides, pale eyes calm. He was of medium height, his build somewhat slender. I wanted to think I could take him if it came to a fight, but after what I'd just seen him do…

Keeping the weapon trained on him, I shot a quick glance up the alley to where Smirks and his two guards lay motionless. At the distant mouth of the alleyway, people were clearly starting to notice.

"I'm not here to hurt you, Haldin," the man said, his voice every bit as tranquil as his composure. I glanced back to him. He tilted his head in the direction of the gathering crowd and said, "But we need to leave. Now."

I hefted the pistol to remind us both who was in charge. "Not the first time I've heard that tonight. Who are you? How do you know my name? And what the scud were you doing at my house tonight?"

"I'll tell you everything once we're safe," he said, waking his palmlight with a slow, careful movement.

"Grop that." I clenched my teeth, fighting the fear that whispered in my ear to pull the trigger and run. "Why would I possibly trust you?"

"Because I know what Kublich is," he said.

My breath caught.

He touched his palmlight display, and I nearly pulled the trigger out of raw nerves alone.

"And because I know what he just did to your parents," he added.

A flicker of motion above caught my attention. A skimmer descending from the rooftop. A skimmer—I realized as it drew close—that's rear trunk hatch hung ajar.

"That was your skimmer I woke up in," I said quietly, my mind whirling with too many disjointed pieces.

"It was," he said, nodding and gesturing for me to get in as the dark skimmer settled down between us. "Because right now, I'm the only person on Enochia trying to keep you alive."

CHAPTER 6
BULLSCUD

"I assure you, that's not necessary," the gray-haired stranger said, with a pointed look at the gun I held trained on him as he drove.

In the flickering city lights of passing towers and skimmer traffic, I watched his face for any sign of... anything, really. Discomfort. Deception.

There wasn't much to see. I kept the gun right where it was all the same. "You're gonna have to forgive me if I'm hesitant to trust you after..."

I didn't know how to finish the sentence. It was all too breathtakingly gropped for me to even voice out loud. Kublich. My parents. The Sanctum Guard trying to kill me. And now here I was, sitting in the skimmer of the stranger who, for reasons unknown, had basically tried to kidnap me barely an hour earlier.

"Would you prefer I take you back?" he asked softly.

There was no mocking or sarcasm in his tone. Only... regret? Wistfulness?

I said nothing. I had no idea what to make of the man. Just like I had no idea what kind of scud storm I'd somehow fallen dead center of. It hadn't been a smart move, getting into this skimmer. But the scene in the alley had drawn too much attention, and somehow, after everything that'd happened tonight, I hadn't felt safe waiting around for Legion forces to arrive.

Of course, I didn't really feel safe here, either. Hence the gun.

We'd been lucky to clear the alleyway without half an army on our tail.

Whether or not he was aware of that fact, my strange companion had shown nothing but serene calm the entire flight. He practically radiated the stuff.

"Pretty oddly convenient for you, by the way," I said, partly wanting to goad him into spilling something, and partly because the silence was killing me, "bumping into me twice tonight."

A slight frown creased his forehead. "You have no idea how far from the truth that is."

I glanced out the windshield as he guided the skimmer through another turn, noting our location and new heading before fixing my gaze back on his dim shape. "If you're really looking out for me, why did I wake up in a dark trunk?" I glanced at the empty back seat. "Seems to me like there were less insane options."

"I apologize for the shock, but it seemed prudent to conceal the unconscious tyro in my vehicle while departing from Sanctuary. Time was of the essence." He gave me a concerned glance. "You weren't supposed to wake up so soon."

Indignation boiled up, hot and bitter. "Oh, well so sorry to ruin your plans. Next time, I'll be sure to be a good little kidnap victim."

He only drove on in silence. The man was damn good at silence. It was the last thing I needed right now. What I needed was answers. Maybe the gun wasn't helping with that—not that my companion seemed overly troubled by the weapon. Still, I was already beyond screwed anyway, right? What could it hurt?

Everything. But what did that even mean anymore?

I wasn't sure. So, with a long breath, I lowered the gun and deposited it in the door's storage compartment.

"Okay." I spread my hands, demonstrating their emptiness. "Okay. I got in the damn skimmer. The gun is down. I'm flying across Divinity with a guy who can apparently jump off buildings and shoot gropping Alpha beams from his hands, and tonight, the High General of the Alpha-damned Legion turned into a—a monster and—and killed my..."

I stopped, fighting back a wave of lightheadedness, hot tears pressing at my eyes, right on the verge of breaking down in front of a complete stranger. A stranger who, for all I knew, might be planning to finish what Kublich had started.

Alpha be damned, it had been a long night.

I wanted to curl up in the skimmer seat—to give in to the exhaustion that hung on my shoulders like a cape of pure softsteel. But I couldn't give in. Not now. Not with Alpha knew how many legionnaires searching for me out there. Not with my odd companion watching my little outburst with nothing but soft pity in his crinkled brow.

"You said you'd tell me everything," I said, dropping his gaze. "So tell me. Who are you? What are you?" I swallowed against the burning ache in my throat, my parents' faces hovering in my mind. "What the scud is going on?"

He slowed the skimmer, checked the mirrors one more time, then guided us down a ramp to a bay door that looked to lead underground. I glanced around one more time before we disappeared from traffic completely and decided we were somewhere near the southern harbors of Divinity, alongside the Red River. I turned back at the sound of a faint hum to find the bay door opening and my mysterious companion watching me.

"My name is Carlisle," he said, guiding the skimmer through the open doorway into a tiny underground lot. "The rest is considerably more complicated to explain."

I looked around the dim lot as the bay door crawled shut behind us. The space was cramped and empty. The stranger—Carlisle, if that was even his real name—tapped at his palmlight display, and the wall in front of us parted diagonally across the center and began to slide open with a mechanical hum. Beyond, a tunnel stretched into darkness, just large enough for a skimmer to pass. Unless my sense of direction was more confused than I thought, the tunnel looked to pass beneath the Red River, to the wilds beyond.

My hand gravitated back toward the gun at my side. "Not to sound indignant, Carlisle, but I think I'd prefer a little more than that before we go flying down any dark tunnels."

He chewed on that for a long moment, fiddling with a small, round pendant I hadn't noticed hanging at his chest. "I'll try to answer what I can," he finally said. "Where did you want to start?"

That was a good question. And now that he seemed good and ready to give me his undivided attention and open up, I couldn't seem to answer it. As outlandishly overturned as my world had been in the past hours, I was still half-hoping I might just wake up soon.

Compartmentalize. That's what I needed to do. Just like they'd always taught us in training. Except I was so far outside of any scenario we'd ever trained that the idea almost kicked a frantic laugh out of me. Compartmentalize? I could hardly form a cohesive thought right now, beyond the drowning rush of one grand question.

Why?

Why was this happening? Why my parents? Why me?

"That thing that attacked us," I found myself saying. "You said you knew about it. Was that really Adrian Kublich?"

"Yes, and no. It was certainly General Kublich's body that attacked you and your parents, but Kublich himself likely had no control over his actions —probably hasn't for some years now. The General's body has been commandeered, for lack of a better word."

"Commandeered…" What the scud did that mean? "Commandeered by what, exactly?"

Carlisle gave me a long, measuring look, his eyes lucid and piercing, like he was trying to decide what I could or couldn't handle—or maybe whether I could be trusted. Finally, his expression dropped to weary resignation.

"A raknoth."

"A what?"

"A raknoth," he repeated. "I can't tell you much about them other than that they seem capable of turning any host they invade into a walking puppet. A heavily modified puppet, as you had the misfortune of observing."

I thought back to the red eyes, the claws, and the odd green hue that'd tinged Kublich's skin at the end. Dizziness swirled through my head. The High General of the Legion, under the influence of some kind of… what? Some kind of demonic super parasite that somehow no one had ever heard of?

"That's not possible."

Carlisle studied me. "Would you rather I tell you he's been taken by a demon of the nether?"

I'd rather be home, asleep in my own bed, life thoroughly un-gropped, not worrying about any of this. Because this was all total bullscud. It had to be.

And yet I had seen Kublich sprout claws—seen the fire awaken in his eyes. I'd watched the High General of the Legion, a friend and ally to my father, brutally murder both my parents.

Was I losing it? I clamped a hand over my eyes in a futile attempt to calm my spinning head. It only made things worse. "How the hell could something like that go unnoticed?" I growled. "Those eyes weren't exactly hard to miss. There's no way."

"The raknoth wouldn't be very good parasites if they couldn't hide their existence." He gave me a peculiar look. "And they're hardly the only oddity that's escaped Enochia's notice."

Was he talking about himself? The impossible fall? The arcane snap flare? He pressed on before I could ask.

"I'm guessing you'd never noticed anything particularly off about Kublich, had you?"

I resisted the urge to glare at him. "You mean like gropping flaming eyes? No. Not really."

He tilted his head. "Just so. And by my guess, Kublich has likely been infected for nearly a decade. Worse, he's not the only one."

My stomach sank, my thoughts drifting back to Carlisle's impossible feats and the nightmare where he'd sported his own set of red eyes.

"And you?" I said, inching my hand closer to the gun at my side. "Who's pulling your strings in there?"

"I assure you," he said, tapping at the side of his head, "I'm still me in here. Just another Enochian, more or less."

Another Enochian. Right.

"May I keep driving while we talk?" he asked.

I eyed the opening ahead, doubt pulling at me from every direction. I needed answers—needed to take stock of my situation, come up with a plan. But where on Enochia could I go? Who could I trust?

I didn't even know where to start.

"Where are we going?" I asked.

"I have a safe place outside the city. Kublich and his servants won't find us there."

I chewed that over. Every bit of rational training I'd ever had told me to take my gun and walk. Get to the streets. Find a node. Call Johnny. Call anyone. Maybe something had happened to Kublich, but the rest of the Legion would sort this out. Right?

Maybe. But then why had four Sanctum Guard and that odd smirking bastard tried to kill me tonight? And what in demon's depths had Smirks even done to me back there, with the paralysis and the whispers in my head?

It was all too much to process. And while my rational mind might be telling me to get out of the skimmer and run, my gut, for some reason, was telling me to do the opposite. Carlisle clearly hadn't told me everything, but I also didn't think he wanted to hurt me. For one thing, if he'd wanted me dead, he'd already had two chances tonight to sit back and watch it happen. That was something, at least. Plus, he had answers, even if they did sound like wild bullscud.

I couldn't trust him. Not until I understood why he'd been there to pull my ass out of the fire in the first place. After everything that had happened, I'm not even sure I could have trusted the High Cleric himself right then.

But for now, sticking with Carlisle sounded better than trying my luck on the streets. So I gave a wary nod of concession to my patiently waiting companion and did my best not to fidget as he guided the skimmer into the tunnel. The tunnel entrance slid shut behind us, leaving nothing but the skimmer's headlights to illuminate the way through the darkness ahead. The fit was tight, and the angle gradually descended over the next few minutes. We were almost definitely passing under the Red River.

I tried not to think about it.

"You're not just another Enochian," I said, in part to distract myself from thoughts of a horrible, drowning death in the dark tunnel. "I saw the things you did."

The skimmer's flight shifted subtly as the tunnel leveled out then began slowly ascending.

"I did say more or less," Carlisle said.

"Yeah, because shooting snap flares from your hands and surviving falls from Alpha knows how high are such tiny little extras."

"Those things I can explain much more thoroughly than the raknoth." He looked over at me, brow creasing in a frown. "In fact, I fear I might have to, considering. And sooner than later."

"What do you mean? Considering what?"

"Considering you're like me. Gifted."

I stared at him in the dim lighting of the skimmer's controls, searching his face for any sign of trickery. There wasn't any. So instead I looked for the cracks in Carlisle's sanity. Because, clearly, they had to be there. But the man who calmly met my gaze looked all too sane, and honest right to his core.

"Is it too late to turn around?" I said.

Carlisle's lip twitched upward, and he tilted his head toward the windshield.

Ahead, the darkness of the tunnel was peeling away along a widening diagonal slit. Another lot, it looked like, probably underground like its counterpart behind.

"Sadly," Carlisle said, "I believe it may be."

I said nothing, trying to collect my thoughts as we approached the light at the end of the tunnel. I suppose I should've been worrying about whether this might be the part where Carlisle led me into an ambush—where I found out he'd been working with Kublich all along, toying with me. But I was too tired. Too confused.

Fortunately, when we exited the tunnel, there were no armed men or red-eyed monsters waiting for us. Or anything else. The lot was larger than the one we'd come from, but similarly empty. I waited until Carlisle had settled the skimmer to the pavement and killed the power before I spoke.

"What do you mean I'm like you? I don't even know what you are, but I'm pretty sure I would've noticed if I was packing some kind of… gifts, or whatever you wanna call them."

"You might have, had your gifts not been dormant."

I shook my head, starting to think I'd made a mistake in trusting my gut. The things Carlisle was saying were insane. I should have just found a node and called Johnny, or anyone else in Sanctuary.

Except Kublich *had* killed my parents. The Sanctum *had* tried to kill me. It didn't make a damn bit of sense. But it had happened—was happening. So what if the rest was true?

What if one of these raknoth things had taken control of Kublich? Twisted him to its will? What if there were more of them? What if the entire damn Legion was after me, with or without Kublich's say so?

No. That was the nerves talking again. It had to be. But what if it wasn't? What if the entire Legion had been compromised?

What if there was no one left to fix this problem?

That was truly crazy talk. Almost as crazy as Carlisle claiming I had some kind of dormant sorcery floating around inside.

"Look…" I started, unsure where I was going with it. "I, uh, appreciate the help, but I think I need to get to a node and sort this all out for myself."

"You could do that," Carlisle said, bobbing his head thoughtfully, "but I'm afraid you'd quickly find yourself in another situation like the one in the alley."

"I grew up in Sanctuary, I know how to avoid their attention."

"I don't doubt that. But what you don't understand is that you've undergone a change. Like it or not, your mind is a veritable spotlight right now for those who know how to look. Go out there before you're ready, and they will find you."

I rolled my eyes. "Because I'm *gifted*, right? This is insane."

"Crazy, maybe. But not insane. You already encountered another practitioner of the art. The Seeker back in the alley. Tell me, did he speak to you when he had you under his control?"

It was several seconds of staring at Carlisle before I realized I'd stopped breathing.

"I…" I raked a hand across my buzzed scalp, thinking back to the terrifying stint of Smirks playing puppet master with my body. "I don't know what I felt."

But I did know. It just didn't make a single iota of sense.

"I understand," Carlisle said. "It's a lot to take in. Especially after everything that's happened tonight."

"It's bullscud!" I cried, and I was surprised by the anger in my voice.

"I could give you more tangible proof." He gave me an apologetic look, and I nearly cried out in surprise when his voice continued on in my head. *If that would make any of this easier to process.*

"Sweet Alpha," I whispered, pressing back against the skimmer door.

His lips hadn't even twitched, but I'd heard him all the same. And it was damn creepy.

Carlisle held his hands up in peace. "It's okay. You're safe here. I just needed to show you that this is real. It's why they were able to find you in the middle of a crowded city. You might have even felt them looking once you escaped the trunk." He frowned at the skimmer's console. "Sorry about that, by the way."

"It's, uh…"

What? Okay? Okay that he'd kidnapped me?

That was real healthy thinking.

"Look, I don't know what's going on, but I'm just another Legion tyro. That's all."

Carlisle studied me for a long moment then turned to climb out of the skimmer. "Come. There's something you need to see."

I grabbed the pistol from the door compartment on the way out. Carlisle was waiting for me by the skimmer's trunk hatch, which was still ajar from my earlier escape.

"Did you at any point stop to wonder how it was you managed to open a locked hatch from inside without the remote?"

I hadn't.

Between the escape itself and everything else that'd happened that night, I'd been far too occupied to even think about that miraculous little detail. Carlisle waved me closer, holding the dangling hatch open for my inspection. I leaned in for a look, a funny feeling creeping into my gut.

It didn't take a trained mechanic to explain why the trunk's lock had failed. The latching mechanism wasn't broken as I'd expected. It wasn't faulty. It hadn't been jarred loose.

It just wasn't there anymore.

It had to have been there when I'd woken up. The hatch wouldn't have been closed otherwise. But now, in the place where it should have been, there was only a disfigured lump, as if the latch had simply melted into the composite material of the trunk hatch.

"It appears," Carlisle said, watching me closely, "that I'm not the only one who broke the rules of what is and isn't possible tonight."

I stared at the too-smooth surface where the latch had previously been, trying for several seconds to think of some explanation as to how it had simply vanished. It had to be a fluke. Or a trick—Carlisle manipulating me into believing this story of his for... for what? It didn't make any sense. None of it.

Was it possible I'd done this?

It couldn't be. It was impossible. But that very thought was starting to lose meaning for the sheer number of times it'd passed through my head that night.

"Let's say I chose to believe you about any of this," I said, looking at Carlisle. "How, by the light of Alpha, have I never heard a whisper about... people like you? Or the raknoth either?"

"Probably because the existence of people like *us* has been one of the Sanctum's most vehemently suppressed secrets for the better part of a millennium. And as for the raknoth, they seem quite adept at blending in, though I believe their arrival here was also much more recent."

"Their arrival to Divinity?"

Carlisle gave a polite smile and shook his head.

He couldn't mean...

"You're not saying...?"

He gave an almost apologetic little nod.

"To Enochia? You're saying the raknoth came from another gropping planet?"

By way of reply, Carlisle placed a hand to the skimmer's rear hatch and closed his eyes, and I stared on in disbelief as the lump of the would-be latch wriggled to life—twisting, stretching, and readjusting until it had reformed into a passable if not perfect latching mechanism. Then he slapped the trunk closed with a light thud.

It held.

Carlisle met my eyes.

"Welcome to the secret war for Enochia."

CHAPTER 7

TEMPORARY LODGINGS

I eyed the bowl of food Carlisle offered me with what must have been a dubious expression.

"If I had ill intentions," he said, waving the bowl for emphasis, "I wouldn't have tried so hard to keep you alive tonight."

The thought had already occurred to me more than once, but I was still off balance in the face of his seemingly good nature. I took the bowl and mumbled thanks. As far as I could tell, Carlisle was on my side for now—I felt more confident about *that* than about what side I was actually even on at this point.

Allegiances aside, I was surprised to find I was starving despite having had a good helping of my mom's meat and gravy pie only a few hours ago. The last helping I'd ever have, I realized. Our last supper together.

The thought hit me like a falling brick, pushing any thought of food from my mind. My stomach, however, deftly ignored my inner turmoil and rumbled unapologetically at the smell wafting from the warm, cheesy pasta concoction in my bowl. Apparently my escape had taken a lot out of me.

I picked up the fork mostly to appease Carlisle. My first bite was minuscule—partly out of some pretense at caution, but mostly because it somehow felt wrong to concern myself with something as insignificant as food after everything that'd just happened. Then the wave of savory flavor hit my tongue, enlightening me as to just how hungry I really was, and I dug in voraciously.

"I'm sorry the best I have to offer is from the fab," Carlisle said, as if he hadn't noticed me attacking my food like a wild animal. He returned to the fabricator in his rudimentary kitchen station and began extruding another helping into his own dish. "You probably won't be surprised to hear it's not so easy to keep a secret hideout well stocked with fresh groceries."

"I grew up in Sanctuary," I managed past a mouthful of pasta. "I'm used to it." I took another look around Carlisle's self-proclaimed secret hideout from my perch on the corner cot.

The room was fairly large, half of it housing a modest living space and the other half mostly empty floor space—which actually might have been the most interesting part of the room. Instead of the permacrete that was nearly ubiquitous in modern Enochian architecture, the floor was made from slabs of dark, almost black stone, the like of which I'd never seen outside the Sanctum's White Tower. That alone was enough to make me wonder where on Enochia I was, but there were plenty more oddities around the room.

Most of it was benign enough—the tiny kitchen space, the household hydrocycler unit, the pristinely ordered desk and its three large displays on the opposite wall. Some of it, though, was much more interesting. Like the small workbench to my right, with its haphazard collection of tools, odd, mismatched trinkets, and—most interestingly—multiple ingredients I knew could be used in homemade explosives. Then there was the miniature armory past the foot of my cot—a mismatched amalgamation of blades, batons, a few odd firearms, and related supplies.

Taking the sum of its pieces, the room looked like the hideout of an apostate terrorist, or maybe some kind of idealistic—possibly deranged—vigilante. Or maybe both, I thought, looking at Carlisle. Though I was still uncertain about the deranged bit.

"And you're sure about the *secret* part?" I asked.

"This place has served me well for some time," he said, looking around the room with a subdued fondness. "We're as safe here as we could be."

I had no delusions that *safe as we could be* meant *truly safe*. Not with my people probably looking for us. But I kept my mouth shut about it. Whatever this place was, it beat a Divinity alleyway for now.

"Been hiding out for a while then?" I asked.

"Most of my life."

There was a subtle sadness to the statement.

"Because of the raknoth?"

Carlisle collected his own dish from the fab and went to his desk chair before answering.

He moved with the grace of a dancer, or a master martial artist—smoothly enough that I wondered if I'd been overconfident in assuming I could handle him in a fight.

"More because hiding out is simply what Shapers do," he said as he sank into his chair.

Shapers?

Before I could ask, Carlisle continued. "Though the arrival of the raknoth certainly hasn't helped my situation."

My fork paused in the bowl at the reminder of his extraterrestrial theory —or insanity, rather. I still wasn't sure he wasn't just screwing with me. Theories about life elsewhere in the universe had come and gone in the past, but the results were in, and the ruling of the Sanctum was clear. Enochia was Alpha's chosen planet—the one place in the universe he'd deigned to create life. We were it.

And even if these raknoth creatures were real, why reach beyond our planet for an explanation? They might simply be an undiscovered species. Or, Alpha be sweet, they might well be genuine demons. I'd always taken the Sanctum's tales mostly as metaphor, but maybe this was exactly what they'd feared. Maybe that explained why the Sanctum Guard were shooting first and asking questions later. Demons were not to be suffered.

It actually made a certain amount of sense. More than Carlisle's wild story, at least. Still, I knew what I'd seen. I'd never forget Kublich's beastly visage—the unholy fire in those eyes. And that wasn't to mention the things Carlisle could do, and the things he seemed to think I could do as well. I swallowed an enormous mouthful of cheesy foodstuff and decided to dig further.

"Let's say I choose to believe the whole alien thing for a minute. Where did these raknoth things come from? How did they get here?"

Carlisle took his time finishing his own bite. "I don't know. I only inferred their origin from something they said the first time I encountered their kind. Although it seems others have reached the same conclusion."

My eyes widened as his words kicked a thought loose. "Kovaks. Sweet Alpha, was this what he was talking about all along?"

Carlisle tilted his head as if to say *maybe, maybe not*. "I didn't know Andre Kovaks. But, judging by the nature of the allegations against him and the content of his journals, I'd guess that, yes, he might've pieced together at least some of the raknoth puzzle."

I frowned. "But why would the Sanctum make a spectacle of that? They had to think he was a madman. Why not just take care of him quietly?"

Carlisle raised his brows, inviting me to answer my own question.

"Unless…" I said slowly, working through the pieces, the food forgotten in my hands, along with my appetite. "No…"

"Because the raknoth wanted to put the very real fear of death into whoever else might be on their trail," Carlisle said. "That was my thought as well."

"That's—"

"Not possible? But why not? They knew it was no risk to them. Who would actually listen to what no doubt sounded like the ramblings of a madman?"

"But that would mean…" I felt hollow. "They've infiltrated the Sanctum as well?"

Kublich was the High General. If the raknoth controlled him, they effectively controlled the Legion. And if they could do that…

To my horror, Carlisle nodded. "I believe so. It's nearly impossible for me to identify human from raknoth without getting close to them, but I'm afraid the raknoth have delved their way quite deeply into Enochia's infrastructure, which likely means they hold at least one high position within the Sanctum. Maybe more."

I stared at the remnants of my cooling food with unseeing eyes.

I wanted to call Johnny, to see a familiar face.

I wanted my parents.

A dull ache spread through my insides. A powerful longing for my mom's smile and her warm hands on my face. For my dad's unshakable faith and resolve. A powerful longing I'd never see fulfilled again.

Because I was alone now.

I'd never be able to turn to them for comfort or security again. Kublich had seen to that. And after tonight, I was pretty damn sure he had every intention of finishing the job with me.

No Mom. No Dad. No Legion at my back.

I was all alone.

"Why my parents?" I finally asked, my voice barely above a whisper.

The question had been burning through my mind all night, over and over. But I'd held back, afraid of the answer. Or maybe just afraid there was no answer at all.

Carlisle dropped my gaze, as if to pay respect to the aching in my chest. "I can't say for certain, but I imagine Kublich must have suspected they knew too much. I doubt he would have acted so openly unless they were a tangible threat to his position."

I'd already figured as much, I realized. Ever since I'd first stumbled into the living room and seen those fiery red eyes. Some part of me had just been hoping Carlisle would have another answer. A better one. One that would've been easier than the truth.

"My dad. He was onto Kublich. He knew."

It explained everything—my dad's behavior over the past cycles, his unusual reaction to Kovaks' execution. He'd known about Kublich. Maybe not everything, but enough to realize that something wasn't right with the High General.

"Your father was a more clever man than his colleagues, it seems."

And here I'd spent the past days questioning his activities, doubting his loyalty to my mom. I felt ill. Even more so, when I recognized the anger rising in my gut. Because if Johnny and I had spotted him with Kublich's servitor, how many others had? How could he have been so careless?

As repugnant as the thought was, I found myself wishing it *had* simply been adultery. At least then my parents would still be alive.

Carlisle's pitying eyes seemed to see right through me. "He couldn't have known what he was exposing your family to. I'd wager he suspected Kublich of something much less sinister. Abusing his command, or trading Legion secrets, for instance. If he'd realized the true gravity of the situation…" He dropped his gaze to the floor. "I clearly didn't know him, Haldin, but it seems to me that your father was a good man, just trying to do the right thing. I'm sorry I couldn't save your parents."

I said nothing. Some part of me wanted to tell him that it wasn't his fault. The rest was stuck watching the scene unfold on repeat, recalling the way Carlisle had become the monster in my nightmare after the fact.

He took my dish and set to cleaning them in the small sink, the hydrocycler unit kicking on with a low hum. I watched in numb silence, my thoughts spiraling nowhere but downward.

"Why were you at my house?" I was almost surprised at the strength of the accusation in my tone. "Why did you know my name?"

Carlisle shut off the water and turned to face me as he toweled his hands dry. "I snuck into Sanctuary to confirm my suspicions about Kublich. I had to confer with a few of Sanctuary's inhabitants to figure out when and where I might track him down in relative privacy. Your name arose from those questions." He frowned. "It wasn't a good plan. But"—he waved a hand at me—"at least some good came of my presence this evening."

I studied him closely, looking for any hint of deceit. The way he'd chosen the word, *confer*, made me wonder exactly how he'd extracted the information.

"I didn't hurt anyone," Carlisle said, seeming to catch my train of thought. "And they won't remember me."

That raised a few more questions, but my head was spinning too much to press the matter. I leaned back against the wall, fatigue weighing nearly as heavily in my limbs as it did on my mind. "I guess I probably should have thanked you by now."

"A forgivable oversight, I think, all things considered." He searched my face, then glanced at his palmlight. "You should try to get some sleep. You must be exhausted."

I glanced at my own palm only to be reminded my device was gone. It was an odd feeling, being without it. Almost like I'd left one of my appendages behind. But how could I really lament the loss of a communications device when I would've given all four of my limbs right then and there to get my parents back?

"Apologies about your palmlight," Carlisle said, apparently having noticed my fixation on my blank palm. "They would have tracked it far too easily."

I dropped my hand and shrugged, too occupied with thoughts of my parents now to care. The fabbed food settling in my stomach only deepened my exhaustion. There were no windows in the room, but I knew it must be somewhere around midnight, if not later.

"One more thing," Carlisle said, moving over to rummage through a set of drawers on the workbench. A few moments later, he turned and offered me a thin necklace, complete with a pendant similar to the one at his own breast.

"I think it would be prudent for you to get used to wearing one of these."

I took the pendant and turned the small disk over in my hands, tracing my fingers over its two concentric circles, the smaller of which was able to turn like a dial between two positions. A symbol had been etched into the disk with red lines, it's meaning completely foreign to me.

"And this is?"

"A precaution," Carlisle said. "Like I said, your mind is a bit of a spotlight to people like us right now, and the raknoth are particularly powerful telepaths. I imagine Kublich caught your mental scent, so to speak, and then there are the Seekers like the one you met back in the alley."

Powerful telepaths.

I wanted to laugh at the notion. But I couldn't. Not after the way Smirks and Kublich had each made a helpless puppet of me, or the way Smirks had whispered his thoughts straight into my head.

My heart picked up just thinking about it.

"They can't, uh, sense me right now, can they?"

Carlisle patted the air in a pacifying gesture. "We're safe for now. Even strong telepaths couldn't hope to consciously reach this far. Even a mile would be unheard of. But sleep has a way of opening the mind and amplifying one's telepathic sensitivity, especially in those new to their gifts and unlearned in shielding their minds. Hence"—he patted at his own pendant—"precautions. We don't want them tracking and influencing you while you sleep."

I nodded slowly, still staring at the odd pendant.

It occurred to me it might be wise to tell Carlisle about my nightmare, where the attack had been twisted so that he'd been the monster who'd taken my parents. Could Kublich have had something to do with planting those seeds of doubt in my head? I didn't know, and I didn't really want to broach the topic right then either.

Instead, I turned the pendant dial so the odd red etchings all lined up, assuming that was the *on* position, and slipped the necklace over my head, not bothering to reflect on how utterly ridiculous this all should've sounded. As soon as the cord settled on my neck, the pendant grew cool to the touch.

"What the scud?" I whispered, half to myself. "How does this thing work, exactly?" I looked up at Carlisle, remembering his cryptic remark from earlier. "And what in demon's depths are Shapers?"

Carlisle gave me a tired smile. "I was under the impression asking questions was against Legion tenets."

The reminder of my home was a bitter ache in the back of my throat. It must've showed on my face, because Carlisle's expression immediately softened.

"We'll talk tomorrow. You're liable to die of exhaustion if I try to answer all your questions before you sleep." He pointed at the pendant on my chest. "For now, just know that as long as the lines of that rune are unbroken, your mind will essentially be closed off to the outside world."

With that, he dimmed the lights and settled to work at his desk node, flicking through newsreels on the central of the three displays.

I wanted to protest—to demand he keep explaining until neither of us could keep our eyes open any longer. But my eyelids were feeling awfully heavy now that we'd paused, and my mouth expelled a yawn instead of words when I tried. So I lay there in a stupor, studying the strange man who'd probably saved my life and trying my best not to think about everything I'd seen that night.

What would the reels have to say about my parents' murders? About my disappearance?

It was too much to think about right now. And I'd probably find out tomorrow anyway. The thought deepened the pit in my stomach. It exhausted me.

Yet sleep wouldn't come. Not for a long while. I couldn't have said how long, only that I seemed to be caught somewhere between—not quite awake but certainly not asleep either, terrible fragments of half-thoughts ripping their frantic ways through my mind. And through the swells and troughs of chaotic noise, three thoughts rose above all others.

My parents were dead.

I was alone.

And, as harrowing as the night had been, I was certain the scud was only just getting started.

CHAPTER 8

COLD TRUTH

I was surprised to wake the next morning, given that it meant I'd somehow fallen asleep the night before. Surprised, groggy, and more than a little disoriented. Everything came back all too fast, though, when I looked around the quaint stone room and saw Carlisle sitting cross-legged on a spacious blue sparring mat, his back turned to me.

"Good afternoon," he said, not turning. "How did you sleep?"

Afternoon?

In futility, I glanced at my lightless palm. "Okay, I guess." I must have if it was afternoon already. I sat up, trying to rub the sleep from my eyes. "What time is it?"

"Three past midday."

Scud.

The thought of even sleeping in past sunrise was like a stun prod to the Legion tyro inside me. But it wasn't like that mattered now. There were no doceres here to chastise me. No Mathis to scornfully point out that my captain daddy had never been late a day in his Alpha-blessed life.

No Dad to tell me to believe in myself and in Alpha above all else, no matter what opinions others may hold. No Mom to laughingly tell him to stop being so serious for a minute every once in a while, lest he make a severe old man of me before I'd even made legionnaire.

The pain couldn't have been any more real if my stomach had actually cramped up and folded in on itself.

Carlisle rose smoothly from the mat and turned to look at me. "You can rest more if you'd like."

I shook my head, trying to push the pain down. "I need to figure out my next move."

I made it as far as my feet before it properly dawned on me that I had no idea where to go from there.

"I've been thinking about that as well. What did you have in mind?"

I just stared at him, utterly lost for words, the weight of how screwed I was cascading down on me like a bottomless bucket of ice water. No matter what I did—who I turned to—Kublich could be watching. Every direction my thoughts turned, the way was untenable. Blocked.

I was trapped.

Sure, maybe if I was really clever about it, I could find a way to sneak a message to someone I knew forward and backward, which at this point pretty much meant Johnny.

But what then?

It wasn't like I could tell him to come pick me up and bring me back to Sanctuary. If Kublich wanted me found, the only place I'd be safe was under a very well-hidden rock. Leave that rock, and he would find me. Reach out to anyone I knew, and he'd find me. Do anything. He'd find me.

I sank back to the cot, burying my head in my hands. "I need to tell someone what happened. If I can convince one of the other Generals..."

The Generals who all answered to Kublich.

"... Or I could turn to the Sanctum."

The Sanctum whose elite Guard had tried to kill me.

If I could just get my story to the right ears, I wanted to say. But how by the light of Alpha was I even supposed to know which ears were the right ones? And if I made one wrong move...

The image of Kovaks' body swaying limply from the gallows came to mind, unbidden. This must've been exactly how he'd felt when he'd realized something was horribly wrong on Enochia.

And now I was the madman no one would be willing to listen to.

Of course, some part of me protested, I also still couldn't be sure Carlisle's story was true—or that anything I'd seen was even real. Alpha be damned, for all I knew, Carlisle could've dosed me with a hard hit of alussein vine and kidnapped me from my house. I could have hallucinated all of it. But that thought was every bit as crazy as the truth I was trying to avoid.

I knew what I'd seen last night. What I needed to do was make sure I wasn't the only one, which meant finding hard proof that Kublich had murdered my parents. That was the only place to start.

But Kublich had already had the entire night. He would've tried to cover up his crime, right? Probably. But there'd been screams. Gunshots. It couldn't have all gone unnoticed. Not in Sanctuary, of all places. Right?

"We need to see what they're saying on the reels," I finally said.

A tangible place to start. That was good. And, whatever happened, it'd be a valuable test of just how wide and powerful Kublich's influence actually was. I started to stand.

Carlisle ghosted forward and pressed a hand to my shoulder. "Haldin." He looked concerned. "You won't like what you see. I'm not sure you're ready to—"

"I need to know," I said, shrugging his hand aside and pushing past him to the displays above his desk.

I waved one to life, navigated through the menu to Divinity's local WAN reel, and scanned headlines and images, an odd mixture of eagerness and dread swirling through me.

There. It was timestamped from the previous night, maybe two hours after the attack. An image of me and my parents from the Legion promotion ceremony we'd all attended a few cycles ago. Seeing their faces, alive and happy… it was like a knife twisting in my gut.

Then I read the headline beside the image.

Tragedy Strikes: Legion Officer and Family Killed in Accidental House Fire.

Carlisle had appeared beside me like an apparition. "You don't have to watch it."

I ignored him and played the story.

"And now," the caster was saying where the vid picked up, "grim news from Sanctuary, where what currently appears to have been a faulty energy cell led to tragedy for a loyal Legion officer and his family."

The caster's voice blurred to a background buzz as I numbly gaped at the bold, white letters of the banner across the bottom of the feed.

Family of Three Burns to Death in Accidental House Fire.

It took three or four tries for the words to register.

Three deaths. Accidental.

It couldn't be.

"Legion officials have identified the remains of Captain Martin Raish," the caster was saying, "along with those of his wife, Klara Raish, and son, Haldin Raish."

My insides turned to ice.

"The investigation is ongoing, but preliminary reports have indicated the fire may have started due to a mechanical failure in the home's backup energy cell. Officials are still working to con—"

The vid paused.

I turned to Carlisle, who'd gestured the command. He met my eyes with an apologetic expression.

"What—How could he—I don't..." I clutched at my buzzed scalp in some vain attempt to keep my mind from exploding.

Kublich was the High General of the Legion. Sanctuary all but belonged to him. I knew that. But for him to warp the facts so quickly and so completely, and on the WAN no less... It was unthinkable. The Word of Alpha Network was the premier news source for all of Enochia. They were the mouth of the Sanctum, which was in turn the law of Enochia. They wouldn't be bullied into lying by one man. Not even the High General.

Which meant this had to go deeper—entire networks of Legion soldiers and WAN newscasters either willfully lying or masterfully manipulated. I could barely wrap my head around the depth of that kind of corruption. And then there was the other part.

"They found a third body."

My voice was flat, but Carlisle heard the unspoken question anyway.

"If the universe was kind, Kublich merely saw to it that the right people lied about what they found."

"And if the universe wasn't kind?"

A shadow fell over his expression. "There are plenty who live hungry in the streets of Divinity. I doubt a raknoth would have trouble procuring a body on short notice, and it wouldn't be too much of a stretch for the investigators to assume such a body was yours if they had trouble identifying it after a fire."

I leaned shakily against the desk for support. "He can't. He can't just get away with this."

"I'll do my best to see he doesn't," Carlisle said quietly behind me. "But... I trust you realize you can't go back to Sanctuary now. Kublich knows you're alive. His servants will be looking for you. Probably the rest of the raknoth too. They don't tend to leave loose ends."

I said nothing. Part of me wanted to argue out of spite. The rest just stood there, stupefied, as the full weight of the situation settled on my chest.

I hadn't expected returning to Sanctuary would be a safe option anytime soon. But the situation was so much more complicated than that now.

Everyone I knew thought I was dead. And if they found out I wasn't, it might well land them in Kublich's crosshairs.

So much for reaching out to Johnny.

I stared at the frozen reel.

Johnny.

What would he have done when he'd heard the news? Would he be at lessons right now? Or would they give him the day?

I saw him in my mind, grieving, hiding the pain behind his jokes when they asked him if he'd like to speak about me at the funeral the Legion would no doubt put on in my family's memory.

Kublich would speak at that funeral. I had no doubt about that. He'd look down on the people who'd known and loved me and my parents, and he'd spout words of respect for my father. Words of praise for me and my mother.

My hands curled into painfully tight fists. "I'm going to kill him."

I didn't mean to say it out loud, but once the words were out, I knew that I meant them to the core of my being.

The life I'd known was over.

My parents were gone. I was alone. Alpha's light, I was *dead* according to the WAN. There was no going back. All I had left was the fear and the rage —the red hot pressure, building, building with each beat of my racing heart. I was going to burst with it.

I was going to make Adrian Kublich pay for what he'd done.

Carlisle was watching me silently, his expression guarded. "You should take some time to process everything," he finally said, turning to go busy himself at the fab before I could answer.

I watched him, unsure what else to do, as he moved about, preparing two bowls of some fabbed bean concoction.

Take some time? Time was the last thing I needed right now. What I needed was a plan of attack. Clear targets. An objective, for the love of Alpha.

I needed to do something.

And yet here was Carlisle, depositing the two bowls at the small table and settling down to eat, like the High General of the Legion hadn't just gotten away with murder.

"Join me, please," he said after a few bites, when I was still standing there gaping.

"I'm not hungry."

I couldn't imagine I would be for some time.

"For mental digestion, then," he said, sliding a chair my way.

"I can't," I snapped before I even knew what I wanted to say. I took a breath and tried again, more calmly. "I can't just sit down and pretend like this isn't happening. I need to do something about it. Right now. You snuck into Sanctuary for Kublich. That doesn't happen by accident. You must have a backup plan, right?"

Carlisle set his spoon down in his bowl, the movement precise and deliberate, just like everything else about him. The slightest crease formed in the brow of his otherwise impassive face as he thought. "Several. Most of which fell to pieces the moment Kublich attacked your family. The rest of which"—he gestured at the bowl—"involve subsisting long enough to find another way."

"We could sneak back on base. It's the last thing they'd expect us to do."

"Us." Carlisle looked troubled by the notion. "And tell me, even if that were to happen, provided the operation didn't fall apart in any number of the thousands of ways it likely would, what would you do once you had the High General alone in a room?"

I thought back to how Kublich had shaken off multiple gunshots—the ease with which he'd manhandled my mom's body and broken my dad's neck. I leaned against the table, suppressing the acidic swell that rose in my throat at the memory.

"You stopped him. You said I was gifted too."

He looked like he wanted to say something, but he stopped himself, waiting for me to say what he clearly knew I was going to say next.

"I want you to teach me to do what you did. Teach me to be a Shaper, or whatever you wanna call it."

He stared at me for a long stretch before finally dropping his attention back to his food.

"No."

And, just like that, he took another bite of the bean stuff, tranquil as ever—like he hadn't just cold-heartedly denied my plea for justice.

"No? What do you mean, no?"

He closed his eyes and let out a deep breath, as if bracing himself for coming unpleasantness. "Let's not make an issue of it right now. You need food and time to clear your head before we discuss it."

Anger flared through my clenched jaw down to my painfully flexing toes.

An issue of it? A tiny little issue of wanting justice for my murdered parents? Was that what I was making?

"Haldin, I think you should—"

I grabbed him by the front of his tunic, barely thinking, barely seeing. I yanked him up from his chair... and promptly found myself stumbling backward for balance, grip broken and forearms burning. The shifty bastard.

I threw my first punch almost before I knew it. Nothing but thin air. He'd barely moved, but the miss was so clean—the punch so wild—that I staggered for balance. Missing pissed me off. But Carlisle's reaction? Not bothering to retreat or press his advantage? Just standing there with that maddening calm?

Something took hold of me then—something I'd been holding in since last night. Something I'd never let loose in all my years of training.

A wordless cry erupted from my throat, and I threw myself at Carlisle like a wild demon.

CHAPTER 9
THE HARD WAY

I might as well have been dancing with myself in an empty room.

All the pain. All the helpless rage I'd been sitting on, too stunned to even process. It all came out. And Carlisle couldn't be troubled to care. He evaded two crisscross punches without even moving his feet. Slipped the savage rib kick that followed with only a small step. I threw a flurry of jabs. A strong cross. Launched into a wild flying knee.

Carlisle calmly pivoted clear of each successive blow and spun outside my flying knee with an ease that dropped it from devastating attack to laughable farce in an instant. As salt to the wound, he even clipped my back leg as my knee flew past his chest. I tumbled to the ground in an awkward roll, bounced back to my feet, and hovered there, burning with embarrassment and the throbbing trophies of my stone floor landing.

Demon's depths, he was fast. Unquestionably faster than anyone I'd ever sparred with. Too fast to bother blocking my attacks. He didn't even have his guard up.

It was infuriating.

"Not bad," he said. "But if I were a raknoth, you'd be dead right now."

So he was assessing me now? What was this, smashball tryouts?

"You know I'm a trained soldier, right?"

The words sounded especially pathetic after Carlisle had effortlessly dismantled my wild offensive, but he just dipped his head in agreement.

"Indeed. And you've learned what they've taught you quite well, I think."

Was he mocking me now?

"What's that supposed to mean?"

"That you appear to be an adept study. But also that your teachers have been slow and brutish."

"Maybe I'm just reticent about hitting an old man."

A hint of amusement tugged at his eyes and mouth. "I think you'll find me sufficiently spry."

I had no doubt about that. The man had survived a fall off a damn building, after all.

"Your base is strong," Carlisle added, starting to pace a leisurely arc around me, toward the more open half of the room, "but it will never be as strong as a raknoth's. Not even close. Your rigidity does you no favors."

"Rigidity is power."

"Power?" Carlisle raised an eyebrow. "Show me."

It was a trap. I wasn't too angry to see that—just angry enough to think I could show the bastard anyway. I lunged into the hardest punch I could throw, driving through my planted foot and up through the kinetic chain that ended with my fist flying for Carlisle's open sternum.

He blurred to the outside of my punch, caught my wrist, and tugged all in one liquid flow. It was a simple move, but his timing was perfect. I staggered forward to regain my stolen balance. He reversed direction before I could find it, pivoting sharply and flicking his wrist. The world blurred, and I crashed to the floor. Hard. Had it been on the stone, I might have broken something. Instead, and probably not by accident, it was Carlisle's pale blue practice mat I slammed down to, which left everything intact. Everything but my pride, at least.

"You call that a punch, tyro?" I heard Docere Mathis' voice in the back of my head. *"You think daddy would've fallen for that bullscud?"*

Some trained soldier I was.

"Okay," I muttered, picking myself up. "You're fast. I get it. You're really fast and I'm not gonna be killing Kublich with my bare hands. Was there supposed to be a real point here?"

His face took on a shadow. "I have no doubt you'd fare well in a fair fight, but this isn't that. What happens when you find yourself facing five men? Twenty? A thousand? If it were only the raknoth, they'd already have us outnumbered and outmatched, but it's far worse. They have the Legion. They probably have the Sanctum. Their power is vast, they're far stronger than us, and they are very hard to kill."

I flinched inwardly at the intensity in his voice. It was the closest I'd seen to him getting upset. But there was something else.

Us.

He'd said *us*. Not singular.

I swallowed. "So does that mean I passed tryouts?"

He let out a sharp sigh. "You're not ready for this."

And with that, he went to sit at his desk, leaving me alone with my thoughts.

I wanted to be angry. Maybe I should've been indignant. But it was hard to be much of anything other than embarrassed after how effortlessly he'd just kicked my ass. So I watched, waiting to see if he'd say more, but he was immersed in the reels as if the entire incident was already gone from his mind.

"Look, I get it," I said. "The odds are stacked."

"That's putting it quite lightly," he said, not bothering to unglue his eyes from the displays. He hesitated, then added, "There are places on Enochia you can go to escape notice. I can help you get that far. It'll be better that way."

Better for me? Or for him?

Now probably wasn't the time to push it. Right now, all I wanted was to be alone. To think. To get out of this room and see the Alpha-blasted sun.

"I'm going for a walk."

Aside from the mag lift that led to the skimmer bay below, the room had only a single door—a thick steel one that looked at odds with the ancient stone of the room. It had to lead outside, to fresh air and open space.

"Haldin."

I paused at the door, expecting Carlisle to object—to tell me it wasn't safe or that I might be spotted. Instead, he went to the kitchen unit, filled a water jug, and tucked it into a small satchel along with some dried goods and a hand lantern.

He returned and offered the parcel to me without a word. I took it, feeling even more embarrassed now for having lashed out at him, and nodded my thanks. A few seconds of awkward fumbling later, I threw open the heavy door's latching mechanism and exited into a dim stone tunnel. I pulled the door shut, thought about digging out the hand lantern, and decided by the faint glow of daylight up ahead that I probably didn't need it.

The hall led me to the top of a dilapidated stairwell. More daylight crept in below, where the structure looked to open to a larger space. I picked my way down the crumbling steps… and gasped.

Compared to Carlisle's little hideout, the chamber was enormous. It was also in ruins, but somehow that fact didn't mar the majesty of the place.

Gentle daylight poured in through several cracks and holes in the high walls, giving life to a vibrant network of vines, mosses, and even a few flowers throughout the grand old space. On the far wall, an open doorway and two empty spaces higher up that might've once housed ornate windows gave me the impression of eyes and an open mouth. Ground stone dust seemed to coat everything, and, strewn throughout, the crumbled remains of sculptures and great stone pillars lay cold and forgotten, majestic in their own way.

Rough sand shifted under my boots as I crossed the room. The place must have been decaying for a long time. Outside, the story was similar. What looked to have once been great works of stone art lay dying slow deaths in the golden glow of the afternoon sun. I picked my way through the crumbling maze and the wild undergrowth that threatened to swallow it whole, heading for a large hill to the west of the ruined temple.

The climb felt good. Fresh air in my lungs, sweat on my brow, and the pleasant burn of light exertion in my legs. For a little while, I didn't have to think about anything else. But then I reached the crest of the hill, and there it was in the distance. Divinity.

The sight of the city filled me with a powerful longing, and an equally strong fear. For a moment, I was tempted to take cover behind the two massive oaks that'd made their home on the hilltop. But that was ridiculous. No one would spot me over here, miles away across the wide expanse of the Red River—which, despite its name, sparkled clear blue in the afternoon sun.

So I sat beneath the oaks, staring at the sprawl of Divinity. From my angle, I couldn't help think the skyline of the tallest skyscrapers bore a vague resemblance to a giant hand, reaching for the descending sun and the heavens beyond. Maybe it was just my subconscious giving shape to the will of the monsters I now knew were right there at the heart of the city, pulling strings and orchestrating Alpha knew what kind of evil.

My gaze drifted to the highest-reaching finger of the vague hand. The Sanctum's White Tower. The very tower where they'd executed Andre Kovaks just... two days ago?

Alpha be sweet, had it only been two days?

Two measly days, and my entire life had exploded.

I sat there for a long while, idly watching the sun descend on the Divinity skyline. The tears came almost by surprise, soft and silent at first, then building until I was sobbing into the rough bark of the oak, expelling everything I'd been holding back since the attack.

Eventually, the sobbing and the gentle touch of grass and sunlight carried me off to sleep. Their faces swam before me, telling me to run, to find a safe place and never come back. Telling me that this wasn't my fight.

Then a red-eyed Kublich appeared to rip them away from me, and I snapped awake, panting and sunburnt. My stomach gave a mournful groan, and I realized I still hadn't eaten that day. The sun was low in the sky now, its traces peeking through the taller buildings of Divinity and illuminating the Red River in a manner most fitting to its name.

I tore hungrily into the dried fruits and jerky Carlisle had given me, contemplating his warnings and those of my dreamt parents. Maybe they were all right. Maybe I was another innocent bystander, just like my mom had been—a victim of horrible circumstance. Maybe this wasn't my fight at all. In fact, it definitely wasn't. I hadn't asked for any of this. Hadn't done anything to deserve it.

And maybe I still could get out. Alpha knew there was a part of me—and not a small part—that longed to just give in, scud my pants, and run for the mountains. I'd been around career soldiers all my life. I'd seen loss. I was living it. And I knew how much more lay ahead if I tried to take up the very fight that'd gotten my dad killed.

My dad. The celebrated hero of the Dorrin Uprising. And Kublich had broken him like a twig.

I was afraid. I wasn't ashamed to admit that much.

And I could still get out. It's probably what my parents would have wanted. But as I sat there staring at Divinity, thinking about Kublich and the rest of the raknoth lurking in the city, something strong and sure inside of me calmly decreed that walking away was no longer an option. I might never be the man my dad was. Maybe no one would. But that didn't mean I couldn't do my damned best to see to it Kublich paid for what he'd done.

And that wasn't all. If the raknoth truly controlled the Legion through Kublich, and if even half of what Carlisle said was true, then I could only assume that they were planning something big, that my parents had been only one tragic piece in the makings of a much larger disaster. If they could take control of the High General of the Legion, Alpha knew how wide and deep their resources stretched.

Even if I ran, could I really expect to escape the raknoth?

And what about the millions of people in Divinity, and the billion more scattered across Enochia—all utterly clueless of the looming threat?

When it came down to it, it was hardly a choice at all. Whatever they were up to, the raknoth had to be stopped. And, fair or not, it was starting to look like Alpha had seen fit to drop the smashball in my corner of the court.

But not just mine.

For better or worse, the gray-haired, pale-eyed enigma waiting for me back in the temple was effectively the only friend I had left on Enochia right now. Or the only one I could talk to, at least. I just had to make him understand.

So I rose in the fading daylight and marched back to the ruined temple, determined to say the words, to make him understand. When I made it back to the hideout and found him engrossed in what appeared to be a live broadcast of some big flashy press conference, though, my curiosity got the better of me. Especially when I recognized the speaker at the podium as Alton Parker, charismatic CEO of the biomedical tech giant, Vantage Corp. The very same Vantage Corp whose offices had been repeat targets of Andre Kovaks before his execution.

"Don't tell me..." I murmured.

"I'm not yet certain," Carlisle said, absentmindedly shaking his head.

Could Kovaks have been right about Vantage? Were the raknoth controlling Enochian biotech as well? There was a disturbing thought.

"—new factory will create five thousand jobs for the citizens of Divinity," Parker was saying, "as well as increase the efficiency of our distribution pipeline, allowing for more available—and, more importantly, more *affordable*—life-changing solutions for the people of this great city."

He spoke with the practiced conviction one would expect from a businessman or a politician.

"We'll see," Carlisle mumbled. He waved the vid closed and turned my way, waiting to see what I'd come to say.

I opened my mouth and froze, unsure where to start. "You... think the raknoth are controlling Vantage?" I said, suddenly apprehensive about coming straight out of the gate with my demand to partner up.

He studied me for a few seconds, those pale eyes seeming to see straight through my hesitation. "The pessimist in me thinks there are probably few major players they don't have leverage on, either through direct infiltration or other means. Manipulation. Blackmail." He waved a hand. "Even legitimate, everyday business operations."

"That sounds kinda paranoid."

"But does it sound wrong?"

"I don't know. Maybe not." I shook my head. "I don't know what to think anymore."

Keep going. Say the words.

Why was this suddenly so hard?

I clenched my toes and forced myself to spit it out.

"I just know that you can't take them alone."

There it was. Out of the bag and into the argument.

I half-expected him to grow dismissive, but he only studied me more closely. "Nothing like a Divinity sunset to clear your mind, hmm?"

Was he testing me? Mocking me?

I swallowed. "I don't care how fast you are, how high of a fall you can survive. You need me."

He watched me impassively, maybe disinterested, maybe assessing.

"Teach me how to use this thing inside me," I said, fingering the oddly cool pendant at my chest. "We can help each other. You can't truly wish to fight them all on your own."

Up until then, I hadn't actually been positive that Carlisle didn't have allies somewhere—fellow operatives who shared this hideout, or even a larger network of insurgents within the city. But the way his expression shifted at my words, falling into... what? Fear? Guilt?

It was a subtle change, but I was sure then. Carlisle was a loner. Which made his hesitation understandable. But maybe I wasn't making myself clear enough.

"I'm not gonna stop," I said. "You can't stop me. I'm going to kill him. All I need to know is whether you're going to help me."

He closed his eyes and let out a deep breath, heavy sadness falling across his face. He stayed that way for some time, clearly thinking. I resisted the urge to pester.

Finally, he opened his eyes and met mine with cold, calm resolve.

"Very well," he said with all the weight of a cleric passing a death sentence. "Let's get started, then."

CHAPTER 10
THE NEW NORMAL

"Breathe, Haldin," came Carlisle's maddeningly calm voice. "Focus."

"Focus on what?" My eyes snapped open, arms thrown out in exasperation. "This is pointless!"

That's when the floor shot up beneath me. Again. I tensed reflexively, arms and legs shooting out to brace even though I knew there was nothing to brace against. I was hanging two feet up from the sparring mat, suspended on nothing but thin air, Carlisle watching me with that damned unshakeable calm.

"This," he said slowly, "is the first step to control."

Whatever was holding me vanished then, and I plopped back to the mat with a fresh dose of shocked wonder riding on top of my building frustration. If Carlisle took any pleasure from flaunting his arcane powers, it didn't show.

"Keep trying to open your mind," he said, closing his eyes again.

So try, I did. I tried, and I tried. It felt like *trying* was about all I was capable of these days.

Open your mind, Haldin. I'd heard it a thousand times in the past five days. That was the key to unlocking my abilities, according to Carlisle. Unfortunately, after nearly half a cycle of my fruitless flailing, he couldn't seem to say much else of prodigious helpfulness, outside of the occasional, *Still your mind, Haldin. Focus, Haldin.*

So began my training with Carlisle. The results had been about as encouraging as Docere Mathis on eval day. But at least the failure didn't end there. Because there was also the sparring.

Each morning, I'd rise, eager to escape my increasingly familiar nightmares. Carlisle would already be up, meditating on the big blue sparring mat. I was beginning to wonder if he slept at all. I'd take the decadent luxuries of relieving myself and maybe having a sip of water, and then we'd spar. No good mornings. No idle chatter.

We trained, and we did it hard—or he did, at least.

It wasn't that Carlisle was unnecessarily rough. Far from it. It was just that, as our first brawl had made abundantly clear, he was embarrassingly beyond my skill in hand-to-hand combat.

Sparring quickly fell to the pattern of him exposing my weaknesses and us practicing how to eliminate them, only to do it all again. It was tedious, often awkward work, adapting what the Legion had hardwired into me so that I could take advantage of Carlisle's far more fluid methodologies. After a few days, the only thing more bruised than my body was my pride. But I did my best to take each bruise as a lesson of what not to do when I faced Kublich.

Of course, that didn't stop me from losing my temper at times. Only that morning, I'd gotten defensive when he'd pointed out I was still relying too much on meeting his strength outright with my own. "What if it were Kublich you were fighting?" he'd asked.

"Strength isn't the problem," I'd growled back, the frustration of several missed strikes burning on my chest and shoulders. "You're faster than me, not stronger."

A minute later, after he'd hammered me to the mat with a sequence of blows that'd fallen with the weight of crashing skimmers, I'd decided it'd be wise to pick my battles moving forward.

"Point taken," I'd grumbled, climbing laboriously back to my feet. "You can beat up a teenager. Good for you."

For a moment, tension had crackled between us. Then his lip had given one of those damn little twitches, like his smile button was broken, and suddenly I'd been laughing, and he'd been chuckling for the first time I'd seen.

Nice as the moment of kinship had been, it hadn't taken long for the sobering reminder to set back in. We weren't doing this for fun. We were preparing to take on the raknoth and half of Enochia with them—preferably without dying. So I didn't complain about being tired and beaten. I welcomed it. Anything to keep my mind away from the thoughts of my parents.

It was just the hours of fruitless mental exercises that were starting to get under my skin.

I couldn't help but wonder if Carlisle was holding back, if this was simply another test, subtler and more nefarious than the one five days ago, when he'd looked into my mind to ascertain, as he'd put it, whether I was his new partner, or just the grieving tyro who'd get us both killed.

Neither one of us had been thrilled about that test. Carlisle had actually seemed more hesitant than me, taking special care to clarify ahead of time exactly what it meant to have another telepath in your head, your every thought and memory—even control of your own body—all utterly vulnerable to their whims.

It wasn't the first time he'd acted as if he were almost hoping I'd simply give up and walk away. But grop that. I needed his knowledge to fight the raknoth, and he'd seemed to believe he needed some assurance I could be trusted with it. So I'd agreed to the test, and we'd set to it.

I'd be lying if I said it wasn't all that bad, having someone poke around in your head. But Carlisle had been quick, and a scudload gentler than Smirks had been back in the alley. Really, it'd almost felt like I was simply letting my mind drift through random memories—right up until I'd tried to control the stream and remembered with a twinge of panic that those flitting memories weren't random at all, and that I wasn't the one controlling them.

Then things had gotten a little uncomfortable.

But Carlisle had given me space, talking me through it. Together, we'd revisited a handful of memorable moments from my past. The times the doceres had scolded me. The times some of the more vicious tyros had mocked me for riding daddy's rank. The gratitude I'd felt when Johnny had shut one of them up with a sucker punch, and the kinship when we'd both refused to let the other take the fall and had ended up scrubbing the tyro privies together.

He'd studied my memories of worship, and my feelings of uncertainty during Andre Kovaks' execution. I hadn't really seen the rhyme or reason to Carlisle's prodding, but maybe I'd just been too busy trying to make sense of the odd tendrils of foreign presence I'd started to notice there in the spaces between my thoughts, gently guiding and nudging.

It had been a little unsettling.

But then the memories had shifted to my parents, and I'd forgotten everything else. It had started innocently enough. A cup of hot silverleaf tea my mom had brought me when I was sick. My dad's modesty in the face of the hero's spotlight. But, surely enough, it had slid out of control with the inexorable certainty of a slow-motion skimmer wreck.

The floor had fallen out from under me, one thought speeding to the next, from my dad's best intentions straight through to the moment I'd watched a red-eyed Kublich break his neck in two. All of it flashing through my mind in one impossibly infinite instant, as vivid as if I were right back there, reliving the worst moments of my life.

I'd come to my senses on my feet, drenched in cold sweat, Carlisle hovering in front of me, hands spread wide, apologizing profusely. I believed him when he said he hadn't meant to drag me back to that night. I just didn't want to talk about it.

Apparently I'd passed his test. I tried to tell myself that was all that mattered. Except here we'd been ever since. Five gropping days, and not an inch closer to me figuring these damned abilities out. I was starting to feel like—

"You're drifting," came Carlisle's voice, tugging me back to the present.

"Probably because this isn't working," I grumbled, opening my eyes.

"You've been at it for a grand total of five days," Carlisle said, looking faintly amused. "Perhaps you should let me be the judge of what's working."

"Perhaps *you* should remind me why you're so sure I'm actually gifted at all."

"Because skimmer trunk latches don't spontaneously transmute themselves." He gave me a pointed look. *"And because you wouldn't be able to hear this if you weren't."*

It should've been encouraging, maybe. But it wasn't.

"These things take time," Carlisle added with the ghost of an apologetic smile. "You have to understand, you've spent your entire life living within the confines of your physical body, solidifying your perspective of where you end and the rest of the world begins. Opening your mind, dropping the distinction between self and non-self… that doesn't come overnight."

"Well maybe if you'd actually give me something other than, 'Open your mind, Haldin…'" I waved a hand in frustration. "That right there was more than you've said in days."

He watched me placidly. "And did it help?"

I scowled at the mat. "I don't know." I thought about what he'd said. "You're saying I have to change my… my perspective of myself?"

"Something like that. It's different for everyone, but in essence, you must find the wall your mind has built to separate you from your surroundings, and drop it. Let go. Allow yourself to become one with the world around you."

I stared at him. "Can you just remind me real quick that I haven't actually lost my mind?"

"You haven't actually lost your mind," came Carlisle's voice in my head.

"Not sure if that's better or worse."

A faint smile touched his lips. "Just remember, extending your sense of self can be quite uncomfortable at first. You'll feel extremely exposed. But, eventually, you'll get used to it."

I nodded dumbly, certain that—while it sounded good in theory—I had no idea how to even attempt the process he was describing.

"Right, then." Carlisle waved me on. "Back to it. Close your eyes and try to find my mind with yours."

Closing my eyes, I could manage at least. The rest...

I tried. I really did. In my mind's eye, I imagined my consciousness like an amorphous blob. I coaxed it to unfold from my body, oozing out toward Carlisle, and—

"Haldin."

I opened my eyes to find Carlisle watching in either amusement or sympathy.

"You don't get bonus points for bursting blood vessels. Try to relax. Quiet your mind until you forget that it's there. Until you can simply let go."

My face grew warm. I'd been so concentrated on the imagery that I'd barely noticed how hard I'd tensed up.

"In fact," Carlisle said, with a discreet glance at his palmlight, "perhaps we should take a break. It's... nearly time."

I swallowed against a suddenly dry throat, looking around in futility for an excuse, for some escape from the inevitable.

I'd known it was coming—had been dreading it since we'd first seen it mentioned in the reels a couple days ago. Carlisle had originally suggested I simply take the day off. I'd refused, preferring the distraction. Not that it had helped. Because when Carlisle handed me his tablet and I saw the live feeds starting to pour in, the acid just about ate through my stomach anyway.

It was time.

The Raish family funeral had come.

~

ALPHA BLESS HIM, Carlisle didn't say a word when I took his tablet outside to view the service alone. Even without anyone watching, it took me a while to work up the will and actually open the feed.

It was a lot to take.

Sanctuary was overflowing with the mournful pageantry. It seemed like half of Divinity had funneled into the base to pay their respects. Tears gathered but didn't fall as I watched friends and acquaintances say the kindest of words about me and my parents.

Even Mathis found something nice to say.

My heart ached when a downcast Johnny took the stage. It was the least I'd ever heard him say about anything, and by far the most forlorn I'd ever seen him look. Every bit of me longed to throw demons to the wind and send him a message then and there on the tablet—to tell him everything.

I could do it anonymously. It could work.

Except there really was no such thing as anonymous messaging over the lights. Not if the Legion cared enough to spend time digging. I was no tech expert, but I knew that much. Contacting Johnny could be a death sentence for both of us. It was out of the question.

But the thought slid to the background anyway when Kublich took the stage.

I'd thought about that noble, strong-jawed mask of his every day since the attack. I'd cursed his name. Envisioned his throat in my hands. But it was only then I realized the true intensity of the rage that had been growing in me since that night.

If all that monster had done was rob me of my parents, it would've been more than enough for me to hunt him to the depths and beyond. But it wasn't just that. It was the life of service he'd accepted from me, from my dad, from all the tens of thousands of men and women of the Legion. It was the ease with which he took that blind loyalty and bent that just service to his unjust will.

By the light of Alpha, he had to pay. For all of it.

The very sight of him smiling and waving down the crowd's applause nearly made me hurl the tablet against the nearest stone column. It was the masochistic desire to hear what he had to say that stayed my hands. But his words only fanned the flames—kind and civil, exactly what one would expect from a respectful, lamenting superior.

They became a dull buzz in my thrumming ears after the first sentence or two. I wanted to scream. To cry. To beat my fists bloody against the temple wall. But none of that would hurt Kublich. And that bastard needed to pay.

So instead, I killed the feed and set the tablet aside. I drew my legs in tight, closed my eyes, and focused on the one thing I could control in that moment—the one tool I could harness against him when the time came.

Quiet your mind, Carlisle had said. *Until you forget that it's there. Until you can simply let go.*

Let go.

A kind of violent calm settled over me as I began repeating those words in my head, over and over. This was it. I could feel it deep down, beyond the realm of conscious understanding—an ethereal flutter in my gut, a silent promise from the spirit of justice itself that Kublich would pay.

All I had to do was let go, starting with Carlisle's cloaking pendant.

I barely hesitated. Carlisle had explicitly told me to keep it on anytime I left the cloaked hideout, but this was more important. I knew where Kublich was right now. I knew what had to happen. Demons to the wind with everything else.

I slipped the pendant off and dropped it to the ground beside me. The calm was deepening, seeping through me like a living thing, loosening my limbs with that silent promise.

He was going to pay.

I acknowledged my body once last time, relishing the pleasant soreness of the past days' exertions. Then I sank deeper, melting into my breathing, each exhalation draining the extraneous thoughts from my body, pulling me in further, further. Again. And again. Breathing until I forgot about my body. Breathing until I was barely aware of the ground I sat on.

In and out.

Over and over.

I'm not sure if it took me five minutes or fifty. Time ceased to register. I breathed until everything in my world was condensed down to that singular rise and fall. Until, somewhere deep in my trance, it simply came to me out of nothingness, like a first waking thought.

Let go.

It nearly snapped me out of the trance completely. I teetered there on the edge between my worldly senses and everything else. Then the balance tipped, and my world disintegrated.

Calling it an out-of-body experience wouldn't do it justice. Everything I was simply blurred into my surroundings like an expanding ball of gas, and for the briefest moment, I could *feel* everything that it touched—could feel it in overwhelming detail. My mind reeled at the colossal influx of information. It was too much.

Hot and cold. Light. Darkness. Crushing imprisonment. Boundless openness. Musty dirt, and porous stone, and—

I hit the grass with a strangled yelp, head spinning with all the sensations that… weren't there anymore? I patted dumbly at my body, reassuring myself I was still whole. I felt weak. Cold sweat plastered my face. For a second, I lay there, too disoriented to move. Then I lurched to my feet, did a double-take to grab my pendant and the tablet, and set off for the hideout at a run.

Carlisle shot to his feet when I burst in, but I was too overwhelmed to care.

"Uncomfortable my ass!" I snapped. "I felt like I was gonna evaporate out of existence!"

He searched my face, surprise flashing in his eyes, shortly followed by something like awe. "Well I believe I did use the word *extremely* at some point," he finally said. "How do you feel?"

I wiped cold sweat from my forehead. "Kind of sick. I didn't realize it was gonna be like… well, like that. And after… after everything else, I just…"

He waited to see if I'd say more, his gaze tracing suspiciously down to the pendant I'd slipped back on. He looked worried. About the pendant? No. About me. I saw it in his eyes when he met my gaze again. He was worried I was about to crack.

"I think maybe you should rest," he said slowly.

Grop that. I shook my head and went to sit on the mat. I wasn't going to back off now. Not when I was finally starting to get somewhere.

"It's going to take an enormous amount of practice," Carlisle said, though I hadn't asked. "Acclimating yourself to your extended senses is one thing. Learning to focus them enough to begin Shaping will be another. I've seen some take to it in a few seasons. A few cycles, even, once. But most take years to develop any appreciable mastery."

"How long did it take you?"

He didn't answer.

"Cycles, huh?" I said. "Guess I have an easy target in sight, then."

I closed my eyes and took a few deep breaths, preparing to start.

"Haldin."

I opened my eyes to find Carlisle watching me, his expression torn.

"If you'd like to talk about the funeral… about any of it…"

My jaw tightened against the confused swirl of emotions rushing through me. For a second, I even thought about telling him—about the things Kublich had said, about how damned deflated Johnny had looked. About the way I'd felt, seeing my parents' urns being honored less than ten feet away from the monster who'd murdered them. But I couldn't. Not now.

So I closed my eyes instead, reaching for that place of calm again, determined to keep honing this new ability of mine until I couldn't anymore.

Carlisle didn't try to stop me.

CHAPTER 11

MEMENTO

"So why Vantage?" I asked the following night as we supped on fabbed meat and potatoes. Whether out of pity over the funeral or the fact that I'd been up most of the previous night practicing opening my senses, Carlisle had let me sleep the morning away. The rest of the day had fallen quickly to training. "You think they're trying to poison us all in one fell swoop or something?"

Carlisle shook his head and patiently finished chewing his food. "Not particularly. If the raknoth wanted to simply kill us all, I imagine they would have done it by now. There are any number of ways they might pull it off. No, I think they intend to use our kind for something more."

I chewed on that for a while.

As the producer of probably at least half the pharmaceuticals and medical equipment on Enochia, Vantage was unsettlingly well-positioned for working any number of insidious misdeeds on the population. Which was probably why Carlisle had spent so many hours studying them in the reels the past few days. The possibilities were endless—and most of them horrifying.

I idly skewered a bit of potato on my fork. "So we're still at paranoid suspicion, then?"

"My specialty," Carlisle said with a faint smile. "But it is interesting that both Andre Kovaks and my contact in Divinity seemed to reach similar conclusions."

A contact in Divinity? So Carlisle did talk to someone, at least.

How many more were out there, circling the impossible truth of the raknoth?

Probably not that many. And I was guessing the others couldn't move things with their minds, either.

"How did you even get pulled into this thing to start with?" The question fell out of my mouth almost before I knew it. I'd hesitated to ask Carlisle much in the way of personal questions since we'd met, which I suppose was a bit ridiculous considering he'd literally been inside my mind. But maybe it was for good reason.

He was staring off now, spoon forgotten in his hand, the silence lingering too long.

"If I'm, uh, prying, you don't have to…"

"No, no." He shook his head and composed himself. "Parts of the story may be useful. I'm just wondering where to begin. Like you, I lost what family I had at the hands of the raknoth. I was brought into the world of Shaping when I was young. Ten or eleven, maybe. My teacher, Cassius, found me living on the streets when… well, at a time when I truly needed to be found. He was a strange man, to say the least. But he saved my life, in more ways than one. It wasn't a hard decision to follow him across Enochia. I had nothing to lose and a world to learn."

"Sounds kind of familiar."

Carlisle smiled, but it was a pained thing.

"The raknoth… took him from you? Cassius?"

He gave a tired nod. "Along with the few other friends I had in this world."

"What happened?"

He idly fingered the cloaking pendant at his breast. "We made these."

At my frown, he pushed on.

"The notion of hiding one's mind from other telepaths had been a problem for Shapers ever since the Sanctum came to power and started indoctrinating its Seeker core to secretly hunt their own kind. All it took was a few whispers, or some unfortunate timing. A Seeker would be sent to confirm, and suddenly a Shaper would have half the Sanctum Guard bearing down on them."

"I don't understand. Do the Sanctum Guard all know what's going on, then? Those soldiers back in the alley must've known what Smirks was, right?"

Carlisle tilted his head in a mini shrug. "Difficult to say who knows what."

"Well it'd be pretty hard for them not to notice when they try to bring in some harmless-looking civilian type"—I waved at him—"and the guy starts flinging things around with his mind, right? People must ask questions. Even Sanctum Guard."

"Perhaps. But few Shapers are actually that adept at using their skills in combat. Most go down without much commotion. It's possible the higher tiers of Legion command have some inkling of the Seekers' existence and function, but you'd know better than I do."

I shook my head. "The tyros sure as scud aren't hearing anything about it."

"Honestly, I wouldn't be surprised if Legion command wasn't either. People tend to believe what's comfortable to believe, and sparse as our kind have become, the Shaper hunt would hardly be the largest operation the Sanctum's ever obfuscated from the eye of the Alpha-loving public."

It all sounded a bit like the gossip of madmen and old crones who swore their felines talked to them, but then again, what didn't these days? Kovaks had sure sounded like a madman, after all, and here I was following in his footsteps. Was it possible the Sanctum had been bending the word of Alpha even before the raknoth came to Enochia?

I kind of wanted to ask. But, then again, I kind of didn't.

"So these cloaking pendants, then," I said. "How'd they lead you to trouble with the raknoth?"

"That was dramatically ambiguous of me to say," Carlisle admitted. "It wasn't the pendants themselves, but rather what happened after we succeeded in crafting them. We knew immediately we had to share our discovery. Cassius and I had lost multiple friends to the Seekers over the years, and those Shapers weren't the only ones."

"How many Shapers are there?"

"Precious few these days. And most live on the run, with their ties loose and their heads down."

I frowned. "And no one else managed to make one of these cloaks in the past thousand years?"

"Not that we knew of. Though Cassius believed we'd only rediscovered a lost art of the Emmútari."

"The Emmútari?"

A soft smile touched Carlisle's mouth. "They were a powerful order of

Shapers, back before the Sanctum's rise. A long story, and one for another time, I think, if we want to finish our current one."

I reluctantly nodded my agreement.

"Suffice it to say," Carlisle continued, "our breakthrough with creating long-lasting runes was unheard of in our circles. To put it into perspective, it was something like the Shaper's equivalent of shifting from hand arithmetic to node programming."

He thoughtfully rubbed his pendant between thumb and forefinger.

"At any rate, as dangerous as it was to assemble multiple gifted minds in one place, the rune technique, and its application for mind cloaking, was important enough to risk it. Once we were all together, we knew we could cloak our collective presence anyway. We were careful. We had everything planned. The only thing we didn't account for was the arrival of the raknoth."

"They found the gathering?"

From the distant look on his face, I wasn't sure he even heard me.

"The raknoth are far more skilled at hunting than any Seeker, you see. Powerful telepaths, yes. But their other senses are preternaturally sharp as well." He shook his head. "I don't know if they scented in on one of the others, or… I suppose it doesn't matter now. All that matters is that they found us, five of them, and that it was a slaughter. Eighteen Shapers gathered. I was the only one who made it out."

I sat tense and quiet, waiting. I hadn't been expecting a war story.

"How did you get away?" I finally asked, softly as I could.

"Cassius told me to run." His gaze dropped to the floor. "I wasn't nearly as skilled then, and once the fighting started and it became clear how outmatched we were… Well, Cassius ordered me to run. And I listened."

I wanted to say something. That there was no shame in a wise retreat. That he'd done the right thing. But it wasn't my turn to speak—I could feel it. Not quite yet.

"Three of the younger Shapers tried to run as well," he said quietly. "They didn't make it far…" He straightened in his seat, visibly pulling himself from his memories. "And so I've trained on ever since, nearly twelve years now, hunting them just as they've continued to hunt me."

Alpha, had he been alone all that time? Even if he did have occasional communication with his contacts… what did that do to a person?

"Thank you for telling me." It was the only thing I knew he might hear, but I couldn't help saying the rest anyway—the stuff the survivors always seemed to brush aside. "I'm sorry about your friends, Carlisle. About Cassius. But I'm sure there's nothing more you could have done."

Carlisle showed me a polite smile, dismissive and only surface deep. "Thank you, Haldin, but I'll be quite fine." He rose to collect our bowls. "And now you know."

Somehow, his response comforted me. Maybe because it assured me he was human after all.

"I still can't believe I've never heard a whisper about this stuff..." I said, moving to help him clean up. "I'm still not sure I even understand what Shaping is, exactly."

That seemed to amuse Carlisle. "I'm sure I don't either. But I can tell you with some certainty that, in the end, it all comes down to channeling energy from one place or form to another. For instance..." He filled a glass less than halfway with cold water and gestured for me to step back from the counter.

"Watch closely," he said when I was in position.

Something as invisible as thin air but as tangible as the arms of a pro smashballer wrapped me tight and lifted me from the floor. Carlisle smiled at my startled curse and waved my attention to the water in the glass.

I rose further, and the water turned icy.

"Do you see?" Carlisle asked.

He waved to the floor as if in invitation, and the invisible force floated me gently back down.

In the glass, the ice had thawed.

"I... definitely see. I'm just not sure I understand. You lifted me because the water froze?"

"I would put it the other way around, but yes. Energy reshaped to a new purpose. In this case, thermal energy"—he waved the glass of icy water—"into kinetic energy."

"Right... I guess that..."

That what? Alpha, was I about to say that that made *sense*?

Red-eyed monsters. Voices beamed straight from one mind to another. And now freezing water to lift unsuspecting tyros. Sure, why not?

It was starting to feel like my bar to the impossible had been permanently damaged.

"I guess I get it in theory. Maybe. But..."

"You have a few questions?" Carlisle said, offering me the perspiring glass I was still staring at.

I laughed. It was too much. Mind boggling. I didn't even know where to start.

"A few," I agreed, taking the glass.

Carlisle dried his hands and retired to his desk. "Perhaps we should come at it tomorrow with fresh minds. You'll be needing more practice with your extended senses before you attempt any energy channeling anyway."

He probably had a point. I'd made some progress over the past day— each time, finding my way to the quiet place a little more quickly, keeping my senses extended just a little longer.

For a few moments, I'd feel it all—my very sense of being intertwining with the pores of the cool stone floor, the fibers of the sparring mat straining under my weight, the tiny swirls of air dancing about the room, so gentle I couldn't have possibly felt them. Except I did—for those few moments, at least.

Then I'd drift too far, my sense of self blurring, too diluted for comfort, and I'd fall back to the safety of my body with a shudder and a rush of nausea.

It was definitely going to take some getting used to. And as incredible as the experience was, it also wasn't particularly fun, repeatedly meditating until I could open myself to a sensation of disembodiment that quickly became unbearable. But I'd done it again and again. For hours. And now it was time to do it some more.

There was just one question lingering in the dark corner of my mind.

"Carlisle?"

He turned from his displays.

"If eighteen Shapers weren't enough to take five raknoth," I said slowly, "what in demon's depths are two of us supposed to do?"

He gave a grave nod, like he'd been waiting for that very question. "I don't have a good answer for you, Haldin, aside from that we'll do whatever we can. I've trained hard these years, strengthening my abilities, learning to fight with them. You have a tremendous amount to learn, and I wager time is on our side about as much as the odds are in our favor. But we'll try."

As pep talks went, it wasn't much. In fact, it was pretty damn scuddy. But it was a solemn promise I could get behind. So I nodded my agreement, letting him return to his work, and I dropped back to the mat with the steady burning resolve to do the same.

～

THAT NIGHT, I woke to find Carlisle gone.

After the initial surge of panic, I decided I wasn't sure what to make of it. For the half-cycle I'd been there, so had he. We each went outside at least once a day to get some air and sunlight —sometimes together, mostly on our own. But other than that, we trained, and he researched. I still wasn't sure he even slept. I'd wake up from nightmares most nights to find him still poring over his displays or pacing thoughtfully around the room.

Waking up to find him gone in the middle of the night didn't feel right. Especially not after he'd spent the day giving me almost too much space for having witnessed my own funeral. I scanned the room for clues and noticed the message on the central of his three displays.

<<Errands. Back soon.>>

Just to be sure, I took the mag lift down to the underground bay.

The skimmer was gone.

"Son of a bitch," I whispered.

Errands...

Maybe he'd simply needed to fetch supplies—fresh filters for the cycler, more nutrients for the fab. But then why in the dead of night? And why not take his stir-crazy trainee along?

Something told me Carlisle wasn't shopping out there, which probably meant he'd gone on recon and left me behind. That kind of made me want to hit something. But there wasn't much I could do about it now. So I returned to my cot, feeling more irritated and cooped up by the minute.

I couldn't sleep. Couldn't think about anything but Carlisle out there, potentially in danger. Without backup. The patronizing bastard.

Eventually, though, my anger cooled, and I found myself thinking about my last moment with my mom, her warm hands on my cheeks, wet with dishwater. Her tender kiss on my forehead. I thought about how much I missed Johnny and how he and the rest of our friends would slowly be getting back to routine now. Getting back to laughing, to checking out girls. Getting back to their lives.

Assuming, of course, that Johnny believed the newsreels. I'd wondered about that a million times. What if maybe—just maybe—he'd pieced things together and seen that something wasn't quite right about the whole situation? Johnny had never been one to question the order of things. But he'd known Kublich was going to be at our house that night. And house fires weren't all that common in Sanctuary.

What if he'd had his doubts?

I looked over to Carlisle's desk node. It was hardly possible. And yet I couldn't bury the thought now in the dead silence of the empty hideout.

What if Johnny had figured it all out and tried to contact me?

Accessing my personal messages here would be a risk, as Carlisle had been sure to point out more than a few times. But considering how many levels of redirects he'd routed his connection through, even he had to admit the risk would likely be a relatively small one.

Still, I'd agreed to leave it alone. Just like he'd agreed to take me on as his partner.

And where the hell was he now?

Running around doing Alpha knew what while he left me to sleep. That's where.

Grop it.

I sat down at the desk, waved the displays to life, and made sure the redirect measures were enabled. Heart thudding with nervous energy, I navigated to the messenger login and typed in my identifier and password before I could lose my nerve.

Several unopened messages, all automated notifications they'd simply forgotten to shut off, from the look of it—Sanctuary announcements, reminders of assignments and other obligations. All but one.

A message from Johnny. Alpha be damned. It was dated from yesterday, only a few hours after the funeral. I tapped it open, too anxious to even breathe.

❧

Hal,

I DON'T KNOW *why I'm writing this. Alpha, I hope no one walks in and finds me writing this. My parents are already concerned enough. If my mom tells me one more time that it's okay to cry, I'm gonna shoot my own wrinklies off.*

It still doesn't feel real. I mean, scud, I set my alarm to read, "He's gone," every morning after I showed up for drills the first day and realized it hadn't all been a gropping dream and that you really weren't coming.

Okay, upon writing that out in text, I'm starting to see why my parents might be concerned. Pretty gropped up... But I'm okay. I just miss you, broto.

I don't know what else to say. Least. Useful. Message. Ever...

Wherever you are, though, I hope it's good. If it's a party up there, maybe you can find a way to give me the heads-up so I know to be extra good for the next seventy or eighty years. Especially if there are hot girls up there. Definitely then.

Ah scud, who am I kidding? Let's make it twenty or thirty years. We both know I'm not that careful.

I don't know why I'm joking about this. Or writing any of it at all (again). So I guess I'll just say goodbye. Maybe I'll see you around someday.

I LOVE YOU, buddy.

-Johnny

P.S. If you boys at comms stumble across this message, don't you dare tell a gropping soul. Hal, you have my explicit permission and plea to haunt the scud out of anyone who doesn't heed this warning.

I BLEW out a shaky laugh and wiped the brimming tears from my eyes.

I'd already swiped over to reply before the rational side of my brain reminded me that logging in with my identifier had already been bad enough and that, for both our sakes, I couldn't write back to him.

That didn't stop me from staring at the waiting cursor, agonizing over the decision for several long minutes. Eventually, though, I powered down the node and crawled back onto my cot.

I wasn't sure if Johnny's message had made me feel better or worse. Mostly, it just made me want to talk to him—to tell him about everything that was going on and to hear him make his jokes about my being shacked up with an older man for six days straight.

But I couldn't. Not while Kublich was still breathing.

At some point, I must've drifted back to sleep, because the next time I roused enough to take in my surrounding, Carlisle had returned. He was also, to my shock, asleep. For the first time I'd seen, he lay supine on his cot, brow furrowed and eyes flicking rapidly beneath his eyelids.

The guy looked less peaceful in sleep than he did awake.

It occurred to me that I should probably let him rest. Given how little I'd seen him sleep, it seemed safe to assume that, if he was doing it right now, he probably had great need of it.

But I was also pretty damn irritated at being left behind, and I wanted answers.

"Rough night of errands?"

My guess that he'd be a light sleeper wasn't wrong. He came awake with a sharp inhalation, eyes snapping straight to me.

He blinked a few times. "Yes. Rougher than I was expecting, at least." A hint of guilt crossed his features. "I'm sorry if you woke to find I'd disappeared on you. I… Well, after our talk last night, I needed to do something. I decided to visit the last office Andre Kovaks broke into before he was apprehended. I didn't go inside. I certainly wasn't expecting a fight, but, well…"

"You found one?"

He sat up and leaned his elbows against his knees, looking more exhausted than I'd ever seen him. "In a manner of speaking."

"Gee, if only you'd had some backup you could've taken along. Alpha be damned, man. I don't know what I'm doing here if you aren't gonna trust me to cover your back when you need it."

"I made a mistake," he said.

I paused, mouth half-open, caught off guard by the admission.

"And I'm sorry for that," Carlisle continued. "It won't happen again."

I closed my mouth, suddenly unsure what to say.

"Did you learn anything?" I asked finally.

"Two things," he said. "For one, Alton Parker is a raknoth."

I stared dumbly down at him. "That's… You're sure?"

He rose to go wave his desk displays to life. "Uncomfortably certain."

"Right." I rubbed at my jaw, thinking that over. "And the second thing?"

"The second thing," he said, swiveling around to face me, "is that we need to find out what Vantage is doing with this new factory of theirs. And we need to do it now."

CHAPTER 12
CONTACT

I hopped into the passenger seat of the skimmer, eager for an adventure —or at least to escape the hideout for a little while. Carlisle, slipping into the driver's seat, was markedly less excited.

"Tell me again," he said.

"Seriously?"

He gave me a look that asked plainly enough whether I really thought he'd be one to joke about such things.

I sighed and waved the dark spectacles in my hand. "Until we get to your contact, the shaders stay on. I avoid talking, keep my hood up, keep my head down. If you say run, I run. And if anyone asks, you're just a kindly good-fellow who promised me sweets to follow him to his skimmer."

He arched one silvery eyebrow.

"I made that last one up."

"This is hardly inspiring confidence in your ability to behave maturely and discreetly."

I held my hands up. "So I'm excited to be doing something other than hanging out in a stodgy temple with an old kook for a day. Someone arrest me."

"Someone may," he said, but he powered up the skimmer and started toward the tunnel nonetheless. "Stodgy…" he said quietly. "I thought it was cozy."

"I'm just kidding, Carlisle. The temple's great. In small doses, though, seeing other people is okay too."

"Yes," Carlisle said as the darkness of the tunnel engulfed us and we began the descent beneath the Red River. "We wouldn't want you going kooky too."

The tunnel tresses sped by in the dark, jumping into existence at the edge of the skimmer's lights one moment only to blink back out the next. I focused and managed to catch a glimpse of the startlingly crushing weight of the Red River above in my extended senses before falling back to my body. It was getting easier.

"Best activate your cloak before we get any closer to the city," Carlisle said.

"Right." I dialed the pendant to its active position. "Who built this tunnel, by the way?"

Carlisle shrugged. "My best guess is smugglers looking to bypass the Red Bridge back before skimmers." I could just make out his smile in the dimly-lit cab. "I doubt it was intended for freedom fighters."

Freedom fighters. Was that what we were?

That answer might depend on exactly what Vantage was up to.

"So this guy we're meeting…"

"Franco."

"Franco, right. He's a friend of yours?"

"I'm not entirely sure I have what many would call friends," he said slowly, "but if I do, then Franco might top the list. After you, I suppose."

"Aw, you're gonna go and make me cry, boss."

The jest came easily enough from my inner-Johnny, but, in truth, Carlisle's words made me ache for the man. Twelve years on the run from the raknoth, the Sanctum, the Legion, and apparently the rest of the world, too. I couldn't imagine how lonely he must be.

"So you trust this Franco, then?"

"As much as I can trust anyone whose head I haven't been inside. If nothing else, we can trust his obsession with collecting information. Especially that pertaining to the raknoth. They were responsible for his wife's death."

"Sweet Alpha," I muttered. "How deep does their pile of dead go?"

"Deep."

The way he said it made me want to shudder.

He tapped his palmlight, and the tunnel exit began to resolve out of the darkness ahead. The tresses flew by slower and slower, then we reached the small bay beneath the streets of Divinity, and Carlisle set the skimmer down.

I straightened the faded green canvas jacket Carlisle had given me and double checked that my new palmlight—also a gift from Carlisle—was set to private. Not that it mattered. Carlisle was the only one who knew the forged identifier the device was linked to. The device was primarily in case some unforeseen emergency separated us. I doubted that would happen, but it was a relief to be wearing one again anyway—even if I couldn't reach out to Johnny or anyone else with it.

On a whim, I gestured at the windshield to display the passenger cam feed and take a look at my appearance. It was only then I realized I hadn't had a good look at myself since the night Carlisle had found me.

Seven days hadn't changed all that much. My cropped brown hair was still plenty short enough to pass Legion regs. I still had my mom's hazel eyes and angular features, and my dad's thick eyebrows. Everything looked more or less the same. And yet there was also something different there. Something more, or maybe something less.

My face looked thinner, the skin around my eyes darker. As tyros, we'd been expected to shave daily. Seven days hadn't yielded as much growth as I would've thought, but the doceres still would've lost it at the stubbly afternoon shadow on my face.

I looked rougher. Older. Or maybe it was only that I felt that way.

"You still recognize him?" Carlisle asked.

I shrugged. "Same old kid, right?"

I pulled up my hood and slipped on the shaders before he could answer, then looked again and barked out a laugh. "Alpha, I might as well stamp 'rebel' on my forehead. I look like I walked straight off a wanted poster."

Carlisle smiled, slipping on his own pair of darkened spectacles. "It's not as bad as you think. Trust me, this look is not unusual in the less glamorous districts."

"If you say so."

"And so I say."

Carlisle slung a small pack over his shoulder, and we headed up the ramp to a street-level door. The sharp clicks of the door unlocking ushered the first real twinge of worry into my gut. Then Carlisle pulled it open, and the roar of voices filled the dank bay, along with the whoosh of traffic and the half-charming, half-repulsive swirl of the city's aroma.

"Remember," Carlisle said, turning his dark spectacles on me and pulling his own hood up, "we are but two individuals in a sea of millions. As long as we don't do anything out of the ordinary, we'll be fine."

I nodded, an eager grin spreading across my face, and together, we stepped through the doorway and onto the bustling streets of Divinity.

～

AFTER DAYS OF QUIET ISOLATION, the throng of the city was cacophonous. Thousands of people scuffled to and fro along the wide walkways and the pedestrian conveyor lines beneath the shade of the towering buildings to either side. Overhead, a mag train whooshed by. Higher still, hundreds of skimmers and cargo transports soared along the air traffic lanes.

So many people. So much activity.

I wiped sweaty palms on my trousers and tried to ignore the suffocating feeling of it all.

It wasn't only the fear of being discovered. As a child of Sanctuary, I'd grown up in a sort of cocoon within Divinity, a small military city nested within a much larger civilian one. And while Sanctuary had been plenty busy, there was a distinct difference between its bustle—always ordered, never without direction—and that of Divinity's, which was a far wilder beast.

I'd never particularly enjoyed the latter.

That said, it was still nice to see people who weren't Carlisle and to smell food that wasn't from the fab. A few minutes into the chaos, I even began to relax a little bit. Carlisle led us northeast, away from the river and toward the heart of the city. We got a few curious looks—and a few disdainful ones —but, mostly, people ignored us. At least until we reached the fringes of the financial district. There, the crowd's attire quickly shifted toward business dapper, which we most certainly did not match.

A curious look from a Legion enforcer nearly stopped my heart cold. Carlisle barely seemed to take notice as he gracefully navigated through the crowd. Thankfully, he cut northwest after the next block, and the crowd quickly began to thin out.

Thin out *and* degrade, that was.

I wasn't an expert on Divinity locales, but I didn't need to be to know we weren't headed toward the rich side of town. The clothes grew patchier and less flashy. Grizzled men with the uniforms and looks of physical laborers went about their business. Entirely too many people seemed to be stumbling into or out of taverns for the late morning hour. Homeless men and women sat on the cracked walkways outside several such establishments.

"You bring me to the nicest places," I said quietly, when the traffic thinned enough that I could draw up beside Carlisle.

"I'll remind you that I grew up in the streets," he said.

Heat flowed into my cheeks, but when I looked over, he was wearing a small smile.

"As charming as this place may be," he said, "we're almost there."

Grimy sheen and smart comments aside, I actually found myself more at ease here than I had back on the main line. At least here, no one seemed to give a scud about how we were dressed. Plus, the Legion presence was far lighter. If the raknoth had eyes out for us, I doubted this would've been their first choice of location.

A few beggars approached us as we went. Carlisle gave them gentle smiles and a touch on the shoulder here and there, but nothing else. I wasn't even sure he had money to give. Now that I thought about it, for all I knew, he could've stolen everything he had at the hideout. The thought bothered me, but I pushed it aside for the moment.

"So what does Franco do, exactly?"

Carlisle hadn't told me much about the man other than that he might be able to get us a look behind the curtain at Vantage's new factory—permits, shipping manifests, and other similar manners of exhilarating tedium.

"In a past life, he was a legal counselor. These days, he mostly trades information."

"Sounds shady."

Carlisle gave a noncommittal shrug. "He has his ear to the ground."

I followed him as he turned down an unremarkable side alley.

Halfway down, he stopped at a metal door, pulled off his hood and glasses, and held his palmlight over the small panel beside the door.

Nothing happened.

I looked around and realized the alley was not as unremarkable as I'd thought. Multiple security cameras monitored the heavy-duty door and the length of the alley as well.

Apparently this Franco wasn't overly trusting of his potential visitors.

I tried to wait as patiently as Carlisle. The place made me uneasy. But finally, after half a minute or so, the door panel flashed green, and Carlisle pulled the door open—or started to before pausing to look back at me.

"When the questions start, you don't have to tell him anything you don't want to." He frowned up at one of the cameras. "He'll probably figure it out anyway, but telling him is your choice."

The warning didn't help my uneasiness. But I nodded, pulled my own hood back, and followed Carlisle inside through the reinforced doorway into a narrow stairwell.

Now that my threat meter was inching up, I couldn't help notice that the lone door at the top of the stairs was also reinforced, and that the stairwell itself would've been a great kill zone for anyone looking to spring a trap. When the door shot up in its tracks with a mechanical hiss a few feet ahead of our arrival, I jumped, hand shooting to the thigh where I most certainly didn't have a sidearm.

"Jumpy," rumbled a deep voice from the room beyond.

Carlisle ignored the speaker and turned back to me. "It's okay. They're perfectly friendly."

Great. Now I looked like a frightened pup as I followed him into the small, bare room beyond the door. Two men waited inside. Their outfits— dark long sleeve shirts and tan pants, not quite matching but close enough —didn't say *friendly* so much as scream *private security*. Their faces, on the other hand…

Beneath a thick dark beard and a balding dome, the bigger of the two wore a weary, no-nonsense expression that said he'd dealt with one too many scudspouting delinquents in his day. Classic ex-enforcer, through and through. The smaller blond guy, though, wore a wide smile and was nearly bouncing with energy.

I couldn't help but think of a weary old hound and bright-eyed pup.

"Mister Carlisle!" the small guy exclaimed. "So good to see you again!"

He bounced forward so eagerly I half-expected him to throw Carlisle into a hug, but he pumped his brakes and extended a welcoming hand instead.

Behind him, the bigger man rubbed at his brow in irritation.

"Likewise, James," Carlisle said, shaking James' outstretched hand. "And you as well, Phineas."

The bear of a man, Phineas, gave a neutral grunt, his dark eyes fixed on me.

"And a guest, too!" James said, following Phineas' gaze to beam at me.

I tilted my head in greetings, still not sure what to make of these two.

James mirrored the motion, though I'm pretty sure his head bobbed a lot more than mine had. "Let's get you up to Franco," he said to Carlisle. "He'll be happy to see you!"

"I'm sure," Carlisle said, unslinging his pack and offering it out to James. "You can hold on to these while we meet with him if you'd like."

James took the bag and was about to check its contents when Phineas stepped up to me, cutting off my view of everything but his broad chest and shoulders. I tensed, but managed to meet his gaze without flinching.

"Arms out," he said in a deep, gravelly voice.

Carlisle leaned around Phineas' bulk to indicate I should comply. I frowned at Phineas but raised my arms out and away from my body. He swept his palmlight around the perimeter of my body in a quick, practiced manner. As he added a few physical pats around my torso and legs, I noticed a faint, mechanical whir and realized one of Phineas' sizeable arms was a prosthetic.

Finally, he stepped back, looking almost disappointedly satisfied and leaving me wondering, between the fortifications and the muscle, exactly what kind of information broker Carlisle had brought me to.

Whatever. I was here now.

Even so, I found myself bracing as James went to the door at the opposite side of the room, still grinning wide. I don't think he'd stopped since we'd walked in, which put the average disposition between him and Phineas right around neutral.

Somehow, it only made me feel all the more like I was about to walk into the lair of a classic storyvid villain when James unlocked the door and turned that grin on us.

"Right this way, my goodfellows!"

CHAPTER 13
SMOOTH MOVES

Franco's quarters were not some storyvid villain's dank lair or roughened den.

Words like *lair* and *den* were far too harsh. And, as we followed James from the bland security room and the kill zone stairwell into an elegant entryway, I decided I might've let Phineas' gruff tone and thorough pat-down color my imagination a shade too far.

The place was far larger than I'd expected, given the glum neighborhood outside. Artificial sunlight poured from above, illuminating the walls pale gold and more than making up for the lack of windows. I took in intricate wooden banisters and a trail of lush red carpet that led up stairs to a balcony with fancy darkwood walls.

There was even a small fountain in the entryway corner, burbling happily away.

James started up the stairs, indicating we should follow him. Phineas dropped onto a couch in the entryway and waved the display on the opposite wall to life to reveal one of those tragically dramatic daytime vids I thought were only watched by aging housewives. I wanted to laugh when Phineas settled into the couch with a sigh and made no move to change the feed, but I had a feeling the man wouldn't take kindly to that.

Instead, I padded up the soft, thick carpet of the staircase on Carlisle's heels. At the top, I saw that what I'd taken for a balcony was actually just the connection between the entryway and the two sides of the second floor. The place was huge.

James paused in front of the door ahead. "Do you guys need anything? Privy? Refreshments?"

His words landed squarely on the full bladder I'd been holding since the financial district. "I could use a privy," I said, glancing down the hallway and back to Carlisle. "Assuming there's time."

He waved a hand. "By all means."

James pointed down the hallway to the left. "Down this hallway and to the right. You'll see it at the end on your right." He hooked a thumb at the door behind him. "Just come on inside when you get back."

I thanked him and headed down the hall as James and Carlisle stepped into what must've been Franco's office. I couldn't help but take my time and admire the decor.

Had the ornate woodworking of the walls been bare, it still would've been plenty to hold my eyes. Thanks to the artwork lining the hall, though, I barely noticed the walls after the first few feet. I shuffled slowly along, trying to take it all in without dallying too long. When I finally turned the corner, though, I found the stretch of art only continued.

Sweet Alpha.

There'd been very little art in Sanctuary—mostly just the pictures we'd seen of some of the classic works during our studies. These might not have been the classics, but there was something to be said for seeing the paintings in person. The vibrancy of the colors. The textures that rose from the canvas, and the way they subtly shifted under the light as I moved past them. It all added a whole new intriguing dimension I'd never really experienced.

I stopped to study a painting of a bare-backed muscular hero-type confronting a great, serpentine beast. He faced the beast's gleaming yellow eyes from a rocky crest, defiant despite the fact that his foe was easily as large as the mountain upon which he stood—so massive that its full extent was lost to the darkness that pressed in, threatening to smother the singular beam of light that shone down upon the hero's skyward sword.

"You and me both, broto," I muttered.

"Looks like he's pretty screwed, huh?"

I jumped at the voice and had scrambled two steps back and into a fighting stance before my rational brain caught up. Then I took in the speaker, and my brain went fuzzy anyway.

She was beautiful.

That was about all I managed to process.

Raven dark hair. Strikingly blue eyes.

So striking that I couldn't seem to remember where I was and what I was doing there. Eyes that looked… like they were evaluating my sanity. I practically fell over myself trying to stand back at ease, as if doing so quickly enough might somehow negate my ridiculous overreaction.

"Yikes!" she said, a cautious smile tugging at her lips. "I'd hate to see what happens when somebody unexpectedly touches you on the shoulder or something."

Heat cascaded through my face, and I could only assume my face was currently competing with Johnny's hair for the title of Reddest Thing on Enochia. "Sorry, I was, uh—I mean… You kinda scared the crap out of me."

"I think that's supposed to be my line here"—she gestured to my face—"seeing as you look like you came to steal the household silvers."

If it was possible, I think my face may have gone redder.

The shaders had done their job so well that I'd completely forgotten I was wearing them. Maybe that's why Phineas had given me grief. I probably looked like some cheesy storyvid thug.

I pulled the spectacles off. "They're, uh… easy to forget."

She was tall, I realized now, and built like some of the female tyros in my class. Except none of the tyros ever made me feel like the floor was falling out from under me when I made the mistake of meeting their sharp blue eyes for a moment too long. I tore my gaze away, heart racing, and peered around the hallway, desperately trying to find something to appear interested in.

"So you live here?" I guessed out loud.

"Wouldn't you like to know?"

I tried to think cool thoughts. I had zero experience being cool or casual around girls that weren't either tyros or Johnny's sister. Especially not girls with such cute smiles and such intriguing—

Say something!

"I would."

Smooth. Real smooth.

She just kept inspecting me, half-curious, half-amused. "Were you looking for something?"

"No, I was just…"

Why had I come over here again?

"Wait. Yes. I was told there may be a privy around these parts?"

Great. And now I was asking her where I could relieve myself.

She didn't bat a lash. "I may be able to confirm or deny that rumor. For a small price, of course."

I couldn't suppress my stupid grin. "Do go on, goodlady."

"Tell me who you are."

"I'm, uh, not sure I'm supposed to make it that easy."

"Oooh, so mysterious…" She parted from the wall and stepped closer. "Are you sure you don't wanna tell me, though?"

Her voice was as soft as her face was sweet, and my desire in that moment to give her anything she wanted nearly trampled the voice of good reason reminding me it was far better for everyone if no one knew Haldin Raish the dead Legion tyro had been here.

"Sadly, yes." I dropped her gaze and placed my hands dramatically over my heart. "Quite sure, goodlady."

"Oh, stop."

When I looked up, she rolled her eyes and pointed out a door at the end of the hallway without looking away, a faint smile pulling at her lips. "It's that one."

Once again, I held her gaze a breath too long, and once again, gravity did strange things to my stomach, a lovely hazy cloud settling over my brain.

I broke our eye contact. "Thanks. I, uh…" I swallowed. "Yeah. Thanks."

"You're quite welcome, my shady goodfellow."

Carlisle was probably wondering what was taking me so long.

"Well," I said slowly, not really wanting to leave, "it was nice meeting you…" I bent an eyebrow in question.

"Oh, no." She shook her head and leaned against the wall to give me room to pass, all the while smiling a smile that made me want to do back-flips and wrestle bears just so she could see it. "No way I'm telling you my name after all that."

"Aww…"

I gave her my best puppy face. Or had started to when Phineas' unmistakable voice rumbled behind me.

"This kid bothering you?"

I only just avoided jumping out of my skin.

The girl, meanwhile, was eyeing me critically, as if giving serious thought to his question.

"Nah, he can live, I guess," she finally said. "For today, at least." The smile crept back into her eyes as she pointed me to the door again. "Go on, you. Go be mysterious somewhere else."

I stepped past her, fighting an odd mix of urges to grin at her like an idiot and to flee Phineas for my life. I think I failed on both accounts. Just like I failed to refrain from looking back when I reached the cycler room.

She was watching me, head slightly tilted, a thoughtful look in her eyes. Then I caught Phineas' guard dog expression over her shoulder, and my big stupid grin died quickly enough.

"I'll find out who you are anyway, you know," the girl said.

My wits failed me, and I resorted to giving her what I hoped was a cool, nonchalant shrug before fleeing Phineas' passive glare into the privy and closing the door behind me.

A minute later, as I stood in front of the mirror washing my hands and running over the conversation in my mind, I realized I was so flustered that I'd forgotten to even relieve my indignant bladder.

I chuckled at myself, shaking my head, and shut off the water to go try again.

WHEN I RETURNED to the hallway, I was sad to see the raven-haired girl had gone—and much less so to see Phineas had done the same. But it was probably for the best. Carlisle would definitely be wondering what was taking me so long by now.

I headed back to the entryway, thinking I should probably try to focus on something other than the memory of her face, but not really wanting to. Phineas was back downstairs watching his sappy vid when I came back to the central balcony. He didn't look up as I made for the door Carlisle and James had entered.

The first word that struck me when I opened the door was *opulent*.

The room had the look of a study. Darkwood furniture that probably cost as much as Carlisle's skimmer but looked less comfortable than its lowly polymer seats. Around the regal collection of furniture was an assortment of rich rugs, more artwork, and—perhaps most impressively—shelves full of real, hardbound books.

Not something you saw every day.

Carlisle and James sat in front of a massive oak desk. A third man with thick, carefully-styled dark hair sat across from them, his strong jaw contrasted by a thin, dark mustache that curled slightly upward at its ends. He had tan skin and olive green eyes.

Franco, I presumed.

I tried to push the girl out of my head and rein in the idiotic smile plastered on my face. Ditching the smile became a lot easier when the three men turned toward me.

"Uh, hello," I mumbled, feeling suddenly sheepish.

James smiled and hopped out of his chair to offer it to me. "Found the cycler okay?"

"Yep. No problems."

Alpha, were my cheeks as red as they felt?

I turned to the man behind the desk, trying to avoid Carlisle's piercing stare. "You have a beautiful collection out there, sir."

The man regarded me for several seconds, his expression neutral. Finally, he traded an amused glance with Carlisle and stood to offer his hand to me. "And you good taste, young goodfellow. I'm Francesco Fields. Franco, if you like. Pleased to make your acquaintance."

His handshake was firm, his hand strong and warm. "Likewise, sir—uh, Franco. Pleased to meet you."

He held my hand a second longer, waiting to see if I'd offer my name, then gestured for me to sit and did the same himself.

"I see you've told our young friend to be careful with whom he trusts, Carlisle. A wise decision, I'm sure. Though, I have to say, he bears a striking resemblance to the son of that poor family who died in the Sanctuary house fire last cycle. Tragic, that."

There was no scorn or mockery in his voice, but I tensed all the same—I couldn't help it. Franco didn't miss it. So much for keeping a secret.

"Tragic is surely not a strong enough word," Carlisle said. "Come now, Franco. Let us not play hurtful games."

Franco sighed and nodded, his calculating look shifting to one of sympathy. "I'm sorry about what they did to your family, Haldin. I don't know how you escaped, but I'm glad Carlisle found you."

He made it sound like he'd seen through the house fire cover up right from the start.

Did that mean he already knew about the raknoth?

"I didn't escape," I said, unsure what else to say. "Carlisle saved me."

I wasn't sure why I chose to make the distinction, but there probably wasn't much point in withholding details now.

Franco didn't look overly surprised by the news. "I suspected that might have been the case."

"Rest assured, we're all duly impressed," Carlisle said.

Franco inclined his head as if Carlisle had just made an obvious point. "Straight to business as usual, then?"

"I wouldn't know what to do with myself otherwise," Carlisle said, with a soft smile.

"Does anyone need anything?" James asked. "Water? Sweetfizz?"

Franco watched us for a second before turning to James. "I think we're set, James. Thank you."

James shot us a wave and one last smile then bowed out of the room, pulling the door closed behind him.

"So…" Franco steepled his fingers and touched them lightly to his chin as he studied us. "What's on your mind, Carlisle?"

"I think we need to have another look at Vantage," Carlisle said.

"Ah, yes. Your favorite demon-hunt." Franco turned to me and gestured at Carlisle. "Anyone else who came to see me about Vantage would be trying to get their hands on trade secrets, valuable medical breakthroughs. But not Carlisle. He's too busy seeing alien plots in his grain bowl." He looked back at Carlisle. "We've been over Vantage. I won't say they're clean, and I don't doubt Alton Parker's a slimy scudspout. But a raknoth? I don't know…"

"I do," Carlisle said.

Franco arched an eyebrow. "Do go on."

"I went to have a look at their Divinity headquarters last night. The plan was to sense what I could from outside and leave. I didn't expect to encounter a telepath there in the middle of the night."

Apparently, the existence of telepaths was no big surprise to Franco.

"And it was Parker?" he asked.

Carlisle nodded.

"You're sure?"

"I saw him through the window while we were… tangling."

Was that why Carlisle had been so exhausted this morning? Some kind of telepathic brawl with a raknoth?

Franco stroked thoughtfully at his mustache, pondering, and finally paused. "So maybe Alton Parker is a telepath, but—"

"A strong telepath," Carlisle said.

"Yes, but that doesn't mean he's one of them."

"An incredibly strong telepath," Carlisle amended. "I assure you, the feel of a raknoth mind is not something one easily mistakes."

"Okay," Franco said finally, clearly not overjoyed. He started stroking at his mustache again. "So what are you thinking?"

"This factory they're building," Carlisle said, "we need to know everything. Who they're contracting with. What permits Divinity's granted them."

"I'm sure it's occurred to you that any dangerously interesting bits may well be absent from the records."

Carlisle sat back in his chair. "You know I didn't come here to talk about public records. Do what you do, and point me in the right direction. I hope you'll trust me when I say there's almost certainly something of dire importance to be found here. We need to find out what they're working on."

"So why don't we just go take a look at the labs?" I said before I could stop myself.

They both turned to me, assessing whether or not I was serious.

"What?" I asked. "We can all agree that that's probably where the evil plan is unfolding if it actually exists, right?"

"That's probably true," Carlisle said, woefully unconvinced.

"But the problem," Franco added, "is that Vantage's main facility is probably the most heavily fortified non-Legion installment in this hemisphere."

"Which Haldin no doubt already knows," Carlisle said, watching me, "which in turn leads me to wonder what masterful plan he might be holding up his sleeve."

I pointed at Carlisle, then to myself. "You break into fortresses, and I know how to guard them. I'm sure we can figure something out."

Carlisle looked none too impressed.

"What if their plan has nothing to do with this factory?" I pushed on. "What if the factory's actually a legitimate operation? We could spend a whole season chasing a dead end while they're still doing Alpha knows what out at the labs. If we're gonna take a shot, why not pick the most likely target?"

The room was silent for a stretch. Carlisle turned his frown on Franco, perhaps looking to see that he too recognized my reasoning as naive bullscud. But Franco was smiling.

"It wouldn't be easy," he said, stroking his mustache. "Vantage's security could probably more accurately be called a private military." He looked at Carlisle. "Frankly, I'm surprised you didn't have more trouble untangling yourself back at the offices."

"It wasn't exactly a moonlit stroll," Carlisle said.

Franco shook his head in admiration. "I don't imagine it was…"

The silence returned, and I could tell both men were thinking about it—were maybe even glad that a naive kid had been there to propose the idea first.

It was like my dad had always said, right?

Do what you think is right, Hal—in your eyes, and in the eyes of Alpha. Pay no mind to what anyone else thinks about that. Do your best. Believe in it. That's what men follow.

I doubted I'd be convincing Carlisle or Franco to do anything they didn't want to, but at least the idea seemed to have caught.

"What do we expect might actually be found out there?" Franco asked no one in particular.

"Answers," Carlisle said. "To what they're planning as well as to several other questions."

Franco drummed his fingers on the tabletop. "Well," he finally said, "you know me. There's no way I could pass up a chance to see what Alton Parker the raknoth has tucked away in his shiny little lab. If you're actually thinking about doing this, that is."

"Perhaps we should explore both avenues for now," Carlisle said. "If we had more information on the labs…"

"We could procure floor plans without too much trouble," Franco said, tapping something into his palmlight. "Info on security specifics will be trickier, but I'll see what I can do." He glanced at me then back to Carlisle. "I take it you might have some field support moving forward?"

Carlisle looked at me with the same heaviness he took on every time I asked him when we'd make our first move. The thought bothered him. That much was clear.

I tried to show him a reassuring smile. "One deceased Legion tyro, reporting for duty."

Carlisle said nothing.

"Very well, then." Franco rapped the desk with his knuckles. "I'll get started immediately. The sooner we can inform ourselves enough to get planning, the better." He looked between us, thinking, then added, "You two might as well stay here in the meanwhile, if you'd like. Alpha knows we have the space."

It was embarrassing how quickly the invitation conjured my hopes of seeing the raven-haired girl again. I couldn't help it any more than I could control the thrill of nervous excitement wriggling through my chest. At least until I took in the expectant arch of Franco's dark eyebrows and realization hit me like a splash of cold water.

That was Franco's daughter I'd met.

It must've been. What else would a girl my age be doing here?

"Perhaps next time, my friend," Carlisle was saying. "Haldin and I have business elsewhere."

My cheeks grew warm. Here we were talking about unmasking a

raknoth plan to destroy Alpha knew how many lives, and I was busy daydreaming about a girl. The thought should've sobered me. And yet, even as Franco stood to shake our hands, jesting that Carlisle was all business and no fun and that we should both find the time to appreciate the finer things and so on, all I could seem to think about was how I wished I could have told her my name.

CHAPTER 14
STONES

"What I said to Franco about us having other business…" Carlisle said once we'd returned to the skimmer below the streets of Divinity. "I'm concerned things are about to get dangerous fast, and your training has only just begun. I know you're perfectly capable as you are," he pushed on when I tried to protest. "But you don't yet understand how much stronger you'll become over the years with proper training." He shook his head wistfully. "If only it were years we had."

"We'll just have to do what we can before the scud plops, then," I said. "I'd be lying if I said I'm not a little scared, but what else can we do? We work with what we have, right?"

Something about my words seemed to alleviate a fraction of Carlisle's concern. He tilted his head in concession and started the skimmer. "We work with what we have."

We navigated the subterranean tunnel in amicable silence.

"Franco and his people seem like… good people," I said as we pulled into the bay beneath the ruined temple. I wanted to ask him about the raven-haired girl but was mildly mortified to broach the subject. If it just happened to arise by "accident," though…

"Better, I take it, than you expected for those involved in Franco's current line of work?"

I gave a guilty shrug as we walked to the mag lift. "Something like that."

"They're good people." His lip twitched. "Even Phineas."

"Yeah, what's his deal?"

"Truth be told, I'm not sure," Carlisle said, tapping the lift controls. "He was a Legion enforcer in a past life, but he doesn't talk much about himself. Or much at all, for that matter. Franco calls him the Hammer."

I thought about the big man with the prosthetic arm and the friendly disposition of a brick wall. "Seems appropriate."

The doors slid open to the hideout I realized I was beginning to think of as home base.

"It's actually his last name," Carlisle said. "Phineas Hammer and James Bell. The Bell and the Hammer. Franco's dynamic duo."

I laughed. "You've gotta be kidding me. Did they have their names changed or something?"

He smiled and went to set his bag down at his desk. "Sometimes, cosmic fate is just a wonderful source of amusement, I think."

"I guess so..."

I was wondering how to prod further when Carlisle shot me a knowing look. "And then there's Elise too."

"I—How do you always do that?"

"Well, judging by how long it took you to find the privy and the cloud you walked in on when you finally joined us, I had to assume you'd either met a lovely lady or that you are entirely more fond of art than I'd imagined."

I swallowed, trying not to wilt under his stare. "Oh, you have no idea. I just go kooky for those brush strokes."

He smiled a little, but there was reservation behind it.

"She's Franco's daughter, isn't she?"

"She is."

Elise. I turned the name over, savoring the sound of it.

"What do you know about her?"

"Haldin..." I could've sworn Carlisle looked more uncomfortable than I felt. "If we want to win this fight, your training is more pressing now than ever. As callous as it sounds, we can't afford distractions, not to mention complications in our dealings with Franco."

Heat flashed through me, roiling from embarrassment straight to anger with startling speed. "That's not what I was—What do you mean, 'if we want to win this fight?' You're seriously gonna throw that in my face after that son of a bitch killed my parents? You think there's anything I won't do to make him pay?"

Carlisle's gaze dropped to the floor. "I'm sorry, I didn't mean to insinuate..." He sighed and sank into his desk chair. "You asked what I know about Elise. I know that her mother died because she was mixed up in business like ours. I know that, if your interest were to become clear to him, Franco would likely make it his business to keep you away from her. He'd do anything to keep Elise safe after what happened to her mother."

He met my eyes, his expression apologetic. "I know it's not fair, but it would be best if you could put her out of your mind."

I opened my mouth only to close it and shrug. "Fine. I was just curious. Forget about it."

He looked like he wanted to say something more, but he only nodded instead, agreeing to drop the matter.

"I'm going for a walk," I said, needing to be away from him, if only for a little while.

Carlisle didn't argue.

Outside, the air was fresh and calming.

Bitterness aside, it was hard to deny the beauty of the day as I walked in the woods beside the temple. Sun pierced through the canopy of leaves, giving rise to thousands of tiny lances of radiance that shimmered and danced across the soft forest ground as the foliage above likewise danced in the gentle breeze. The air smelled of soil and bark. I took deep breaths, enjoying the peaceful quiet after the bustling chaos of Divinity.

A peculiar stone caught my eye, so smooth and round that I mistook it for a small bird's egg at first. I scooped it up and continued on, absentmindedly flicking the stone into the air and catching it as I went.

Carlisle was probably right about Elise. I knew that. I didn't even know her, for Alpha's sake, and I'd seen to it that she didn't know me. Besides, I had far more important matters to worry about—matters of life and death. But no matter how logical my inner voice sounded repeating those thoughts, I couldn't seem to rid my mind of her.

Eventually, my meandering brought me to the southern bank of the Red River. I stood there for a while, rubbing the smooth stone between my palms. The running water looked cool and refreshing, the sun playing off its surface in a mesmerizing dance of shimmering light. I cocked my arm back to throw the stone into the water but paused, changing my mind.

Sanctuary wasn't visible from this side of the city, but I stared for some time at the place where it would be, thinking about Kublich and my parents and the raknoth. Finally, I turned back for the temple and resumed my simple, soothing game with the stone.

Flick. Catch. Flick. Catch.

It was time to get back to training.

~

"I'm ready," I told Carlisle when I made it back to our home base. "What's next?"

Carlisle looked relieved. He glanced at the stone I still held in my hand. "That's perfect."

"This?" I said, holding it up. "Perfect for wh—Gah!"

The stone flew out of my palm and straight into Carlisle's waiting hand without a second's warning.

"I want you to try to move this stone with your mind."

I frowned from my empty hand back up to him, waiting for more. "Really? That's all? What happened to mastering my extended senses first?"

"Well, seeing as a brash young tyro seems determined to move our timetable up"—he tossed the stone back to me—"I think it's time we enroll you in the accelerated program."

"Right." I stared skeptically at the stone between thumb and forefinger. "Does that program come with directions this time, at least?"

"Only the most basic. Remember the water glass. I chose to channel thermal energy from the water to lift your weight from the ground, but that was only one of hundreds of ways I could've accomplished the task. At the end of the day, the only hard rule is that energy is conserved. To expend it in one place or form, you must take it from another. Past that, I'd rather not restrict your thinking. I could give you pointers, but most Shapers find their own ways of doing things. It's probably best you do too."

"You're some teacher, you know that?"

"Take it as a vote of confidence," he said, turning back to his displays with the faintest of wry smiles, "and rest assured, I'll be here if needed."

That seemed to be my cue to get started. Unsure where else to begin, I placed the stone in front of me on the mat and closed my eyes to focus. Finding the stone in my extended senses seemed as reasonable a place to start as any.

Of course, that was easier said than done.

By now, reaching out was becoming as easy as a careful thought and a few deep breaths. Bit by bit, that fear of drifting away into nothingness was fading away too, and I could reach out for longer and longer. Where at first it'd been impossible to pick out more than a wild jumble of disjointed details, I was even beginning to make sense of at least some of what I felt. It was just my control that left something to be desired.

It was starting to get better, I thought. Maybe. Instead of simply bleeding out like that ball of expanding gas, now my senses at least seemed to move in the general direction I most strongly focused on. I'd even noticed that the sharper my focus became, the less thinly-stretched I felt.

Most of the time, though, it still kind of felt like trying to land a transport flying dead stick. Which was why I spent the next twenty or so minutes sweeping around, through, and past that damned stone like a rudderless ship, catching glimpses of its smooth round surface but never quite managing to get my hooks in and stay there.

I was about to withdraw and try again for what felt like the hundredth time when I bumped into something unlike anything I'd ever felt—a vibrant energy that burned like a fog beacon, hard to miss, but also somehow hard to get a perfect fix on.

I was still unfruitfully trying when Carlisle's voice came to me. *"Careful. That's my mind you're trying to invade."*

I recoiled in surprise. *"Oh scud! Sorry, I didn't mean to..."*

I almost laughed when I realized I was still immersed in my senses and merely thinking the words rather than speaking them.

"Sorry about that," I repeated out loud, reeling in my senses and opening my eyes. "I didn't mean to..." I trailed off at the look Carlisle was giving me.

"Yes," he said slowly. "You said that already."

"I know but... Wait." A quiver of excitement ran through me. "You... you heard that?"

A slow smile spread across his face. "A pessimistic man might point out that you were *supposed* to be working on the stone..." His smile widened. "But I think this might be adequate cause for congratulations, all the same."

He was positively beaming now. I couldn't help but smile back, my head whirling with what had just happened.

"It's still only the beginning, mind you," Carlisle said, reining his smile in just a fraction, "but this... this is encouraging, Hal. You're doing far better than I'd dared hope for."

"I, uh... Thanks." I frowned. "I think." I thought about what I'd just done, trying to solidify the feeling in my head for future reference. "So, when I was trying to focus in on you..."

"I wasn't letting you. You've already experienced firsthand what it feels like when such a link goes unchecked and abused."

"That's what would happen if I kept pushing?" I asked, uneasily thinking about the complete helplessness of Smirks—and Kublich before him—holding me hostage in my own body. Just the memory got my heart racing.

"Only if you pushed hard enough to break my defenses. It's also possible to form a harmonious sharing between minds. Possible, but dangerous. I don't have to explain to you how vulnerable you are once a telepath is past your defenses. But you should also know that, once they have that foothold, it's nearly impossible to drive them out by force."

"Nice of you to point that out now," I muttered.

"You were never in any danger from me," Carlisle said. "But you have to understand, uncloaking your mind in the presence of another telepath is essentially making a wager that your will is stronger than theirs, or at least strong enough to hold if they decide to fight you for control."

I fingered my cloaking pendant nervously. "So shouldn't I learn to protect myself?"

"Soon, yes. Like everything else, it'll take a good deal of practice. Eventually, though, you'll be able to protect yourself with little more than an afterthought. For now, though—"

"I should focus on the other stuff?"

He cocked his head. "I was going to say you should simply keep your cloak on at all times in the outside world. But, now that you mention it..." He waved at the stone in front of me, his smile spreading. *That stone isn't going to move itself.*

CHAPTER 15

WHITE LIE

I'd spent my nearly eighteen years of existence seeing the world through a pin prick in the blindfold. That's what I realized on the day my mind brushed against the thrumming turbulence of the fly.

It had been three days since Franco's, with little news but that he was confident he'd have something for us soon. The waiting was killing me. Though, to be fair, it might have had less to do with the waiting and more to do with my stubborn abilities.

I'd yet to so much as budge that thrice Alpha-damned stone.

My extended senses, on the other hand, were quickly becoming the gateway to a whole new world. A world where I could apparently feel a fly from across the room with my mind, I realized, as the tiny buzzing mass in my senses settled onto the cool stone wall and held still long enough for the details to begin falling into place. The chitinous edges of delicate wings, so fine and yet so pristinely ordered. The intricate ridges between the hundreds of hexagonal units of its eyes. The bristly hairs on its body. The warmth of its blood.

All of these things, I felt from halfway across the room—as clearly as if I were inspecting a man-sized fly with my own hands and eyes.

It was impossible. It was incredible. But perhaps most of all, it was distracting. Because how was I supposed to convince myself to keep bursting blood vessels trying to move a confounded pebble when I'd suddenly discovered entire new worlds upon worlds to explore within that very room?

Not well. That's how.

And that's not to say I didn't spend hours trying. I'd lost count of how many times I'd held the stone firmly in my senses, imagining it lifting from the ground, willing it to be so. More often than not, there was vigorous brow-wrinkling involved as well. But time and time again, nothing happened. Not on the first try. Not on the hundredth.

It was maddening.

My thoughts darkened by the hour. Some small voice insisted I shouldn't be hard on myself. Demons to the wind, I *had* learned to feel a fly's wings from across the room with my freaking mind in just nine days, after all. Where would I be in just another few days, at the end of a full cycle? How long until I was shooting snap flares from my hands and catching myself from Alpha-blessed hundred-foot falls?

Probably a damn long while if I couldn't even move a scuddy little stone.

I clenched my jaw and kept trying. I'd like to say I eventually took a deep breath, backed up from the situation, and solved the problem like a scholar. But, in truth, it was only when I'd snapped—when I'd already plucked the stone from the mat, intending to whip it across the room—that inspiration finally struck.

Carlisle turned from his displays, calmly considered the stone I held ready to hurl across the room, then went back to his work without a word. I was too busy unpacking the tangle of excited thoughts racing through my head to worry too much about what he might be thinking.

Energy.

I'd been thinking about it all along—about Carlisle's words, and shifting energy from one place to another. But I'd been thinking about it all wrong. I'd been straining until it felt like I'd blow a valve trying to produce that energy, but that'd been all I was doing. Unfocused, undefined straining, paired with hopeful visualization. But maybe all I needed to do was lift the stone—without touching it.

I wanted to mock myself for the simplicity of the thought. That's what I'd been trying to do all along, right? But it shouldn't be this hard. I was sure of that now.

So I dropped the stone to the mat and forced myself to sit back, breathing calming breaths. I reached for the stone with a small tendril of my mind, finding its smooth surface for the millionth time, the sensation as real in my mind as if it were actually pressed to my flesh. I focused on that sensation and started redirecting, willing the feeling of the stone from my abstract mental space back toward my physical body, down toward my hand.

It took several minutes to find the exact feeling I was searching for. Finally, though, I convinced myself. I knew the stone wasn't in my hand. But, at the same time, it also *was*. I could feel it there. It was real, I told myself. I had to believe it. If my hand moved, so too would the stone.

So I raised my hand.

A surprised laugh from across the room startled my focus, and my eyes snapped open just in time to see the stone wobble in midair, on level with my upraised hand, and fall back to the mat with a happy little plop.

Even seeing it, I didn't quite believe it.

I'd moved something with my freaking mind.

And sure, there'd been many unbelievable moments while exploring with my extended senses. And yes, I'd already seen Carlisle work more impressive feats and tell me I'd eventually be able to do the same. But it wasn't until that moment that I truly started believing all of it.

"How did you do it?" Carlisle asked, positively beaming.

"I just, uh, pretended the rock was in my hand." I glanced down at the hand in question, still trying to process. "And then I just moved it."

"Marvelous! First with the telepathy and now with the telekinesis..." He shook his head, still smiling. "You have to understand, Haldin, when I said earlier that it might take cycles, I was sure I was being unrealistically optimistic."

I couldn't help but laugh. "Alpha, thanks for the vote of confidence."

He was still shaking his head. "You mistake my meaning. Most take several seasons to do what you just did. Some take years. This..." He waved a hand, lost for words, then hopped up with sudden energy. "Here." He pushed his chair toward me on skittering wheels. "Why don't you try to lift this now?"

I considered the chair, then shrugged and reached out with my mind. Just like before, I concentrated until I could believe my palm was actually planted on the bottom of the chair, then I raised my hand. There was more resistance this time, as if...

As if I were lifting a desk chair instead of a pebble. It was so obvious.

Grinning, I raised my hand higher and opened my eyes in time to watch the chair topple over with a crash.

Carlisle looked down at the fallen chair and gave a few slow claps. "Do you understand what's happening now?"

"I'm... connecting things to my hand so that I can move them from a distance? The chair must have tipped because my focus wasn't centered on it right."

"That is specifically what you're doing, yes. But how would you explain something like this?"

The chair righted itself and lifted from the ground to hover a few feet in the air. Carlisle stood there, calm and relaxed, as the chair orbited once around him and settled neatly back to the floor.

"I don't know," I said slowly, trying to reason through it.

He waved me on, inviting me to speak my thoughts.

"Okay. You didn't move at all, so you weren't using force from your muscles to move the chair like I did. But you must have been using energy from somewhere, because things don't just move without energy. So, it came from... I don't know. Somewhere else in your body, I guess?"

"Very good," he said, nodding. Then he grinned and pulled a small energy cell from his pocket. "I was actually using this, but you're right, I could have drawn energy from my body or our surroundings in any number of ways."

I blew out a light chuckle. "Cheater."

He shrugged, clearly amused, and clearly in better spirits than I'd seen since... well, since ever.

"So there are a lot of ways to do it," I said, "but it always comes down to moving energy from one place to another?"

"That's precisely the essence of Shaping. Channeling energy from one place to another, often from one form to another, to"—he raised his eyebrows—"re-Shape reality. Get it?"

I smiled at Carlisle's unusual energy. "So where else could I draw energy from? How did you use that cell?"

"You can channel it from anywhere, really. Energy is always around us, in one form or another." He waved the energy cell. "There's chemical energy in this cell, and in the generator's fuel..." He pointed at the fab. "Even in our food. There's the electromagnetic energy flowing in from the solar panels outside. The thermal energy of the air and that of our bodies. Even the atomic energy of matter itself, though I don't believe any Shaper has ever dared try to control such a force. The first question is whether you can figure out *how* to channel what energy you find and Shape it to serve your purpose. It's mostly a combination of practice and creative thinking."

"And the second question?"

"Is whether or not your body can withstand channeling the amount of energy required to accomplish your goal." He sobered. "That's where things can get unpleasant."

"What happens if I can't? Withstand it, I mean."

"Channeling energy can be quite dangerous. Lethal even, in some cases, if a Shaper tries to handle too much at once. Fortunately, most of us who take more than we can manage tend to pass out before much serious damage occurs. Most of the time."

"Oh, the relief," I muttered.

"Not to worry. You'll find your limits quickly enough, just as you'll notice they begin to grow as you push them and further explore your abilities. Remember…"

He waved a hand in invitation, and four knives sprang from the pile of weapons by my cot, flew across the room, and pulled into tight orbit around him.

"… you're only just getting started."

"Only if you remember you're a big old show off," I mumbled.

"I'm sure I don't know what you mean."

As he said it, the knives pulled into tight formation then broke off and began whizzing around like skimmers in battle. At least he kind of looked like he had to focus for that display.

Maybe he was human after all.

"Practice and creative thinking," he repeated as the knives continued their dance. "Those are the keys. That's why I wanted you to figure out how to move the stone on your own."

"Right…" I said slowly, too deeply ensconced in Carlisle's display to say much else until he grew tired of his game and landed the knives back in their proper places. "So what should I do next, then?"

"Practice," Carlisle said with a smile, "and think creatively."

By supper the following evening, the training had invaded my life to the extent that Carlisle had me try using my utensils with telekinesis instead of my hands, just to practice fine control. A few dozen spills and food-laden spoon pokes to the face later, I even started getting the hang of it. Or spilling a little less, at least.

Clumsy as it was, it was good to feel like I was actually getting somewhere. Especially after I'd spent the afternoon trying to telekinetically pluck things out of the air and finding out that objects in motion were still well past my skill level. Carlisle had told me not to berate myself and reminded me that I was doing beyond exceptionally well, but somehow I couldn't seem to hear anything but Mathis' voice in my head, asking me what Captain Daddy would have to say about my difficulties.

I was being hard on myself. Some part of me knew that. But even so, I couldn't help but think my mental Mathis had a point. Sure, my dad hadn't been able to move things with his mind, but he'd been an Alpha-blessed hero of Sanctuary. He'd been smart and skilled and careful.

And Kublich had still broken him like a twig.

So I'd be damned if I was going to sit back and congratulate myself on lifting a chair—telekinesis or no. This fight wasn't going to be won by lifting pebbles and chairs. I had to work harder. Get better. Get stronger.

I had to kill Kublich.

But for now, I knew, I needed to start by mastering the basics. So I summoned a sponge from the sink to manage the growing pile of my accidents.

"A man could get pretty lazy practicing this stuff," I said, wiping up the mess before floating the sponge drunkenly back over to the sink.

"It wouldn't exactly be the first time we humans had abused amazing abilities," Carlisle said, tapping pointedly at his palmlight.

"Guess not." I absentmindedly fingered my spoon, contemplating our special brand of amazing abilities and a question that had been rolling around in my head all day. "Before, when you said the Sanctum had covered up certain truths in the past…"

"You're wondering why it is they hunt our kind?"

I nodded. "I can understand why people like us might be feared, but… I don't know. How did this happen? How has the Sanctum kept this whole thing a secret?"

"The short version is that they haven't. Not truly. But I assume it's the long version you'd like to know."

"I might settle for medium."

Carlisle smiled but quickly sobered. "You're familiar with the prophet Sarentus and the demons of his scriptures, yes?"

"Yeah, everyone is, but…" I frowned, thinking of the giant statue of Sarentus in front of the White Tower. "You're not saying…?"

Was he implying that the demons of Sarentus' Holy Scriptures had in fact been Shapers?

The Sanctum made no jest in warning us of the perils of demons, even now, a thousand years after Sarentus had unified Enochia and helped cast them back to the nether at the turning of the dark ages. Like most people, though, I'd assumed that the modern day demons discussed in Sanctum services were mostly meant as metaphor for the lingering temptation to commit sins in the eyes of Alpha.

Yet, now that I thought about what vague details I could recall from the scripture—the talk of demons corrupting men to their will, calling upon unholy forces for strength...

"You'd never heard of the Emmútari before I mentioned them, had you?" Carlisle asked.

I shook my head.

He looked supremely unsurprised. "Few have these days. I often wonder whether the High Cleric himself is even aware of his heritage."

I didn't like the sound of this. Apparently, my feelings showed.

"Are you sure you're ready to hear me disparage your Sanctum?" Carlisle asked.

The way he said it—*your* Sanctum—made me even more uneasy. But I needed to know. It might only be his version of the story, but the Sanctum had tried to have me killed, and I needed to know why.

"Tell me," I said. "Please."

"Very well." He laid his hands on the table, preparing himself. "Over a thousand years ago, before the Sanctum came to power, there was an entire order of men and women like us. The Emmútari. Conquerors feared them for their command over the elements, and for over a hundred years, the Emmútari used their power to keep peace across Enochia."

It sounded pretty much like the beginning of any number of the old fae tales, but I refrained from pointing that out.

"You've heard plenty about how Sarentus unified the twelve nations of Enochia under one deity to conquer a great evil," Carlisle continued. "What's no longer told is that it was really the Emmútari he was uniting the world against, playing on the mutual fears of the old nations. A strong Emmútar could have stood alone against dozens of soldiers in those times, you see. It wasn't the kind of power many kings liked seeing outside of their control. You can imagine how the world might've been looking for a reason to turn against the order. Sarentus simply struck the flint at the perfect time, and in marched the armies."

Neat and tidy. Just like every other tale. And yet...

I looked at the ancient stone surrounding us. "Was this supposed to be their temple, or something?"

"I don't actually know," Carlisle said, following my gaze around the room. "Maybe an outpost, if anything. Maybe a relic of some other dead and forgotten sect. The main temple of the Emmútari, though, was allegedly destroyed beyond any recognition. With most of the Emmútari still in it, I might add. Yet they refused to fight."

"To keep the peace?"

He shrugged. "I think they realized there never could have been true peace on the other side of bloodshed. The people of Enochia no longer wanted the Emmútari, and so the order surrendered. They offered to disband and live quiet lives."

"And that wasn't enough?"

"The people's fear was too strong. The united armies called for blood. Of course, not all of the Emmútari were present at the temple when it came under siege. Those who survived went into hiding. And, once the ashes had cleared with Sarentus on top as the mouth of Alpha, the one true deity of Enochia, he condemned any surviving Emmútari as practitioners of black magic. Demons of the nether."

"And the Emmútari killed him for it," I said, bridging the gap between his story and the one that said Sarentus eventually sacrificed himself to banish the last and greatest of the demons.

To my surprise, Carlisle didn't deny it.

"So the story goes," he said. "The order of the clerics took charge, and the surviving Emmútari were hunted for the rest of their days. Thankfully, some of them found new generations of gifted and decided to pass on what knowledge they could. The art became known as Shaping, and those teachings trickled from generation to generation until I heard all of this from Cassius."

"And now I'm hearing it from you."

"So it continues." He smiled. "Perhaps this means I've served my purpose."

"I dunno. I might need you around for another few days, at least."

Joking aside, his story disturbed me. Not because I believed it, necessarily. It was more just that I couldn't see a better explanation for why the Sanctum would be hunting Shapers in the shadows. And if there was one thing I couldn't deny anymore, it was that Shaping was absolutely not a wild figment of my imagination.

Still, it was hard to believe something as monumental as an entire world order of Shapers—or Emmútari, or whatever—could be so completely burned from history. Even if it had been a long, long time ago. And even if it was the all-powerful Sanctum we were talking about.

"How could the Sanctum and the Legion not know about all of this?"

"Perhaps some of them do," Carlisle said. "Surely the clerics overseeing the Seeker core have at least some inkling of the truth." He cocked his head. "Though, to be fair, I can't pretend I'm positive our version is the complete truth either. What we know for sure is that we are the ones being hunted. And it's clear enough that Sarentus held the pen of history. Is it so hard to imagine the Sanctum's story is… incomplete?"

"I…"

I didn't know what to say to that—what to even think about any of it. I wasn't sure I wanted to. Better to focus on the threats I could be sure of for now.

"How are we even supposed to use our abilities out there if dropping our cloaks is going to light us up for any nearby Seekers or raknoth?"

Thankfully, Carlisle didn't seem to mind my changing the subject. "A valid question," he said, rising to go rummage in the workbench drawers. "I think the time has come for you to wear this."

He tossed a small something my way.

Another pendant, with equally cryptic runes etched across its surface. I traced my finger over a series of notches that progressively increased in length around the circumference of the disk, like an antique volume dial.

"Is this a signal booster or something?"

"Sort of the opposite, actually. When the dial is at the maximum setting, this rune will cloak you as tightly as your current pendant does. As you dial it down, though, the cloaked area expands like a bubble, effectively increasing your sphere of influence without opening yourself to everything else outside."

"So it's kind of like an intensity setting, then." I frowned. "Except, isn't that kind of backwards? The longest notches mean I'm fully cloaked? I'd think that should mean the cloak is fully extended."

"You're quite free to make your own variable range cloaking pendant if mine is unsatisfactory."

I swapped the old pendant out for the new with a sheepish smile. "I guess this old clunker will have to do. What kind of range are we talking about at max—sorry, at *minimum*—setting?"

Carlisle rolled his eyes and mumbled something about ungrateful teenagers under his breath.

"That one should give you a range of about forty feet. You can deactivate it completely if you need to go further. And I should also point out that extending the cloaked area will require more energy. You noticed your old pendant was cool to the touch when active, yes?"

"Because it was drawing energy to form the cloak?"

I tried to say it as if I hadn't just then realized it.

"Indeed. When activated, these pendants absorb heat from their surroundings to generate the cloaking field. It's a minor effect when the field's small, but as the field grows, the heat requirements grow significantly." He tapped the pendant resting over his tunic. "Direct skin contact can get uncomfortable."

That was fine by me. Getting the chills wasn't a bad compromise for being able to use my abilities without completely exposing myself. Curious, I dialed the cloak out as far as it would go.

Within seconds, the pendant was icy cold. Not totally unbearable, but I could see what Carlisle meant about direct skin contact. By the time I dialed the cloak back in, the air around me had grown a few degrees cooler, too.

"Pretty damn cool."

"Just remember, if it comes to a fight, you'll still be vulnerable to any telepaths inside your cloaking field. Hopefully it's not something we'll have to worry about anytime soon, but we should start training your mental defenses nonetheless."

That sounded good to me.

I still shuddered at the memories of Kublich and Smirks playing puppet master with my body. Enough so that I was about to suggest we start the lessons right then when Carlisle's desk node emitted a light chirp and one of the displays awoke with a notification.

"Franco?" I asked as he crossed to check it.

"The one and only." He glanced down at his palmlight. "We should move. We can be off the streets before the suspiciously late hours if we leave now."

"We're going tonight?"

My obsession with mastering telekinesis had mostly held the thoughts of Elise at bay throughout the day's training, but the prospect of returning to Franco's threw open the floodgates to fanciful thoughts of fair skin and mischievous smiles.

"Whatever we decide from Franco's information," Carlisle said, "it'll probably require a couple days to plan and prepare. And time is of the essence." He gave me a shrewd look, as if only then noticing I'd sounded a few notes too excited about the new plans. "Please don't make me regret the decision, Haldin."

I scowled, praying my cheeks weren't as red as they felt. "Please. I know how to control myself. Soldier, remember?"

"Tyro," Carlisle amended, looking less than convinced, but he said nothing more.

I accepted the slight without argument and gladly turned my attention to packing a few days' supplies, more than ready to see what the night would bring.

CHAPTER 16

FIRE AND STAVES

We made it to Franco's unmolested under the rambunctious cover of the Divinity nightlife crowd. I made a point of removing my hood and my specs at the door this time.

"Hey, guys!" James cried from the top of the steps.

It was like being greeted by an excited puppy.

"Hello, James," Carlisle called.

I raised a hand in greeting and returned James' smile. It was kind of hard not to.

"No pat down?" I asked when James beckoned us through the antechamber and straight into the house.

An embarrassed look crossed his face. "Oh, Phineas just wanted to make sure, umm… That is, we don't normally—"

"It's quite all right, James," Carlisle said. "These are dangerous times."

I nodded my agreement when James turned his gaze to me, and it seemed to assuage his concerns. He bounced on through the doorway, waving for us to follow.

We passed Phineas—who roused from his couch-lounging only enough to respond to our greetings with a low grunt—and headed up to Franco's study. I glanced each way at the landing, hoping I might discreetly catch a glimpse of Elise.

No such luck.

My spirits fell as James shuttled us through the ornate door and into the study. Franco sat behind his big oak desk, poring over a tablet. He didn't speak as we sat. Just tapped a few commands on his tablet and waved a hand at the holodisk in the center of his desk.

A three-dimensional map sprang to life over the desk, slowly rotating to reveal a huge complex surrounded by a perimeter wall that nearly rivaled Sanctuary's.

"That's the Vantage facility?" I asked.

I already knew the answer. I'd seen images of the place before. It just looked a tad more intimidating after I'd suggested breaking into the place.

Franco nodded absentmindedly. "They take their privacy quite seriously, as you can see."

"Sweet Alpha, I guess so. I can't imagine they'd take kindly to us poking around for answers, either."

"No," Franco agreed, "I think not."

"You have details on security?" I asked.

"Not as many as I'd prefer," Franco said, looking irritated about the fact. "Vantage has done an unusually good job of tightening their loose ends. Their security is run completely in-house these days, and apparently with very few weak links. But I did manage to persuade an old contractor of theirs to provide us with some plans and rough estimates. Sounds like they've assembled even more of a private military than I'd realized in the past few years. If I wasn't drooling to see what they're hiding in there beforehand, well..."

"Are we to take it your investigation into the factory was largely uninteresting, then?" Carlisle asked.

"Oh, I wouldn't say uninteresting. Just unresolved. Something's off, and my instincts are telling me that the labs are where we'll find our answers."

"I see." Carlisle drummed his fingers on the arm of his chair, thinking. "Any clever ideas on getting past that private military, then?"

Franco shifted his frown between us. "I was hoping that might be where our ex-soldier and our world-class Shaper might come in. Let me tell you what I know."

Over the next hour, he broke it down for us. The size of the complex. Specifics of the perimeter wall. The estimated population of the scientists and crew living onsite. Peak hours of activity. Anything and everything else he'd managed to scrounge up from his contacts and from various records—some public, some not.

Franco had gathered an impressively large amount of information in an impressively short amount of time. We had plenty to discuss throughout the briefing.

The complex was essentially a tiny city in its own right. Our target, the main research building, spanned about a third of that complex, ten floors high above ground, and five floors deep below.

While our information on the building's interior was about as thin as our actual understanding of what we were looking for, we were all in agreement that the secure labs below ground were a likely target. Franco even posited there might be additional underground floors missing from the building plan, based on some minor inconsistencies between some permits and some old contractor's records he'd somehow dug up.

It sounded a bit paranoid at first. But we were dealing with red-eyed monsters who actually had their clawed hands on several of Enochia's most prominent strings, weren't we?

We'd left paranoia miles behind.

We talked into the night, discussing options, infil and exfil routes, the security measures we'd most likely encounter, and what we might actually learn once we were inside. James and Phineas could run support and handle our transport in and out. Franco was supremely confident he'd be able to decrypt whatever information we pulled from the facility, though he admitted it would likely take some time.

Without anyone outright saying it, it was clear we'd all hopped on board this crazy expedition with both feet first. Demons to the wind.

After a couple hours of brainstorming, a rough plan was taking form, along with a list of the equipment we'd likely need for the job. As invested as I was in the conversation, I couldn't help but let out a yawn during a particularly long pause in conversation.

"You should get some rest," Carlisle said.

I tried to work up the will to be indignant, but I was too tired. "You might have a point."

But I was still hesitant to go.

"Don't worry," he said, "I won't go slinking off into danger without you this time."

I nodded, rose to my feet, and made it as far as the door before realizing I had no idea where I was going.

"Take a right out the door, then a left down the next hall," Franco said. "There are two guest rooms at the end. You should find anything you need in there."

I said my thanks and shuffled out of the room and into the dim hallway, trying to rub the sleepy haze out of my eyes and idly wondering how long they would stay up strategizing.

More than that, I wondered how comfortable Carlisle would actually be bringing me in on the action when it was time.

Whatever he might say, I could still see the hesitation in him. Trained or not—soldier or not—he felt like he was bringing a helpless teenager into a dangerous conflict. But then again, maybe I was just projecting my own doubts onto him.

I was ready to put my life on the line and cover his back. I was sure about that. But that didn't make the prospect of breaking the law, infiltrating a fortress, and actually wading into the fray against the raknoth any less terrifying.

Much as I longed to make Kublich and the rest of the raknoth pay, I could feel my rage slowly smoldering, more vulnerable with each passing day to the creep of cold fear. I needed something to sink my teeth into. Infiltrating Vantage hadn't been what I'd had in mind when I'd signed up for this fight, but I could only pray it was the right move to make.

At the end of Franco's directions, I found myself peering through a dark doorway, too lost ruminating over everything and nothing to step in and look for a light. A heavy sigh escaped me.

"A nugget for your thoughts, stranger?"

The voice was soft in the calm, dark hallway.

Elise.

My heartbeat picked up.

"Just the one?" I asked, not turning.

"I guess that depends on how good these thoughts are." Her voice was closer now. "I might be convinced to make it a knot. I'm open to negotiation."

I turned to take her in, powerless to prevent a ridiculous smile from splitting my face.

Her raven hair was barely discernible from the darkness of the hallway, but I could see her fair face just well enough to make out the outline of her smile.

She drew up to me and leaned her shoulder against the door frame. "So, thoughts?"

"My thoughts…"

Blue eyes crinkling in a smile. A subtly sweet scent I wanted to breathe in until it consumed me. And… what was it I'd been sighing about a moment ago?

"… are pretty great now."

And they were.

Just like that, all the heavy burdens of Kublich and the raknoth and Vantage had slid to the sides—not gone, but temporarily overruled by the urge to make her smile.

She just wrinkled her nose. "I won't lie, I think you'd be lucky to even get half a nugget with a gem like that."

"Hey, a deal's a deal, right?"

She conceded the point with a tilt of her head.

Alpha, how was her every movement so intriguing?

A small silence passed between us, more exhilarating than uncomfortable.

"So," she said, "why are you in my house in the middle of the night, sighing in dark doorways?"

"Uh…"

Always be honest, Hal, came my dad's voice in my head. *It's the only real secret to being a good commander, a good husband, a good person. Tell it as it is.*

Except I was pretty sure telling her I was trying to stop shadowy monsters from wreaking havoc on Enochia was absolutely not an option.

Scud.

"Nothing."

"Nothing?" She looked pointedly from me to the guest room. "You got a thing for dark rooms or something?"

"What? No, I just—Well what were you doing out here, Lady Inquisitor?"

"My lurking creep senses were tingling," she said without missing a beat. "Had to come check the silvers, make sure there weren't any shady characters about. You know how it goes."

"Sure, sure. Look, Euh…" I only narrowly reined myself in from dropping her name, which I probably shouldn't have known, being *not* a creep and whatnot. "I know this probably looks strange, but I'm just here with my boss."

She mouthed the word, *boss,* studying me with a small frown. Finally, she shrugged. "You just look like you've got some heavy stuff going on in there. Thought maybe I could help."

"And maybe learn a juicy secret or two while you're at it?"

Her frown darkened to a scowl.

Alpha, why in demon's depths would I say that?

I'd done it. Just like that, I'd said something stupid and offended her.

But then she cracked a wicked grin. "Who says I can't do both?"

I laughed. I couldn't help it. Something about her energy…

Before I could say anything, she straightened and held up a finger to silence me, cocking her head as if listening. Then pulled the guest room door silently shut, grabbed my hand, and tugged me down the hallway without warning.

"Phineas is coming," she whispered lightly against my ear.

We pulled up to the intersection, and she peered around the corner before looking back to me. "Wanna talk where the troops won't find us?"

Somewhere, beneath the part of me that was still goop-brained from the feel of her breath on my ear and her hand in mine, Carlisle's warning flashed through my head. For all of two seconds.

It was just a talk, right?

"Yeah," I whispered. "Let's scoot!"

She made a horrified face. "Let's what?"

"It's something my dad used to… It's—Never mind!"

She shook her head and pulled me forward.

I went along, just glad she probably couldn't see the reddening of my cheeks in the dark hallway.

There was a faint creak from the next hallway as we passed—maybe from the staircase?

We didn't stick around to find out.

Elise dragged me to the end of the hallway, past the painting I'd been admiring the previous day, and pushed me through the farthest door on the left. It was a large bedroom, somewhere between posh and cozy, lit by what appeared to be flickering firelight.

That's about all I had time to process before Elise nudged me against the wall and expertly swung the door shut without a sound.

"What's the big—"

She stepped in and silenced my whisper with her hand, eyes focused somewhere distant like she was still listening.

I don't know if it was the look on my face or that she only then realized she'd just dragged me down the hall and clamped a hand over my mouth, but she dropped the hand, and her face broke into a silent giggle.

Then we both tensed at the soft thump of heavy footsteps approaching on the carpet outside.

Definitely sounded like Phineas.

Only in the last few feet did he make any attempt to quiet his footsteps, but I still felt him pause outside the door.

I held my breath, pretty sure that Elise was doing the same.

We stayed there, faces only inches apart, unable to speak, nothing to do but stare at each other.

So I stared.

I couldn't have looked away—couldn't have even breathed if I'd wanted to.

My head was spinning. I was falling, my stomach informed me, even though my feet were decidedly still planted on the floor. I was going to explode with the raw energy burning through me.

And then she was letting out a deep breath. Stepping back.

I swallowed, trying to pull myself together.

Outside, Phineas' footsteps were retreating down the hallway.

"Ta-da!" she whispered, waving her hands in a flourish.

"Not bad," I whispered, smiling. "You normally sneak around your own house like special forces?"

She shrugged. "We're big on secrets around here."

"No kidding." I looked around the room, taking in the details I'd been too distracted to register.

A darkwood bed sat across from the door, its rosewood red canopy in tune with the room's carpeting. To the right, the room opened up to the sizable space where the flickering light was coming from. My gaze lingered on a few solid-looking staves propped in the far corner of the room, past a large work desk.

"Are you also big on professional staff-fighting in your spare time or something?"

"I don't know if I'd say professional, but I wouldn't wanna meet me in a dark alley."

"Hey, a dark hallway didn't seem so bad."

Her lip quirked. "Night's not over yet. You still have to make it back past the hallway watch."

I frowned in Phineas' general direction. "Yeah, what's up with that? Are you under house arrest or something? Are we meeting under peril of death right now?"

"Eh." She pretended to think about it. "Maybe half of us. The old bear's pretty protective. Hates cocky pretty boys, especially."

I followed her around the corner and saw that the flickering light was coming from her holodisplay, which was dancing with the imitation of an ancient wood fireplace—crackles and all—in front of a long white couch.

"Are you calling me cocky?"

She looked me up and down. "No. I don't think I am."

And with that, she plopped down on the couch in front of the crackling facsimile of a fire, legs up, and gestured to the end of the couch, where she'd left just enough room for me to fit between her feet and the couch arm. To the consternation of the small Carlisle-voice in my head, I sank to the soft white cushions.

"So," she said, "how'd you get into the business of creepily lurking about strangers' houses?"

I told her it had just sort of crept up on me, and we ran from there.

We talked well into the night, steering clear of anything personal—even as basic as our names—by some unspoken agreement, electing instead to joke and debate about matters of little consequence.

It was the best I'd felt since the attack, by far. I hadn't realized just how starved I'd been to talk to another human being like the world wasn't in danger of ending.

Watching the would-be firelight dancing across her slender features, I completely forgot how tired I'd been. I was just happy to listen to her talk. To see her face glow whenever I cracked a particularly competent joke.

Eventually, though, the blur of fatigue returned. Elise was curled into a ball at her end of the couch by that point, looking as if she'd nod off at any minute. My palmlight display informed me we'd been at it for four hours.

"Sweet Alpha," I murmured. "I better get some sleep."

Whatever tomorrow had in store, it looked like I might be facing it without much rest.

"Mmm," Elise purred back, partially asleep already.

I stood to leave and paused in front of her curled form, uncertain what to do.

"Hey," I whispered, patting her on the shoulder, "do you want a ride to bed?"

She made no response.

Down for the night.

I pulled the blanket from the back of the couch and was preparing to drape it over her when she went full plank—legs out, arms to her sides, head lulled, and tongue out as if feigning death.

I laughed at the silly spurt. "Is that plank-speak for yes?"

"No, I think this one means *pass the plank salt*, actually."

"Okay," I said, moving to scoop her up. "Come on, you."

Before I could, she arched her back nimbly over the couch arm, reached down to the ground with her hands, and deftly sprang from the couch into a backward handspring.

She landed on her feet and shook her head at me, clearly amused by my wide-eyed surprise. "Cocky pretty boys, I'm tellin' ya."

Damn. Maybe she *could* kick my ass with one of those staves.

She reached a hand toward me. "Walk me to the bed, my heroic goodfellow?"

"Who me?" I asked, circling the couch to offer her my arm, which she took with an exaggerated curtsy. "See, I was actually hoping you might escort me past the perils of the hallway. Rumor has it there's a bear roaming around out there."

"Hmmm," she purred. We reached the bed, and she gave me a grin and an affectionate pat on the arm before falling to the soft-looking blankets. "Sorry, I think you're all on your own this time. Best of luck out there."

"My hero," I murmured.

I must've hesitated a moment too long, because she rolled over and met my eyes with a curious look. I thought to move to the door, suddenly feeling quite embarrassed and awkward, but something about the look in her eyes held me there. Something serious. Tender.

Something that dropped my stomach into free fall and put wild thoughts in my head.

I dropped her gaze, my heart thudding so heavily that I was sure she'd hear it.

"Goodnight, Elise."

Ah, scud.

"Someone's been doing some digging, hmm?"

I looked up to meet her inquisitive stare. "I'm certain I have no idea what you're talking about."

She smiled. "Right. Of course not. Well, you'd best be on your way, then, stranger."

I tipped an imaginary hat, decided it was the stupidest, least smooth gesture ever, and turned hurriedly for the door.

"Goodnight, Haldin Raish."

I froze.

She knew. But how much? My face had been plastered all across the newsreels not so long ago. If she knew my name, did she know about my parents? Did she know I was supposed to be dead?

How could she not? She was Franco's daughter.

I turned to find her watching me with… was it concern? Sympathy?

"I recognized you the moment you showed up in my hallway," she said, dropping my gaze. "Even with those shaders on. I just thought maybe you'd rather not, you know, feel like a victim or whatever. It's, uh"—she looked back up—"nice to meet you, for what it's worth."

Emotions flashed through me, too quick and turbulent to make sense of. Shame. Anger. Sadness. As she held my eyes, though, the negativity began to burn away, and I was left with gratitude.

"I…"

I was glad she knew, I realized. And even more glad that she'd elected to treat me like a person instead of an injured puppy.

"… Thanks, Elise."

"Any time, Haldin. Blessed dreams."

We shared one last smile, then I stepped into the dark hallway, closed the door behind me, and padded back to my guest room, feeling lighter than I had in cycles.

CHAPTER 17

BOILING POINT

He knew, I decided as I smashed to the padded floor of Franco's impressively-equipped training room with an undignified thump and felt Carlisle's knee press into my back.

He had to know.

Carlisle had woken me in the early hours of the morning—maybe two hours after I'd finally made it to bed—and insisted we train while the rest of the house slept. I'd groggily dragged myself out of bed and followed him across the house to the training room, where I'd promptly wondered if Franco really needed such a big room to work out.

Now, though, all I could think about was the mat pressing into my face and Carlisle's knee digging into the back of my shoulder.

"You're slow today," he said, his voice maddeningly calm as I struggled uselessly against his superior leverage.

"New environment," I grunted. "Very distracting."

I heard a small sigh, and I swear I could feel him shaking his head in exasperation. "Why do I worry your distraction lies elsewhere in the house?"

Embarrassment filled me at my failure to heed his warnings. Anger that he wanted me to stay away from Elise at all. Or maybe, at the heart of it, it was just that some part of me knew he might be right.

But I sure as hell wasn't about to prove his point for him.

With my free hand, I dialed my cloak out. Then, with stubborn focus, I extended my senses, telekinetically grabbed for a weighted training ball on the nearby rack, and did my best to fling it at Carlisle's head.

I think I surprised myself more than Carlisle.

He twisted deftly out of the ball's path. I stifled my surprise and took advantage of the distraction to likewise twist out of his hold and throw a sweeping kick, which he in turn dodged with an aerial cartwheel. I rolled out of the kick and popped back to my feet with a few feet of breathing room.

"Better," he said. "Much better."

The adrenaline helped clear the hazy exhaustion from my head, and I held my own for the next several bouts after that.

It was still early when Carlisle ended our match and left me alone in the room. He returned a minute later carrying a wooden cutting board and a shiny metal pot filled with water.

"What, time for cooking lessons already?"

He dropped the cutting board on the matted floor and placed the pot gently on top of it, apparently in no mood to be joked with at the moment. "Time to learn thermal conversions. I want you to boil the water."

With that, he turned to leave.

"Just like that?" I thought after him.

He paused but didn't turn. *"Better you find your own path. You know that."*

I did. But I also didn't want him to leave. I just wasn't really sure why that was yet.

"Carlisle?"

He turned to regard me, waiting.

I hesitated, not sure which I should ask of the two questions that surfaced. Not really sure I even wanted to hear the answers.

"Not that I want to be the naysayer after I kind of started it, but are we really sure we're best off risking our necks on Vantage?"

Carlisle glanced at the open doorway and back to me. *"Not so loud."*

"Right. Sorry. I just mean, with Kublich controlling the Legion, they wouldn't really need to be that clever to get what they want, right?"

"Perhaps not. But it's impossible to say without first knowing what it is they want."

There was something there. Some flicker of a painful memory.

"Is there something you're not telling me?"

With a resigned look, he crossed the mat back to me and sat cross-legged close enough that we could talk quietly. I sat opposite him, waiting.

"All I really know," he finally said, "is that Alton Parker is most certainly a raknoth, that he's building a factory for some unknown purpose, and that there's been a precipitous rise in disappearances around Divinity in the past year."

"I hadn't heard that."

"I wonder why that would be."

I frowned. "Why do you think the disappearances are connected? What would they want with a bunch of kidnapped humans?"

His gaze had gone distant. "The same thing I imagine they want with the rest of us. I think this factory is only the first step. I think they want to take this world for their own, enslave every last one of us, and use us like cattle."

Where was he getting this from?

Not that I had any great reason to doubt him. The raknoth were ruthless, evil bastards from where I sat.

But something about the way he said it…

"How do you know?"

His eyes focused back on me. "Because Cassius told me."

"What? I thought Cassius was… I mean, I thought the raknoth got him."

A pained expression crossed his face. "I don't know that he died. Not for sure. He used to come to me sometimes. In my dreams."

"After the attack?"

He nodded. "A couple cycles later, when I thought it was safe, I went back to look. For Cassius, for any of the others. I never found anything. I'd been looking for seasons when the dreams started. I never found out if it was actually Cassius or if they were just particularly lucid nightmares. All I know is there was something horribly wrong about those dreams. I began to fear that, even if it truly was Cassius somehow reaching out to me, the raknoth must have done something to him. I worried they were using him to find me."

Carlisle's breathing was slightly ragged now, his arms crossed protectively. I'd never seen him this rattled.

"I began to sleep less and less," he continued. "I figured out ways to get by without it for days at a time. I… I ran away from him. Abandoned him for years."

I sat in silence, unsure what I could possibly say to ease his pain. Finally, I reached out and laid a hand on his shoulder. It felt woefully inadequate, but it was all I could think to do.

His slumped head raised at my touch. He regarded my hand for several seconds, then finally looked up at me. "I'm sorry. It's still quite troubling to me, even after all this time."

I removed my hand from his shoulder, suddenly feeling awkward about the contact. "He must've been like a father to you after everything. I can appreciate what it would feel like to try to shut that out. But maybe those dreams really were just nightmares, like you said. You'd obviously been through a traumatic experience."

"It's possible, yes. But I don't really believe it. It's why I've never stopped searching for Cassius. Years ago, once I'd confronted my fears and come up with contingency plans, I began allowing myself to dream from time to time. He never came back to me. Perhaps he truly is gone now."

I didn't know what to say.

If Cassius had been alive and free, I assumed he would have found Carlisle. If he wasn't dead, the only other likely possibility was that the raknoth had had him prisoner somewhere all this time. Either way, it seemed a safe bet that Cassius was lost.

"I'm sorry, Carlisle."

He gave me a wan smile. "Thank you, Haldin. I can only hope we'll find some of the answers we seek at the labs."

I nodded.

He started to rise and paused. "Was there something else?"

I thought of Elise for all of a half second before shaking my head. Carlisle was right. We needed to focus on the mission, and we needed to figure out what those red-eyed bastards were up to.

"Good," he said, his usual tranquility returning. "Try to boil the water. We can talk more later."

With that he headed for the door.

"Oh, and I'd recommend against channeling your own body heat for this challenge," he added telepathically as he disappeared into the hallway.

"What the hell do I use then?" I muttered to the empty room.

I bent down to inspect the pot, still churning through the details of Carlisle's story.

Cassius, still alive.

Was it possible?

Probably not.

Weren't we just two of a kind, though? Gifted orphans, fighting for something we could never have again.

I dipped my fingers into the pot. The water was icy cold to the touch.

Great. Couldn't let it be too easy, right?

I scanned the room for energy sources to channel.

There was the heat of the air and everything else in the room. There were the lights and the electric lines that ran through the walls to power them. What else?

I was surrounded by free weights and other exercise equipment, but that stuff was for expending energy, not collecting it.

Except where did that expended energy go?

The weights.

Perhaps I could put gravity to work for me and channel the kinetic energy of a falling weight to heat the water?

It felt like a real breakthrough moment for all of two seconds. Then I remembered how damn hard it'd been to channel energy from a moving object the day before. The mental image of me tipping over one of Franco's pristine weight racks and watching a few hundred pounds of hardsteel crash to the floor killed the idea outright.

I heaved a sigh and decided to try the least complicated option first.

Carlisle had advised me not to use my own body heat, but it wouldn't hurt to test the waters, so to speak.

So, I dipped my fingers back into the water, closed my eyes, and concentrated on the reservoir of heat at my core. Slowly, carefully, I willed it to flow down my arm, through my fingertips, and into the water.

It worked.

The water in the pot grew less icy around my fingers. Soon enough, though, a visceral chill touched my insides. It wasn't unbearable. Actually, I was pretty sure I had enough in me to boil a lot more than a pot of water before I'd be in serious trouble. But I also didn't feel like flirting with hypothermia, so I released the link with a shiver and moved on to my next option—the air.

Focusing on the thermal energy in the air proved an awkward feat, the metaphysical equivalent of trying to grab a box that was plenty light but simply too large to fit my arms around. As was becoming customary, though, I sat there and tried again and again, mentally toiling until I found the right mindset to make it work.

Finally, I managed to get moving by focusing on one small patch of air at a time.

Focus. Open channel. Drain heat from air to water. Repeat.

With my extended senses, I could feel air densities shifting and swirling to equilibrium with each patch I drained. The faintest breeze touched my face, and a smile pulled onto my lips.

It was slow going, and not without frustration. I was filling a leaky, seemingly bottomless hole, and I'd forgotten my shovel.

Slowly, though, I was able to drain larger and larger patches of air. The water grew warm. Soon enough, it was actually hot. Tendrils of vapor were beginning to rise from the still surface when a voice came from the doorway.

"It just gets stranger and stranger with you, doesn't it?"

Elise.

I dropped the link to my current patch of air and retracted my senses, pleased to find my focus had barely slipped at the unexpected arrival, but unsure how to play being caught staring at a pot of water.

Franco clearly knew about Carlisle's abilities, if not mine, but it was entirely possible Elise knew nothing about Shaping. It didn't seem like something one casually talked about.

"What's with the pot?" she asked, padding closer.

"Oh, you know…"

I turned to face her and lost my train of thought.

She was wearing dark workout clothes that, while not exactly revealing, clung to her athletic form in a way that made it hard to keep my eyes from roaming. Harder than boiling a pot of water with my mind.

"… just, uh, seeing if my glare is strong enough to boil water."

"Uh-huh." She scrutinized me, then placed a hand on my shoulder and leaned over to inspect the water, which had ceased steaming now that I wasn't pouring heat into it.

My brain couldn't quite seem to decide whether that was good or bad, what with the distraction of Elise's hand on my shoulder and her dark hair brushing gently against the side of my face as she leaned.

Either way, I had to imagine I kind of looked like a crazy person.

"I'm not sure we're supposed to be talking," I stammered.

"Hmm," she said. "Well, you should probably figure that out then."

I looked up at her, hovering over me, wonderfully close.

She showed me a smile that took my insides for a ride and tilted her head toward the pot. "Looks like your glare needs to step its game up, by the way."

I was scrambling for a clever reply when another voice spoke behind us.

"Ah, children."

Franco.

I sprang to my feet, perhaps a little too quickly. Carlisle was with him, as well as another man I didn't recognize. The newcomer was short and tan and had a long, cylindrical container slung over his robed shoulder. He kicked off his sandals before stepping onto the padded floor.

"Elise, I see you've met our new friend," Franco said, his eyes fixed on me the entire time.

"Sure have!" She waved to Carlisle and the newcomer, chipper as a bird. "Blessed morning, Carlisle. Master."

Master? Master of what?

They both returned her greeting, the mysterious master coming to join us on the mat, his movements radiating discipline.

He offered me a small, courteous nod before turning his attention to Elise. "You're ready?"

"Always," she said.

I considered the long case he carried, my thoughts drifting to the staves I'd seen in Elise's room the previous night.

"Haldin." Carlisle's voice pulled my attention away. "We need to talk."

I scooped up the pot of warm water and the wooden board and scooted by Elise and her master, who eyed the pot of water uncertainly, granting me a small sense of amused satisfaction. Maybe I liked having some mystery going for me too.

Elise caught my eye and mouthed what looked like, *Have fun.*

I was too conscious of Franco's watching eyes to make any response as I went to join him and Carlisle.

Whatever Elise's mysterious master started to say to her was lost to me as I followed the others out of the gym. Franco led us down the hallway and into a shiny, surgically clean kitchen, complete with several pristine metallic appliances and dark marble countertops.

James was bustling about in an apron that read *Kiss the Cook* in big, red letters under a set of matching red lips.

I would have laughed if Franco and Carlisle hadn't looked so serious.

"Hey, Haldin!" James said. "Let me take those for you."

He took the pot and cutting board without comment, as if it was perfectly natural I'd simply be walking around with them.

I joined Carlisle and Franco at the wooden dining table, my stomach rumbling at the alluring scent of frying bacon and the sweet undercurrent of hot griddlecakes.

My mouth began to water.

"We've decided we should move sooner than later," Carlisle said.

That got my attention. "How soon?"

"Tonight," Franco said. "We'll have everything we need by then. Every day we wait past tonight is just another chance for them to notice someone's been digging."

My shock must've shown, because Carlisle did something very un-Carlisle-like and patted me on the shoulder.

"Eat," he said as James lowered a sizeable tray of griddlecakes and bacon onto the table. "Then we'll talk about it."

I nodded dumbly.

Tonight.

Ice crept through me.

All my training, all my resolve, and yet this fight hadn't truly felt real until that moment. Tonight, though… Tonight, Carlisle and I would venture into the lair of a very real, very dangerous monster.

Suddenly I didn't feel so hungry.

That must've shown too, because James almost looked apologetic when he set utensils and an empty plate down in front of me.

"Get 'em while they're hot."

CHAPTER 18

WRONG SIDE

Whether the holo plans we'd seen had been totally complete or not, they at least hadn't lied about one thing. For a biotech research lab, the Vantage compound sure looked a lot like a military fortress.

Carlisle and I lay in a cold, dark ditch a hundred yards west of the perimeter wall, watching the guards patrolling along the top.

"Ready?" came Carlisle's voice in my mind.

"Ready."

It wasn't just a reflexive response.

Before we'd left, Carlisle had taken his last crack at trying to convince me I still had a chance to walk away from this fight. The flight over had been for what nerves remained. And there'd been plenty of them.

But now, huddled in the dirt next to my partner in vigilante crime, it was finally time to act.

Carlisle planted his hands, preparing to spring. *"Just as we planned, then. Wait here until the ascent is clear."*

And with that, he leapt forward and took off for the wall, moving faster than I'd ever seen a human move.

I'd known he was going to use his abilities to bolster his speed. Expecting it, though, didn't keep my jaw from dropping. It was preternatural. He covered the hundred yards in a blur, gathered himself, jumped a full thirty feet in the air, and caught onto the outside edge of the perimeter wall, agile as any acrobat.

I could only gape as he hung there patiently, waiting for the next guard to pass.

Clearly, I still had a lot to learn about my abilities.

I raised my sidearm—one of the fancy compact pulse guns Legion specters sometimes used for covert ops—to watch more closely through the sight's connection with the equally fancy microelectronic lenses Franco had lent me, thanking Alpha for the hundredth time Franco had seen to outfit us with his impressive resources.

The guards we'd observed on the wall so far had all been as well armed and armored as Sanctuary patrolmen, their movements organized, disciplined. They weren't screwing around here.

Carlisle waited until the approaching guard passed, then deftly vaulted over the lip of the wall and applied a stun baton to the man's neck. The guard went rigid with the shock, then slackened as the baton sedative began taking effect. Carlisle caught him before he crumpled to the ground, checked his surroundings once more, and flashed me a thumbs up.

I killed the scope feed in my lenses with two upward blinks and checked to make sure the grappling module was still properly fitted to my gun.

Time to move.

If I had any complaint about our gear, it was that I felt a little vulnerable, what with all the big guns around here and nothing but James' comparatively flimsy armor skin for protection. But at least I was able to move fast.

I covered the stretch between the ditch and the wall at a dead sprint—which is to say, moving about half as fast as Carlisle had. At the wall's base, I took careful aim and fired.

The pulse gun's magnetic accelerator hummed, and the grappling bolt blurred noiselessly upward and dug into the permacrete with a tiny thud. I flipped on the external coiling motor and held on tight, using my feet to skitter up the wall as the motor whisked me upward with a faint electric whir.

From the walkway atop the wall, Carlisle reached a hand down. I killed the motor, clasped his hand, and scrambled over the wall to hunker down in the walkway while I disengaged the grappling bolt and reeled it back in.

Carlisle removed one of the unconscious guard's gloves, and I held the exposed hand up so he could scan the man's fingerprints with his palmlight.

I was glancing around for promising dark corners to hide our sleeping friend when Carlisle scooped the guard up and tossed him over the wall.

I jerked up to the edge. *"What the grop are you—Oh."*

On the other side of the wall, the guard wasn't falling to his death, but rather drifting gently to the ground on Carlisle's telekinetic ride.

"Sweet Alpha, man. A little warning next time?"

Carlisle tilted his head in concession and pointed to the stairwell halfway down our section of wall. I set my weapon to stun rounds and set off beside him at a crouching jog.

We paused near the stairwell. Carlisle dialed his cloak out, went vacant for a second, then dialed it back in and shook his head. *"Two guards down there. Over the wall, it is."*

He waited for my affirmative, peered over the lip of the inner edge, and lightly hopped off the wall to the compound below. He would slow his descent, I knew, but it was still kind of alarming to watch.

I hooked the grappling bolt into the wall, waiting for his signal. Too long. There must be a guard hovering nearby, or maybe—

Scud.

Or maybe my cloak was dialed too close for me to communicate with Carlisle below.

As soon as I dialed it out, his voice came to me. *"Ah, good. I was worried I was going to have to come back up there."*

"Yeah... Sorry. Still getting used to telepath comms."

"Better to be safe. Get ready."

As foolish as I felt, he had a point. If a Seeker or any of the raknoth—say, Alton Parker—happened to be nearby, all it would take was one careless slip-up to bring the entire facility down on us.

"Go," came Carlisle's voice.

I vaulted the wall, grappling module gripped tight, and descended to join him on the ground.

We stuck to the shadows behind a stack of shipping crates, waiting for a clear approach to one of the unobtrusive side doors we'd identified as an ideal entry point to the research facility—sufficiently removed from both the heavy security of the front entrance and the residential activity at the back of the complex.

A few guards walked by on patrol. In the distance, a skimlift was moving racks of shiny canisters onto a heavy transport. Other than that, things were as quiet as we'd hoped they'd be in the dead of night.

The patrol passed, and we darted across the yard, sticking to the shadows as much as possible. We pulled up beneath the security camera posted above our target door. Carlisle planted a little routing chip on its housing and keyed his earpiece as he sank back into the shadows beside me. "We're ready, James."

"Right," James' voice crackled in my right ear, "just a second, guys."

I activated my lenses' zoom and kept my weapon at the ready, watching the distant guards on the wall, as we waited for James to get in and loop the feeds of the nearest cameras. Beside me, Carlisle readied the fingerprint scans we'd procured from the guard on his palmlight.

Above, one of the distant guards turned down the section of wall near us and began marching closer. I tapped Carlisle's shoulder, and he extinguished his palmlight.

"James?" he said, his voice low and calm. "The sooner the better."

I trained my weapon on the approaching guard, grip tight.

"Almooossst…" James said. "Crap. Almost there!"

My heart was hammering. Even shrouded as we were, the guard was probably close enough to see us now. All he had to do was look this way.

I rested my finger on the trigger.

Too long. It was taking too long. I had to take the shot.

"Got it!" James said. "Go!"

Carlisle pressed his palmlight to the access panel, which flashed green after a moment's hesitation. The door slid open, and we hurried inside.

"Merciful Alpha," I hissed once the door was closed behind us and we were alone in the entryway.

That had been too close.

"I got you guys!" James said, sounding more confident now. "Okay, so now you need to—Oh crap."

Carlisle lifted his head like he'd sensed something and stared somewhere down the hall the entryway led to. I carefully dialed out my cloak and reached out with my extended senses.

Several minds were approaching. Three—no, four—of them.

"Incoming," James said. "Four guys. Unarmored. Two lightly armed. Can you hide?"

"Not really," Carlisle said quietly. He glanced at me. "I suppose we're somewhat in need of directions anyway."

I could hear the voices now, drawing closer.

"Uh, you mean you wanna—"

"Ask these goodfellows for directions," Carlisle said. "Exactly. Get ready."

"Oh boy," came James' voice.

I leveled my weapon at the entrance to the hallway beyond and waited, forcing a few deep breaths. Carlisle stood at ease ahead, stun baton loosely concealed behind his forearm.

Skilled and scary as he was in action, I still couldn't believe Carlisle had declined to bring a gun, insisting his body and mind were the only weapons he needed—and, apparently, a stun baton for good measure. Personally, I wished he would've brought a real weapon. But I wasn't the master Shaper here.

Either way, I was damn glad for the reassuring weight of a gun in my hand as the voices reached the intersection.

They were making quite the racket as they strolled into view, the first of the pack vigorously animated in his description of just how badly the attractive woman—my word, not his—from the tavern last night had been begging for his beardsplitter.

They froze when they saw us.

Then Mr. Chivalrous broke the spell and went for his holstered sidearm. I shifted my aim to him and squeezed the trigger with pleasure.

The magnetic accelerator hummed, the pulse gun gave its strange recoil, and Mr. Chivalrous went rigid as the stunner found its mark on his chest.

His three companions came to life as he crumpled. Carlisle telekinetically yanked one of them past him and toward me as if in offering, then he dashed forward to meet the other two.

My opponent did an admirable job of catching his balance, considering he had no way of understanding what had just happened. He groped for his sidearm and drew. I caught his hand and directed the weapon away from me, pivoting in to deliver an elbow strike to the side of his head.

He stumbled with the blow. I pressed the advantage, twisting his gun free and clubbing the back of his head with it. He hit the ground with a thud and didn't get back up.

I spun, nerves humming, ready to assist Carlisle.

But he was already dragging his two limp opponents back into the entryway, where they wouldn't be as immediately visible.

"Well done," he said, glancing at the guard I'd taken down. "Any trouble?"

"All good." I didn't sound as shaken as I felt.

All the drills and sims in the world apparently couldn't quite capture the real thing.

"Good work, guys," James' voice crackled through the comms.

I gathered myself and dragged Mr. Chivalrous back into the entryway by his limp legs. Carlisle was crouched over the guy I'd taken out, prodding at him experimentally. The guy gave a disgruntled moan.

I felt slightly guilty, watching the man's feeble attempt to rouse. We might be doing the right thing here, but that didn't make me feel any better about beating up on guards.

"Asking for directions?"

"In a manner of speaking," Carlisle said, closing his eyes and placing a hand to the man's forehead.

The poor guy gave a shudder, and I suppressed one of my own as I realized what Carlisle was doing—sifting through the man's memories for what we needed instead of bothering to talk it out of him.

Quickly enough, Carlisle appeared to find what he was looking for. His eyes drifted open, and the Vantage guy slumped back into sleep or unconsciousness.

"I think Franco was right about the extra floor."

"How do you know?"

He laid the guy gently down. "This man's recall of the facility is nearly crystal clear. Impressively so. Except near the lifts at the bottom floor. There, his memories are muddled, like they've been tampered with."

"Sounds like it's worth checking out."

Especially since we'd already been leaning toward heading down first anyway.

"Let's get to the lifts and find out," Carlisle said.

We set off through the facility, James following from afar, looping the camera feeds ahead of us and unlooping those behind just in case someone happened to be paying extra close attention. A couple times, he had us duck out of the path of incoming guards or night shift researchers.

The scenery was highly repetitive—mundane, sterile-looking hallways linking lab after lab, which themselves all looked pretty damn similar. All I saw were long, dark countertops full of expensive-looking equipment and rows and rows of beige shelves and cabinets, full of all manner of containers and chemicals.

Something about the place made my skin crawl.

The sight of the mag lifts was a relief for all of five seconds. Then we boarded, and I couldn't help but start worrying about what it was we were headed to find.

I punched the icon for the bottom floor, anyway, and wasn't too surprised when the lift display protested. *ERROR: I.D. REQUIRED FOR CLEARANCE - ACCESS LEVEL 5.*

"You don't say," I muttered. "James? Think you can—"

"Try to break into the lift controls?" James said. "I'm working on it."

"Thank you, James," Carlisle said, "but there may be an easier way if I…" He planted a hand on the wall of the lift, eyes drifting closed. "Hold on."

I gripped the hand rail and kept my mouth shut, trusting that he knew what he was doing.

Good thing, too.

I was about to ask what he was thinking when the lift car gave a metallic groan and dropped out from under my feet. My stomach flew into my chest, my grip on the handrail pulling tight against the sudden free fall.

I narrowly contained the wild yell fighting to escape my throat.

Carlisle knew what he was doing.

The lift car kept plunging.

But he knew what he was doing.

Right?

We were about to find out.

Right when I was sure I'd lose my grip on the panic, the lift car began to slow, the floor pressing up to gradually reclaim my weight until I had to tense my legs to brace against a hard halt.

"Alpha be damned with the warnings, man!"

Carlisle's lip twitched. "I did say 'hold on.' I believe we've reached true bottom."

"Wonderful. I don't suppose you have a trick for opening the door now?"

He held up a finger to tell me to wait, his eyes still closed. I fiddled with my gun and was starting to wonder exactly what we were about to find on the other side of those doors when Carlisle gave a sharp gasp.

It didn't sound right coming from him, as unshakeable as he always seemed to be. But his face had blanched, and his expression was shocked—horrified, even—his breathing ragged in the suddenly too-tight space of the lift car.

What in demon's depths could make him react like that?

I reached for my pendant, thinking to explore with my own senses.

Before I could, though, the doors slid open, and my jaw dropped.

"Sweet Alpha," I whispered.

CHAPTER 19
BLOOD DRIVE

Two things immediately struck me about the room beyond the lift doors.

For one, it was enormous. By the dim light that drifted up from below, I could barely make out the room's ceiling and sides from my viewpoint in the lift. The back wall was far enough to be lost to darkness.

The room's size, though, quickly fell background to the feeling in my gut.

There was something terribly wrong about the space. Some sickly haze that clung to the greenish-yellow air. A cloying scent I couldn't immediately place.

Carlisle caught my elbow as I started forward. "This... will be disturbing."

I met his gaze, and he reluctantly released my arm.

We stepped cautiously onto the catwalk platform outside.

No signs of movement.

The room was cavernous—the ceiling at least thirty feet above us, the ground floor a good fifteen feet below. A network of bare-bones metal staircases and catwalks led around the room's perimeter, providing access to the rows of dark cylindrical somethings lining the walls.

Aside from the low, steady thrum of running machinery, all was still and quiet.

Almost remorsefully, Carlisle stepped to the railing ahead and indicated that our interest lay below.

The first thing I noticed was how neatly the rows of equipment were arranged on the ground floor. Then I got a closer look at the equipment, and I had to clamp onto the railing to keep my knees from buckling.

People.

Those were people down there.

Dozens of lifeless human beings, strapped to rows and rows of rectangular white racks. Sickly pale. Each one stripped to their undergarments. Each assaulted by a mess of tubes—respirators, waste collectors, IVs. All of it.

I was going to be sick.

What in demon's depths were they doing to these people?

"They're alive," Carlisle said quietly beside me.

"What are they—"

I clutched at my stomach, fighting down a fresh wave of nausea.

Carlisle was right.

The rise and fall of respirator breaths was faint but discernible in a few of the closer chests. I dialed my cloak, reached out with my extended senses, and felt life, horribly frail as it was. And it seemed to be fading.

I studied the dark red line that ran from one woman's arm, down and under her neighbor's rack, where it joined his dark red line. It went along like that, rack by rack, until the common line of the ten racks in that row emptied into a tall cylinder at the end.

"They're... draining their blood?"

Carlisle didn't seem to hear me.

"But... why?"

He turned for the stairs. "Keep your eyes open."

I followed him to the ground floor in a trance, unable to pull my eyes away from the unwilling donors, wired up to their apparatuses. There was something disturbingly mesmerizing about the sight.

They must've been drugged. Their sleep looked almost too serene, yet still there was some faint unease—as if, deep beneath the surface, they wanted to cry out for help, but couldn't.

It was horrifying.

There was a roughly equal mix of men and women, mostly early twenties to late fifties. My stomach turned at how pale and weak they looked. As we approached the first row of racks, the respirators greeted us with a steady chorus of mechanical sighs.

Alpha forbid one of their victims stop breathing before they'd finished sucking them dry.

"Liquid nutrition." Carlisle's voice snapped me out of my haze. He was tapping at a node console beside several large drums whose tubes ran to the thin frames above each row of racks. "Heparin... barbiturates... Some of these people may have been here for cycles already. Maybe longer."

"We have to get them out," I heard myself say. "We can't leave them like this," I added when Carlisle turned to me.

"We also can't make it out of here with forty-some comatose victims." He seemed to age thirty years before my eyes saying it. "We need to route James into one of these nodes, pull what data we can, and figure out how to stop this from happening to thousands more like them."

I stared at him dumbly.

We had to try. These were people we were talking about. Real human beings. Of course we had to try.

I walked over to a console near Carlisle's and woke it up before I lost my nerve. "James, I need you to help me see if we can wake these people up somehow."

"Uhhh..." James said.

"Do it, James," Carlisle said. He crossed to my console and connected another routing chip, along with an external storage drive. "Just get the transfer started first. We'll look around while you work on that."

"Right." James sounded relieved. "I'm on it."

A directory window popped up over the display's request for a valid user ID and passcode and promptly came alive with a long string of digital commands.

"Hold tight," James said. "Should only be a minute or two before I'm in."

I looked around, wondering where best I could apply myself while we waited. I didn't have the first idea about how to help these people. Yanking tubes and hoping for the best didn't seem like a great bet.

My gaze drifted to the rows of cylindrical structures that lined the walls along the perimeter catwalks, just too far removed from the light to clearly see. "What are those things?"

"I don't know," Carlisle said, already starting for a nearby staircase. "But we better have a closer look while we can."

Ascending to the first row of cylinders, I was able to start making out more details. Thick panels covered the front of each tube. Glass, maybe? They were dark, but I thought I could see something in the closest one—a dark shape subtly contrasting against the surrounding darkness.

I was reaching for my hand lantern when Carlisle conjured light from his palm and shined it onto the nearest panel. Definitely glass. The light pierced easily through to illuminate a tank full of some thick green fluid and—

"Holy scud!" I whispered.

"I'll be damned," Carlisle agreed quietly.

At first glance, the thing floating in the tank looked like a man.

At second glance, it clearly wasn't.

The details were all horribly wrong—face reptilian, lips nearly non-existent, eyebrows and facial features all at harsh angles. Large patches of its skin had a scaly texture, and its fingers and toes ended in claws rather than nails.

It looked just like Kublich had when he'd attacked my parents.

A cold shudder gripped me, along with a sudden intense desire to be far, far away from this place. "Is that thing alive?"

"Yes," Carlisle said. "But it appears to be unconscious. Are you seeing this, James?"

"What?" James' voice crackled back. "No, I was—Holy crap! What the scud is that thing?"

"It looks like a raknoth," I said.

"But it's not," Carlisle said. He closed his eyes. Placed a hand to the glass. "It's… I'm not sure what it is. A new breed. Some manner of hybrid between raknoth and human, maybe."

I traced the row of cylinders with my eyes until it was lost in darkness, counting rows, estimating the arithmetic. "They're building an army."

Carlisle opened his eyes, nodding slowly. "I think you're right."

"But they already have the Legion."

It didn't really add up unless…

"Perhaps discreetly manipulating the Legion through Kublich was becoming too cumbersome," Carlisle said.

That was it, all right. None of this added up… unless the raknoth were planning on wiping out our Legion and replacing it with theirs.

"The blood." I glanced back down at the lines of pale victims, slowly bleeding dry. "You think that's the first step of… whatever this is?"

Carlisle shook his head and raised his light until I could see the lines at the top of the cylinder. "I think it's the food."

I couldn't decide if that was better or worse. My brain could barely manage a single thought, aside from the one.

Whatever was happening here, we had to stop it.

"Guys?" James said. "I'm in. Data's transferring."

I turned and started back down the stairs to his console. "Do you see any way to wake these people up?"

"Working, working."

I reached the display and saw files transferring to the external drive in the background while James remotely navigated through a visually hectic interface of vitals, ID tags, and a couple dozen other metrics I couldn't make easy sense of.

"Guess it was too much to hope for a *wake up* button, huh?"

"Actually…" James said, still flicking through menus. "Yes! Look. There's an arousal subroutine that… scud."

The tiny flutter of hope died in my chest as I studied the display and realized what James had seen. The shortest option on the list, the emergency arousal protocol, would take a full hour, with most of the actual projected waking times being well over that.

Scud was right.

"Can you see if there's any way to—"

A series of loud, electronic cracks and the sudden flare of floodlights above hit me like an electric shock to the spine.

Before my brain could catch up, I had my sidearm drawn and at the ready, sweeping the now fully-illuminated reaches of the enormous room for any incoming threat, adrenaline coursing through my veins.

Were we caught? Trapped down here, surrounded by Alpha knew what manner of monsters? I didn't see any sign of imminent danger, but—

"We need to leave, now," came Carlisle's voice as he ghosted down the catwalk stairs toward me. "James," he added quietly as he joined me and reached for the external drive, "can you finish the transfer remotely?"

I only half-registered his words, still tensed, trying to look everywhere at once, feeling entirely too much like a rat in a cage.

"Only if you can give me an hour's uninterrupted access. The drive's a hundred times faster than—"

"Well, well," crackled a voice from above, distantly familiar. "What do we have here? Interlopers. Oh, dear."

I scanned the high catwalks, looking for the source of the suave, self-satisfied baritone. Nothing. It must've come from amps in the ceiling.

"That sounds like Alton Parker," Carlisle sent.

That was it. Alton Parker, CEO of Vantage and, infinitely more importantly, raknoth.

"Oh crap," James was whispering in our ears. "Oh crap!"

"You, I've been half-expecting, Carlisle," Alton continued. "But is that the Raish boy I see? Oh, the General is going to love this."

"Spare us the theatrics," Carlisle called, his voice firm but admirably calm. "What are you doing to these people?"

"He hasn't stopped going on about your mother, Haldin," Alton continued as if Carlisle hadn't spoken. "Swears she's the sweetest he's ever drank. Won't stop talking about it. Well, that and how much he's looking forward to having you for comparison. Honestly, it's getting to be…"

He kept talking, some corner of my mind noted. But rage had taken me, roaring through my veins, through my ears, drowning out everything else. I was already lurching forward, opening my mouth to cry that, if Kublich wanted my blood, the son of a bitch was welcome to try for it. Something tugged me back before I could. A hand clamped to the back of my neck. Carlisle's hand, I realized, just as something I could only describe as liquid calm flowed into me from the spot where his skin met mine, restoring some semblance of rational thought.

"Ah, what spunk," Alton was saying above. "Delightful."

"He's baiting you," Carlisle sent. *"Trying to keep us here for something."*

"And you, Carlisle," Alton pressed on, "yes, we know who you are. I knew you the moment I saw you the other night. Your dear old master told us all about you. After all the torture, of course. Ugly business. My colleagues are what you might call monsters, you see."

He was a smug son of a bitch.

I felt Carlisle tense at the mention of Cassius, but, unlike me, he held his composure. *"We're leaving,"* he sent, reaching for the external drive though the transfer on the display read only eighty-seven percent complete.

"But these people—"

"These people are lost for now. The entire base will be on us in minutes." He slipped the drive into his pack, turning for the mag lifts. "James?"

Nothing.

"James?"

"Your friend cannot hear you," Alton said, all traces of amusement gone from his voice now. "No one will hear you." Above, the doors of our waiting lift car slid shut with the finality of a gun cocking against the head. "But I do have something to show you, if you'd be so kind."

A series of mechanical pops sounded from along the walls, followed by a string of sharp hisses, like pressurized gas being vented. I didn't have to look to know the sounds were coming from the cylinders holding those monstrosities. Carlisle grabbed me by the strap of my pack and pulled me toward the stairs to the closed mag lifts.

"I said I have something to show you, humans," Alton Parker growled after us. "You've been such curious little boys so far. Don't tell me you're losing your nerve now?"

I couldn't process what was happening—what was about to happen. Couldn't look away from the poor souls still bleeding on the racks.

"We can't leave them, Carlisle."

And yet the sounds of venting gas and draining liquids from cylinders all around us told me we had no choice. Never mind the Vantage army no doubt waiting above. We'd be lucky to make it out of this room alive. Because I had a bad feeling I knew what came next.

Across from us, the first cylinder popped open with a victorious chime.

Inside the tank, its inhabitant gave a shudder. Then the creature's eyes snapped open, pale and red and hungry.

"Awaken, children!" Alton called. "Awaken, and bring these interlopers to me."

CHAPTER 20

NIGHTMARES

The air crawled with an unholy cacophony of eager hisses and guttural roars, punctuated here and there by those Alpha-cursed chimes that each announced the arrival of yet another monster to our underground death trap. Terror froze my brain, held me in a stupor. Three of them hit the floor across from us, wetly smacking down from the catwalk—falls that should've broken limbs. They just loped straight for us, none the worse.

Those eyes. Those hungry, gaping mouths, all full of sharp, utterly inhuman fangs.

"Haldin!" Carlisle snapped.

I'd drawn my gun, swapped to lethal rounds, and put two neat holes in the closest creature's chest almost before I knew it, the old training finally kicking in.

The creature dropped to the floor with a wet-sounding gasp, which only enraged its two companions. One sprinted straight for us at an alarming speed. The other hauled a supply tank off the ground and hurled it at me.

Reflexes rolled me out of the tank's path. Judging from the impact when it crashed to the floor behind me, it must have weighed a couple hundred pounds, but that hadn't stopped the creature from throwing it like a smashball.

They were strong.

Carlisle stepped to meet the one charging us. It threw a wild, clawed slash that probably would've killed him, but he pivoted in perfect control, slammed the creature to the ground on its own momentum, and pinned it by the arm while he liberally applied his stun baton to its neck.

After several seconds of growling and spasmodic convulsing, the creature lay still.

The one who'd thrown the tank roared an awful challenge, preparing to charge Carlisle. I gunned it down before it got the chance.

Several more chambers were popping open around the room now, their ghastly inhabitants stumbling out, shaking off their disorientation. Focusing on us.

"The lift," Carlisle sent. *"I'll get the doors. Let's move."*

I wasn't going to argue. Especially not when the first creature I'd shot stirred and began pulling itself back to its feet, and the others shortly followed its lead.

Definitely time to go.

We ran for the mag lifts, Carlisle falling in on my flank as we reached the stairs. At the top, I spun to fire on our pursuers and cover Carlisle, but he was already there. I backpedaled toward the lift with him, firing off a few choice rounds, and nearly fell over backward when one of the creatures crashed to the platform almost on top of me from the catwalk above.

The swipe it took at my head, I ducked more out of luck than anything. Then my brain caught up, and I drove a high kick straight into the thing's face.

It was like kicking a hardwood statue. The reaction force sent me staggering backward for balance, but at least the creature stumbled back too. I prayed for it to hit the railing and flip over to the floor below. Instead, it caught its balance and shook my chest with a furious roar.

I raised my gun as the creature lunged. Before I could fire, though, the creature halted in midair, caught by some invisible force, and was flung off the catwalk to the ground floor below with a strangled screech.

"Move, Hal," came Carlisle's voice.

I turned to cover the last stretch to the mag lift at a sprint, thanking Alpha that Carlisle had already pried the doors open. They closed as soon as I was through, and it was only then I saw that we were standing not in the lift car we'd rode down in, but the dark, empty shaft. I toggled my torch on and saw that the lift cars were all waiting several stops above now, probably at ground floor.

Carlisle looked down from his own inspection with a frustrated furrow in his brow and considered me. "How are you doing?"

I almost wanted to laugh—right until something hit the shaft doors with a harsh bang.

Trapped in a lift shaft. Bloodthirsty monsters pounding on the door. A private army most likely waiting above.

I swallowed. "I'm doing great. Just grea—"

Another something slammed into the door, followed by violent pounding. The lightsteel was starting to dent inward when a hum from above announced the enemies outside might be the least of our worries.

The mag lifts were descending toward us. All of them.

"Flowers and gropping sunshine," I growled.

"Don't move," Carlisle said, his eyes already shut in concentration. "I've got it."

Monsters pounding at our backs. Alpha knew how many hundreds of pounds of lift car speeding down on our heads. I did my best to refrain from pointing out that he'd better have it in the next two seconds and instead reached out, preparing to try to help him play catch.

There were a pair of tiny thunder cracks—which I hoped to Alpha were the motors blowing—then the brakes engaged, and the lift car lurched to a halt fifteen feet above us with a hair-raising screech. The shaft filled with the acrid scents of burnt rubber and electronics. I was about ready to cheer when the adjacent lift cars reached the bottom of the shaft on either side of us, boxing us in.

But at least we weren't smashed.

Then another crash and the wrench of deforming metal yanked my attention to the shaft doors, and my relief evaporated. Pale red eyes appeared at the dented crack in the shaft doors, followed promptly by a frustrated howl.

"Up," Carlisle said, moving into position to give me a boost onto one of the lift cars beside us.

I took the boost without question, scrambled onto the bare top of the car, and was just turning to offer Carlisle a hand up when he flew up from the darkness and landed beside me.

"Which floor?" I asked, readying my grappling module.

"James," Carlisle said to his earpiece.

Silence.

"James? Phineas? Do either of you copy?"

I glanced at my palmlight. Nothing. "They're probably—"

"Jamming communications down here?"

"And waiting with their entire guard core above," I added.

Carlisle looked up. "We need to get to the roof."

It was a deviation from the original exfil plan, and it might leave us in a tight spot if we couldn't contact James and Phineas above, but I agreed. Better that than take our chances against Vantage's private army on the ground floor. Our armor skins would theoretically stop at least a few slugs, but they'd still hurt like demons' danglers, and it'd be a whole lot more than a few slugs we'd be dealing with if we played into their hands like that.

As if we'd needed any more encouragement to get moving, a pair of clawed hands snaked through the widening gap in the shaft doors below, blindly groping about for any nearby flesh.

To the roof it was.

The red warning light on the grappling module's rangefinder was informing me we didn't have enough line to make it more than about four floors at a time when Carlisle laid his hand over my gun and moved in as if to embrace me.

For a brief moment, I was just shocked. Then he said, "Hold on tight," and understanding set in.

My shock barely had time to shift flavors before we left the roof of the lift car and rose into the open shaft above, propelled only by Carlisle's will and energy. It was a bizarre ride, gliding smoothly upward through thin air, held in a tight embrace by a man with whom almost all my prior contact had involved one or both of us trying to inflict bodily harm on the other.

It struck me as laughable that I could actually manage to feel awkward about a hug even as we underwent telekinetic flight between a hostile army and a pack of bloodthirsty monsters. Then a door a couple shafts over and a few floors down pried open to admit an armored head, and the world righted itself straight back to Grop Town.

"They're in the shafts!" the head cried. Then he seemed to process our flight. "They're... They're... Never mind!" The head disappeared and the doors began to slide back shut, but not before we heard, "Just get in the lifts, you steel sippers!"

The shaft filled with resonant humming, and within seconds, every lift but the one Carlisle had wrecked was arriving at the ground floor, ready to carry a good six or eight soldiers each straight up to join us.

Carlisle deposited us on a shallow ledge several floors above, reaching for his pendant. He paused, seeming to think better of whatever he'd had in mind.

"Scud," he whispered.

I think it was the first time I'd heard him swear. It didn't inspire confidence.

"This will have to do," Carlisle said, extending a hand toward the door across the shaft. The door parted with a reluctant groan. A placard on the wall beyond declared we'd reached the sixth floor. "Get to the roof and hail Phineas and James. I'll be right behind you."

I tore my gaze from the lift cars. "Wait, what are you gonna—"

But he was already plunging down the open lift shaft, arms spread wide and tunic billowing in the wind. He did something that slowed his fall and sent one of the waiting lifts plunging downward as he landed on its neighbor.

"Go!" his voice drifted up to me.

I looked from him to the stomach-clenching drop between me and the sixth floor. I couldn't just leave Carlisle to handle the lifts and Alpha knew how many soldiers on his own. But I probably couldn't get down there fast enough to help, either. And none of it would matter anyway if our ride wasn't there when we needed it.

Demons to the gropping wind.

I drew the pulse gun. Judged the toss as best I could.

"Carlisle, catch!" I cried, lofting the gun and its grappling module gently his way.

He looked up from the smoking wreck of his current lift car, and the plummeting gun shot to his hand like a magnet. I didn't wait to see what happened after that. I steeled my stomach and leapt across the open shaft.

For a terrible second, there was nothing beneath me but empty space and the promise of a horrible death. Then the dark shaft gave way to bright hallway lighting. My feet hit soft carpet. I tucked into a roll and popped up, fists raised in challenge to a blessedly empty lift bank that looked to empty into administrative offices.

I drew my backup sidearm, took the first stairwell I found, and climbed at a sprint. Three floors up, James' voice crackled into my ear.

"—uys hear me? Hello?"

"James! Sweet Alpha am I glad to hear your voice."

"Hal! What's going on? Are you guys okay?"

"Sort of. They must've jammed communications below. Tell Phineas we need exfil from the roof."

"The roof?"

I turned the last flight of stairs and paused, speaking between panting now. "Small army problem on the ground floor. I don't think we're getting back over the wall without your help."

"Ah…" James said.

"It's fine," came Phineas' unmistakable rumble. "We'll meet you on the roof."

"Thank you, Phineas," I said. "I'm almost there now, but Carlisle went back to slow them down. I don't know if I should—"

"Don't," Phineas said. "You might just slow him down. Clear the roof and keep your head down, kid. We're heading in."

I bit back an indignant retort. Keep my head down? I'd just fought my way out a lab full of mutant beasts and they were talking to me like I was a damned child. Still, he wasn't wrong about the plan. Carlisle had the grappling module, we needed to know our getaway route was clear, and I was only half a floor away.

Roof first. Head back for Carlisle after that, if necessary.

The first flicker of hope touched my chest as I cracked the rooftop door and the cool night air kissed my face, sweet and welcoming after the smell of slow death in the lab and the stagnant dark of the lift shaft.

We'd gotten what we'd come for. We'd escaped the monsters below. Now we just needed Carlisle to make it up here.

I pushed the door the rest of the way open, sidearm raised, sweeping the closest of the ventilation housings and other obstacles for any hidden surprises first.

Something prickled at the edge of my awareness. I swept my weapon around and was about to reach out with my senses too when I caught sight of the dark figure at the far edge of the rooftop.

My stomach fell.

Even wreathed in shadow, I was sure I knew who it was. The figure turned, a faint red glow lighting the darkness where his eyes should be.

"Well, well," a smooth baritone called. "The rooftop escape, a timeless classic. And all alone, I see. Whatever happened to our dear friend Carlisle?"

"Phineas," I murmured quietly to my earpiece, "sooner is better than later."

Across the rooftop, Alton Parker stepped into the dim lighting and began stalking towards me with a murderous smile.

CHAPTER 21

SHOWDOWN

"**S**ay again?" James' voice crackled in my ear.

"Alton Parker's here," I said quietly.

"Get out," Phineas rumbled. "Find Carlisle."

Watching the ember-eyed demon strolling leisurely my way across the rooftop, I sincerely considered listening to him. But I couldn't. I had no idea where Carlisle would be, for one thing. If I went running trying to find him, there were any number of ways we could pass each other without realizing. And that was assuming Alton didn't just put on a burst of raknoth speed and catch me before I even made it down from the rooftop.

Running from a predator wasn't a smart idea. Not that *not* running was a brilliant idea, either. But I wasn't completely helpless prey, was I? This was what I'd been training for—with Carlisle, and for all my life before that.

Whether the Sanctum realized it or not, I knew now that demons were absolutely real. And I was staring straight at one.

"I'll handle it," I said softly.

"Don't be an idiot, kid," Phineas said in my ear. "He'll kill y—"

I muted my earpiece with a double tap.

That was probably the most idiotic decision of all, considering it might mean missing a life-saving bit of information in the next minute or two. But if I was going to survive, I needed to focus, and that wasn't going to happen with a three-hundred-pound bear rumbling in my ear that I was going to die.

"Handle me, will you?" Alton called, still taking his time.

Alpha, had he heard that? He was still a good fifty yards away, and I'd been nearly whispering. But that hardly mattered. What mattered was surviving.

I'd keep him talking. Take my shot if I found it.

Scud, maybe I could throw him off the roof with telekinesis if I played it right. Of course, that would mean extending the sphere of my cloaking field enough to let Alton in, which was something Carlisle would've no doubt vehemently recommended against. But still…

An idea was forming in my head—a ploy to lead him closer to the nearest edge—when he rendered the plan moot and covered most of the remaining distance between us in an impossible thirty-some-yard leap.

His impact shook the permacrete beneath my boots. Demons below, how strong were they to be able to move like that?

"Tell me, Tyro Raish," he said, flexing clawed fingers, "how exactly do you plan to handle me?"

I had no gropping idea. But I needed to keep him talking, so I went with, "Just like we handled your scaly children downstairs."

That seemed to amuse him. "You know," he said, shaking his head, "I was thinking I'd hand you over to Kublich when he gets here, but this is all starting to—"

"The General's coming here?"

The world collapsed down around me, condensing on that one idea. Kublich. Here. Tonight? I squeezed my gun tight, the familiar rage creeping into my heart.

Alton Parker sneered at me. "That's right, Haldin. Mommy and Daddy's killer is on his way to finish the Raish tree. Does that anger you? Does it fill you with rage? Will you beat your chest like the rest of these ridiculous humans and—"

I raised my gun and shot him in the face. Or tried to.

I'd been hoping to hit an eye, figuring that was the only spot my suppressed, subsonic rounds might actually do real damage. But Alton jerked defensively at my motion, and my slug hit his raised hand instead.

"Gah," he growled, shaking the crumpled slug free from his hand. "Petulant little fly. I might actually enjoy killing you with my own hands."

His eyes were fully alight with scarlet demon fire now, and a change was coming over his face—the skin darkening, the angles shifting to something reptilian, like the creatures we'd seen below.

The sight flashed me back to the night of the attack, and the change that had come over Kublich as he'd torn my parents apart. Fear gripped at my limbs. Quickened my breath. Laughed away all attempts I made to talk it down as he prowled forward.

"They're not yours," I said, almost without meaning to.

That caught him off guard. "What?"

I barely even knew where I was going with it at first. But the words came. "Those hands you want to rip me apart with. They don't belong to you." I shook my head. "None of this does."

It was hard to tell past his increasingly alien appearance, but that seemed to genuinely amuse Alton. "No? I suppose it's your Alpha-given right to rule this planet, yes? To harvest your crops and eat your livestock." He chuckled and started forward again, showing me glistening fangs. "How perfectly human of you to condone your own morals simply because you are no longer at the top of your own food chain."

I searched for something to say—anything to derail him a minute longer. But the talking was over. Alien or not, I could see it in his movements.

So I raised my gun and fired.

He threw his arms up and dove at me like a humanoid wrecking ball. I hit the permacrete and flinched at the sound of him smashing straight through the ventilation housing behind me. Alpha, he was powerful. But at least I was faster to my feet. Before I could think better of it, I charged in and threw a heavy kick at the recovering raknoth.

His head might've been a softsteel punching bag for all it yielded.

The glint of a red eye was my only warning as Alton spun into a savage backhand aimed at my head. I dropped into a backward roll, too off-balance from the kick to duck without falling.

Alton stomped at my retreating form hard enough to rattle my teeth through the permacrete.

I rolled to my feet with an angry raknoth bearing down on me, eyes ablaze.

Telekinesis crossed my mind, but there was no way. No time.

I ducked a brutal swipe and put a pair of slugs in each of Alton's knees. Fine shooting. But not fine enough to drop a raknoth.

He threw his arms wide and let loose an utterly inhuman roar. The sound hit me like a thumper blast.

I took the best snap shot I could at his gaping mouth.

Judging by the cracking sound and the pained screech that replaced his roar, I'd gotten lucky and hit his fangs. The small victory, however, evaporated when the stairwell door I'd come from burst open and three guards rushed onto the rooftop, weapons raised.

"They're here!" one shouted. "Tell th—"

It was like the three guards had been hit by an invisible skimmer. Two of them went flying, while the third merely hit the permacrete with a startled cry.

A flicker of hope in my chest.

Then the shaking permacrete of a charging raknoth.

I leapt away without thinking and narrowly avoided Alton's grabbing arms. I tried to backpedal, set my feet, but he was on me, and he wasn't letting up.

I ducked one punch. Twisted past another. In the corner of my eye, I saw Carlisle rising from the downed guards, rushing toward us.

Then my foot caught on the corner of a ventilation fan.

Alton's fist flew toward me. My world condensed around that fist.

There was no avoiding it.

It was like what I imagined being struck in the chest with a sledge-hammer might feel like. If not for James' armor skin, I thought I might have died on the spot. Then again, I wasn't entirely sure I hadn't.

I might've lost consciousness momentarily. There were scrapes and jarring impacts, but I only half-felt them, like I wasn't quite there.

Then there was a flash of the rooftop edge and I tore back to awareness as I realized I was headed over it.

Arms out, legs down. I scrambled frantically to find some purchase and stop my wild roll.

Too late.

My heels kicked against nothing but open air.

I was falling.

I tried to scream. There was no air in my lungs. All the air in the world below me, and none in my lungs. I couldn't think. Couldn't breathe.

I was on my way to die when I crashed into something strong and unyielding and decidedly not there. An invisible platform of thin air.

Carlisle.

Before I could be properly astounded, the miraculous construct flung me upward and dished me back onto the rooftop. I landed in a heap of pain, fire spreading through my chest as I gulped for air with a raknoth-hammered diaphragm.

Across the rooftop, Alton was closing on a distracted Carlisle. The raknoth snatched the arm Carlisle had extended my way and wrenched violently.

There was a wet cracking sound, and a heavy grunt from Carlisle. I waited for him to miraculously reverse the tide, but Alton drove him to the ground, still cranking on his broken arm.

I caught sight of the pulse gun I'd left for Carlisle. It was right there on the permacrete, where Carlisle must've dropped it. The fire in my torso flared brilliantly when I tried to move. The pain was bad—worse than I could recall having felt. But I couldn't let it stop me.

Carlisle was in trouble.

I reached for the gun with my mind. Willed it to my hand. Then I rolled over and fired five stun rounds at Alton's back. Four hit. He went rigid as the rounds delivered their shock charges.

The brief distraction was all Carlisle needed.

He sprung to his feet, spun past Alton's convulsing form, and drove a foot into the back of the raknoth's knee. The leg buckled, dropping Alton to his knees. Carlisle drew a dagger from his tunic with his good hand and plunged it into Alton's back, right where his heart would be—assuming he even still had one.

The knife didn't pierce far into Alton's dark suit and scaly hide. The stun bolts had nearly depleted their charges, too, judging by his shift from spasms to wild thrashing. Apparently the sedative portion of the rounds wasn't having much of an effect on him.

Trying to score another shot was a stupid risk. I didn't have a clear line, and my hands were far from steady. But the raknoth was clearly recovering, and, with both of us injured, I didn't see things improving from there.

So I took careful aim, exhaled, and squeezed the trigger twice.

My last two stun bolts caught Alton on the side and locked him up for another few seconds while Carlisle reset behind the knife and drove into it again. He must've added some serious telekinetic juice, too. The dagger drove through Alton's tough hide like a pneumatic press.

Carlisle yanked his dagger free and leapt clear of Alton's frenzied screeching and thrashing.

I prayed it was the bastard's death throes I was witnessing. But I wasn't counting on it. And for good reason.

Alton lurched back to his feet with a few choice curses and went at Carlisle like a wild animal, grabbing and swiping and biting and cursing. Carlisle kept a step ahead, despite the left arm hanging uselessly at his side.

I tried to push myself to my feet, but the pain was unbearable now. Something—several somethings, maybe—were broken inside of me.

So I watched helplessly as Carlisle thrust a hand at Alton and lit the air around the raknoth's head with dozens of explosions of startlingly bright light, each accompanied by a loud pop.

I didn't understand why he was wasting his energy. Neither, apparently, did Alton.

"Enough of your damned trickery," the raknoth roared from inside the brilliant light show, blindly swatting. "Come meet your end like—"

A heavy black skimmer came soaring out of the night sky and plowed straight into the raknoth with a thick crunch. Alton sailed across the permacrete like a skipping stone and toppled unceremoniously over the edge with one last furious roar.

The skimmer settled, and James and Phineas climbed out.

"Let's go," Phineas said. "Now."

He didn't need to tell me twice. He just, as it turned out, needed to peel me off the permacrete and half-carry me to the skimmer. Carlisle made to pick me up first, but Phineas growled, "Your arm," and that was the end of the discussion.

At least I mostly managed to keep from crying out in pain.

I didn't feel right. My head swam, my vision darkened. I nearly fell back over, but Phineas' grip was strong.

That had been one strong punch.

Carlisle watched me with a worried look as he went to open the rear skimmer door for us. I didn't understand how he wasn't passing out from the pain of his shattered arm. I didn't understand much at all right then besides the pain and the nausea it was bleeding over into.

"Come on, kid," Phineas rumbled. "You're almost there."

Alton had made a pretty mess of the skimmer's armored hood. Damn, the raknoth were tough. But we'd taken one down tonight. There was that. And now we just had to get out of here before—

The rushing thrum of approaching craft drifted over the rooftop.

I knew that sound. Would know it anywhere.

"What's that?" James asked, frantically scanning the dark sky.

"Legion transports," I grunted, then stiffened as Alton's words flashed back to me.

... hand you over to Kublich when he gets here, he'd said. *That's right, Haldin. Mommy and Daddy's killer is on his way to finish the Raish tree...*

Kublich. He was in one of those transports.

"Dammit, kid, we have to go," Phineas growled.

I resisted his pull, looking to the dark sky.

There. The outlines were closing on the rooftop now.

The door burst open behind us, jarring my attention. Several armed guards poured out, weapons at the ready. In front of us, more troops were arriving by another door.

Phineas gave up on playing nice and hauled me into the skimmer, barking at the others to get the grop in. Carlisle slid in beside me and slammed the door shut as Phineas dove into the driver's seat and did the same. James appeared in the front passenger seat just as the guards opened fire.

Slugs pelted off the skimmer's armor with sharp cracks and twangs. No one spoke a word as Phineas scrambled to bring the engine to life and lift off.

The first Legion transport reached the rooftop, swiveling around to give its passengers access. And there he was, tall and proud in the frame of the open side door.

High General Adrian Kublich. Alpha damn his black soul.

I forgot the pain coursing through my body. I forgot the guards and the slugs pelting us and everything in my world except for my desire to sink daggers into the appraising dark eyes Kublich directed my way.

Carlisle's hand clamped down on my wrist.

"Go!" he barked at Phineas.

I tried to yank my arm free. Carlisle held tight. I tried to push past him, toward Kublich, mindlessly growling and flailing and—

Phineas threw power to the engines, and, for several seconds, I was powerless to do anything but press into the seat like dead weight as we shot off into the night sky.

When I could move, I whipped around and strained against Carlisle's grasp, watching Kublich's stern face shrinking in the rear window.

"No," I whispered through clenched teeth.

"Hal…" Carlisle's face was plastered with concern, his voice thick with it. It only amplified the desperation in my chest, the roiling inferno threatening to overwhelm me from the inside.

The skimmer veered downward, and Kublich was lost to the night.

"NO!"

My voice broke with the force of the scream. The skimmer jerked in Phineas' hands.

A fit of coughing seized me, each one a harsh bite on my raw throat. When it was done, my hands were flecked with blood.

They were all watching me. Carlisle. James. Even Phineas studied me in the mirror before turning his focus back to flying.

I'm fine, I thought to say. *It's fine.*

But instead, I slumped into a wretched ball in my seat, hugging my legs against the nausea riding in on the returning tide of pain—physical and otherwise.

I closed my eyes.

Hold it together.

I felt like I was going to burst. Going to die.

Hold it together.

I'd never been in this much pain.

Carlisle's hand settled on my back.

The first hot tears streamed silently down my cheeks. And there, in the dead silence of the skimmer's cabin, I squeezed my eyes tighter and let the sobs rack my body until there was nothing left but to give in to the inexorable weight of my exhaustion.

Carlisle's hand never left my back.

CHAPTER 22
SWEET DREAMS

When I woke in my soft bed, I couldn't remember how I'd gotten there. Only that I was at Franco's. And that I felt warm. And good.

Like, really good.

My head was tingling pleasantly, my brain floating in warm honey. Honey. Honeyhead.

Was I on drugs?

I squinted up and found two clear bags hanging on the bedpost and a thin tube that ran to a bandage on the back of my hand. An IV.

Huh.

The sight should've bothered me. I was pretty sure about that. But I was also pretty sure that, in fact, all was well. Definitely not cause for concern. The pain when I tried to shift in bed, on the other hand… That was unpleasant. It rose through the warm honey fuzz like an invading army. It flashed me straight back to Vantage. To the racks. The monsters. To Alton Parker.

And to Kublich.

I sat up with a drunken growl. Or tried to, before the pain doubled and I flopped back to the bed with a gasp. I lay there, trying to hold on to the rage —wanting to steam with it. But I was tired. So tired. The urgent need for action dissipated, gently but insistently pulled away by the warm weight of the drugs.

I slept. At some point, I might've felt Carlisle's presence hovering near. He might have come and gone between fitful bouts of sleep. Time passed erratically.

When next I truly climbed to consciousness, a hand was resting on mine, warm and soft. I cracked an eyelid and spied Elise at my bedside, worriedly nibbling at her lower lip.

I did my best not to move.

This was good, right?

Yes, my honey-brain decided. Yes it was. Maybe, if I was careful, I could just lie there forever, enjoying the tender warmth of her hand on mine. That sounded pretty damn good to me.

"Haldin?"

Apparently I needed practice at playing dead.

I opened my eyes. Elise was on her feet now, leaning over me, her right hand still on mine. "You're awake."

Alpha, she was beautiful.

I tried to blink the bleariness from my eyes.

"Elise," someone whispered.

Was that me?

A drunken smile pulled at my lips.

"Oh, thank Alpha," she whispered, smiling back at me.

It didn't seem possible that that smile should triple her beauty. Maybe she had powers of her own. It was uncanny. I wanted to tell her. *Should tell her*, said honey-brain. Needed to tell her.

"Yurr...most beau—ful..."

She laughed and abruptly wrapped me in a tight hug. Or tight enough to send a wave of pain through my torso, at least.

"Sorry!" she said in response to my groan. "I'm sorry. You just..."

All at once, her demeanor flipped, and she released my hand and gave me a sharp flick on the forehead.

"Ow... What the scud, lady?"

"I was worried sick! No one tells me a damned thing around here. I just found you lying half-dead in my house, all hooked up like we're running an Alpha-blessed medica here." She shook her head. "You didn't look alive."

"You should see the other guy."

She looked like she was thinking about giving me another thwap. Instead, she sighed and pulled my blankets down to the waist.

My breath caught.

It was like Divinity's premier abstract artist had gotten ahold of my torso and had nothing to work with but purples and blues.

"You were saying? About the other guy?"

I could only stare at my bruises in horrid fascination. At least the sight sobered my fuzzy thoughts a bit.

"What were you guys doing out there?"

I finally tore my gaze away and met her eyes.

What was I supposed to say?

"We were… trying to figure out what some bad people are planning."

She searched my face, looking for more, then shook her head. "Oh, good. I was worried for a second there you were gonna be super vague about the whole thing." She bit back her next comment. Then, more calmly, she said, "You can trust me, you know."

I dropped her gaze, not sure what to say. Keeping her in the dark wasn't fair. I sure as scud didn't want to do it.

But it wasn't my call, was it? And if there was even a chance that keeping her away from the truth of the raknoth would keep her safe…

I wasn't so sure I blamed Franco for wanting to keep her away from the entire mess.

"So did you?" she asked.

"Huh?"

"Did you find out what your bad people are planning?"

I thought back to the grotesque abominations in the lab and to the poor souls still trapped on those blood racks, and guilt filled me.

"Sort of."

"And the other guy?" She pointed at my bruised torso. "The one who did this to you?"

I watched in my mind's eye as the skimmer plowed Alton Parker off the rooftop. The impact alone would've been more than enough to kill any human. Alton, I wasn't positive about, but the ten-floor fall that followed?

"We took care of him."

She considered that with a grim face. "Good," she finally said. "I know my dad wouldn't involve himself in this kind of thing unless the people on the other side deserved it." She shook her head. "But I still can't believe he would let Carlisle bring a kid into… whatever this thing is."

I bristled and was promptly rewarded with a wave of aching pain.

"I'm not a kid," I grunted.

She fixed me with a level look, sage beyond her years. "We're both kids, Haldin."

I bit back my decidedly kidlike retort and shrugged. "Maybe so, but I can take care of myself just fine."

She arched an eyebrow and stared pointedly at my bruised body.

"This is different," I insisted.

This was only because I'd been fighting a super-powered—apparently bloodsucking—demon. But I couldn't say that, could I?

"Look, it's not their fault. Carlisle's tried to talk me out of this thing more than once. I have my reasons for being here."

The look on her face—part guilt, part sympathy—told me those reasons were no mystery to her.

"Your parents," she said quietly. "It wasn't just an accident, was it?"

An aching lump formed in my throat. I shook my head, fighting back unexpectedly abrupt tears.

Damn drugs. Or maybe it was Elise. Somehow, having her ask about them felt completely different than if it had been Carlisle or Franco or anyone else. Beneath her caring gaze, I felt open and vulnerable and—

Elise closed me in another hug, more carefully this time.

"I'm so sorry, Haldin," she whispered.

I didn't know what to say—didn't have to say anything, I realized. She knew enough. She'd lost her own mother to the raknoth, after all. Only she probably didn't even know that.

It wasn't fair. But all I could do was hug her back tightly.

She rested her cheek against the top of my head, and, for a long while, we stayed like that, and I felt warm and safe and cared for.

Tears weren't far away when the door opened and Carlisle slipped into the room.

Elise and I quickly broke apart, but Carlisle paid little mind to our intimate moment. He just looked relieved to see me awake.

"How are you feeling?"

He took in the extensive discoloration of my torso, which probably gave him all the answer he needed.

I forced a smile. "Kind of like I was the one to fall off the building. But other than that, not so bad."

"Someone fell off a building?" Elise asked.

Carlisle hesitated, glancing between us. "Yes. But I'm sure your father wouldn't appreciate us regaling you with the story."

Elise flashed him a charmingly conspiratorial smile. "Aww, come on. We're all friends here, right?"

Carlisle's lips twitched, but he wasn't to be convinced. "I'm sorry, Elise, but could I talk to Haldin alone for a few minutes?"

She rolled her eyes, not bothering to hide her irritation. "You know what? I was on my way to go train anyway. So go ahead. Have fun talking about all the secrets poor, helpless Elise mustn't know. Please, don't let me get in the way here in my own house or anything."

She gave a scathing curtsy and marched for the door.

"Thank you, Elise," Carlisle called after her, his tone apologetic.

She wasn't gentle with the door on her way out.

"Why can't we tell her anything?" I asked.

Carlisle sat down next to my bed. "I suppose we could, but to what end? Whether it's sensible or not, Franco wishes to shield her from all of this. It's not our place to deny him that, especially while we're making use of his resources and hospitality."

The fact that I'd arrived at a similar conclusion didn't lessen my desire to argue. It simply wasn't fair for her. But I wasn't sure what to do about it right now.

"Fine. What have I missed? How long have I even been out?"

I glanced at my palmlight to answer my second question. Well into the afternoon already. I'd slept for about fourteen hours, by my guess.

Carlisle tilted his head in deference to the palmlight. "A good while, but I expect you'll be needing plenty more rest. You haven't missed much. It'll take quite some time to decrypt most of the data we retrieved. Franco says Vantage's digital security is every bit as thorough as the physical."

"Yeah, that's easy to say for the guy who didn't have a roomful of hungry lizard people trying to eat him."

It might have been funny if the underlying reality wasn't so horrifying. The guilt pressed heavier as my thoughts shifted back to the pale, helpless men and women still bleeding out in slow motion on those racks.

"All those people back there…"

"You tried, Hal. There was nothing more we could have done."

"I don't think that's much comfort to them."

"All the more reason to stop the raknoth as quickly as possible. Many of those victims will likely survive for cycles to come. Maybe longer. There might still be hope."

I wanted to believe that. Something told me I shouldn't hold my breath.

"Where do you think Alton got them? And those creatures…"

"Hybrids."

I frowned.

"A designation we've been using for now, at least," he explained. "Thinking back on how they felt in my senses, that's my best guess. Part human, part raknoth. And what little we've uncovered so far suggests many of the hybrids and the blood donors were actually Vantage employees not too long ago."

My frown deepened. "Why in demon's depths would they do that to their own people?"

He cocked his head. "Well, aside from the observation that the raknoth don't seem to greatly value humans to start with, I suspect these particular employees might've known too much. More efficient to make use of their loose ends rather than kill them outright."

"Well how gropping responsible of them."

Alton Parker's sneering face arose in my mind, calmly declaring humans the new livestock of Enochia. I felt like I was going to be sick.

Carlisle started saying something, then seemed to change his mind. "We'll get to the bottom of it when we decrypt the contents of that drive. Luckily, you should have plenty of time to rest and heal before then. We couldn't make out everything on Franco's scanner, but you have some cracked ribs at the very least. James administered nanites while you were out, but you'll still need a few days' bed rest."

My aching body and its obscene gallery of bruises told me he was absolutely right about that, but it was the last thing I wanted to hear—the last thing I wanted to do, lying here while Vantage continued draining their own people and turning out Alpha knew how many more of those hybrid creatures.

Carlisle hesitated over his next words.

"There's one more thing. A rather frustrating piece of news."

"Couldn't all be flowers and sunshine, huh?"

Carlisle just gestured the display on the opposite wall to life and navigated to a WAN newscast dated from that morning. My stomach sank at the headline.

Apostate Terrorists Raid Vantage Research Labs.

Both of our images—taken from Vantage's upper floor cameras and, admittedly, pretty damn terroristic with the battle gear and the tense expressions—hovered over the caster's shoulders as he explained how the two of us had broken into Vantage planning to secure materials to synthesize bioweapons for terrorist attacks on Divinity.

Vantage security, of course, had oh-so-heroically routed our evil efforts.

"Alpha be damned," I growled under my breath.

It was a win-win for the raknoth. No doubt the public would fear the two of us now, and be on vigilant lookout. But Vantage also got to look like the shining, trustworthy hero—certainly not the kind of company that would devour their own employees to build and feed a monstrous army that apparently drank human blood.

"It gets worse," Carlisle said quietly.

I wasn't surprised to hear I'd been recognized from the footage they'd captured on our way out. What did surprise me was the part where the caster explained that my mysterious resurrection had Legion authorities speculating I'd been responsible for the fire at my house. Responsible for the death of my own Alpha-blessed parents. Along with the help of my mysterious partner, of course—the man known only as Carlisle.

I said nothing.

At least until the caster went on to reveal that, while tragically injured in the attack, the magnanimous CEO, Alton Parker, had bravely attended to his people in the aftermath and now had something to say. With that, the feed cut to a posh medica suite to show Alton in a cushy hospital bed, very much not dead.

"How is that son of a bitch alive?" I growled.

But Parker was already launching into his usual ludicrous fluff—apologizing to the families of the guards we'd allegedly brutalized, insisting that he didn't know what it was we'd hoped to gain from a facility whose *only* goal was the advancement of medical science but that he sincerely hoped we'd be caught by the authorities before we had the chance to harm any more innocent people.

"I'd hoped we had ended him as well," Carlisle said, pausing the feed. "Next time, we'll be more thorough."

Next time…

I studied Carlisle, calm and poised as always, and it made me feel a small measure better.

Next time, it was. Because we were just getting started, rough as that start had been.

"How's your arm?" I asked.

"Healing quickly after a less-than-pleasant setting." He moved the arm a little to demonstrate. "I had the nanite treatment as well. Should probably still have it immobilized, but…"

I blew out an amused huff. Carlisle was about as likely to back off as I was to stay in this bed for a few days' rest. At least for today, though, I might not argue.

After he gingerly assisted me to the privy, Carlisle moved to take his leave, but paused at the door. "You did good back there, Hal."

I didn't realize until he said those words just how completely I disagreed with him. All at once, though, it came flooding out. "I didn't do scud," I said, staring at my hands. "Didn't help you. Didn't save a damn single one of those people. All I did was nearly get you killed trying to save me."

For a long moment, there was silence. I couldn't bring myself to look at Carlisle. All I could think about was what Docere Mathis would have to say. About what my dad would've done if he'd been there. About how he would've found a way, or at least gone down fighting for what he believed in.

Captain Martin Raish wouldn't have left those people to die.

I tensed when Carlisle laid a hand on my shoulder. I hadn't noticed him move from the door.

He waited until I forced myself to meet his eyes.

"I left them there too, Haldin. I was afraid too. This isn't about which one of us scored the most points out there. We're one step closer to bringing this operation of theirs down. And I, for one, was glad to have a partner in there. I'm not so arrogant as to believe I couldn't have frozen or missed something had you not been there to cover me."

He was pandering to me. He had to be. There was no way he would've frozen down there.

I just shook my head, pushing it aside. "Whatever. I still couldn't take him. How am I supposed to bring the High General of the Legion down if I can't even hold my own against an Alpha-cursed biotech CEO? He's probably, like, the pansy of their evil empire or whatever."

Much as I didn't mean to be joking, I couldn't help but smile a little as I said it.

Carlisle smiled too, holding his healing arm up. "I'll remind you that that pansy took me by surprise as well."

"Only because you were busy catching me."

"Haldin." He kneeled so our eyes were level. "You survived your first fight with a raknoth. I can't name a single person outside of this room who can claim as much. That's not so bad for a seventeen-year-old tyro."

"Ex-tyro, I think it's safe to say."

He smiled and squeezed my shoulder. "You'll only grow stronger from here. Have faith in yourself, Hal."

I was hardly convinced, but he didn't appear to plan on leaving until I gave him something, so I mustered a curt nod to appease him.

When he was gone, I closed my eyes and finally allowed myself to think about the failure I hadn't given voice to.

Kublich.

Back on the rooftop. The ultimate failure of the night.

His stern visage floated up in the reddish darkness of my eyelids. He'd been so close. So damned close. Never mind that Carlisle and I had both been injured. Never mind that a knife to the back, a skimmer to the front, and a ten-floor fall apparently wasn't enough to end a raknoth.

Kublich had willingly come within my reach, and I hadn't been strong enough to do a damn thing about it. And now we were terrorists in the eyes of Enochia. All for trying to help.

Fourteen days. Barely more than a cycle since I'd sat at supper with my parents and that murdering bastard, and now I was officially a wanted man. A public enemy, on the run, fighting a war I never would've believed existed just fourteen short days ago.

I cursed as I realized that Elise would have almost certainly seen the news on the reels before we'd talked. There was no way she'd have missed news of a terrorist attack. And yet she'd said nothing—only listened to what I'd had to say.

I should have told her more. I wished I could have.

I let out a heavy sigh and sank deeper into the bed, weariness making itself known throughout my battered body.

I'd make it up to her somehow. Just like I'd pay Kublich back. Somehow.

And, somehow, we'd stop the rest of the raknoth too. Stop them from turning all of Enochia into blood banks and breeding grounds for their monstrous hybrid army, even as the people of Enochia called for nooses on our necks.

But for now, my body insisted, I'd have to start with at least a few more hours' sleep. From there, we'd see.

Somehow.

CHAPTER 23

SUNSHINE AND FLOWERS

T he next morning, I gritted my teeth, removed my IV, and pulled myself out of bed. Having officially reached my limit at thirty hours of bed rest, I sidled gingerly out to the hallway to find the others, refusing to be waited on a moment longer.

I headed for the kitchen, figuring I might find them at breakfast, and ran into James halfway there, carrying the tray of bacon and eggs he'd been bringing to me. After only minimal fussing, we adjusted course and joined everyone else in the kitchen, where a choir of relieved smiles and well-wishes greeted me. Even Phineas gave me a stoic little nod, which was more of a greeting than I'd ever merited before.

Maybe the beating I'd taken had earned me an ounce of respect in his eyes. Or maybe it had something to do with Franco having made it clear that Carlisle and I were officially welcome residents of their home, terrorist status or no.

Much as I blessed his name for that, he also made it clear, with a pointed look at Elise as I joined them, that we wouldn't be discussing business over breakfast. Elise rolled her eyes at the look, but said nothing.

I don't think talking would have accomplished much anyway without more information. Clearly we needed to stop Vantage, but how? Destroy the facility? What about all the innocent civilians? And what if they'd already built another one, or several? We didn't know the first thing about what they were truly up to, or how extensive the operation was. Until we did, anything we had to say would be blind speculation.

So we tried with limited success to enjoy a normal breakfast. *How are your ribs feeling, Haldin? Cough up any blood lately? What do we do if the Legion comes knocking, asking about our harbored fugitives?* You know, normal.

With the aid of the nanites, I did heal remarkably fast over the next couple days. Elise probably deserved a good chunk of the credit too, keeping a smile on my face in the many hours my recovering body proved too exhausted for me to train even with my mind.

I apologized to her for trying to keep quiet about Vantage. She shrugged it off and said it wasn't like I owed her anything, and that she might have done the same were our situations reversed. She still might've been a bit hurt underneath the bravado, and continuing to keep secrets from her ate at me, but I didn't know what else to do.

Mostly, I trained with my abilities, day in and day out.

In addition to refining my Shaping, Carlisle began instructing me in the basics of guarding my mind. As usual, we started off with Carlisle encouraging me to simply follow my intuition and try to keep him out as he telepathically probed for weaknesses in my defenses.

There were a lot of them.

It didn't grow any less bizarre or unpleasant with practice, having another sentience break into my mind. Carlisle kept his own mental barriers tight, as he claimed an enemy telepath would when invading. It made it feel like a nameless, faceless entity rooting around in my head with the wispy tendrils of its presence rather than my caring mentor. Still, I recalled my experiences with Smirks and Kublich well enough to know that Carlisle was still taking care to be gentle each time he invaded.

"Let someone make it this far," he reminded me, *"and you'll likely belong to them until they see fit to release you."*

As testament to his claim, he had my body begin hopping in place, up and down without a single thought from me. I watched in morbid fascination as the hops continued despite my attempts to stand still. I honed in on Carlisle's wispy presence and tried to force him out to no avail.

Up and down. Up and down.

I gasped as he released me. "Agh sweet Alpha, man, that's sick! Agh!"

"Would you prefer a fowl dance next time?"

I glared at his faint grin. "Ha-ha. How about you just tell me how the scud I'm supposed to actually stop you? And if you say practice and creative thinking, you're gonna have to break into my mind again to stop me from killing you."

Carlisle fought back a smile, but the effort only made him look more amused. "Right. I won't say it, but you know how this goes. It's best you find your own approach. Personally, I like to cover my mind in a slick, oily film that's impossible to grab onto. Imaginary, of course." He smiled at some memory. "Cassius used to focus so thoroughly on the mental image of a stone that there was simply nothing left on the surface for another telepath to find."

"A stone? Like a plain old, side-of-the-road stone?"

He nodded, his smile reaching his pale eyes in a way it rarely did. "One in particular that he'd picked up one day and carried for years after. The perfect stone, he called it. Cassius was an interesting goodfellow."

"Sounds like it."

But what was my tactic going to be? What would be my stone?

"How does one manage to fight while thinking about nothing but a stone?" I asked as I deliberated.

"Not easily, at first. No matter what trick you find, it's going to take practice to do much else while maintaining your guard. But it's necessary to safely use your abilities around the raknoth or the Seekers. With enough practice, it'll become second nature."

"And here I thought I was starting to get the hang of all of this stuff."

"At every step, another fork," Carlisle said, his expression sympathetic. "Try to remember that you've already come a tremendous way, Haldin. And in under two cycles, no less."

It hardly felt like a tremendous way in light of my all-too-recent failures at Vantage, but I nodded, sat down, and settled into a meditative state, searching for the thing that could be my rock. Elise came to my mind unbidden. For a second, I thought about emulating Cassius' technique. But no. It would be beyond foolish to put her image out there to anyone intending me harm.

Something else, then. Something safe.

I found myself thinking about the fortifications I'd grown up around— the thick walls and massive gate of Sanctuary. The two gargantuan dark-steel doors, so heavy and well-guarded that they were only closed during times of emergency.

Who in their right mind would ever march on Sanctuary anyway?

Acting on instinct, I pictured those great doors nestled between the walls of a barren canyon—a canyon that made its narrow, winding way to the outside world from the landscape of my mind. I solidified the image until, sitting behind my impenetrable gate, sheer stone walls rising a hundred feet high on every side of me, I was sure I was ready for Carlisle's attack.

This time, my mental sanctuary didn't fall so easily.

He came slowly at first, the tendrils of his mind brushing lightly at my gate, seeking any cracks through which they might slip. Finally, he withdrew—only to return a moment later in a violent rush.

The weight of his mind crashed against my gate. Somehow, it held. He pushed harder, and I braced the gate with everything I had. Somewhere, far away, fingernails were digging into my palms and sweat was trickling down my forehead. Carlisle's attacks only grew stronger until, finally, my gate gave way.

I swore and slapped the mat in frustration when he released control back to me. He told me to relax so we could try again.

We went on like that all afternoon. The more time I spent huddled in my mental fortress, the more comfortable I grew there, and the more durable my defenses became. As they strengthened, though, so too did the power of Carlisle's telepathic assault.

There never seemed to be limits with him.

When one of our bouts had stretched long enough, I thought maybe I'd done it, that maybe he had nothing else to throw at me. Then some distant warning whispered to me, and something hit my chest. As deeply immersed as I was in our mental battle, I hadn't felt Carlisle's shove coming.

My eyes snapped open, and I teetered backward, oddly unable to pull out of my slow cross-legged tip back to the matted floor, like the inevitable tumble of a felled tree. I realized what was happening and threw myself back into my mental defenses.

"Too late," Carlisle's voice echoed from within my mind.

"You cheated!"

Carlisle returned control return to me, and I indignantly righted myself.

"There is no cheating," he said. "Not when it comes to fighting for your life."

I bristled with a hot retort, but Carlisle held up his hands in peace.

"It was a great start, Hal. I was concerned about your reliance on brute force of will, but your defenses were getting rather strong at the end there. Surprisingly so for your first time. With practice, it'll become nearly impenetrable, and with even more practice, you'll learn to hold it in the background so you can focus on fighting."

I exhaled, forced my aching body to relax, and nodded. "All right, then. Bring on the practice."

$\sim$

JUST THREE DAYS after waking up in a sea of bruises, I'd healed well enough that I only felt as sore as I might have after a particularly rough sparring match with Carlisle. Wonders of modern medical technology.

Franco's machines were still hard at work on the Vantage data decryption. None of us were entirely sure what we were hoping to gain from the drive, aside from leverage to either dismantle their operations ourselves or expose them to the public somehow.

Franco plainly leaned toward the latter.

"Not to sell us short," he said as we discussed it in his study one day, "but we've seen what they can do. I think it's safe to say that we're outmatched at this point. But exposing them could change that."

Outmatched? Of course we were. We always had been. They had not one, but *two* armies now, one of which was playing outside the rules of nature. The question wasn't whether we could take them head on. The question was how we were supposed to expose an enemy that had control of the Legion, the Sanctum, and apparently the WAN too.

What could we possibly do that they wouldn't just sweep under the rug? And even if we could get word out, what could we say to actually convince Enochia that their leaders were either malicious demons themselves or, at the very least, being controlled by them? We had our own footage from Vantage, of course, but it wouldn't be hard for someone to claim it was all just make-believe storyvid effects.

"Clearly, convincing the world that some of its most prominent leaders are in fact red-eyed monsters would be a problem," Franco admitted. "We'd need undeniable proof of who they are and what they're doing to those people at Vantage. Hard facts others can dig up and verify themselves. And we'd need to broadcast it in a way that can't be brushed aside like they did with the Vantage break in, or with..."

"With my parents' murder," I said.

Franco nodded apologetically.

I tried to keep us moving past it. "So what you're saying is we'd basically need to compile the world's best propaganda vid and commandeer one of the Legion's emergency broadcast bunkers?"

I couldn't help but snort at the thought.

After another half hour of discussion, we all agreed we needed to have a look at the drive's contents before we could settle on any real plan. Worse, Franco wasn't even sure how much longer it'd take, other than that it would hopefully be less than another cycle.

It was not an encouraging meeting. But at least I was ready to return to full training with Carlisle that day.

We sparred. We Shaped. And the next day, we did it again.

On the third day of our sparring, Franco wandered in to watch us spring about the mats, trading blows back and forth. James poked his head in a minute later, followed shortly thereafter by Phineas. Carlisle didn't seem to mind the spectators while we sparred but asked for privacy when it was time to move to our Shaping exercises.

The following morning, they came back, and Elise came with them. She stole my attention as she always did when she walked into the room. Carlisle rewarded my distraction with a firm kick to my newly-healed chest.

I went with the blow and managed to transition into a backward handspring, sparing another brief glance at Elise as I landed back on my feet. Her concerned look quickly shifted to a devilish grin and a tilt of the head that seemed to say, *Not half bad.*

After that, I was back in the fight with vigor.

Just like that, our morning sparring became something of a daily entertainment event for the household. On the seventh day of our public showing, once we'd finished sparring, Franco surprised me by asking if we'd mind putting on a Shaping demonstration. Carlisle surprised me further by agreeing. Most surprising of all, though, was the fact that Elise didn't appear to be the least bit confused by the conversation—merely excited. She knew about Shaping. Which meant I'd kept one more thing from her that I probably hadn't needed to.

At Carlisle's behest, I telekinetically shot weighted training balls at him, flicking my wrist with each throw mostly for dramatic effect. One-by-one, he pulled them into planar orbit around himself, forming an impromptu model of our four-planet solar system. Then he closed his eyes, and a radiance spread outward from his body, growing until he resembled a large sun at the center of his orbiting planets.

I laughed while the others clapped and let out appreciative *ooohs* and *ahhhs*, gaping at Carlisle's solar mimicry in open wonder. Even Phineas looked like he was dangerously close to cracking a smile.

And then there was Elise.

I don't know if it was the way the glow of Carlisle's sun was reflecting in her wide blue eyes or if I was just excited to be openly showing her this side of myself, but inspiration struck me as her eyes met mine.

I kneeled and placed my palm to the mat, feeling out along the floor with my extended senses until I found the stone at Elise's feet. Before I had time to think it through, I tapped into the energy from the lights above and let it flow through me, willing the image in my mind to reality.

There was an intake of breath across the room—Elise's, I thought. I kept the energy flowing and felt more than saw the small tendril of stone begin to sprout from the slab at her feet. The lights dimmed then flickered as I drained their energy to my purpose. For a few seconds, the room was lit only by Carlisle's light.

My head and chest buzzed with the crackle of channeled energy—more than I was used to handling. A chill crept through me. And, in the yellow glow of Carlisle's sun, we all watched as the stone stem thinned and blips slowly emerged to form into the shapes of petals and leaves.

I released my energy sources, and the lights shot back on in the room, brightly illuminating the surprisingly passable stone flower I'd just grown out of the floor. I stared at the tiny sculpture, every bit as stunned as everyone else.

James gave a few excited claps, then stopped at the look Phineas gave him. Franco was staring at the flower as if he were assessing whether its presence were some kind of security threat.

I'd made a mistake.

It was only a flower. But I knew that the feelings that had called it forth were not simply friendly ones, and judging from the tension in the room, everyone else could see that too. Everyone, maybe, except Elise, who was still fixated on her flower, face alight as she traced the stone petals beneath her fingers.

Her eyes found mine and, for the briefest moment, it was just the two of us in that room. Then my racing heart pulled me back to the painful silence. It had stretched too long. Why wouldn't someone say something?

I glanced desperately back at Carlisle, whose radiance had dimmed, his planets now stationary.

"Help! I didn't mean to do it."

He frowned a little, and I thought he might leave me to flounder.

Thankfully, he wasn't so cruel.

"I hope you all enjoyed the rousing finale," he said, allowing his radiance to die out completely and his stationary planets to shoot over and resume their existence on the shelves as ordinary training balls, "but I think Hal and I better get to our own practice now. As impressive as Shaping flowers is, I can't imagine it's going to be much help in the coming days. Allow me to fix that for you."

He extended a hand, and, across the room, the stone flower gave a sad twitch and reluctantly melted back into the floor, restoring the grainy gray surface to its original state.

I kept my mouth shut, embarrassment and gratitude and indignation all warring for position inside.

The unmaking of the flower, along with Carlisle's peaceful words, quelled whatever troublesome thoughts were brewing in Franco's mind—or drew a cordial smile out of him, at least. "Of course, of course. Thank you for letting us watch. It took me back."

Took him back? To what, exactly?

Now didn't seem like the time to ask.

Elise's gaze lingered on the spot where the flower had receded into the floor, then she gave me a sad smile and turned to join the others as they left.

"How bad was that?" I asked when they'd gone and we were sitting down to move on to telepathic sparring.

"It could have been worse," Carlisle's voice came to me, *"but you need to be careful, Hal. Mindful. Respectful. For the mission, if nothing else."*

I hesitated. *"Are you displeased with me?"*

"The situation would be less complicated if the two of you could set these feelings aside," he finally replied. *"But no, I'm not upset with you. I only ask that you avoid stepping on Franco's toes like you just did. My approval doesn't matter. For now, his does."*

"Thank you," I sent, hoping he could feel the sincerity of the thought.

I wanted to correct him and point out that Elise and I were only friends anyway, despite what I might feel. But the thought of broaching that topic with Carlisle made me want to squirm, despite the fact that he'd been inside my head multiple times in the past days.

"How did I even do that, by the way? Everything else I've learned has been so deliberate, but I didn't even think twice about it. It just kind of happened."

"You were inspired," he sent with a tone suggesting it was the most obvious thing in the world. *"Most refer to what you just did as Expression. You've seen how Shaping can be approached one simple transfer at a time, each with fairly predictable laws and balances. If what you've practiced so far is the hard science of Shaping, then Expression is the art."*

I frowned. *"I don't understand. I mean, I still drew energy from the lights. It was still a transfer."*

"Yes. The laws of conservation will always apply. It's more that, in the right context, with the right emotions and strength of will, Shapers can sometimes accomplish more abstract, complex feats than they might otherwise be able to frame accurately in their minds, based on their limited understanding of physical law."

"Ah. That kind of makes sense. I guess."

He studied me thoughtfully, looking like he had more to say on the matter. Finally, though, he dropped whatever it was, and we settled in for the day's lesson.

CHAPTER 24
SLIP

That night, after a hard day's training and a perfectly civil dinner with the others, my wandering feet carried me back to the training room. I sat for a long while at the edge of the matted floor, fingers tracing the cool stone slab where I'd coaxed the flower into existence earlier that day.

Even after Carlisle's explanation about Expression, I still didn't quite understand how I'd done it. I wished he hadn't erased it, but I didn't really blame him. Idly, I wondered if I'd be capable of recreating the sculpture. I didn't see why not, but I also wasn't remotely sure how I'd even start.

"We're gonna have to get another training room," came Elise's voice from the doorway.

I barely managed to contain a startled jolt, absorbed as I'd been in my ruminations. She was leaned up against the doorframe in her dark, form-fitting training clothes, studying me.

"Provided I ever wanna get another productive session in, at least," she added.

"Sorry, I was just, uh…" I glanced at the flower spot, unsure what to say.

"I know," she said, her expression softening. "It was beautiful, Hal. Probably the nicest thing anyone's ever made for me." She smiled. "And when I was younger, Phineas made me this super kick-ass wooden pony, so that's kinda saying something."

I snorted at the thought. "What is it with you and that old grouch? You seem to be the only person on Enochia he likes."

"Nonsense," she insisted, furrowing her brow.

"Oh yeah?"

"Well… he's at least slightly fond of James. Though I don't think he'd ever admit it."

I smiled. "So those two have been with you that long, then?"

"My happy little family, ever since Mom passed," she confirmed. "Three grown men trying to raise a girl," she added with an exaggerated roll of her eyes. "What a fun twelve years it's been."

"Has it really just been the four of you all these years? I mean, do you at least get to, you know, get out sometimes?"

"Sometimes." She wrinkled her nose. "Although Daddy Dearest almost always sends Phineas with me, sooo… Not so easy, making friends and whatnot when you have a grumpy old bear for a shadow. Not that I don't have any friends or anything, but…" She shrugged and tried to laugh it off. "Okay, so maybe I don't have so many friends."

"Hey, no, I'm not trying to say…" Alpha bless my awkward bones. The last thing I'd wanted to do was hit a nerve or sound like I was judging. Somehow, I'd just managed to accidentally do both. "I mean, I can count on my fingers alone the number of times I'd stepped outside of Sanctuary before this all started. I just meant…"

Her eyes crinkled with a smile as she watched me fumble.

"… that that sounds lonely, I guess," I finished, almost certainly blushing now. "But hey, I'm right there with you these days."

Her smile widened. "And aren't I just sooo lucky for that."

I met her eyes, and her expression sobered a few shades.

"I really am glad you're here," she said softly.

"Me too."

I only half-heard my own words, on account of her eyes doing that thing they did sometimes where they'd pull me in and then drop me off the side of a cliff. The gaze lingered. Any moment, my thundering heart was going to pop out of my throat, and yet I couldn't look away.

She was the one to break our eye contact this time, an honor that normally went to me. I'd gotten the impression she actually rather liked watching me squirm in these quiet moments.

Had I done something differently this time? Something wrong?

I looked back at the floor, trying to still my racing heart. "Sorry about your flower."

"No, I'm sorry about the way my dad..." She was staring at her feet, searching for the words. Finally, she gave up and threw her hands to the air. "I just don't know what he expects me to do, trapped in here like a prisoner all the time! Like"—she spread her hands to the house around us—"what is this?"

"This... is a training room. Pretty nice one, too. Though I hear it may have a lurker problem."

It was a bad joke. I admit it. But I had nothing else. I just wanted to make her smile. So, I held my breath on the end of her incredulous stare, waiting.

When she finally did laugh, I'm pretty sure it had more to do with the look on my face than my joke, but I counted it a win anyway.

"Alpha, you're such a dolt!"

I rolled to my feet and pointed a finger menacingly. "Take it back!"

She arched an eyebrow in a rather alluring fashion. "Or else?"

Lacking a clever response, I decided to go for shock factor instead. I crossed my arms dramatically and channeled the necessary energy to bring the air around us to a gusting swirl that tugged at my tunic and set Elise's ponytail dancing.

"Oookay..." she said as the buffeting wind died down.

"Are you sufficiently impressed?"

"Maybe," she said, her eyes bright and curious. "How does it work, exactly?"

I uncrossed my arms. "What, Shaping?"

She nodded.

I hesitated, but the expectant look in her blue eyes broke me before she even had to press the matter. She already knew Shaping existed. From there, I couldn't see how explaining the specifics would really matter.

Mostly, I was just excited to finally tell her something of substance without feeling like I was breaking the rules.

"Well, it basically all comes down to energy exchange. You take it from one spot and use it to make something happen somewhere else. Like just now, I drained heat from the air and used that energy to push other patches of air around, which started a kind of cascade of different air densities and temperatures all trying to stabilize."

"That's..." She frowned. "Oh."

"You seem disappointed."

"No, it's just... Well, from the stories I've heard, it just always sounded more magical, you know?"

I cocked my head. "What stories *have* you heard, exactly? And where from? I'd never heard a peep about Shaping before I met Carlisle."

"My dad does trade information for a living. Or did, at least, before he decided to bolt the doors and hole up with a pair of dangerous terrorists."

I swallowed, my stomach sinking at the unanswerable questions I expected to follow.

Instead, Elise continued on as if the whole terrorist thing wasn't worth concern. "He's heard all kinds of stories. He used to tell me tales about the Shapers, and the, uh… Em-yoos… Em-yute… Agh, it was something…"

"The Emmútari," I offered.

"That's the one. He was fascinated by them. Used to talk about 'em a lot." She shrugged. "I guess I was fascinated too. I'm not surprised he wanted to help Carlisle with… whatever this thing is that you're all doing."

She looked away abruptly, her jaw quivering.

I cringed, realizing her casual comment about us being terrorists had been anything but. This situation was taking a toll on her. Not that I could blame her one damn bit for that.

When she turned back to me, her eyes were wet and imploring.

"I'm scared, Hal." Her voice was quiet, desperate. "And not just because you could have died the other night. The only other people I really care about in this world are all caught up in this thing, too. And meanwhile, everyone just expects me to sit quietly in the corner and… and do what, exactly? Pray that you won't all be dead next cycle? Grop that."

Her tears were spilling over now.

I watched the clear rivulets flow, working my mouth noiselessly, praying for the words to defuse the situation. I wasn't sure they existed. So instead I reached out to take her hand.

"I deserve to know," she said quietly.

Seeing her crying, so clearly in pain, I felt the aching tug of my own phantom tears. I couldn't stand it anymore. She was right, and I wanted nothing but to explain to her what was happening. But I couldn't say the words.

So I closed my eyes and thought them instead.

"It's the raknoth, Elise. We're trying to stop a bunch of demonic parasites from destroying Enochia because we're the only ones who can!"

It was a cowardly move on my part, and I hated myself for it.

I knew she couldn't hear me. My message wouldn't make it to her, and some scuddy part of me would still get to feel like I'd tried somehow—like I wasn't just going to stand there and watch her cry her eyes out over an undeniably scuddy deal. Despicable.

Only she wasn't crying her eyes out when I opened mine again.

She was just gaping at me, eyes wide.

"What…" She took a step back, holding a hand out as if to keep me at bay.

It wasn't possible.

She took a sharp inhale to clear her runny nose. "What in demon's depths was that? What's a raknoth?"

It just wasn't possible. And yet she'd clearly heard the telepathic message she had no way of hearing.

Alpha only knows whether she caught the next one.

"Oh, scud."

CHAPTER 25

FIRE AND ICE

Carlisle and I trudged the streets of Divinity in pouring rain, watching the shadows for unfriendly eyes.

"It was reckless," he sent, not pausing ahead or even looking my way.

I wasn't quite sure if he was referring to my actions over the past hour, or to Franco's. Probably both.

"She wasn't supposed to hear," I sent back. *"It was only supposed to..."*

It didn't matter now. The damage was done.

"Let this be a lesson on all reasoning that begins with 'supposed to.'"

I scowled at a puddle underfoot, fighting the temptation to argue.

"How is it possible she heard my thoughts?"

"You know the answer to that."

"She's gifted?"

He walked on silently ahead.

"Did you know?"

There was a shift in him, something like the equivalent of a mental sigh. *"No. Franco has never allowed me to test her for any latent ability. But it was a possibility I might have been wise to inform you of. It might have even played some intangible hand in the... affinity you so quickly felt for one another."*

"But why suspect it was a possibility at all?"

"Elise's mother, Liandra. She was a Shaper."

For some reason, the answer didn't really surprise me. Not as much as the implications, at least.

"But my parents…"

"The gift is not always passed directly. It might skip generations. It might not even be hereditary, for all we know. But there's a reason Elise has been wearing a cloaking pendant since Liandra died."

"I hadn't realized she—Wait…"

Something had clicked in my mind. Something Carlisle had said about Franco's wife losing her life mixed up in business like ours. And twelve years ago. That's when Elise said her mom had passed. Twelve years.

The same twelve years since Carlisle had seen seventeen Shapers slaughtered at the hands of the raknoth?

"Was… Did you know her before? Liandra?"

This time, Carlisle did stop. He pulled into the shadows of an alleyway and waited for me to catch up, face buried beneath his hand in what could've been exasperation—or overwhelming sorrow.

"Now is not the time to discuss this, Haldin. Suffice it to say that Elise was not the one I originally crafted that cloaking pendant for. After Liandra… was taken, I gave it to Franco, delivered the news, explained what pieces he didn't already know. He was devastated, of course. But he took the pendant and told Elise that it had been her mother's and that she must wear it at all times so that Liandra could always watch over her. It was enough. He never wanted to know if she possessed the gifts that had been the death of her mother."

It was a lot to process.

I tried to picture whether Elise had been wearing her pendant tonight when my thoughts had slipped. She must not have been. But why? What had motivated her to remove it after all these years, tonight of all nights?

I thought of the stone flower and her questions about Shaping. Of her tears, and her talk of her family.

"I take it Elise doesn't know any of this?"

"I'm not sure what Franco's told her. She clearly has some inkling of the existence of Shaping, but I'd not be surprised if Franco had kept the rest hidden."

No. I wouldn't be either.

Since we'd left Franco's, I'd been trying to understand exactly how in Alpha's good graces things had unraveled as spectacularly and rapidly as they had. Suddenly, though, it all made a lot more sense.

The man had come completely unhinged when he'd realized what I'd let slip to Elise. I'd never forget the dark look on Franco's face when he'd thrown open the door and stormed into my room, growling accusations.

I'd tried to apologize. Tried to explain that it had been an accident and that it turned out Elise had an incredible gift. Of course, knowing what I knew now, his subsequent explosion was a bit less mystifying. He'd even taken a few swipes at me.

Now, I kind of wished I would have let one of them land. Maybe it would have helped him get his head on straight. Maybe I even deserved it. I wasn't sure anymore. But when Elise had come running, defending me, yelling at him to stop… that had been the final straw.

Franco had screamed at me to get out. I'd tried to talk reason into him—to remind him of the raknoth and ask him what any of this would matter if we didn't stop them. Then the furniture-throwing had started, and Carlisle had appeared to tell Franco we'd simply go back to our hideout for the time being.

Too bad we'd left our skimmer waiting a couple miles away in Carlisle's underground lot.

It wasn't exactly a smart idea for the two of us to be wandering the streets of Divinity. In fact, given our brands as wanted terrorists, it was plain stupid. But at least it was dark, and the pouring rain had cleared most of the usual foot traffic out of the streets tonight.

So, hoods up and heads down, we trudged on.

I didn't know what our next move was—how long it might be until I saw Elise again, when and where our next shot at the raknoth might come. The persistent rain didn't help my spirits, either.

I hastened to catch up to Carlisle in the yellow glow of the streetlights and the pale blue of the various displays that plastered the building sides and rained their own downpour of advertisements on the few pedestrians who skittered about trying in futility to keep their heads dry.

"I'm sorry," I sent as I drew up beside Carlisle. *"I should have been more careful."*

"I won't argue there." Another mental sigh. *"But it's not you I'm upset with. I understand what losing Liandra did to Franco, but the man has simply lost all reason where Elise is concerned. Trying to keep her safe from the truth was one thing at the start, maybe, but after everything we've learned? And wanting to keep her true nature hidden all the while? Bah."*

"He'll come around, right? He's too smart to think he can just sit under his rock and hope the raknoth play nice."

Plus, he still had all the Vantage data. I had a feeling Carlisle wouldn't take no for an answer where that was concerned. None of us could afford to sit back and ignore what the raknoth were up to.

"I trust he will. It's just a question of how much time he needs and how much time we—Stop walking."

I almost didn't register his words in time to slow down beside him as he drew up and pointed up at a big, bright ad display ahead of us. An ad display for some kind of feminine product.

Something was wrong.

I didn't see anything, but I trusted his instincts just as much as my own, if not more.

"Seekers," he whispered in my mind.

Cold fear clutched at my stomach.

Then I saw it—a distortion in the air, maybe fifteen feet to our left, where the walkway lines and the falling raindrops subtly warped around what appeared to be empty space. The telltale sign of an optical shroud. And once I'd spotted it, I noticed another.

Specters?

I did my best not to react.

Whoever it was, they had us caged against the building, holding perfectly still now, probably waiting to see if we'd actually noticed them or if Carlisle just had an odd fascination with women's hygiene.

"How many?"

"Two Seekers, four guards. You focus on the guards."

Six on two, us unarmed?

I tried to keep my expression neutral.

I couldn't see them, but the tension in the air was palpable now. We'd been paused for too long. Any second, they'd throw demons to the wind and jump us. We couldn't wait for that.

Carlisle was of a similar mind. *"Close your eyes."*

My last glimpse was of him raising a foot as if to stomp the ground. Then a violent white flash lit the darkness, nearly blinding even through my eyelids, and a gust of rain and air slapped my face on the tide of an odd, magnetic thrum that washed over me in a sea of tingles.

Six forms had appeared in the street when I snapped my eyes open, most of them reeling from Carlisle's flashbang, trying too late to cover their eyes. A few of their shrouds were still sputtering out.

Where I'd expected the dark armor plates of the Specters, four wore the white and gold of the Sanctum Guard. It wasn't hard to figure the other two were the Seekers, one in a dark gray long coat, the other—

My stomach fell as I recognized the slick face and green canvas jacket.

Smirks.

Before I had time to dwell on it, Carlisle stepped forward and telekinetically hurled a thick hunk of ice he'd apparently conjured from the rain water at the two Seekers. Smirks shoved Gray Coat aside and dove the other way himself to avoid the projectile.

No time to see what happened next.

I charged the nearest of the Sanctum Guard, dialing my cloak out as I went. He was still squinting from Carlisle's blast, but his rifle was shifting my direction.

I gathered my strength and gave myself a telekinetic boost as I leapt, flipping in the air, and landed right behind him. In a smooth motion, the Guard dropped a hand from his gun, drew a knife, and jabbed it back at me, reverse-grip.

He was quick. I was quicker.

I caught his forearm. Kicked the back of his right knee, driving him down to the ground. I planted my knee against his knife arm and yanked. Bone cracked with a sickening sound. His scream turned my stomach, but I forced myself to grab the knife from his now-limp hand and drive a hard kick into the back of his helmet.

He crumpled to the rain-soaked street, and my rising guilt was quickly snuffed by the sight of the three Sanctum Guard who now had a clear line of fire on me.

I tucked into a diving roll to put the Seekers and Carlisle, who was somehow swatting aside Gray Coat's fireballs with his bare hands, between myself and two of the soldiers.

That left only the third Guard to worry about for the moment.

I rolled back to my feet and chucked the knife at him. He deflected it with an armored forearm, but by the time he brought his rifle back to bear on me, I was nearly on him.

Just not nearly enough as I felt his finger tighten on the trigger.

Without thinking, I threw myself horizontal, legs first. The rifle barked. I twisted in the air and kicked, not entirely sure if I'd just been shot or not. My foot connected, then I slammed to the pavement with a grunt.

The guard swore as something clattered to the pavement several feet away. He was reaching for his sidearm. I scurried back to my feet and kicked him in the armored chest as hard as I could, then I thrust a hand out and added a strong telekinetic shove to propel him straight into Smirks.

My head and arms buzzed with the surge of channeled energy as the two men crashed to the ground amid growled curses. I scanned for the next threat, and my insides went cold.

The other two Sanctum Guard were flanking their way around the Seekers' brawl with Carlisle, and they'd have a clear line on me in about two seconds.

Too much space between us. Not enough time.

I needed cover. But there was none.

They raised their rifles.

I didn't know what to do. I raised my hands helplessly, willing them to stop—willing it all to stop.

They opened fire.

The first slugs hit like rapid fire punches right into the center of my being—half a dozen in the blink of an eye, each one a small inferno. Only...

I gaped, taking in the sight ahead.

… Only the slugs hadn't hit me. They hung motionless a few feet in front of my outstretched hands. And that fire pouring through me? Energy, I realized.

I'd caught their slugs.

The Sanctum Guard, who looked as shocked as I felt, recovered their wits and tensed behind their weapons, ready to fire again.

I focused my will and let the absorbed energy go with a thrust of my palm and wordless cry. My telekinetic lance caught one of the men and sent him corkscrewing to the pavement. His partner stumbled in the wake but quickly recovered.

Head swimming with the exertion, I reached out and telekinetically ripped the rifle from his hands. It caught on his back by the strap. I pulled more energy, steam rising around me now, and hurled the rifle down with enough force that the Sanctum Guard went with it, face smacking to the pavement.

The other Guard was getting back up now. My vision was darkening. I reached out to slam him to the pavement with telekinesis anyway, and... nothing.

Without warning, I'd lost him like someone had slipped a blindfold over my extended senses. I tried to reach out again. Couldn't.

And that's when I realized I couldn't move, either.

"Got ya, you little scudder," a voice growled in my head.

My stomach fell through the floor.

I threw myself behind my mental defenses, but it was too late. Smirks had me, and I could only watch helplessly as the Guard ahead regained his feet.

At the edge of my vision, Carlisle slammed one of the Seekers to the ground. Apparently not Smirks, though, because I remained immobilized.

The Guard took aim.

To the left, Carlisle caught Smirks in the side of the head with a glowing, outstretched palm. The Seeker sagged into a motionless pile. Control returned.

Too late.

The rifle roared, and something punched into my side, frighteningly abrupt, as I dove.

I hit the ground like a sack of bricks, stunned senseless. It took the pain a surprisingly long time to come. I swear I saw the blood first. It stained a wide swatch of my shirt, running thick from my sleeve down my hand to mix with the rain into thin, watery streams of pinkish-red that dribbled from my fingers to the pavement.

Drip. Drip.

"Hal!" Carlisle's voice snapped me back to reality.

And with it, the pain—sharp, fiery agony that blossomed in my right shoulder and screamed its way through the entire side of my body. I tried to focus

After that, my account of the fight was hazy.

The Guard who'd shot me tried to shoot Carlisle. Ended up shooting Gray Coat somehow thanks to a clever move on Carlisle's part. Gray Coat died in wide-eyed surprise, a neat hole in his forehead.

Carlisle extended a hand, the wrath of Alpha in his eyes, and the shooter rocketed into the building behind so hard that he might have died on impact.

All threats accounted for, I laid my head on the rain-soaked pavement and closed my exhausted eyelids. In the aftermath of the fighting, the street was wonderfully silent, save for the steady patter of the rain. It was comfortable, in a way. Comfortable enough to sleep.

Something slipped under my head. A hand.

"Hal." Carlisle, shaking me gently, his voice brimming with urgency. "Haldin? Hold on. I'm—" His attention snapped elsewhere. He raised a hand, and there was a smack and a groan from someone before he turned back to me. "I'm going to stop some of the bleeding."

Pain lanced through my side as he placed his hands to my right shoulder and arm and announced, unnecessarily, "This is going to hurt."

Searing heat pierced from his hands. I screamed.

The pain doubled. Quadrupled.

My scream outlived the air in my lungs.

Then, just before I lost consciousness, Carlisle withdrew his hands, and the heat faded.

My throat was raw, and I smelled charred meat in the air. The pain was breathtaking. Enough that I kind of wished I had passed out.

"Can you walk?" Carlisle asked. "We have to get to Franco's."

Whether or not I was losing less blood now, I felt even weaker than I had before Carlisle had decided to "help" me. My vision was swimming, my thoughts thick like syrup. I couldn't imagine pulling myself to my feet right now.

I tried to say so but couldn't seem to get much further than, "Nnnn…"

He laid a hand on my chest. "Come on, Hal."

"—don't think Franco will be—"

"You let me worry about Franco," he said. "Now I'm going to help get you moving. Try to take it easy."

Take it easy?

I could do that. Easy.

In fact, I was already fading into unconsciousness. At least until Carlisle's hand did something tingly to my chest, and a bolt of pure adrenaline pulsed through me. I gasped at the intensity, bolt upright and eyes wide before I knew it.

"Holy scud!" I scrambled up to my feet. "What was that?"

"Just a little boost," Carlisle said, rising. "It won't last long, though, so let's move. Just be careful with your wounds."

"Right! Yeah. Makes sense. Let's do it, then. Let's go! Damn, this feels better."

I had to consciously try to keep the words from pouring out of my mouth.

My hands. I needed to be doing something with my hands—or the good one, at least. I started drumming on my leg as Carlisle walked over to Smirks' unconscious form. He removed the Seeker's palmlight and tossed it to the pavement. I shifted my weight and started tapping my feet.

Sweet Alpha, I was twitchy.

I couldn't help but think of James, and before I knew it, I was giggling about it.

Carlisle scooped Smirks' unconscious form over his shoulder and started back toward Franco's. "Come on, Hal."

I bounced along beside him. "Prisoners? We're taking prisoners now?"

"Just the one," he said, turning down a narrow alleyway. "I'm not sure how they found us, but I don't want to leave him to do it again."

Made sense. As did the detour.

There was no way our fight had gone unnoticed. True, we'd been in a seedy area, and there also hadn't been a soul in sight when the fighting had started. But there'd been gunfire. Reinforcements would already be on the way.

I gladly matched Carlisle as he sprang into a light run, Smirks bobbing limply up and down on his shoulder. We stuck to the back alleys as much as possible, not keen to be spotted by any curious eyes. Especially not with an unconscious man in tow.

At first, the going was easy, and I barely even noticed the pain that had been excruciating only minutes earlier. With each passing minute, though, the boost waned.

By the time we drew up to Franco's door, my exhaustion had returned, stronger than ever. My body felt oddly distant and vaguely gelatinous, like I might lose form and melt into the ground at any moment. A deep, throbbing ache was taking root across the right side of my body, and my mind felt fried, as if I hadn't slept for days.

"Weee're baaack," I called at one of the cameras.

Carlisle shushed me, and I let out a little chuckle.

So maybe I was getting a bit loopy.

Carlisle waited another few seconds then turned to the camera I'd addressed. "If you can't see, allow me to point out that Haldin's been shot. Twice. He needs help, and I strongly suggest you give it to him."

Even in my altered state, the intensity in his voice was a little bit frightening.

"Sweet Alpha, Carlisle," I mumbled. "That's not gonna make—"

The door panel flashed green.

"Huh."

Carlisle pulled the door open and helped me in, balancing Smirks on his shoulder all the while. I was stumbling up the stairs with Carlisle stabilizing me from behind when the door at the top hissed open and Elise came running out with a protesting James close on her heels.

"Hal?" she cried, rushing down the steps to meet us.

She pulled my left arm over her shoulders, slipping her right arm around my waist to support me the rest of the way. Carlisle followed silently, and James hung at the top of the stairs, fretting.

In the entryway, Phineas gave me a once-over and turned to Carlisle. "You brought a guest?"

Carlisle dropped Smirks to the floor with a muffled thump. "We'll need to have a chat. Can you find a spot for him?"

Phineas wordlessly scooped the Seeker from the floor and carried him off, past the stairs.

"Phineas?" Carlisle called. He removed his cloaking pendant and tossed it to Phineas. "Make sure that stays on his neck for now. And that he can't see anything that might give our location away."

Phineas gave an affirmative grunt and turned back to his business.

I was fading fast now. Elise all but hauled me up the stairs and toward my bedroom. My foot caught on the carpet, and I stumbled against her, my vision clouding with nebulous dots.

"Sweet Alpha, Hal," she said softly, with only a slight waver in her voice. Her face was pale, and I was pretty sure her fragile smile was solely for my benefit. She shifted my weight on her shoulders and pulled me forward again. "I can't leave you alone for ten minutes, can I?"

I think that was the moment I realized I loved her.

But maybe that was just the blood loss talking.

A small chuckle escaped me. Then my foot refused to take the next step, and I lurched forward.

Elise braced herself, but Carlisle's arms snaked in and caught me before I fell into her.

Together, they carried me the rest of the way. James was already bustling about the room, unpacking and organizing their assorted medical supplies. My stomach shriveled at the sight of the scalpel and forceps on a white sterile pad next to the bedside.

My escorts lowered me gently to the bed.

"Go to sleep, Hal," Carlisle's voice drifted to me from somewhere. "You're safe now."

I squinted and groaned at the glare of the overhead light James had clamped to the bedpost. It beat down on my face, unpleasantly warm and bright.

Then Elise's face slid into view, cutting out the light. The radiance outlined her face, giving her a positively celestial beauty as she leaned down and planted a light kiss on my forehead.

"I'll see you soon, stranger," she whispered.

There might have been worry behind her smile, but my eyes were already slipping closed, the corners of my mouth tugging contentedly upward for the simple presence of my raven-haired seraphim.

Blessed sleep took me.

CHAPTER 26
THE CALM

The field was lush and colorful, alive with the sounds and smells of nature. I took it in, squinting against the radiance of the clear afternoon sky. A shimmering lake stretched in front of me, calm and beautiful. Beyond its crisp blue depths, mountains rose to meet the sky, their peaks high enough that many of them were lost to distant accumulations of clouds.

A secure warmth pressed against my side.

Elise.

She smiled up at me with startlingly blue eyes, her chin resting on my chest. "Hey, stranger."

Alpha, did she make my heart race.

My cheeks warmed as I realized she could probably feel it, too.

"You're here…" was all I could think to say.

Her smile widened, which was inarguably a marvelous thing. And yet…

What was she doing here? What was *I* doing there?

"Where are we?"

She raised her head from my chest and looked around, frowning. "I don't know…" She brightened. "Isn't it wonderful?"

I laughed, and the nagging feeling diminished. "It is! It really is…"

She nestled in, and I lay back down, happy to enjoy her warmth. We basked contentedly in the sun, and I wished all the while that it could be that way forever.

But it couldn't, said the nagging thought. I wasn't sure why, but I knew this was only temporary. We weren't safe there. I could feel it.

As soon as I had the thought, the day began to darken. We traded an uncertain look and sat up.

A wall of dark clouds was rolling in over the mountains. But, no. That wasn't right. The storm clouds weren't passing over or around the mountains. They passed straight through, emerging out of them as if they'd arrived at one side and had simply refused to trouble themselves with circumventing the great, unyielding bodies of stone.

Movement below drew my eye. A dark figure, striding toward us over the surface of the lake. The storm clouds were following him, I realized. Bound to him. I knew before I could see his face that it was General Kublich.

He glided over the water, refusing the pull of gravity even as his storm clouds ignored the physical barrier of the mountains. At each point his boots touched the water, a turbid stream of crimson rippled outward, expanding as he continued forward until he glided along at the point of a murky, blood-red spearhead.

Elise was clutching my arm now. "Hal… Hal, what's happening?"

Kublich's eyes came alive with red fire. "Come, boy," he called, his voice booming off the backdrop of the mountains. "Let us finish it. Or will you run for a third time?"

I was on my feet before I knew it, anger and shame and outrage pulling me toward Kublich like a force of nature, apathetic to the icy fear clenching at my chest.

"Hal!" Elise cried out. "Don't!"

And then, inexplicably, she was shaking me. "HAL!!"

I snapped awake with a gasp. Cold sweat covered my forehead, and Elise held my left hand in a painfully tight grip, her eyes wide and alarmed.

I scanned the room.

No red eyes. No raknoth. Just a wide-eyed Elise, a good deal of pain beneath the warm haze of whatever drugs they'd given me, and the uncomfortable weight of sweat-soaked blankets.

I was in my bed at Franco's.

Elise gave her head a shake as if to clear it. "What the hell just happened?"

She looked like she'd just woken up as well.

"I don't know." I tried to throw the blankets off and found my right arm was fixed in a blue sling. "I was having a nightmare, I think."

"You think?! Was that The High General of the Legion?"

My mouth fell open. "You... you saw that? General Kublich?"

"On the lake," she added, nodding.

We stared at each other, mouths agape.

"Did we just—"

"Share a dream?" I said. "I think so."

"Oookaaay..." Elise let go of my hand and stood to start pacing the room. "But..."

"Telepathy," I said with more assurance than I felt. "Our minds are more open to it when we're sleeping, so we must've, uh, found each other, I guess."

Elise paused her pacing and spread her hands. "Oh, sure. Basic stuff, right? That was freaking weird, Hal! And why The General? Is he one of them? The raknoth?"

I hesitated.

"It's okay, Hal. My dad and I had a long talk while you were out. He's not thrilled, but I made it clear I'm not just gonna keep my head in the dirt anymore. He won't give you two the boot again. Plus"—she threw her hands up in exasperation—"maybe I deserve just a little bit to know why you keep coming back here half dead."

"You're right. You do." I reached out to her with my free hand.

She took it and sat back down, waiting.

"Kublich is one of the raknoth. He's... the one that killed my parents. Would have killed me too if Carlisle hadn't shown up. That's why I'm here."

"To make him pay?"

"Alpha willing, yeah. But, I don't know. It's more than just that. They're gonna eat this planet alive if no one stops them. Revenge or not, I can't just watch it happen."

She ran her free hand lightly over the bandages on my arm and shoulder. "You also can't stop them if you're dead."

"Well, if I don't—if someone doesn't—we're all dead anyway."

"That doesn't... I mean, Alpha, Hal"—she laid her hand on the side of my head— "things were turning dark in there."

I dropped her gaze. Tried to shrug it off. "I'm still not even sure how you got in there."

A glance at her neck confirmed her cloaking pendant was still absent.

She noticed my focus and touched the empty spot at her breastbone almost self-consciously.

"You should probably..." I started, before realizing I was about to walk myself into a corner.

But she was good. Much better than me. It took her all of a half-second to process the inconsistency.

"Son of a... You already know, don't you?"

I swallowed, afraid to answer. "I just found out about your mom tonight, or"—I glanced at my palmlight for the time—"last night, I guess. After the scudstorm."

She released my hand, studying me, her expression pensive.

"I wanted to tell you the minute I found out," I pressed on. "There are so many things I've wanted to tell you, Elise, but... Well, I did end up getting shot when I finally let something slip, so maybe my fears weren't totally unwarranted?"

She stared at me blankly then finally rolled her eyes, lips twitching upward. "Oh, boo-hoo..."

I showed her a guilty smile.

"Anything else you want to tell me?"

"I guess the first thing is to emphasize that you wear your pendant at all times from now on. It will keep you safe from—"

"Unfriendly minds. I know, I know." She frowned at herself. "Alpha, that still sounds weird. But yeah, that was the first thing Daddy Dearest told me when he'd calmed down enough to revert back to spoken language rather than interpretive furniture flipping. Carlisle gave me the same spiel an hour later, while I was watching James dig a slug out of your shoulder."

"Ah. Right. So then..."

"Well, I was hesitant to leave with you all..." She waved a hand helplessly. "And he said he had me covered for the moment anyway, so I just..." She shook her head. "I don't even know why I took it off in the first place yesterday. I barely ever do, but... Well, it was an interesting day. And now, finding out about my mom and everything, I just feel, I don't know, betrayed. And when Dad told me this thing was keeping my abilities hidden... It's just a lot to process."

"I'm sorry, Elise."

She shrugged, though her expression was bleak. "Hey, you started the revolution. Once you blew the lid off, he didn't really have any choice. He told me things he's been holding in pretty much my whole life. Being the last one to know obviously sucks, and I'm still pissed about it. But I don't know, it's kind of amazing. My mom, a Shaper. And now this." She tapped the side of her head. "It's crazy. I really just want to find out what else I can do."

I swung my legs over the edge of the bed. "Now that's something I can help you with. You know, as long as no one's gonna shoot me for it."

Taking to my feet, I decided I was getting entirely too accustomed to working through the pain of fresh injuries. As brightly as my two slug wounds lit up, though, it wasn't nearly as bad as walking around post-raknoth-smashing had been.

"Easy there, master Shaper," Elise said, hovering beside me. "I don't think you're in any shape to be hitting the mats right now."

I chuckled. "Maybe not, but sitting gingerly and talking you through some exercises, I can probably survive. We should probably see what the others are up to first, though."

"Yeah, it was a bit tense last night," she admitted as she took my arm to support me out to the hallway. "I think things might be calming down now that everyone's had a chance to at least try to sleep."

Once we got moving, I felt stable enough. Elise kept my arm in hers anyway.

"So did your dad fill you in on what we've been doing here? I mean, more than what I've said already?"

"You mean fighting the evil demons bent on world domination? Yeah, I think he mentioned something about that. Still trying to decide if you guys are all screwing with me."

"I wish I was."

She said nothing. Just glanced at me and quirked an eyebrow as if to say, *Oh yeah?*

For a second, my cheeks out-burned my slug wounds.

We found James and Franco in the kitchen. They looked tired.

Franco stood to face me, his expression guarded, and I tensed. Next to me, Elise radiated exasperation but remained silent.

Finally, Franco stepped forward and laid a hand on my uninjured shoulder. "I owe you an apology, Hal. I overreacted. Maybe by a long shot. It's... hard sometimes to keep a level head when it comes to the safety of your child. I'm just glad you're alive."

"Thanks, Franco." I patted his shoulder in return and immediately felt awkward about it. "I understand."

I wasn't sure I really did, but the apology surprised me, and I didn't know what else to say.

"You guys must be hungry," James said, rising from the table to grab more plates.

I was, I realized. Famished, in fact.

We all sat at the table, and I gratefully dug into a plate full of eggs and toast.

"Where's Carlisle?" I tried to ask around an indecent mouthful of eggs.

"Keeping an eye on the Seeker you two dragged back here," Franco said. He didn't sound thrilled about it. "We're going to have to figure out what to do with him. And quickly. I didn't sign on for holding prisoners, here. Especially not telepathic ones."

"I agree," I said. Which was wholeheartedly true, given Smirks' proclivity for mind-hopping. "Do you think he knows anything we can use?"

Franco shrugged. "I'm not getting my hopes up, but it's worth finding out. Rumor has it there are only twelve of them in service at any given time, so they might be privy to some dirty secrets."

"Only eleven now, I guess," I said quietly, recalling the Seeker who'd taken a bullet while tangling with Carlisle.

"Fair point," Franco said.

I felt Elise watching me with a frown.

"What about the decryption?" I asked. "Any progress?"

"All done!" James said.

Franco nodded. "It cracked last night. The drive just finished decrypting this morning."

"Anything good jump out?"

"There's a lot there," Franco said. "It's going to take some time to pull it into a cohesive whole, but I have a feeling we've got enough."

"Enough?"

"To expose the raknoth," Franco said. He traded an uncertain glance with James before returning to me. "What you said a few days ago, about the emergency broadcast bunkers..."

"Wait, no, that was..." I let out a chuckle. "That was a joke. They're two of the most well-guarded structures on Enochia. You don't just break into those things."

Franco held my gaze evenly. "And what if you had to?"

I tried to entertain the thought and ended up shaking my head. "It's crazy. We'd have to infiltrate Sanctuary or Haven first, either of which will be impossible with everyone already looking for us. And then, assuming we could even make it to the bunker and bypass the security protocols to start a broadcast, we'd have to hold the bunker until the broadcast was complete.

At which point, there'd be the minor issue of escaping from the literal army that would have us surrounded."

"I understand it would be difficult, but—"

"I think the word you're looking for is *impossible*. Unless…"

The others all perked up.

"Unless?" Franco asked.

"Dirty secrets," I mumbled. "Can't go through the gate. Can't go over the wall. Impossible. And there's no such thing as a backdoor into Sanctuary."

Franco leaned eagerly forward, seeing where I was going with this now. "But…"

"But there's no such thing as the Seeker core, either."

Franco was tapping the tabletop, lost in thought.

"You think this Seeker guy might know a way in?" Elise asked.

I shrugged and sat back, speechless, considering the implications of what we were discussing.

Franco started talking again, but I barely heard him.

Sanctuary. My home. The very fortress I'd spent my life training to one day protect. And here I was talking about infiltrating like the apostate terrorist they said I was. It felt wrong. But was that me talking, or seventeen years' worth of tradition and duty and memories, good and bad?

I didn't know. And I also didn't see a better way. The raknoth had to be stopped—there was no question there. Taking them out directly wasn't happening. Not with their twin armies between us and them. Sabotaging their blood racks and the hybrid operation would only slow them down—it wasn't a solution.

We needed the people of Enochia behind us. We needed the Legion, removed of Kublich's command. The raknoth might be vastly more powerful than us humans, but the might of the Legion could still prevail if we could only point them at the right target. Which all sounded great in theory. But could I really go through with attacking my own home just to try to save it?

I found myself wondering if my dad would have been willing to turn against his beloved Legion in order to see justice served.

He had put his own family in danger, hadn't he?

The silent accusation had passed through my mind a thousand times since their deaths. But, as I sat there waiting for the familiar tide of resentment and blame, it was also the first time I also realized with conviction that he absolutely would've cast the Legion into the depths too if he'd truly believed it was the right thing to do.

All this time, something inside of me had been trying to blame him—to hate him, even—for getting my mom killed. For bringing us front and center into this entire mess. He must've realized what his actions might cost, after all. And he'd gone on anyway. He'd invited disaster.

And now, knowing everything I knew about the raknoth, I was sure I would've done the same.

It wasn't his fault. And it wasn't mine, either. But, just like him, I needed to do what was right, no matter the cost. No matter what anyone else might think. Even if it meant people who didn't deserve it got hurt. The raknoth had to be stopped. And if there was another way, I didn't see it.

We needed a way into Sanctuary.

"—right, Haldin?"

I snapped back to the kitchen table to see Franco, James, and Elise all watching me.

"Huh?"

"I said only one way to find out," Franco said.

"Right." I stood from the table, half-finished plate forgotten, as they stared quizzically at me. "Why don't you guys see what you can dig up on that drive?"

"And you?" Franco asked.

"I think I'd better go have a chat with our new Seeker friend."

CHAPTER 27
GARRETT

I went to find Carlisle in what they called the basement of the house. In truth, it was actually a floor above street level, tucked away behind the entryway staircase. But it lay beneath the primary quarters of the house, and they used the space rarely enough that I hadn't even seen it yet, so, at some point, it had become "the basement."

It was a long shot, I knew, hoping that Smirks would have some secret way to get us into Sanctuary. But, then again, who knew anymore? Demons to the wind, there could be half a dozen backdoors. They could be common knowledge to all the specters and high-ranking officers, for all I knew. After everything I'd learned about the Sanctum, the Emmútari, and the Seekers—not to mention the raknoth—I had to wonder just how many unquestionable truths in my life had in fact been lies.

Phineas was sitting outside one of the rooms beneath Franco's study. He regarded the sling on my arm and tilted his balding head toward the door in indifferent invitation.

Inside, the room was empty but for Carlisle, sitting cross-legged on a table at the edge of the room, and Smirks, who was lashed to his chair with an amount of rope that seemed ridiculous until I remembered that, even confined by Carlisle's cloak as he was, he might be able to work his way through any bindings that were physically touching him.

His eyes tracked my entry, cold and predatory in a way that was at creepy odds with the easy smirk on his mouth. I felt the familiar urge to wipe the look off his face. At least there was that for stability in my life. Carlisle opened his eyes and seemed to return from some distant meditation as I scooted gratefully onto the table beside him, fatigue weighing heavy from my wounds.

"How are you feeling?" he sent.

"Hurts a bit. But I'll live."

At second glance, I noticed he was actually wearing his own cloaking pendant, and the one around Smirk's neck appeared to be a replacement, hastily fabricated on a polymer chip with ink runes.

"You did well out there, Hal. If I hadn't failed to keep this... goodfellow occupied, you wouldn't have been—"

"It's not your fault, Carlisle."

He looked less than convinced.

Hoping to lighten his gloom, I added, *"I just need to make it back here in one piece next time or Elise might kill me herself."*

That, at least, got a little lip quirk. *"Have you spoken to the others?"*

I nodded. *"Sounds like we might need a way into Sanctuary."*

Carlisle looked at me questioningly, but then understanding dawned. *"The emergency broadcast system, again?"*

I made a face. *"I'd rather not claim credit for the insanity, but I might have agreed it's our best shot once we have something to show. Think we could do it?"*

"I guess we'll have to if no one has a better idea. Franco's probably right about needing to get the people on our side."

Smirks was watching us like a hungry wolf, his brown eyes calculating.

"Have you learned anything from him?"

Carlisle shook his head. *"Invading an unconscious or sleeping mind can be problematically erratic. I should be able to handle him myself now, but by the time he woke, I figured it was more sensible to be safe and wait for you. I'm starting to get a bad feeling about having delayed, though. Are you ready?"*

"What's the plan?"

"Just think of it like another one of our mental spars. I'll do the brunt of the work this time, but you can see what it's like to attack instead of defend."

"Sounds safe."

"It'll be fine. Once we're in, all you have to do is focus on what it is you want to know."

"Like if he knows a quiet way into Sanctuary?"

"Precisely. Just hold the thought as steady as you can. The first time rooting in another mind can be a bit disorienting."

I imagined that went double for violent sociopaths. The thought of willingly crawling inside Smirks' head made me want to shudder just as much as the memory of him lounging around in mine. But I had a mission.

Carlisle hopped off the table and went to Smirks.

"Time to play?" Smirks asked.

Carlisle ignored him. *"I'm guessing he'll probably try to take your mind in the first few seconds, so brace yourself."*

I took a deep breath and drew the steel gate of my mind shut, preparing to hold against an attack. When Carlisle was satisfied, he adjusted his own cloak and plucked Smirks' pendant from the Seeker's neck. I half-expected Smirks to try to bite Carlisle's hand. Instead, he waited calmly for the cloak to be removed.

As soon as it was, his mind crashed against my defenses.

I held firm. Our eyes narrowed at one another. He slammed into my gate again. He was strong, but not like Carlisle. Even holding tight against him, I had ample focus left to feel Carlisle's mind snaking its way around Smirks'. The Seeker, however, didn't seem to notice until it was too late.

He retreated to his own defenses, eyes widening. Anger roiled up in me, creeping in from those places in my defenses he'd sought to break, startlingly quick and hot. Anger at the pain he'd already caused me. Anger at what he stood for. Anger at all of it. My hesitations fell away. Then I formed my mind into a sharp spear and hurled it at Smirks.

I punched through his defenses like a softsteel slug through roughspun cloth.

The fact that Carlisle was squeezing in on him like a constricting serpent at the time probably helped more than a little bit, but I still wasn't expecting to break through so smoothly. Just like I wasn't expecting the wild flood that rushed over me when I did.

Sights and sounds whirled through my mind, punctuated by a touch here, a smell there—all of it tied up in a mash of emotion. And, riding over all of it, I saw Carlisle and myself from Smirks' perspective. No, from *Garrett's* perspective. Garrett. That was his name. I knew it like I knew my own, just like I knew his anger and his fear.

The latter gave me pause. Then I reminded myself what he was—what he'd done—and I decided with certainty that the shifty bastard was still Smirks in my book. More importantly, he had answers. As if in response to the thought, memories that weren't my own flashed through my mind—or was it ours?—flitting from one thing to the next seemingly at random.

"Focus," came Carlisle's voice.

That's right. I had to focus on what I wanted to know. And as soon I remembered that, I began to realize the fleeting glimpses of Smirks' experiences weren't appearing randomly but rather in response to my own thoughts, as if I were recalling my own memories.

Right, then. Sanctuary.

How would we get into Sanctuary?

"How about you try the gate?" came Smirks' voice. *"Both of you be my guests and—"*

With a focused thought, I pushed his voice down, down, until it faded to a dull background buzz. I tried to keep calm. Tried to keep my focus clear over the rising irritation.

How could we get into Sanctuary, *unnoticed?*

Like that, we flashed to dark water. The Red Ocean, I remembered, as if I'd actually been there. A nighttime skimmer approach off the cliffs on the northwestern edge of Sanctuary. There was something there. A hidden passage. I focused more closely, and it began to unfold in rapid fire.

There was a way. A way Smirks knew by heart, with multiple access points to the Sanctuary subbasements. A way no one knew about, except the High General and a few trusted officers.

Had my dad been one of them?

Smirks didn't know. Didn't care. It was simply a secret between him, his fellow Seekers, their Sanctum handlers, and the High General.

He knew what Kublich was, I realized, delving deeper. But no. Not the entirety of it. He knew that Kublich was a vastly powerful telepath. Suspected that he might be something more, something darker. It frightened him. But not enough to stop. Not after a lifetime of slavery to the Sanctum. Not after the toil and the torture, the years of faithful service that had never once earned him anything other than the Sanctum's resentment and a loaded gun aimed at his back.

He was trapped. They all were. And Kublich was their salvation.

Kublich, and Kublich's master.

Smirks didn't know who the man was. Didn't know how Kublich and his shadowy co-conspirators had managed to avoid detection while ascending to such positions of power. Barely cared. Probably, they'd simply infiltrated the Sanctum first. The Sanctum controlled the Seekers. Who else would even be able to tell?

No, the only thing that shook Smirks at all was the human experiments —those garish super soldiers Kublich and his allies had created to aid their kind in the coming war. But that hardly mattered either. All that really mattered was what Kublich and his master had promised to those Seekers wise enough to join them.

A proper place in the new world, free from fear and condemnation.

"You won't stop us," Smirks growled. *"You or that damned wild hound you call a master. This planet has trampled us underfoot long enough."*

I wanted to laugh. To hit him. To scream at him for falling so completely into whatever bullscud story the raknoth had clearly sold him. Most of all, I needed to know who this shadowy master was. But something had sent a twinge of alarm through me—a snippet of a thought that was gone before I could even process it.

What had it been?

Nothing but defensive silence from Smirks. I started retracing my steps until it hit me like a bursting dam.

The hybrids. Smirks' so-called super soldiers.

A few of them had been out there last night, searching for us, scenting from the shadows while the Seekers and their Sanctum Guard made their rounds. Their noses were preternaturally keen, and they still had our scents from the labs. Just like they still had Smirks' scent.

Raw excitement was radiating from the Seeker now, bordering on hysterical.

They would have swept the aftermath of our fight, caught our scents. Smirks was sure of it. They would lead his allies here. They would be coming for us.

I tore out of Smirks' mind, back into my own body, and locked eyes with Carlisle, who looked to have just returned himself. I saw my horror reflected in his eyes.

"They're coming!" I said.

"That's right, you gropping steel sippers," Smirks snarled. "Let's see how you bastards do against—"

Carlisle slammed his elbow into the side of Smirks' head, and the Seeker slumped in the chair like his strings had been cut. For a moment, there was silence.

Then, outside, the soft but insistent alarm chime began, unmistakable in its message.

Carlisle looked at me, pale eyes bleak.

"They're here."

CHAPTER 28

TRAPPED

We were gropped, good and proper.

That was all I could think as I lumbered up the stairs after Carlisle and Phineas, the chime of the house's alarm taunting me each step of the way.

How many were out there?

How in demon's depths was I supposed to fight with my arm in this confounded sling?

The stairs alone left me panting, sharp pains pulsing from my wounds, driving a hot, sickly ache through my right side.

For now, I gritted my teeth and followed the others left at the top of the stairs. We nearly plowed into James when he came flying around the corner, fumbling assault weapons and a worn leather pack.

He skidded across the carpet like a children's toon character, paused for a shocked moment, then tossed one of the rifles to Phineas and handed the pack to Carlisle. "Load up, guys. We've got big trouble."

Carlisle checked the pack and handed me two energy cells, which I tucked away in my trouser pockets.

"Thought you guys might need the juice," James said.

"Good call," Carlisle said, slinging the rest of the pack over his shoulder. "Where are the others?"

"Elise is in security." James jutted his chin in the other direction. "I'm going to get Franco right n—"

An explosion shook the house, unmistakably from the direction James had just indicated.

We all exchanged a stunned look.

"Dammit," Carlisle muttered. "Let's go, then. Not you, Hal," he added as I stepped to join them.

I started to protest, but Carlisle silenced me with a hard stare.

"Get Elise below," Phineas rumbled.

"We'll get Franco and join you," Carlisle added.

"But I c—"

"You're in no shape, Hal." Carlisle's face was stern and weary. *"Protect Elise. If we don't make it back in two minutes, get yourselves out of here."*

"Carlisle, I..." There wasn't time to fuss or argue. *"Just please come back."*

Carlisle squeezed my good shoulder and went to join Phineas and James, who were already sweeping down the hallway, weapons raised.

I watched them go, then hurried around the corner and down the hall to the security room across from Elise's bedroom. Compared to the rest of the house, it was bare bones—nothing but a couple desks, several security camera displays, and Franco's rather respectable armory.

Elise was alone in the room, studying the camera feeds with dull shock written on her face.

When I got a good look at the displays, I saw why.

There looked to be an entire company of Legion troops swarming the building outside. At least two squads, I decided, trying to assess the feeds with a level head. Well over thirty men.

A sizable hole had been blown in the eastern wall of the building, and soldiers were already grappling their way up. I caught a flicker of Franco retreating from a room. A glimpse of Carlisle and the others rushing down the hallway.

"He went to get the drive," Elise said quietly, her voice flat, as the first few soldiers climbed into the eastern breach.

At the first dull cracks of gunfire, she flinched and appeared to snap out of her shock. "We have to help them."

Part of me wanted to agree. But Carlisle was right. I was in no shape. And I sure as scud wasn't dragging Elise in front of armed men.

"No. They're coming back." I went to the weapons racks, grabbed the pulse gun I'd used at Vantage, and slid an extra feeder into my arm sling for easy access. "Phineas told us to get below. What's below?"

As an afterthought, I grabbed a knife and clipped it to my belt. My hands were surprisingly steady. At least until another explosion shook the house, and the displays revealed a column of men storming up the stairs from street level.

Scud.

Once they were in, they'd be in perfect position to cut us off from Carlisle and the others. And they weren't in the mood to waste time about it, either.

Like its counterpart in the alley, the door at the top of the narrow stairwell was reinforced. They blew through the wall instead. As soon as it went, two of the soldiers peeled off from their allies like wild animals. The first one plowed through the entryway door with impossible ease—for a human, at least.

Hybrids? Could it be?

It was impossible to tell past the Legion gear and the closed helmets the pair wore. But what else could move like that?

Before I could think to answer, the display cut out. Others followed.

They were taking out our eyes.

"Elise, we have to move."

She didn't seem to hear me, staring at a display where Franco and Phineas were hunkered in the training room, Phineas leaning out from the doorway to lay down fire.

Then that display cut out too.

I could hear them now in the distance, shouting orders over the steady sounds of fighting.

"How do we get below, Elise?"

"Are they gonna die?" she whispered. "Are we?"

"Hey…" I shifted the gun to my sling hand and slid my fingers under her chin to direct her gaze to mine. "Hey, stay with me. No one's dying. It's gonna take more than a company to stop Carlisle. And as for us"—I stroked her cheek and shifted the gun back to my good hand—"I'll tear the entire Legion apart before I let anyone lay their hands on you."

Somehow, I managed to keep my voice steady despite the frightened energy I was fixing to combust with. Maybe it was simply that I meant what I said. Meant it to my core.

Her blue eyes searched my face, measuring the truthfulness of my words. Her head slowly began to nod, and then she snapped out of her trance and bent to pull up a flap of carpet.

There, right in front of the weapons racks. A floor hatch.

"An escape route," she said. "That's what's below. There's a tunnel and an old lev tram."

Thank Alpha. We had a way out. I just didn't know how the others were going to get to it with a couple squads swarming the house.

I reached out with my senses and was alarmed to feel several minds headed toward our side of the house from the entryway. The two leading the group felt alien. The hybrids, I guessed.

Before I had time to think better of it, I picked one of the human soldiers and threw myself at his mind as I had with Smirks. I barely even felt resistance. Sights and sensations flooded my awareness, and suddenly I was in the hall, and my fireteam was stumbling into my back as I stood there, motionless.

"What the scud, Derner?" someone snapped.

I tried to look around, and my vessel's head turned in crisp response to my will.

It was eerie. I didn't like it one bit.

But this was survival.

Derner's eyes showed me a house crawling with Legion troops. I couldn't see our friends, but the sounds of fighting were thick from the other side of the house. A snap flare—Carlisle's doing, I guessed—flashed through the hall and bleached my vessel's sight.

I felt disoriented soldiers stumbling into one another. Heard their muffled cries through Derner's ringing ears.

I grabbed the thumpers from his gear vest, pulled the pins, and tossed them blindly toward the head of the group moving for our side of the house. The last thing I felt was two of Derner's fireteam tackling him to the ground as I pulled out of his mind with a shudder.

"What is it?" Elise asked behind me, her voice tight.

I turned and saw with a jolt of surprise that Elise had pushed open a section of the wall to reveal a passage that looked to lead behind Franco's study.

Outside, the thumpers detonated with a pair of thick booms.

"Enemies coming for us." I closed the door to the hallway and locked it, trying to keep my voice calm as I went to pull the escape hatch open. "The hybrids can probably smell me. You need to get below. I'll hold the room until they're back."

She just went straight to the weapons rack, shaking her head.

"No. No way." She plucked a compact rod and gave it a twist. The ends sprang violently outward to yield a dark staff, which she twirled through a few revolutions with a whistling speed that would have been frightening if not for the grace with which she controlled it.

"If you stay," she said, deadly serious. "I stay."

She meant it.

I opened my mouth to say something—I don't know what. That I understood, but that I also couldn't lose her?

Another explosion rocked the house before I could speak.

More gunshots. The shouts of troops charging down the hall.

"Elise…"

There wasn't enough time to convince her. To tell her everything I needed to. So I reached out to her mind and showed her—the way I felt when she was with me, the way my heart soared when she smiled. The way I needed her to be safe now.

The tears welling in her eyes told me she saw it, that she understood. But she didn't climb down the hatch as I'd hoped.

She stepped past it, moving straight toward me.

Outside, the voices were growing louder, the thuds of heavy boots closer. Down the hallway, the sharp crack of splintering wood announced the first breached door.

I reached out to touch Elise's cheek as she drew close. To tell her to hurry.

My mouth was half open when she grabbed the front of my shirt and tugged, hard.

Her lips found mine before I knew what was happening, so alive and warm and vibrant with everything that was her that, for a precious moment, I forgot everything else. The impending danger. The fear and the pain. There was nothing but that kiss. The soft heaven of her lips against mine. The intoxicating closeness of her.

But it couldn't last forever.

Outside, another door splintered.

"I'm still not leaving," Elise whispered as she pulled back, holding my eyes.

"Clear," someone called down the hallway.

Boots thudded our way.

Alpha be damned.

I pulled Elise with me and hunkered down behind the larger of the two desks in the room.

It wasn't much, but it'd buy us a moment or two, hopefully while the men all filed neatly into the room to inspect the suspicious open hatch in the floor.

I counted seven in total as they paused outside the door. Two hybrids. Five men.

"I'll try to take the hybrids down first," I sent to Elise.

She gave an affirmative nod, some of her earlier fire giving way to tight-jawed fear now that the danger was palpable. She also clearly hadn't had time to put her cloaking pendant back on. There wasn't anything to be done about that now.

"Stay behind cover until—"

Something struck the door with a sharp thud. A boot, probably.

One of the hybrids must have taken the second kick, because it only took two.

The door splintered from its hinges and smashed into the opposite wall with a crash, followed promptly by a bone-chilling roar from the doorway.

Then they came.

CHAPTER 29
HARD RIDE

"What the scud was that?" someone cried.

Every instinct I had screamed at me to spin around and open fire as thudding boot falls paraded into the room.

"Hey!" another voice shouted.

Were they yelling at each other? At the hybrids?

Boots approached. Something hissed at the air.

I stayed crouched behind the desk, waiting, watching with my extended senses.

"What's this?" someone asked.

"They must've fled underground," another said.

The moment I felt the last man cross the threshold, I opened the channel to the energy cell in my pocket and telekinetically hurled the other desk at the doorway.

Energy crackled through my veins. A choir of shouts filled the room—soldiers scrambling to evade the heavy projectile.

For the most part, they failed.

The desk missed the hybrids but plowed into the mass of soldiers. In the ensuing chaos, I stood and opened fire. Or tried to, before the spots in my vision darkened and I found myself staggering to my knees.

Behind, something growling thudded into the desk.

Elise spun to her feet and cracked a savage blow to the hybrid's head.

I raised my gun in a shaky hand and fired three slugs at the creature's head before it could shake it off.

Two hit, and the hybrid dropped in a slack heap of scaly limbs.

I rose, glimpsed a weapon moving to the right, and fired without thinking. The shots probably didn't pierce the soldier's armor, but they did give him a seconds' pause. Enough time for Elise's sailing staff to crash into the side of his head, javelin style.

Elise was already flying after the weapon in a low somersault. She moved with stunningly fluid grace, rising, plucking the staff from the floor, and sweeping it into the soldier's chin all in one movement, then bounding without pause toward the soldiers untangling themselves from their ungainly pile under the desk.

The second hybrid watched her go uncertainly, then rounded on me and charged with an eager hiss.

I backpedaled, taking aim.

The hybrid dropped low behind the desk, cutting off my line of fire. Then, with a guttural chuckling noise, it rose and flung the desk at me.

I acted on reflex, casting my mind out, desperately pulling energy from the oversized projectile. The desk crashed down at my feet. My insides crackled with the energy of its halted flight.

I let it loose with a telekinetic blast.

The hybrid hit the floor with an irritated roar. A wave of exhaustion rode in and nearly made me do the same. I was in no condition to be channeling this much energy. Not that I had much of a choice at the moment.

Across the room, Elise's staff was falling on the recovering soldiers with brutal precision. One raised his weapon only to receive lightning-fast blows to gun, arm, and head. She reversed direction without pause and slammed her staff down on another's head.

Still another soldier—partially pinned beneath the desk—was sighting on her with his sidearm. I took a second to telekinetically slam his head into the ground and whipped my gun back up for the recovering hybrid.

Too late.

The hybrid leapt over the desk and knocked me roughly to the ground, setting my wounds on fire. A strong hand found my throat and yanked up until my feet were dangling. I couldn't breathe. I kicked as best I could.

The hybrid slammed me against the wall, expunging what little air remained in my lungs. My right side was a sea of pain. Black spots crowded my vision. The hybrid squeezed harder. I feebly tried my gun, but the hybrid had my arm pinned.

Darkness closed in.

"Hal!" Elise cried somewhere far away.

The pressure on my throat lessened, and the hybrid yanked my head to the side. My vision cleared enough to see the creature had torn its helmet off in preparation to bite my throat out.

Then I caught a flicker of motion, and the hybrid stumbled forward as Elise's flying staff rocketed into its back. I could barely see straight, but I felt my gun hand free as the hybrid planted its arms to keep its balance.

I pressed the gun to the creature's side and pulled the trigger three times.

The hybrid shrieked in pain. I drove my good shoulder into its chest before it could bite. It didn't go far—I was too weak right then to push it more than a few feet. But it was enough.

My fourth and fifth slugs found the hybrid's head.

I shifted my aim to the soldiers, scanning for the next threat, every part of my body burning in protest.

All clear.

I sagged back against the wall, gasping for air.

Then Elise was by my side.

"Are you hurt?" I groaned.

"Seriously? You get put through the wall by *that* thing and you're asking me if I'm hurt?"

A small grin tugged at my lips. "Yeah. Are you okay?"

She gave a shaky laugh, shaking her head. "You're ridiculous."

We both turned to look down the back hallway Elise had opened.

That's when I realized that the sounds of fighting had stopped elsewhere in the house.

Not good.

Two minutes, Carlisle had said. And it had already been at least three.

I reached out. More troops arriving in the downstairs entryway. And there, on one of the few undamaged security displays. Reinforcements arriving outside. Another company, at least.

"We have to go," I croaked.

Elise helped me to my feet, though my words had lit a spark of panic in her eyes—the beginning of the realization that the others weren't coming. That we were on our own.

"But, they're—"

"They might have made it out another way," I said, speaking quickly. "Even if they're captured, we can't help them right now. There are too many out there. We need to get out, regroup."

"No... No, no..." She said the word like she was chanting a mantra against reality.

"We'll find them," I whispered. "I promise, Elise. We *will* find them. But we have to go. Now."

She squeezed her eyes tightly shut and finally gave a reluctant nod. We hurried to the open hatch. One of the soldiers by the desk groaned something, whipping us both around, but then he slumped to the carpet.

I waved Elise to the hatch opening and the long, narrow descent by ladder below. She didn't argue. Just collapsed her staff to a more manageable length and clambered down the rungs. The sounds of approaching soldiers were growing too close for comfort. I scrambled after Elise and pulled the hatch and its cover closed above us without looking back.

For now, at least, we were on our own.

After an awkward and lengthy descent, the narrow ladder-well opened up to a dusty, low-ceilinged space formed entirely of permacrete. Elise flipped a switch on the wall, and a few dim lights flickered on to reveal the small lev tram in the center of the room, a relic of the old Divinity underway lines that hadn't been in common use since well before I was born.

I started for the tram... and paused when a flicker of something tickled at the edges of my senses. Had it been a sound? Just a feeling?

Elise was watching me uncertainly. "What is it?"

I shook my head. It was nothing. We needed to move.

"Come on." I hurried over and palmed the access panel by the tram's doors.

To my relief, they slid open.

Pale lights snapped on as we stepped into the compartment, illuminating lines of sickly green polymer seats along the walls. The contrast between the lights inside and the dimness outside blinded us to everything but our own reflections in the windows and only added to my uneasy sense that we needed to get far away from here, and fast.

"Do you know how to drive this thing?" I asked, moving instinctively toward the front.

There. A control console.

Elise appeared beside me. "I think it's pretty much a go button."

She wasn't wrong. At my touch, the console display powered up with a map of Divinity and a programmed route that would take us somewhere near the city's eastern outskirts. I didn't particularly care about the specifics. Anywhere was safer than our current location.

I tapped the *Begin Route* command and grabbed a handhold with Elise as the tram hummed to life, lifted a few inches from the ground, and began to accelerate.

We'd barely made it ten feet forward when something thumped on the roof.

"What was that?" I hissed, reflexively hunkering down and then shifting the gun back to my good hand as I cautiously approached the rear of the tram, where the sound had come from.

"What?" Elise asked behind me. "I didn't hear anything..."

My hand froze halfway to my pendant, the back of my neck tingling. Something about her tone.

All at once, it hit me, and I threw myself away from Elise, onto the tram seats. Just as her collapsed staff came whooshing through the air at my head.

I landed jarringly on my sling arm. A cry of pain tore out of me, the world blurring with it. Distantly, I noticed the clatter of my gun hitting the floor.

"Elise!" I groaned, awkwardly rolling around to face her.

Her eyes were vacant. Without remorse, she swung the club of her collapsed staff at my nearest knee. I rolled back onto my shoulders and flinched as the blow shattered the polymer seat where my legs had just been.

She moved to reset for another strike, but I rocked forward and hooked my legs around her torso and arms before she could. She struggled soundlessly, her vacant expression eerily unchanging.

I braced my mental defenses as best I could while wrestling to keep her under control. Then I pulled off my cloaking pendant and jammed it down around her neck.

The effect was instant. She gasped and nearly collapsed onto me, eyes wide, panting with the exhaustion she hadn't shown a moment earlier. "Hal, I—"

"Gun," I snapped, pointing to the weapon at her feet, sure now that I knew what had landed on the roof. Or who.

"What?" She looked around, clearly disoriented.

Mind-snatching had that effect.

"Gun!" I shouted this time, sensing the incoming threat.

Something clicked in Elise's eyes. Then the rear window shattered, and Smirks swung in from the tram roof. He landed roughly in the pile of glass.

Elise reached for the gun, but Smirks raised a hand, and the weapon sprang into the air toward him instead. Elise lashed out, lightning fast, and smacked the weapon down with her staff, then she lunged at Smirks, spinning into another strike.

He thrust both hands in her direction and plowed her over with an invisible wave of force.

The son of a bitch.

I rolled to my feet, fear and rage and pain all swirling into something dangerous in my chest. Smirks slammed into my mental defenses, but I held firm. He yanked telepathically at the gun that had fallen under the seats to the left, but I caught it with telekinesis and fought him for it.

Smirks wasn't smirking now.

For a long moment, we struggled on the two mental planes. Then I dropped my hold on the gun and lunged forward.

He caught the gun. I caught his wrist, pushed the weapon aside, and drove a hard kick into his stomach. He doubled over with a grunt. I ripped the gun from his hand. Smacked him across the head with it. Kicked him again.

He hit the rear wall of the tram, hands raised in pitiful defense, nearly toppling through the broken window. I pulled every last scrap of energy I could and helped the son of a bitch through. Or that's what I meant to do, at least. Instead of flinging Smirks neatly through the open window, though, I plowed him straight through the tram's rear door.

He sailed from the tram with a strangled yell, promptly swallowed by darkness, the tram door flapping in the rushing wind as if in pleasant farewell.

Then I hit the deck, exhaustion nearly robbing me of consciousness. Maybe it did for a moment. The next thing I knew, I was staring up into Elise's beautiful blue eyes, trying to place why they were so wide, so frightened—why she was crouched over me, hands clasped nervously to her chest like she didn't trust them.

The tram was quiet but for the rush of air at the open rear. I raised my head and watched the dark tunnel behind us, replaying those last hectic moments in my mind.

Had I just killed a man?

I didn't know. Somehow, I doubted Smirks would go down so easily. Maybe the more important question was whether I'd meant to kill him. Because when he'd attacked Elise...

I pushed painstakingly into a sitting position and met her apprehensive gaze. She hovered there, teetering on the edge, then finally plunged forward and wrapped me in a desperate hug, burying her face in the crook of my neck. I wrapped my good arm around her, holding her tight, lost for words. She was trembling.

"I couldn't stop, Hal," she whispered.

I squeezed her tighter with my good arm. "It's not your fault, Elise. It was Smirks. He… You're okay now. We're okay."

She shook her head lightly against my neck. "But the others…"

I swallowed, unable to find the words. Unable to do much anything other than cling to her as reality set in and cold dread filled my insides. Because as much as I wanted to believe they'd found a way to fight their way out of Franco's back there, what were the chances, really? Even Carlisle had his limits.

For all I knew, our friends were all dead or captured. Which left us alone and on the run. Two teenagers. No resources. The Legion might already be tracking this tram line—might already be waiting for us at the end. And if they weren't, Kublich would see to it we were hunted day and night. He'd find us. Just like the others. Just like my father. Find us and—

Elise shifted against me, startling me from my thoughts, and pulled back just far enough to meet my gaze. I saw my fears reflected in her blue eyes. But there was something more underneath it. Determination. The resolve to make this right.

She touched my cheek. My head wasn't spinning anymore.

"We're okay, Lise," I whispered, pulling her close again.

She didn't resist. Didn't argue. Just settled to the tram deck with me, both of us staring out into the rushing darkness behind, searching for some inkling of reassurance as the lev tram hummed on, carrying us toward Alpha knew what manner of fate.

But we were alive. We had each other.

It would have to be enough.

CHAPTER 30

REFUGEES

Alpha bless Franco was the theme of the day, I decided, as I settled on the darkening woodland clearing below and began guiding the old but serviceable skimmer down for a landing. Alpha bless Franco once for being paranoid enough to keep a working escape tram beneath his home. Twice for leaving this old skimmer waiting in the dusty old underway station the tram had brought us to. And probably more than thrice for having the foresight to load said skimmer's trunk with a neatly-packed kit of water, rations, and several other useful items for two young outlaws on the run.

A few feet into the descent, I glanced over at Elise's sleeping form, thought better of my manual control, and tapped on the autopilot's landing sequence. Despite my hours of sim practice, I hadn't exactly mastered the soft touch of skimmer flight, and the last thing I wanted to do right now was yank Elise out of sleep and right back to obsessing over the fate of the others.

After a long day spent mostly in tense silence, waiting for the Legion to come crashing down around us any moment, we still had zero idea what had become of our people. It wasn't like we could check the reels, or message them and ask. Falsified or not, the Legion would be closing in on tracking our palmlight IDs by now—assuming they hadn't already scanned them back at Franco's. Powering down our devices had been the first move we'd made once we'd gathered our senses back on the tram.

From there, the path had been less clear. Franco kept another safe house in Divinity, according to Elise, but we'd both agreed that, once the Legion started digging, even Franco's extensive precautions in hiding the place wouldn't hold up indefinitely. It had felt like too much of a risk. So I'd proposed we head for Carlisle's temple hideout to the south of Divinity—after taking the better part of the day to bury our tracks, so to speak.

An enormous eastward detour along the Red River later, we'd skirted through the historic city of Humility—a place notoriously light in its Legion presence—then doubled back, crossing over the river to the dense forest wilds that dominated that side of the Red River for hundreds of miles. I'd hoped to make the old temple by nightfall, but, between avoiding the autonav and sticking to the cover of the wilds whenever possible, the going had been slow.

Now, it was too dark to continue without lights or a night lens display, which this skimmer was too old to be equipped with. The distant lights of Divinity were still a good thirty or so miles northwest. Maybe we could've risked the skimmer lights. Maybe it'd been paranoid of me to disable the autonav back in Humility. But I'd seen one too many criminals hauled in by the enforcers for their tiny mistakes.

Tonight, we'd camp in the skimmer. Tomorrow, we'd find the temple and, Alpha willing, our people too. I held my breath as the skimmer descended the last few feet to the grassy clearing, suddenly terrified that the landing would wake Elise. I couldn't even say why. Maybe I just didn't want to admit out loud that we were still every bit as blind and on the run as we had been that morning.

The skimmer touched down, and Elise roused with a startled breath, glancing dazedly around at the thickening woodland darkness. "We're there?"

"Uh, not quite," I said softly. "Close, though. Just didn't wanna flip on the lights and make it easy for someone to spot us looking around for a secret hideout over here."

"Ah. Wait, *looking*? As in, you don't know where it is?"

"I know the landmarks. I'll be able to find it in the daylight. I think."

She looked less than convinced.

I tried to smile. "Don't worry, I've totally got this."

She softly laid forehead to palm. "I'm suddenly understanding where all those jokes about men and directions come from."

The day had left my mind short of witty replies, so I just went with,

"Yeah, well, we should probably eat and get some rest. Some of us have been busy flying all afternoon."

In truth, I'd been more than happy to let her rest, especially after she'd spent the entire morning flying us. But after everything else today, the teasing was the only thing that seemed to feel normal—the only thing that had let either of us crack a smile since the tram.

"Yeah, yeah," she mumbled, apparently too tired for witty replies herself. She reached for the door latch. "Well, some of us need to empty our tiny lady bladders first, if the big strong man doesn't protest."

She climbed out of the skimmer and shambled off into the darkness. I couldn't help but smile a little, cheeks warming, as I thought about the big strong man comment.

It had started at the end of our tram ride that morning, when I'd hopped straight into the driver's seat of the waiting skimmer and palmed the starter panel to no avail. Again and again, I'd tried, until Elise had rapped on the window—nearly startlingly me out of my seat—and made a perfectly polite *get out* signal with her hooked thumb. I'd obliged, she'd taken my place, and the skimmer had groaned obediently to life moments later.

Biometric access, I'd realized. Elise just insisted she had the magic touch. Which, in hindsight, had only made it that much more patronizing when I'd asked if she knew how to fly the thing.

"I do," she'd said, nodding very seriously. *"The big strong men taught me how."*

Amidst the stammering stream of apologetic clarifications that'd followed, she'd tapped the console and, holding my gaze while the skimmer lifted off, added that the skimmer had a full autopilot suite, and that she thought we *might* just be okay if only her big strong man could get the door for her, please.

Despite everything, we'd both been smiling by the time we pulled out.

It hadn't lasted long, and we'd barely talked since then—about the others, or anything else. Tonight, I expected, we might. But today, we'd just needed to survive.

It was maddening, not knowing whether the others were hurt, captured, or worse. The thought of losing Carlisle with my parents so fresh off the pyre was simply too much for me to stomach for more than a few seconds at a time. I could only imagine how Elise was feeling. I glanced at our deactivated palmlights for the millionth time that day, itching to power mine up and check the reels for news. But it was too dangerous.

Instead, I climbed out of the skimmer and went to take my turn in the woods. Afterwards, shyly using the skimmer as a partition, we attempted to wash some of the day's grime off with a bit of water and swapped what dirty clothes we could for the clean spares from the trunk.

"Leave the tunic," she said quietly, coming around the skimmer with alcohol and fresh bandages for my wounds.

I let her work without complaint, glad for her touch, for her scent—the scent that reminded me of the way her lips had felt against mine, even as we'd prepared to face death together. Glad again for the cover of night as she looked up to meet my eyes and the heat in my cheeks intensified.

Supper was more water and dried rations, leaned up together against the open trunk in the deepening darkness. It was a moonless night, with barely a star to see. Nothing but the mechanical act of swallowing the food I barely tasted, and the simple reassurance of Elise's shoulder pressed to mine.

Finally, we pulled the blankets from the trunk, blessing Franco once again for his uncanny provision, and went to make camp for the night in the skimmer.

Goodfellow that I am, I insisted Elise take the back seat of the skimmer, which was much more conducive to stretching out. Astute observer that she was, she noted that I was in far worse shape than she, and that she wasn't so sure my man bits—chivalrous and gargantuan as they so clearly must be— would even fit up front anyway.

She dropped into the front passenger seat before I could protest.

Grateful and warm of cheek, I crawled into the back and spent a few minutes shifting around until I found a reasonably comfortable arrangement. Then, for a while, I simply enjoyed the pleasure of not moving. I found myself wishing for a little starlight. As far-removed from the city as we were, the darkness was disconcertingly complete. I practically couldn't see the hand I held a few inches from my face.

Rivaling the darkness was the silence. Even at the temple, there'd been the low thrum of the electronics, the cycler, the occasional firing of the generator. Outside, in the clearing, there was little but the occasional hoot or rustle of the woodland nightlife. Inside the skimmer, it was almost dead silent. Silent enough that I became uncomfortably conscious of my every movement, of every breath that hung between us.

I could feel Elise there in the darkness, in a way I was pretty sure had nothing to do with my extended senses. *Just the two of us*, I couldn't help point out to myself, as if I could somehow forget. Just the two of us, together alone in the dark night.

When I'd climbed into the skimmer to lie down, I'd expected a long, sleepless night of worrying about our friends and what we should do next. Now, though, I couldn't seem to think about anything but how close she was lying.

I should have been thinking about Carlisle, planning for tomorrow, troubleshooting every possible contingency I could think of. But there was nothing for it. All I knew was that Elise and I were separated by only a few feet of darkness and that, for some reason, it was important I keep the sound of my breathing inaudible, as if the simple need for oxygen had somehow become embarrassing in our quiet closeness.

It was the hardest I've ever thought about breathing in my life.

Elise was equally quiet, and though I couldn't see her, the tension in the air somehow told me she was as restless as I was. Slowly, as if scared my shifting mind might rustle and give me away, I reached my senses out to feel for her. She broke the silence just before I made it.

"Hal?"

Her voice was soft, uncertain, and there was something in it that made my heart pick up.

"I'm here," I said, just as quietly.

Another silence. Then there was rustling in the front, and my seat sank as she propped a hand by my chest. More scrambling, more rustling, and then she slid onto the back seat alongside me, not quite touching. I could feel her there, balanced on her side, hesitating, recalculating.

My heart was hammering, though I couldn't say exactly why. I wanted to say something, to reach out and pull her in, but I couldn't seem to move. Something was different in the silence between us. Something foreign to me.

Just when I was sure she'd abandon whatever flight of fancy had brought her back here, I felt her shift. Then my heart leapt as I felt her peeling away my blanket. Swinging her leg over mine. Straddling me. I couldn't breathe. Then her reaching hand found my tender right shoulder in the darkness, and I hissed in pain.

"Sorry!" she whispered. "Sorry. I, uh…" I felt her hovering over me, afraid to set her weight down. She was about to leave. I'm not sure how I knew it, I just did.

I didn't know what to do. I reached blindly for her cheek in the dark, not understanding what this moment was, or why it was happening. I just didn't want it to end. Instead of the smooth cheek I'd been expecting, though, my hand encountered the soft roundness of her right breast. My cheeks caught fire. I pulled my hand back, an apology forming on my lips.

Elise's hand found mine in the dark and pushed it back against the swell of her chest. Then I gasped as she settled her weight down, straddled on top of me.

"Elise," I whispered.

"Hal," she whispered back, close enough now that the warmth of her breath tickled at my cheek. "I…"

Beneath the soft heaven of her breast, I felt her heart beating against my palm and realized with a shock that it was racing every bit as fast as mine. Then she kissed me, and I thought of little else.

Her hands cradled the back of my head, pulling me hungrily in. I wrapped my good arm around the small of her back, pulling her tight against me, guided by some raw urgency I'd never known, awakening deep in my veins now. Her hips moved against mine, and my entire body roared for me to take control, to do something. She broke from our kiss to plant a trail of smaller ones across my jaw, to my ear, to my neck.

I could barely breathe.

This girl. To feel her against me… For a second, all I could think of was the first day we'd met beside that painting. The first night we'd snuck to her room and talked until the early morning hours. I'd wanted to kiss her then. Wanted her more than anything now. More than I knew what to do with.

I kissed her. Grasped without knowing what I was grasping for. Pulled her desperately to me, breathing her in. She didn't smell like flowers and perfume. Her scent was real, and tinged with pain. I wanted to take it away. Wanted nothing but the two of us alone in the world.

My hips were moving against hers on their own now. Before I knew it, her shirt had come off, and it was her smooth skin beneath my fingertips, and then we were scrambling to tear off what clothes remained. I cursed my blue sling as it got in the way, ignoring the pain, terrified my awkward struggle was ruining the moment. But Elise helped me, planting one soft kiss after another across my body as we fumbled the tunic off in the darkness.

It was only when the bare skin of my body was pressed to the intimate warmth of hers that we grew still and seemed to remember who we were and what we were doing. I held my breath, heart hanging in my throat. Was this really happening?

I didn't know if I should ask. Didn't want to say the wrong thing.

Then, with a soft, sweet kiss, Elise lowered herself astride me. A ragged breath escaped me, and I pulled her forehead to mine, shock and pleasure cascading through my body. This was happening. We began to move together, slow at first, uncertain, then building in tempo as the sensations began to take hold.

I was lost in the feeling of her. Needed more. Needed everything. Without thinking, I reached out and caressed her mind with my own, desperate to be closer. Whether consciously or not, she pulled hungrily back. Excitement screaming through my body and mind, I gave myself over. Completely.

I think my heart nearly stopped.

We shared a sharp gasp as our each and every sensation—our very senses of being—all came crashing together, intertwining into one. We felt it all. Every thought in our two heads. The way we felt about each other, about this moment. The pain, the fear, the hope—all of it swirling in an infinitely complex nebula of everything that was her, that was me. That was us.

We felt it all, together. All at once. All crested by each plunge of ecstasy rushing through my body, and every blissful tingle building in hers.

It was too much to handle.

We clung to each other, mouths frozen breathlessly open, and convulsed as our link took us over the edge, rocketing us into a field of bright, blinding bliss, so intense I thought we'd both pass out.

Then the light began to dim to a soothing, glorious glow, and Elise collapsed on me even as I crumpled back into the skimmer seat, unable to move or speak or do anything other than lie there in one another's arms, catching our breaths, until sleep took us.

CHAPTER 31
EMPTY NEST

The light of dawn struck with a veritable parade of aches and pains marching across my body. It wasn't gentle. That I'd managed to sleep at all seemed a testament to the severity of the scudstorm we'd survived yesterday. Or maybe just a testament to how completely Elise had…

Elise.

It hit me like a bolt.

She wasn't there. Not on my chest, where I thought she'd been for most of the night, and not in the front seats either. I scrambled for the door, found my left leg and arm mostly asleep with pins and needles, and nearly toppled out of the skimmer. My bare feet found the grass just as the blanket wrapped around me snagged on something and yanked taut—helping me catch my balance, if not maintain my modesty. Sniffling to the left spun me around before I could worry about that.

I let out a relieved breath at the sight of Elise sitting against the skimmer. Then I took in her red eyes and runny nose, and my relief soured. She looked surprised by my sudden appearance— not that I blamed her—but there was something else. She was clearly upset, and I got the immediate impression it was the kind of upset I wasn't meant to stumble in on.

I wanted to ask if she was okay. Wanted to vanish and pretend I'd never interrupted. For a long handful of seconds, neither of us spoke.

Then her eyes flicked downward and back up. "You're, uh…"

My cheeks burned hot as my attention returned to the salacious lack of cover my snagged blanket was currently providing.

"Right." I tugged the blanket and freed it enough to adequately cover myself. "Yeah. I, uh."

A faint smile touched her tear-streaked cheeks as she watched me squirm.

"Pants, then breakfast?" I said.

"They teach you that one in tyro academy?"

I couldn't help it. I laughed. The sound brought a little life to Elise's smile, and she waved me on to go get dressed.

"How long have you been up?" I asked as I sat down next to her, clothed and bearing half of our remaining rations.

She took the food I offered her, shrugging. "An hour. Maybe two. Couldn't really sleep after..." She looked at me, then away to the tree line when I held her gaze too long. "I don't know. After everything."

Everything. Everything as in our only friends and family being potential prisoners or casualties of the Legion? Or everything as in us?

Probably both. Everything was everything, after all.

"Elise..."

I didn't know what to say. Was she regretting what had happened between us? Part of me suddenly felt as if I'd taken advantage of her emotional turmoil in allowing it to happen. I wanted to reach for her hand, but it didn't feel right.

She let out a long breath and shook her head. "Sorry, I just... It's a lot to take in right now. I wasn't expecting any of this. And last night..."

"Was a mistake?"

The words slipped out of my mouth without permission, reeking of guilt and insecurity.

Elise shook her head without hesitation, looking startled that I'd even suggest such a thing. "No. No, I don't mean that. I just... We need to find them, Hal. My dad. The others. Last night, I was scared—still *am* scared—and I just wanted to feel..." She shook her head again. "I think what I'm trying very poorly to say is that I'm sorry."

Her? Sorry to me? I couldn't be hearing her right.

"It's... okay?" I shook my head. "Nope, that doesn't feel right. Look"— I took her hand and was relieved when she didn't shy away—"I know it's scary right now, but we're gonna do this thing together. We'll find out where they are, and we'll do whatever we have to."

She turned to meet my eyes, gauging the sincerity of my words.

"And you have absolutely nothing to apologize about, by the way," I added. "No way. *I'm* not sorry that we—I mean, I... I really like you, Elise. You're... Meeting you has been the best—"

She put a finger gently to my lips. A quiet smile had crested her mouth, more beautiful than any dawning sun. "I..." she started. It was only then I noticed the soft sadness behind her smile. "Can you tell me another time? After we've found them? I just... I can't..." Her brow was creasing, her lips threatening to tremble.

"I'll wait," I said, giving her hand a squeeze before standing up. "As long as you want. Whatever you need."

I didn't fully understand, but I wasn't about to press the issue when she needed support more than ever.

She dropped my gaze, looking relieved, and some of the life returned to her smile. "Oh please. I bet you say that to all the girls you swive on the run from the Legion and their evil overlords."

I cocked my head, considering. "You're not wrong. That has been my move one hundred percent of the times I've found myself in this situation."

She shot me a look.

I offered her a hand. "Ready to face the day, outlaw?"

She took my hand and rose until we stood within a few inches of one another, nearly eye to eye. Close enough that I could smell the sweet tang of dried fruit on her breath.

I should have stepped back, given her space. But my body didn't want to —wanted instead to pull her tight, close the spare inches between my lips and hers. Forget about the rest of the world just a little while longer.

She put a gentle hand to my chest, distancing me in gesture more than in physical space. "Renegade outlaws first, teenagers second?"

I forced myself to nod, struggling to rein in the part of myself that wanted to just kiss her anyway. She was right. "They teach you that one in renegade outlaw academy?"

She narrowed her eyes. "Mine was better."

No arguments here, I thought to say. Except I still couldn't seem to back up and look away. Just like I couldn't *not* see the part of her that likewise didn't look away even as she bade me to. Even after everything we'd shared last night, my head spun with the simple closeness of her.

"And if I find myself overwhelmed by the desire to kiss you in the meantime?" I heard myself say, my voice barely a whisper.

She brushed lightly at my cheek with her thumb, then leaned in and planted a soft kiss on the spot before pushing past me to the skimmer.

"Well, I guess you are an outlaw, aren't you?"

~

Despite my bravado that morning, renegade outlaw life, it turned out, hadn't magically become an easy, rewarding venture overnight. Mostly, it continued its long string of tough breaks with a particularly well-placed gut shot.

The temple was empty.

I'd known it as soon as we'd found the place and hid the skimmer, I suppose. But I still held on to hope right up until the moment I pushed the big hardsteel door open to a roomful of silent darkness.

No one flipped on the lights and yelled, *Surprise!* As far as I could tell, nothing had changed at all since the last time Carlisle and I had set out for Franco's… Alpha, had it really only been last cycle? It felt like entire seasons had passed.

Looking around the room, I wasn't sure what I'd been expecting. That we'd walk in and find them all there, waiting, perfectly fine? That Carlisle would turn, clap me on the shoulder, and tell me I'd done a good job? No. Deep down, I'd known this was coming. Elise, on the other hand…

The look on her face made me ache with sympathy.

"Oh," she finally whispered.

"They could still be out there," I said, too quickly. "Lying low somewhere. They might be on their way right now. We should give them at least a day before we get too worried."

I almost cringed at how much it sounded—like I was trying to convince myself.

"Let's just"—I looked around the room, not really sure where I was going with this—"get cleaned up. Have something more than dried fruit. Try to relax until we know more. I don't know about you, but I could really use a hot shower."

Elise's expression was vacant. I wasn't sure she'd heard me at all.

"We need to check the reels."

I glanced at Carlisle's node, wanting to argue but knowing she was right. As twisted and unreliable as the stories surrounding yesterday's disturbances would probably be, I doubted either of us would be able to focus on anything else until we saw what they were saying. That said, I also wasn't sure how Elise would react if and when the news—true or not—was the bad kind. I didn't know how I'd handle it myself.

As short as our time together had been, those four men had become the closest thing to friends and family I had left. Especially Carlisle, who'd given me purpose and saved my ass on more occasions than I could quickly count. I couldn't imagine facing the raknoth without him. But it was more than just that. I cared for the man. He was odd at times. Distant. But he was also kind, and undeniably good.

I wasn't ready to hear bad news. And I was pretty sure Elise wasn't either.

"I can take it, Hal," she said quietly, apparently reading my indecision.

I studied her somber expression and found myself reluctantly agreeing. Ready or not, we both needed to hear *something* right now. So I woke the node on Carlisle's desk. There were no obvious messages waiting for us. I tried not to think about what that meant as the newsreel headlines began populating the display.

It wasn't hard to spot what we were looking for.

The top reels were comprised almost solely of variations of the same story. *Legion Takes Decisive Action Against Divinity Terrorist Cell.* Elise found my hand and gripped it tightly as I waved up the first vid. I wanted to roll my eyes as the reporter began detailing the situation. According to them, Legion officials had tracked the terrorist group behind the recent Vantage attack to their base of operations in Divinity and had been forced to move in to eliminate the dire threat to the city's safety.

"Fortunately," the reporter went on, "the tragic Legion casualties sustained during the raid were not in vain. Multiple key targets were eliminated during the operation, including Francesco Fields, the suspected head of the cell, and the man known only as Carlisle, one of the two perpetrators identified at the Vantage lab attack last…"

The reporter buzzed on somewhere far away. Elise's grip was painfully tight on my hand, her lips trembling. I didn't know what to do—what to say. The story was a lie. A raknoth fabrication. It had to be. Right?

In the background, I vaguely heard the reporter say something about Haldin Raish, terrorist, and his suspected accomplice, Elise Fields, remaining at large. Legion authorities were now offering a sizable reward for any information. I paused the reel, feeling sick, mind reeling.

"They lie," I said, reaching for Elise. "We know they lie."

She pushed my hand away and stumbled a few steps back, tears spilling down her cheeks. "I just… need some time. Alone. Please."

The pain in her eyes hit me harder than Alton Parker's fist. I wanted to pull her to me, take her pain for myself. But the look she gave me told me not to try. Not right then, at least.

So I watched her hurry for the door, fighting the instinct screaming at me to go after her—to hold her close and never let her go. I watched her go, my mind numb, and once she'd gone, I dropped heavily into Carlisle's chair, buried my face in my hands, and wondered what in demons' fiery depths we were supposed to do next.

CHAPTER 32
BROTO

When I was six, my parents had taken me on our first family camping trip. No training. No Legion. Just the three of us, an old, patched-up canvas shelter, and the northern woods right along the base of the Auborean Mountains for four entire days.

As far as I could remember, it had been one of the best trips of my life.

Until the third day, at least, when I'd ventured too close to a patch of wild puffscratch bushes and found out exactly where that ridiculous name came from. That was the day I found out just how itchy my flesh was capable of feeling. I remember being almost in awe of the intensity of it. It was revelatory. And what followed had been one of the hardest challenges of my childhood.

"Don't touch it, sweetling," my mom had cooed as my dad stormed back to our shelter for the gloves and wipes. "You'll spread it and then you'll itch all over. Dad's coming, sweetling. Show mommy your hands and let's just— No, Hal! Don't!"

Some itches, it turned out, are better left unscratched. And that's what I told myself over and over as I sat there in the hideout, trying to accept that Elise needed her space for now. I did my best to keep busy. Cleaned myself up. Got some silverleaf and fresh bandages on my wounds. Tried to meditate. I even fired up a racing sim on Carlisle's node. Nothing worked.

Which left me alone with my dark thoughts.

Were the stories true? Half-true? There was no way to know. Alpha be damned, they probably could've called the raid a training exercise and no one would've questioned it. But what about the others?

I tried to convince myself that Carlisle would've made it out alive—that he was too strong to fall to anything less than a raknoth and that, on top of that, I would've somehow felt it if he'd died when I was anywhere nearby. But how long should we wait here for him? Where else would we even go? And what about the Vantage data, and the raknoth themselves? The question churned in my mind like spoiling dairy, thickening the dread in my stomach.

But on the bright side, I only had an entire day to kill.

I paced until I was ready to burst, then I paced some more. I thought of the puffscratch bushes and my parents until the yearning ache was too much to handle. My thoughts drifted back to Sanctuary. To my old home, my old life. To Johnny.

I realized with a pang of guilt that I hadn't thought of him for days. Realized with another jolt that I'd even missed our graduation, which should've been this past Honorsday. Just two days ago. It felt like a bad joke—my peers swapping their tyro tunics for new posts as active legionnaires even as half of Sanctuary was busy patrolling the streets for me.

Scud, some of my classmates were probably out there with them now.

But what would Johnny be doing? What must he be thinking, seeing all these reels? The Vantage attack. My mysterious resurrection. The raid on Franco's last night. And with nothing but the word of the Legion and the WAN to go by…

Alpha be damned, my best friend probably thought I was a terrorist. He might even be hunting me.

I thought of the message he'd sent, right after my funeral. Wondered if I should have answered it. Before my brain could properly chastise me about the risks, I was already back at Carlisle's node. Maybe it didn't matter anymore. Maybe now was exactly the time to risk turning to him.

Either way, I needed to do *something*.

So I navigated to my personal messages and scrolled through a long line of official-looking Legion notifications detailing just how breathtakingly gropped I was if and when they caught me, looking for Johnny's old message. Something else caught my eye first.

A new message from Johnathan Wingard.

It was dated from yesterday, with a header that was more a running stream of profanity than an actual coherent thought. I probably had that coming. I almost didn't want to know what the rest said, but I took a deep breath and tapped the message open anyway.

❧

H*EY BROTO,*

S*AW the funniest damn thing on the reels today.*

What was it, you might be asking yourself? I'll get to that in a minute. But first I want to focus on the fact that you're asking yourself anything at all. How? Why?

BECAUSE YOU'RE NOT GROPPING DEAD, YOU GIANT, TRAITOROUS BEARDSPLITTER!!! THAT'S GROPPING WHY!!!

Sorry. I'm sorry. I shouldn't swipe in anger at a lifetime friend, right? That would just be downright scuddy of me.

KIND OF LIKE LETTING YOUR BEST GROPPING FRIEND THINK YOU'RE GROPPING DEAD!

Then again, if even half of what they're saying about you is true, I guess I don't actually know if we were ever really friends to begin with. I can't picture it. I honest to Alpha cannot imagine you could do the things they're saying. When did you start planning all this? Why? How could you?

I just can't believe it. Didn't believe it at first. I told myself they must be wrong about Vantage. That there'd been some confusion. But then I heard about the raid this morning and... Well, all I seem to have is evidence, Hal. Evidence, and a dead best friend (who's apparently not so dead) who hasn't seen fit to give ol' Johnny a peep to the contrary. So I guess my friend actually is dead, even if his body is still running around out there, reading this message.

Do you know what kind of scud people are muttering behind my back around base? Do you know what that steel sipper Bucky is saying about us? Command's already called me in five times to question me about you.

Life could be better.

Look, I don't expect you to answer this. You didn't answer the last one. I don't even know if I want to hear what you have to say. Alpha's faded old wrinklies, I could probably get shipped off just for sending this message. (To a guy who's supposed to be dead. Just in case we're forgetting that part.)

I guess I just needed to know that you know, wherever you are, that I wish to the end of Alpha's beard you would have talked to me before it was too late.

You know who I serve. You know where I stand.

If there's anything left of my friend in there, please, Hal. Please don't make us find you.

-*Johnny*
    (Your ex- best friend. In case you forgot.)

PS On the off chance this is all some big misunderstanding and we're actually on a manhunt for your evil twin or something, I actually AM sorry for slinging an angry message at my dead best friend. But, again. Not looking likely.
    PPS You're still my broto for life, broto.
    PPPS But I'm still gonna shoot you. I hope you're gropping happy.

I STARED at the message for a long time. Read it again, just to make sure I had it all. I felt hollow inside. Wanted to cry. Wanted to scream and rage and break something. Most of all, I wanted to tell him not to give up on me yet —that this wasn't me, that there was far more going on behind the scenes. But I couldn't. Reading my messages was dangerous enough. Sending one when the entire Legion was hounding after us would just be plain stupid.

For all I knew, Johnny might report it straight to command at this point.

So instead, I filled a water jug, gathered some food from Carlisle's stores, and set out to go find Elise. Because I needed someone, and she probably did too. And right now, all we had was each other. Just the two of us against the world, like some romanticized storyvid. Except I didn't feel like some ill-fated hero. I just felt ill.

It didn't take long to find her. From the temple ruins, I could just make out the figure at the crest of my favorite hill, outlined by the afternoon sun. By the end of the climb, my breathing was labored, my wounds aching in hot, pulsating waves. But it felt good to be moving.

If Elise saw or heard me approaching, she didn't show it. She sat knees-to-chest under the two oaks, facing Divinity. I sat next to her and offered her the water jug, which she took and drank from deeply.

"Thanks," she said quietly.

I suppressed the urge to ask if she was okay, knowing all too well how worthless the question was right then. Instead, we ate in silence, watching the slow dance of radiance and shadow on city and river as the sun crept low enough to light the White Tower and its shorter neighbors into the flaming, skyward hand I'd often studied in the evenings.

"Do you believe it?" she finally asked, still gazing over the river.

"No," I said—too quickly, judging by the look Elise shot me. "I don't know… I don't know what to do. About any of it."

Her hand found mine, a soft, simple touch. Tears were pressing at my eyes before I knew it.

"Plus I just found out my last friend in the world thinks I'm a terrorist," I droned on, flat, chest threatening to burst. "So there's that."

She wrapped an arm around me, cupping the side of my head, gently nestling me in.

This wasn't right. She was the one reeling from the news of her father, her family. I'd come out here to take care of her. And yet here was my head on her shoulder. Here were her fingers so tenderly stroking my hair.

The first sob racked through me.

"I don't know what to do, Elise," I whispered, hot tears sliding down my cheeks, salty at the corners of my mouth. "I don't… I'm so sorry."

She just pulled me tighter without a word. I wrapped my arm around her, every bit as tight, and then she was crying, and I was crying, and for a while, we were just two children again, afraid and alone in the world.

By the time the tears dried, the sun was retreating behind the horizon, and the air was growing chill and dark.

"We better go back in," I said.

She nodded. I rose and helped her up.

Our hands remained intertwined as we strolled back to the temple, both of us seemingly in better spirits, even though nothing had really changed. Wading through a sea of helpless sobbing had that effect, I guess. But it was more than that. As we'd huddled together, crying our eyes out, it had felt like an unspoken agreement. An understanding that, no matter how bad things got, we had one another. It wasn't any guarantee that things would work out or that we'd be safe. But it was enough for now.

"I never told you how amazing you were back there," I said, tilting my head back toward the city. "I had no idea you could fight like that."

The first traces of a smile tugged at her lips. "I tried to tell you. But hey, how could the pretty little flower *possibly* know anything about fighting, right?"

"Well, in my defense, you are, like, *really* pretty. Maybe too pretty. How was I supposed to know?"

"Sexist!" She threw a playful punch at my good shoulder.

I dodged it, backpedaled her grab, and all of a sudden, we were running through the maze of the temple ruins in a mad game of tag, laughing all the way. I skittered into the temple, conjuring light in my palm. Through the front hall and up the stairs, Elise hot on my heels, until I rounded the corner, extinguished the light, and whirled to catch her in the darkness with a loud, "Aghhh!"

She crashed into me with a startled yip, and then we were laughing again—deep, belly-aching laughter that went on until we were doubled over, panting for breath, eyes wet with new tears. Even when the return to our empty nest sobered our frivolous mirth... even when I glanced at the empty displays and remembered Johnny's words with a dull ache... I thanked Alpha that I had Elise.

We collapsed into my cot, thoroughly exhausted from the tribulations of the past days, content to simply enjoy one another's presence. Soon enough, I drifted into an easy sleep.

Only to snap awake what felt like minutes later.

According to the displays on the wall, I'd actually been asleep for hours. It was the middle of the night. But there was nothing. The room was silent, but for Elise's breathing and—

There. A faint hum. The mag lift, I realized, descending to the skimmer bay below.

Someone was coming.

CHAPTER 33

INSIDER

I leapt from the cot and snatched my pulse gun.

"Hal?" Elise groaned sleepily. "Wha—"

"Shh," I sent. *"Someone's coming. Get behind me."*

I took up position behind the lip of the stone wall. Elise padded up behind me, collapsed staff in hand. The lift was humming back up now. Almost here. I telekinetically killed the lights.

It was just Carlisle. It had to be, right?

"Close your eyes," I sent.

I wanted to believe I was overreacting. That we were safe here.

Safe. Just like we'd been at Franco's. My head was spinning with thoughts of the scent-tracking hybrids and raknoth ripping the temple's location straight from Carlisle's mind.

The lift doors parted with a faint scraping sound.

I thrust my gun hand around the corner, channeled from the hideout's main energy cell, and let loose with my best imitation of Carlisle's snap flare attack. I'd never tried it before, and the effort left my head tingling oddly, but it worked. The dark room flared brilliantly through my closed eyelids. I leaned out, gun raised…

And drew a sharp breath of relief.

Carlisle stood in the open lift car, hands held up in surrender. He appeared quite un-blinded, as did James, who was frozen mid-hunker behind him, arms extended protectively, blinking in confusion.

"Did… Did you just catch a snap flare blast?" James asked.

At the sound of his voice, Elise gasped and poked out from cover behind me.

Carlisle was too busy running his eyes over us and letting out a relieved breath of his own. "Thank the fates you're here," he said, flicking the lights on and lugging a large gear bag out of the lift. "I was hoping, but I… Well, I'm glad to see both of you."

I lowered my gun. "Carlisle?" It felt silly leaving my mouth. Clearly, it was him. But I was too stunned—too overwhelmed with relief—to think of anything else. At least until Elise registered what I hadn't yet.

"Where are the others?" she asked, a slight quaver in her voice.

Carlisle's relieved expression turned somber. I glanced past him and saw nothing but James slinking almost guiltily out of the lift. No Franco. No Phineas.

"You're both safe," Carlisle said, going to deposit his cargo by his desk. "That's no small victory." He turned back to us, reluctant. "The others…"

"We lost them." James' voice was bleak as he joined us, and he looked more grim and deflated than I'd ever seen him. "They had Franco pinned when we got there. We got him, got as far as the training room, but… Well, Carlisle was working on a way out when they overran us. Phineas and Franco were holding the door, and…"

"Are they…?" I didn't want to say the next word out loud.

"They were alive, the last I felt them," Carlisle said quickly, "but the Legion has them now."

"I'm so sorry, Elise," James said, head hung low.

Elise stepped forward, eyes brimming with tears, and wrapped him in a tight hug.

"You think they took them to Sanctuary?" I asked Carlisle quietly.

"Most likely." He frowned. "Almost convenient, in a twisted sort of way."

Convenient was a strong word, but I understood what he meant. Because if we still had any interest in going through the suicidal effort of infiltrating Sanctuary, at least now we could fell two fowl with one slug once we were on base. Except without the Vantage drive, we had no hard proof to broadcast aside from our own accusations and some shaky vid footage of our excursion. Unless…

I studied Carlisle's expression, but it gave little away. "Does that mean…?"

He gave a slight nod. "We stopped at Franco's safe house to pick up a few things."

James stirred at his words, disengaging from Elise, and I felt a flutter of hope at the sudden excitement in his eyes. "I don't think the Legion was all that far behind us," he added, bending down to rummage through the bag they'd brought. "But it was worth it."

From the bag, he pulled a dark, unmarked case and a boxy piece of electronic equipment. He deposited both on the table, giving the latter an affectionate pat.

"Please, Alpha," I said, sinking into a chair and eyeing the ambiguous electronic block, "tell me that's the Vantage data."

"This," James said dramatically, "is the… wait, did you just say—"

"You got the Vantage drive?" Elise asked, snapping out of her reverie to come lean against the back of my chair.

"I…" James looked back and forth between us, taken aback. "Well, yeah, but…" He frowned at his tablet. "I just thought it was gonna be a good surprise."

"It's a great surprise, James," Elise said.

"And a very clever backup system," Carlisle said, his tone unusually affirming.

"Oh." James puffed up a bit and gave a little shrug. "Yeah, well, it's just something I set up in the safe house a few years ago. The tech's a little old, but it works. It's all right here." His face fell. "We're just lucky Franco managed to dump the drive before they got in."

I reached for Elise's hand, feeling her tension.

"Maybe on to the good news, James," Carlisle said.

"Right," James said, tapping at his tablet. "The good news. The good news is that we found something."

I perked up as James turned his device to show us a list of files, each labeled simply with a date. Audio files, I saw. A log of some kind?

"What are they?"

"Journal entries from one of Vantage's head researchers," James said, clearly excited about the fact. "We were lucky to bump into them when we did. There's a *lot* of stuff on that drive. But this…" He shook his head. "This is pretty unbelievable."

"Evidence?" I asked.

"Oh, we've got evidence," James said. "But this is even better. Answers."

Carlisle even looked half-optimistic about these entries. Maybe there was hope yet.

"Tell us," I said.

"Hear it for yourself," James said, setting the tablet on the table.

He started the first entry.

<<ENTRY ONE: My name is Therese Brown, and... Oh, this feels silly, talking to myself like some kind of paranoid... No. No, I chose to do this for a reason.

My name is Therese Brown, and I was recruited eight years ago to join Vantage's regenerative medicine team. Within three years, I was heading it. That's when I was first approached by Alton Parker himself. That's when all of this started. You have to understand, working at Vantage isn't just another—>>

I looked up as the recording skipped and found James swiping the footage forward with his palmlight. "Maybe just the good parts first," he said.

We didn't argue.

<<—the CEO of Vantage himself comes to tell you that aliens—honest to Alpha extraterrestrials—have appeared on our doorstep. That they need help and that—>>

"No..." James murmured, skipping again. "Here."

<<—story went like this: In their past travels, these aliens—these raknoth, as they call themselves—happened across a planet populated by a people not unlike our own. It was there they fell prey to an illness against which they had no immunity— pathogens that apparently posed no problem to the local life but were quite deadly to the raknoth. By the time the raknoth realized they were sick, though, they were already halfway across the galaxy.>>

"That's insane," I said, holding up a finger to pause the recording. "Another planet of people like us?"

"I know," James said, fiddling with his palmlight again. "Believe me, they were plenty skeptical. She goes on about it for a while. But then..."

<<—then we got a look at the samples Mr. Parker brought us, and... Well, I guess it's easy to lose sight of things when you're sitting on the biggest scientific breakthrough the world's ever seen.>>

James swiped forward again. "She goes on about how those samples were like nothing they'd ever seen. Like, totally foreign. Apparently they don't even have nucleic strands. It gets a bit dense, but Alton Parker basically had them in there for five years trying to learn an entirely new branch of biology."

"And they didn't think to tell anyone about all this?"

"That's exactly what these logs are. You have to understand, no one on their team had even left the compound for years at this point. Alton Parker owned these people. Therese was terrified to even be recording this, but I guess she'd seen one too many cracks in Parker's story. Like the fact that they kept receiving raknoth samples even though the raknoth were supposed to be hidden somewhere in the northern wastelands to quarantine this foreign illness of theirs."

"Which, what's the deal with that?" I said, glancing at Carlisle, who hadn't spoken. "Are they actually sick? And what about the rest of it? The blood, the racks, the hybrids?"

Carlisle deferred to James.

"Yeah," James said. "So this is where it starts to get weird."

Elise and I stared at him.

"Weird*er*. Right. So yeah, their samples were apparently chock-full of parvobes astoundingly similar to the millions you'd find crawling around on all of us."

"Why's that weird?" I asked. "Isn't pretty much every living thing on Enochia covered in parvobes?"

"He said similar," Elise pointed out, looking unsettled.

James pointed at her. "Right. Similar to ours, but almost definitely *not* from Enochia, according to Therese. Something about evolutionary branches and..." He waved a hand. "Look, you should probably listen to the whole thing, but first"—he swiped the tablet over to the second audio entry and scrolled through a little ways—"this is important."

<<*We barely knew where to begin. We didn't even know whether those parvobes were actually what was causing the sickness. But it was the best explanation we had. So we started there, trying to eliminate all non-raknoth life from the tissue samples.*

It was no good.

We tried all manner of treatments, from mild to aggressive. Interestingly, the tissues themselves were incredibly resilient to pretty much any harmful substance or stimulus we could think to throw at them, and what little damage we left was usually regenerated within minutes. But that was only short term. Eventually, no matter what we did, they would die. There was talk going on of trying to splice pieces of our own immune systems into theirs when Mr. Parker came to offer another potential treatment.

Human blood.

That should have been the first warning bell. Why human blood? And why in demons' depths was Alton Parker the one suggesting it? It was preposterous. Nonsensical.

And it worked.

Human blood—not swine, not rodent, but only human blood—was able to keep our samples alive and well as we worked over the next few years. It was... Well, the logical side of me always assumed there was some human-specific protein at work there. Maybe a combination of them. It had to be something. But years passed and no one found a satisfying explanation for it.

It was spooky. And—Oh, Alpha be damned, I need to go check on our latest graft assay. I'll be back soon.>>

"So they are sick," I said.

"And human blood is the only treatment," Elise added.

"That's what I took away from all this," James said. "But there's more, too. Therese's team was trying to figure out how to harness the regenerative machinery of the raknoth tissues for medical applications."

"But?" I asked.

"But apparently the raknoth tissues kept pulling some kind of hostile takeover of whatever human or animal samples they touched. Like a virus, almost. And the only thing that could slow the process down was—"

"Human blood?" Elise said.

James nodded uneasily. "I'm thinking that's how the, uh, hybrids might've gotten started. Some kind of early trial. Or an accidental infection, or…"

"A not accidental one?" I provided.

James' swallow was audible, and I didn't blame him one bit.

"There's one more thing," he said, reaching for the tablet.

<<ENTRY THREE: Our allometrist, Doug, told me something today that made me want to lock my office door and curl up under my desk.

We've all been wondering for years what these raknoth look like, what manner of creatures these raknoth are, but we have yet to see one in person, or in… whatever. Doug's best guess, though—from the admittedly small amount of information he has to work back from—is that they're fairly small creatures.

About the size of a human brain, he told me today.

Those were his words. The size of a human brain. We'd already heard his report that the raknoth were likely small, but the way he said it today, it was like there was a reason he didn't just say, "About the size of a dew melon," or something less… creepy. Like he'd been thinking about raknoth and brains a lot lately.

So, after five years of study, here's a quick summary of what we actually know about these things. They're likely damn tough. They somehow exhibit parasitic behavior even at the subcellular level. They seem to require human blood to survive. And, last and maybe creepiest, we have reason to believe they're about the size of a human brain.

This is purely wild speculation, but I can't help wonder: what if the raknoth aren't actually quarantined up north? We've all wondered how they're surviving up there without the human blood they presumably need. I've been assuming that, since we're getting samples, we must be sending supplies to them as well. But what if that's not it at all? What if they're already among the population, feeding? How would they go unnoticed? How would you slip into a totally novel society and hope to blend in?

I think I'd take over one of the natives, if I could. Slip in. Learn from their memories. Take control. Become them. In other words, I think I'd take over one of their brains.

Or take its place...

Alpha, I sound like a delusional nut.

I'm tired. I need more data before I rattle out any more wild conspiracy theories. I just... have a bad feeling. About all of this.>>

I stared at the tablet, my own bad feeling thickening in the pit of my stomach. It sounded like Therese had figured it all out. And if she'd tried to get the word out, as these audio logs seemed to indicate...

"What happened to her?"

James looked at Carlisle, who nodded. With a grim expression, James started the last audio file.

<<ENTRY SIX: I don't... I don't know what's happening, but... Scud. I don't think I have much time. I don't know if you can even trust what I'm saying right now.

Those things I said about talking to Doug, about him happily resigning... I don't think they're true. I can't... It's all mixed up in my head. I don't know how to explain it.

I'm not crazy.

Alton Parker. I think he did this to me somehow. I don't know how. I think the raknoth have converted him, made him one of their own. I think he's—

Thud. Thud.

Oh sc—

Crack.

Hey! What the hell are you doing? You can't—Hey! Stop! Don't—>>

I listened in horror as Therese Brown was roughly dragged away from her recorder, kicking and screaming until James paused the file.

Silence hung in the air.

"Sweet Alpha," Elise finally whispered.

James bobbed his head. "Yeah."

I looked at Carlisle, whose brow was furrowed in a troubled expression. "You think they put her on one of those racks?"

"That would be my guess."

The same racks from which he and I had failed to liberate a single soul back at Vantage. Had Therese Brown been one of those poor victims? The panic in her voice at the end there…

I buried my face in my hands, guilt crashing down on me. I barely even heard what Elise said next. Something about us having kept her in the dark. An apology from James. Some back and forth about what we'd just listened to. I could barely form a coherent thought for the wild maelstrom racing through my head.

This was it. As awful as I felt for Therese and those like her, as worried as I was about Franco and Phineas, these were the answers we'd been looking for. If we could get into Sanctuary, get this out there for the rest of Enochia to hear…

I moved my right arm experimentally, assessing the pain and wondering how quickly I could be back in proper fighting condition.

"Ah, yeah," James said, apparently noticing my cringe. "We grabbed something for that, too." He opened the dark case from the bag to reveal a line of cylindrical vials packed neatly beside a larger injector.

"Tissue scaffold gels," he explained, plucking a vial from the case. "Infused with nanites and other good stuff. Guess it's about time you were conscious for a dose, huh?"

Not really sure whether to agree or disagree, I gingerly followed his gestured directive to remove my shirt. An uncharacteristic calm settled over James as he focused on the task of cleaning my wounds and readying the injector. I only half-noticed. My mind was already back on Therese's logs, and the raknoth.

Aliens. Was it really possible? I'd never stopped thinking of them as demons, but Carlisle *had* said as much right from the start. Maybe that's why I felt so numb to the realization. Or maybe it was just that, much as the revelation would shock the world, I knew it didn't matter anymore because, either way, the raknoth were our enemies.

Our enemies who apparently required human blood to survive.

Was that what this had always been about? Not demons of the nether, spreading misery for the sake of pure evil, but rather a strange race simply doing what they must to survive?

Had my parents died for nothing more than cosmic chance?

I didn't realize I was trembling until Elise's hand found mine and squeezed. I looked up and found James hovering nervously, having paused at his work. I nodded to him, and he resumed without a word.

We needed to move on this. On all of it.

How long before Vantage's new facility was ready to begin harvesting blood and churning out hybrids at Alpha knew how many hundreds or thousands of civilians a day? How long before Franco and Phineas were moved to a permanent detention facility, or slated for execution? Before they were interrogated—assuming it hadn't already happened?

I squeezed Elise's hand back, trying my best to look reassuring. "We'll get them back, Elise."

"I know we will," she said quietly, her eyes somewhere far away. "No matter what."

I glanced at James and Carlisle. "And these logs…"

"We're going to splice them with the footage from the labs," James said, "along with some of the other evidence on the drive. We've already got some of it figured out."

"Will it be enough?" I asked, to no one in particular.

"Alone," Carlisle said, "they could probably bury any single piece of it as a fabrication. Our word versus theirs."

"But Enochia won't be able to ignore all of it," Elise said. "Not all of it together. Not when the reporters start digging, connecting the pieces."

Carlisle nodded. "I agree. The truth will prevail this time."

"Okay," I said, rising and looking around at our ragged crew before pulling on my shirt.

James dropped my gaze when I met his eyes, looking almost abashed as he tucked the injector away and grabbed a fresh bandage. "There's just one more thing,"

"What?" I asked, my stomach sinking.

"We think Enochia should hear your story first," Carlisle said. "What the raknoth did to your family. What they're going to do next. You and your father were respected members of the Legion. Even after everything they've said in the reels, that fact will at least get the people's attention. Then we can hit them with the footage James compiles."

I wasn't sure what to say. Me? Bare my story for Enochia? It sounded… dirty somehow. Not to mention mortifying. At least up until I remembered what they were already saying about me. The world thought I was a terrorist who'd helped murder my own parents. Could it really get much worse?

Probably. But it didn't matter. The world needed the truth. And, whatever they might say about me, my parents' memory deserved better than that.

"Fine," I said, pulling on my shirt and sinking back into my chair, trying to gather my thoughts. "Get the camera."

CHAPTER 34

HOMECOMING

An eerie silence filled the dark skimmer cab, interrupted only by the muffled crashes of ocean waves on rocks. We flew low over the water, skirting along the cliff face parallel to the west wall of Sanctuary high above. Up there, the sky was hazy with the faint glow of Sanctuary lights, and those of Divinity beyond. Down by the water, though, darkness permeated everything.

The only light in the skimmer came from the controls and the dim windshield display that guided James' flying without the need for big shiny skimmer lights. The tug of acceleration joined the anxious churning in my stomach as he swooped the skimmer upward and banked around to the north cliff face.

Next to me, Elise was a silhouette. I found her hand and gave it a squeeze.

Scuddy as the visibility was with just the windshield display, I expected it would take us several slow sweeps back and forth before we had any hope of spotting the concealed entrance we'd gleaned from Smirks' memories. Assuming we found it at all.

In the four days we'd spent planning and training—and, occasionally, eating and sleeping—this had been the part that had scared me the most. Because, as dangerous as the rest would be, if we didn't find this entrance, we were gropped, plain and simple.

Thankfully, we had Carlisle. He must've been searching with more than his eyes, because he pointed to a spot of pure darkness above in short order. "There."

James gently steered us up, up. Under a rocky protrusion, over a large crag, and into a tight tunnel, so dark that James was forced to nudge the skimmer's lights to dim to see anything at all. Perhaps fifty feet into the cliff, the claustrophobic passage opened to a small, unadorned hangar that had been hollowed straight out of the stone.

I wiggled some of the achy stiffness from my arm as James guided the skimmer down. It'd be another cycle or so before I was actually in good shape, but James' gels had done enough. I'd make do. James landed, and we climbed warily out, weapons at the ready.

What I wouldn't have given for a pair of night lenses. But we hadn't had access to Franco's toys this time around. Our lanterns would have to do. We kept them dim, just enough to let us navigate.

The hangar was empty, save for a couple gear crates and a single dark skimmer off to the side. Hopefully no one would be coming for it anytime soon.

One last gear check, and we headed for the only visible door at the rear of the hangar. Pausing at the door, Carlisle and I both checked the way with our extended senses. It was a risk, dialing our cloaks out anywhere in Kublich's domain, but, as long as we were careful, the advantage of effectively seeing through walls probably outweighed the risks. Carlisle had outfitted Elise and James with cloaking pendants of their own to keep their minds safe.

"Clear?" I thought at Carlisle.

He nodded and pulled the door open.

A wash of damp, musty air hit me like the embrace of an unwashed street dweller on a sweltering Midsummer day.

We all exchanged a somber wrinkling of noses and pushed cautiously into the network of ancient and long-disused sewage tunnels beneath Sanctuary. The air was wet and thick on my skin and in my lungs, and it tinted our soft lantern lights a sickly green hue. Vegetation covered more of the arching brick walls than not, and our boots splashed into shallow puddles here and there.

At the first intersection, we paused for bearings. As expected, our palm-lights' nav chips didn't function this far underground. Which meant—also as expected—that all we had to go by were the fragmented images from Smirks' mind, my own familiarity with the base above, and a compass.

I took the lead, turning when and where I could to keep us headed mostly south and a little east, toward the main comms building. A few times, we paused to inspect a startling noise or movement, but each alarm turned out to be false—merely a foraging rodent or the echoes of our own progression.

All except one.

We'd been walking for about fifteen minutes and were passing by the arched opening of an overflow chamber or some such when I heard it. The faintest trace of a low rumble nearby—something like a snore. Or a growl.

My heart was already thudding when Carlisle grabbed my wrist to halt and gravely nodded in the same direction.

"Hybrids," he sent. *"A dozen in that chamber. Sleeping, I think. More ahead. We shouldn't stay down here."*

Gropping right, we shouldn't.

But were we far enough into Sanctuary to ditch our chance at free passage?

It didn't matter. If one of those things caught our scent... better we take our chances slinking in shadows above than getting trapped in these dark tunnels with a frothing horde of bloodthirsty monsters.

Not wanting to risk even quiet murmurs in the vicinity of those monsters, we relayed the need to get above to James and Elise by silent hand signals. They got the gist enough not to ask questions, and we moved on quietly, eyes peeled for access to the base above. Another few tense minutes saw us past another side chamber and an old service room, both full of slumbering hybrids by the sound of it.

What in demons' depths were they all doing down he—

Something prodded my shoulder, and I barely suppressed a spastic jump. It was James, getting my attention to point out a ladder in the next tunnel over. We headed for it, trying to balance the need for quiet with the urge to get the scud out of those tunnels as quickly as possible.

Carlisle ascended first, up the circular well that extended through the tunnel's ceiling. James followed, then Elise. I let out a sigh of relief as I emerged after them into a cramped stairwell and James quietly lowered the hatch behind me, sealing us off from the sleeping monsters below.

"There must be a hundred hybrids down there," I murmured to Carlisle.

"More," Carlisle said.

James blanched at that, wide-eyed, and Elise didn't look much better, though the surprise didn't rock the grim determination in her eyes. I squeezed her shoulder, and she placed her hand over mine for a brief moment.

James swallowed audibly. "Those were… That was…"

Carlisle patted him lightly on the back. "They're behind us for now." He frowned at the floor. "Though this probably means our original exit plan is out of the question."

That went without saying. We were going to have to commandeer a ride out of Sanctuary. But I was too busy thinking about the hybrids—the ones below, and the ones that had attacked Franco's alongside the Legion company.

Had the legionnaires known?

The hybrids had been disguised in Legion gear, sure. But had that been to hide them from the soldiers, or just from any prying public eyes?

From what little I could recall, the legionnaires had seemed surprised when one of the hybrids had lost it and plowed the security room door down, but still…

"What if the Legion already knows?" I asked quietly.

The question hung silently for a stretch.

"If the hybrids' existence were common knowledge here," Carlisle finally said, "I doubt Kublich would be hiding them down there. The more troubling question is when and how he's planning to use them."

He had a point there.

"Either way," he continued, "the rest of Enochia must know the truth. They may yet band together even if the Legion were lost."

It wasn't a comforting thought. But he was right, so we filed up to move on.

Carlisle took the lead in ascending the stairs.

I was expecting outlets to the subbasement levels, but the narrow stairwell led nowhere but up for several flights. Finally, the stairs ended at a small landing and the first door we'd seen. I carefully dialed out my cloak and felt ahead.

Four minds in the next room, blessedly human, noticeably drunk—on power and other substances. An officer's lounge?

I checked that my gun was set to stun rounds and gave Carlisle a ready nod. He pushed open the door. I put stun bolts into the two men by the well-stocked bar to the left as they turned. To the right, the other two were frozen in shock, halfway to their feet.

Before I could tag them with stun rounds, Carlisle telekinetically shoved their heads together with a cringe-worthy *bop*, then walked in and calmly applied his stun rod to each of their necks. Elise and James followed us into the room, their own weapons drawn and ready.

"We should hide these guys," James said.

I almost laughed—out of excitement at how smoothly we'd cleared the room or relief to be away from the hybrids, I couldn't say. Maybe some part of me was simply starting to get a taste for the thrill of real action. Still, I couldn't help but feel guilty and maybe a little treasonous as we each picked an officer and dragged them into the stairwell we'd come from.

When Carlisle swung the stairwell door closed, I saw the side facing the room was actually a false wall panel. I wondered if those officers had had any idea what they'd been sitting next to before we'd popped out. Not that it really mattered in comparison to what we were here to share with them and the rest of Enochia.

I pulled up the map of Sanctuary on my palmlight and took in our position as the others leaned in to orient themselves. We actually weren't in bad shape. Almost a mile into Sanctuary, close to the center of the base. The comms center and its broadcast bunker were less than a quarter mile east of us, and the brig closer to a half-mile away, near the western perimeter.

"You guys are good?" I asked James and Carlisle.

"Are you?" James said, looking concerned.

"We'll do what we have to," Elise said.

I forced a smile. "Yeah, what she said."

It was going to be a much longer trek than I'd been expecting ground-side. Still, better that than trying to creep past sleeping hybrids.

"Remember to mind the towers' lines as best you can," I added for everyone's benefit as Carlisle went to the door to scout the way outside. "The corners mostly watch outward, but you never know when someone's gonna get bored and check out what's happening on base."

Carlisle gave a satisfied nod at the door, indicating the way was clear.

"We'll see you soon then," I hoped out loud.

Carlisle clapped a hand on my shoulder. "I have faith in you, Hal." He turned to Elise and rested his other hand on her shoulder. "Keep him safe just in case?"

The hint of a smile broke through her sober expression. "I'll get him back to you in one piece."

James and Elise shared a quick hug. I clapped James on the back. None of us planned to go down tonight, but we also couldn't ignore the fact that this could be our last goodbye. Before I could lose my will, I grabbed Elise's hand and pushed the door open.

The four of us crept out, sticking to the building's shadow as we skirted to its northern edge. There, we silently waved to James and Carlisle. They turned right and covered the gap to the next building at a crouched run.

Then it was just the two of us.

I steeled myself, squeezed Elise's hand, and turned for the brig.

Munitions crates and parked transports. Shadows and thin prayers. From one to the next, we moved across Sanctuary using whatever cover we could find.

The going was as slow as it was agonizingly tense.

Sanctuary was much less active at nighttime, but that was far from saying the security was light. We waited for minutes at a time, crouched behind boxes—or, once, underneath a supply roller—for passing foot traffic. Twice, I considered mind-snatching to turn someone away from us, but that came with its own set of risks.

When we weren't narrowly avoiding the patrols, I worried one of the tower lookouts would happen to glance our way at just the wrong time.

Finally, though, we reached the dull permacrete length of the brig. We slipped around to the back, putting us adjacent to Sanctuary's western wall and away from most of the foot traffic.

The brig was long and not overly tall—only two stories, with one being underground. Still, the roof wasn't easily accessible from ground level. And the roof was where we needed to be. So, after triple checking no one was approaching on the perimeter wall above, I pushed off the wall, turned, and fired a grappling bolt into the lip of the rooftop fifteen feet above.

I checked again to make sure no one had come running at the dull thud of the bolt, then I held the gun out to Elise and touched her skin to circumvent her cloak. *"One click on the motor. Lie flat when you get up there."*

She took the gun, inspecting its workings, and was about to move into position when I spotted two legionnaires rounding closer to us up on the perimeter wall.

I grabbed her and pulled her tight to the shadows. *"After these two pass."*

The wall was close enough and high enough that we'd probably be out of their line of sight when it mattered. I watched until the two disappeared behind the inner lip to be sure.

With the immediate threat of being spotted past, I dropped my gaze from the wall to Elise, thinking to tell her we'd better wait for them to move on. It was only then that I realized how close she was, pressed tight against me, her face only inches from mine.

She was searching my face for an update. I caught the sweet tang of wild berries on her warm breath and, despite everything, barely managed to restrain myself from kissing her. Other parts of me proved less disciplined.

Her eyes widened a hair, then she raised a hand over her own mouth as if she were afraid she might laugh.

"Eyes up here, please," I sent, cheeks burning. *"I'm not a piece of meat, you know."*

She bent a brow and shifted against me in a way that made me acutely aware of the limited accuracy of my statement as she turned to look at the perimeter. Above, forty yards down the wall, the two legionnaires' bobbing heads had reappeared over the edge, moving away from us. She turned a questioning look my way.

"Go."

She planted a foot on the wall, triggered the coiling motor, and lithely walked her way up and onto the rooftop before reversing the motor to send the gun crawling back down.

I waited anxiously.

If everything was going smoothly for Carlisle and James, they'd be in position to start soon. As soon as I could, I snagged the gun, checked my surroundings, and ascended to the rooftop. Elise was there with a helping hand at the end.

"Why thank you, goodlady." I sent when I was lying flat on the rooftop beside her.

She made a silent flourish. I smiled and tapped my palmlight to send the short range pulse that would let Carlisle know we'd made it. *"Keep an eye out."*

She gave me an abbreviated salute, and I went to prepare our entry point.

The rooftop was dark enough that I'd be surprised if anyone noticed us slinking around, but I stayed prone anyway, trying to estimate the rough location of the brig's main guard station. It had been a long time since I'd been in the brig, and crawling across the rooftop didn't exactly give me the best vantage point.

When I thought I was close, I cautiously dialed out my cloak and reached downward.

Nothing directly below, but… There. About ten feet further ahead. Four minds. Consoles. Walls of displays.

I withdrew my mind, scooted to the proper location, and retrieved the long, flexible tube of scorch dust I'd carefully folded into my pack. I fixed it to the rooftop in a rough circle, about four feet in diameter, half-wincing with every tiny movement. Carlisle had insisted the mixture of finely powdered lightsteel and oxidized whipsteel was safe enough to carry, but that didn't keep my pulse from quickening as I handled it.

Once I was satisfied, I rolled around and crawled back. Elise met me halfway, and we settled in to wait. Assuming nothing had gone critically wrong, our message would be hitting the broadcast system any minute. As soon as it started, we'd need to move, take advantage of the excitement while the base's collective attention was fixed elsewhere.

But for now, I tried to enjoy the last moments of quiet. The warmth of Elise pressed against my side, and the cool kiss of the salty ocean breeze at our backs.

"Life perils aside," I sent, trying my best to radiate calm, *"it's actually kind of a beautiful night."*

I looked over to find her watching me with an odd look in her eyes—some raw outflowing of emotion that pulled straight at my core. I returned her gaze, nearly overwhelmed by the sudden surge of tender feelings melting through me. And that's when it happened.

"I think I love you," she whispered.

Shock rippled through me as she pressed her lips to mine.

She loved me? Truly? I might've glimpsed it during our brief mind meld, but to hear her say the words out loud… it was like a warm honey hit of weapons-grade pain meds, only five times better and without the mental clarity issues. Then the rest registered.

She *hadn't* said the words out loud.

Her lips hadn't moved, except to greet mine. Elise had just tapped into her telepathy. She was drawing back from the kiss, now, clearly confused by my surprise. She didn't know I'd heard, I realized. Which made sense. Our efforts to coax out her new abilities in the past few days had been fruitless—much to her frustration. But now she saw it.

Her eyes widened, her fingers drifting up to cover her mouth. Why did *she* look worried? Didn't she understand how deeply I was already hers? I took her hand, pressed my other palm to her cheek, and reached out to tell her.

The sharp click of Sanctuary's amps coming online yanked us back to the present before I could.

My breath caught. It was starting. Except it wasn't my voice that came pouring from the amps, as I'd expected.

It was the Sanctuary alarm.

CHAPTER 35

REUNITED

"Hello, Enochia," my recorded voice rang out from the Sanctuary amps. "My name is Haldin Raish."

I barely heard it over the blaring of the alarms.

"What do we do?" Elise hissed beside me, our moment forgotten.

I tried to listen to the alarm. Tried to think.

Double tone alarm. Intruders on base. That made sense, but…

We'd expected the alarms. Just not so quickly. Certainly not before the broadcast had even started. But it was going now. Theoretically, millions of people across Divinity and the rest of Enochia were hearing my voice and seeing my face at that very moment.

It would've been bizarre to think about if I wasn't too distracted with the powerful floodlights snapping on across the compound and the shouts of rousing soldiers. Legionnaires began storming out of barracks doors, dressed and armed every bit as quickly as I'd expected. Amp Hal prattled on, twining with the insistent alarm.

And still no word from Carlisle.

"We stick to the plan," I said.

I couldn't initiate contact. Not yet. James' short-range encrypted channel would only hold up for a couple minutes once the Legion caught wind of it, and we were going to have some critical coordination to do when it was time to exfil.

So, I pushed the thought aside, extended my cloak, and reached out for the strip of scorch dust. Tense energy radiated off the four guards below. I almost felt bad about the extra stress I was about to quite literally drop on them. "Get ready."

I fixed onto the magnesium ignition strip and drew energy from one of the cells in my pack. It took more than I expected.

Then a small white flare pierced the night and rapidly expanded to a full conflagration.

To my extended senses, the torrential cascade of the reaction's energy was almost overwhelming. To my body, it was a startlingly hot slap of air to the face. Beside me, Elise gasped at the ferocity of it.

We scrambled to our feet. The inferno was already dying down. With a sound like crumbling rock, the circular section of the roof broke free and fell to the room below.

There were crashes and bangs, shouts and curses.

We reached the charred edge of the hole, and I looped an arm around Elise's waist, not wanting to give the guards below time to recover.

Then we jumped.

The drop was only about twelve feet. Just enough to give me a strong blast's worth of energy when I siphoned it off to slow our fall. It buzzed through me and eagerly sprang when I released it at the first guard I caught sight of.

He flew back, chair and all, and slammed into the console behind him.

We dropped the rest of the way to a shaky landing.

I gathered myself to spring at the next two guards ahead... and froze at the set of blue-green eyes staring back at me from under trimmed, fiery red hair.

His mouth was agape in open shock just like mine.

"Johnny?"

He sucked in a little breath when I spoke, like he was only then confirming I wasn't a specter, returned from the pyre. "Hal?"

"You got brigged?"

Why? Why was that the first thing that came out of my mouth?

There was a moment there where I thought that he might answer, that we might all remain calm and talk it out.

Then the woman beside Johnny went for her sidearm.

I slammed her to the wall with telekinesis.

"What the hell, Wingard?" she growled. "Shoot him! Take that bastard—"

A stun bolt to her chest crumpled her to the floor.

At a crash from behind, I snapped around to see Elise standing over the fourth guard, staff in hand. The man was slumped over his chair, unmoving.

I turned back to face Johnny's raised pistol and raised my own hands in surrender.

"Hal, what the gropping…? What the…" His mouth worked soundlessly.

I felt Elise hovering behind me, ready to strike. In the background, Amp Hal prattled on.

"It's okay," I said, slowly holstering my gun. "Both of you, it's okay."

"The scud it is, beardsplitter!" Johnny cried. "You… You're… What is this?" He glanced at the guard I'd shot. "You just— "

"Stun rounds," I said. "She's fine. Mostly."

He jerked his head, gun hands shaky. "Not the point man! Okay, kind of the point. But what in the gropping scud buckets is going on? If you can't tell, I'm twitchy as a stimmed rabbit right now, so you'd better tell me before my gropping finger slips."

"Or you could put the gun down," Elise said.

Johnny took her in at a glance. "I'd ask who the scud you are, but I don't have to, what on account of you guys being known terrorists." He all but shouted the last two words.

I'd never seen him this rattled.

"Johnny…" I spread my hands. "Things aren't what they seem here. Those questions you had about the night I disappeared, you were on the right track. The Legion's been compromised."

"Bullscud," Johnny hissed, but he was still listening.

"We've got bad people pulling high strings," I continued. "And it goes deep. My dad found out. That's what he was up to. That's why…"

The words stuck in my throat.

"—ut I don't expect you to just believe me when I tell you several of our leaders have been possessed by alien life forms," Amp Hal was saying in the background. "So instead, allow me to present you with some of the footage and audio logs we recovered during our illegal inspection of Vantage labs."

Johnny bent a fiery-red eyebrow. "Bad people, huh? Because it sure sounded like your clone up there just said aliens."

"I know it's crazy, but—"

"Oh, don't sell yourself short, broto. It's straight steel-sipping insane."

I pointed to the main display beside us, trying to keep calm. "Do you remember Andre Kovaks?"

"You mean the mad son of a…" Johnny trailed off as he spared a cautious glance at the display and lingered, his expression shifting from wary to disbelieving to utterly stunned as he took in the scene of dozens of pale, tranquil bodies strapped to the racks below Vantage.

He turned back to me, gun fractionally lowered. "Alpha's tits, I knew I shouldn't have trusted those mushrooms. Any chance I can just convince you two to fly back up that there big hole in the roof?" He glanced at the guard who'd caught our fall, so to speak. "And what the demons' danglers did you do to Erns? What was that?"

Elise touched my arm. "We have to go, Hal."

I gave her a nod. "That's gonna take some explaining as well," I said to Johnny. "But no aliens involved for that one, at least."

Johnny barked a humorless laugh. "Oh good. And here I was worrying my day was about to get weird. We'll just cap it at *dead best friend dropping in with his new lady person to talk about evil aliens and—*"

Somewhere in the distance, an explosion shook the night.

Johnny's eyes went hard, his weapon raising.

Then a new voice boomed from the amps, drowning out Therese's audio log and the alarm tones alike.

"Attention. This is a Code Black."

Johnny growled a stream of curses. I stared at the amp in disbelief, an uneasy feeling creeping into my gut. Code Black? For four people?

"This is not a drill," the amp speaker continued. "Sanctuary has been breached by unidentified hostiles, numbering in the low hundreds and counting."

I traded a wide-eyed look with Elise.

"Hostiles appear to be unarmed but extremely deadly in close range. Repeat, this is a Code Black. All available companies should—"

There was a commotion, hard to make out in detail over the alarm and Therese's voice. What was clear enough, though, was the bloodthirsty roar, and the gunfire that poured through the amps in the seconds before it cut dead, along with the alarm.

Hybrids.

"Tell me this isn't your people," Johnny said, his voice deadly serious, his weapon trained straight at my face.

"Did that sound like a person to you?" Elise said. "Hal, we have to move. Now."

"Kublich's taking Sanctuary," I said before I could really think it through.

When I did, though, I only grew more certain.

"What the scud are you talking about?" Johnny said. "He's High General. He already has Sanctu—"

"Taking Sanctuary with his own army, Johnny. Kublich is not the man you think he is. Now we need to get our friends and get out of here. All of us."

"If you think I'm gonna—"

"Johnny," Elise said, her voice brimming with the threat of an imminent explosion, "take a look at this display."

He frowned in her direction, then went wide-eyed. I glanced over and saw a pack of hybrids charging a disoriented fireteam out in front of the brig.

It was over before I could even think about trying to get out there to help them.

"What?" was all Johnny could manage to say.

"That's what Kublich's been up to," I said. "That's what I'm trying to tell you."

"I don't know what's… I have to help them. Kublich couldn't have—"

"Kublich killed my parents, Johnny. I watched him do it with his own hands. He tried to kill me. And, I promise you, he's the one controlling those things out there. I need your help, Johnny. We need to get our people out of here. Help me get them out, and I'll stay here. I'll fight beside you for Sanctuary."

"Hal…" Elise whispered.

"We can't let him take this base," I said, not dropping Johnny's gaze. "Help me. Please."

"I thought you were dead, man," he said finally, like he was just now seeing me for the first time since we'd dropped in. "Even after the stories started. I knew if you were out there, you wouldn't let me go on thinking you'd…"

He shook his head, looking away. There was pain on his face. Deep, genuine pain like I'd never seen from Johnny.

I'd known he was upset—and understandably so—but seeing him like this… It hurt.

"I'm sorry, Johnny. I didn't—It wasn't safe for me to contact you. I swear I thought about doing it anyway, dozens of times. But I couldn't."

"And now you're just dropping in to casually ask me to commit some light treason."

I flinched. "Yeah. Pretty much." I tried to force a smile. "Aren't you glad to have me back?"

I didn't mention the part where the regime I was asking him to commit treason against might well facilitate his being turned into food at some point if we didn't do anything about it.

"Dammit." Johnny said, curling and uncurling his fists. Then, in his mimicry voice, "Ours is not to ask, children. Don't mind the fire. Don't mind the—Gropping son of a—" He kicked a chair, anger flashing for a split second before he finally looked up to meet my eyes, shaking his head. "Man, if I hadn't already been questioning everything from the High Cleric to my own mother, I would have shot you back at 'You got brigged?'"

"Not my finest first line," I said. "That mean you're in?"

He glanced at Elise, a familiar grin spreading across his face. "She's coming, right?"

And just like that, the first little crack was forming in the wall between us, and I found myself chuckling despite everything. "Yeah, Johnny. She's coming."

He wagged his eyebrows at Elise. "Well, totally worth some light treason, then."

"Elise, meet my best friend, Johnathan Wingard."

"Pleased as sunny petals," she said. "Now can we please find my dad and get out of here?"

"Straight to business, then," Johnny said, going to one of the displays and flicking through a few menus. "Alpha save my soul. Names?"

Elise was just beginning to say "Franco" when Johnny waved her off.

"Kidding. Just checking patrols." He grabbed a riot gun from the rack by the door. "I know exactly who you're looking for. Kind of hard to miss."

Elise stared at him incredulously.

"What?" Johnny gave an innocent shrug, sliding a stunner into the riot gun's chamber. "You know how it is. Gotta keep an eye on us terrorist types."

CHAPTER 36
PRISONERS

"Hal, Hal, Hal," Johnny said as we jogged down the stairs to the brig's bottom level. "What in the name of Alpha's shriveled old man bits have you gotten me into this time?"

"You know," I said. "Saving Enochia. Finishing what my dad started. Just another day in the Legion, really."

"Hey, at least it'll be a good story when we're side by side at the gallows. You guys forced this onto the emergency broadcast channel?" he added, pointing at one of the amps that was still projecting Therese Brown's story through the building.

"Our friends saw to it."

"Sweet Alpha, you guys aren't gropping around, are you?"

At the bottom of the stairs, Johnny reached for the access panel to the heavy hardsteel door and paused. "Two of our guys are down here. Let's take it easy if the talking turns ugly, yeah?"

We agreed. He palmed the access panel, which lit green. Another tap, and the door gave a sharp clack and hissed open on its tracks. I cradled the riot gun I'd taken from the guard room and swept in on Johnny's heels.

The door hissed shut behind us, an acute reminder that there was one and exactly one way out of this level. Elise pressed a hand to my back, experiencing a similar unease by the look of it.

"Let's get your family back," I whispered.

She looked more apprehensive than ever, like, now that we were so close, it was only natural we'd find out that we'd made some critical error and that all hope was in fact lost.

The hallway was wide and brightly lit, spanning most of the length of the building. Rows of viridian cell doors lined each side, and after every block of cells, smaller hallways branched perpendicularly from the main passage.

The two guards Johnny had mentioned were nowhere in sight.

We prowled down the hallway, Johnny on point, Therese's voice ringing off the hardsteel cell doors in a grainy treble. I doubted it would be much longer before the troops broke through whatever surprises Carlisle had left for them and shut the transmission down.

Hopefully the world was paying attention.

I was beginning to worry about where those guards were when Johnny slowed his pace and called, "Hey, goodfellas? I have something to tell you, but I need you to promise to take it easy for a minute."

Elise and I froze.

Ahead, a stout legionnaire rounded into view from a side hall, engrossed in his tablet. "I don't know," he called over his shoulder to someone else, "I'm just gonna go check."

"Let it be said that I really can't stress the *take it easy* part enough," Johnny called.

The guard looked up. "What is it Win—"

He caught sight of me and Elise and went rigid, eyes darting back and forth between me and Johnny a good dozen times in the space of two seconds.

Johnny raised his hands, his riot gun held to the side in an unthreatening manner. "Easy. Eeeasy, Benny…"

Benny didn't take it easy.

The stout man dropped his tablet to the floor with a clatter and made a desperate grab for his sidearm. "It's Raish!" he cried.

Johnny whipped his riot gun into position and fired a heavy stunner into Benny's chest with crisp precision. It was only as Benny flopped to the ground that Johnny seemed to process what he'd done.

"Dammit, Benny! Look what you made me do!"

A muttered curse from around the corner marked the location of Benny's partner.

I pointed to the spot, but Johnny was already marching forward ahead of us, sliding another stunner home with authority. "How 'bout you, Bucky?" he called. "Care to talk for a second?"

A ripple of surprise shot through me. Bucky was only a year older than us. I'd trained with him for years.

Apparently that didn't mean much now.

As we stacked in behind Johnny at the corner, two warning shots thundered, teeth-jarringly loud in the enclosed space, and kicked spouts of permacrete from the wall opposite us.

"C'mon, man!" Johnny called. "We all know something strange has been going on lately. You know Hal, for the love of Alpha! He's not a terrorist."

Another gunshot. Followed by Bucky's wavering voice. "I always had a bad feeling about *both* of you scud heads!"

Johnny turned back to me with a wide-eyed expression that was part indignant, part amused surprise. "Has anyone ever told you you're a bit narrow minded, Buckster?"

As he spoke, he signaled a plan to me.

I nodded my acknowledgment, and before Bairn "Bucky" Bucksworth had a chance to reply, Johnny threw himself across the mouth of the hallway and rolled for the far corner. I rounded the corner, riot gun held left-handed so I could take aim without leaving cover. Not that it mattered.

As expected, Bucky was tracking Johnny's wild roll, which gave me plenty of time to take aim and squeeze the trigger.

The stunner knocked him back against the wall before he crumpled.

Something itched at the edge of my senses.

"Johnny, down!" I shouted, just as a third guard sprang out further down the main hallway, her weapon raised.

Johnny scrambled for cover in Bucky's hallway. The first shot cracked, and my stomach wrenched as Johnny cried out. I swept my gun for the new target.

Elise blurred past me and hurled her staff javelin style at the shooter before I could fire.

The staff struck the guard square in the chest. She fell to her rear with an audible whoosh of air evacuating pummeled lungs, wheezing and clutching at her chest. I drew my sidearm and tagged her with a stun round, feeling none too proud about it.

"Agh!" Johnny cried, pulling himself up against the wall he'd flopped behind. "Son of a bitch, Brie!"

We hurried to him, but he held up a hand to silence our worried questions. "I'm fine, I'm fine."

He showed us the back of his right arm, where a neat trail was torn through his gray brigs tunic. The sleeve was stained scarlet where the slug had grazed his arm, but it didn't look serious.

"Say, Hal, did I ever tell you about the time alliteration nearly killed me? Forgot Brie was down here. Buncha bitter, belligerent bastards." He peered around the corner at Brie's unmoving form, then to the staff, then to Elise.

For maybe the first time in his life, Johnny refrained from saying anything at all. He simply gave Elise an appreciative nod and a look that said, *Not bad.*

She smiled and offered him a hand, which he gratefully took, and we continued on. Now that the shooting had ended and my nerves were coming back down, I noticed the thumping sounds all around us.

Thump. Thump. Thump.

The prisoners, I realized, pounding against their cell doors, probably wondering what in demons' depths the commotion was all about. It just reminded me what was happening to Sanctuary outside.

We took the rest of the main hallway at a run. As soon as Johnny gave the all clear sign and guided us down the second to last side hall on the left, Elise rushed past us.

"Dad? Dad?!"

Tears were welling in her eyes as she spun, looking around at the doors on either side of her, five to each side.

It was only then, seeing the desperation in her eyes, that it truly hit me how much raw emotion she'd been holding down since Franco and Phineas had been taken. The fear and helplessness must have nearly crushed her, and yet she'd manifested the willpower to stick patiently to the plan and to not come running and screaming for Franco as soon as we'd set foot in Sanctuary. I wasn't sure I could've handled myself so well, had I been in her position.

For a terrible moment, there was nothing but the echo of her voice.

Then, "Elise? Sweetheart, is that you?"

A muffled voice. Frail. But definitely Franco's.

Thank Alpha.

"Dad!" she cried, lunging for the door the voice had come from. "It's us! We're gonna get you out!"

She shot Johnny an expectant look at the last part.

Franco's muffled voice came through the door again, but I couldn't make out what he said.

Johnny palmed the panel by the door, which flashed green. He punched an additional command, and the door unlocked with a heavy click that resounded down the hallway.

Elise ripped the hardsteel door open with frantic energy. Hinges groaned in mournful protest, and then there was Franco, crumpled to his knees at the cell's threshold. His face was bruised and grimy. He wore a tattered, blue-gray jumpsuit and a look of exhausted defeat.

Until he saw Elise.

At the sight of his daughter, Franco's eyes lit up, and something between a laugh and a weary moan escaped his throat. He struggled to his feet. She grabbed him and pulled him up forcefully enough that they almost toppled into the doorframe together. Neither of them seemed to particularly care.

Elise clung desperately to her father, and from the look on Franco's face, he might have been under the impression that he'd in fact moved on to the afterlife.

After a long moment, though, he came back to the sight of us standing there, and he sobered. He took in Johnny's Legion tunic suspiciously, then Elise's staff and the rest of her gear.

"What are you doing here?" he asked, his voice hoarse. He gave me a hard look. "How could you bring her here?"

Elise fired back before I could open my mouth. "I'm rescuing my dad. And I wasn't brought here like a piece of cargo. I fought my way in, just like Hal."

"She did," I agreed, failing to suppress a smile of admiration. "She really saved our asses just now."

Franco's studied Elise as I spoke, his brows fighting to meet. "I'm sorry," he finally said. "You know how I worry. You just... You really are your mother's daughter. She would have been so proud of you. Just like I am." He pulled her into another hug.

"Touched as I am to hear it," Elise said, drawing back, "we need to get out of here."

Johnny, probably painfully aware of our pressing time constraints, had already moved surreptitiously to the next cell.

"Let's see what's behind door number two," he muttered to himself. "Maybe *Johnny* gets a hug this time... 'Hey, Johnny! Thanks for turning on the Legion for us terrorist sorts at a moment's notice. It was a really swell move and all.' Oh, yeah... No sweat. Totally. Anytime!"

I smiled at Johnny's monologue.

Franco was staring after him with a confused frown.

"He's an old friend," I said, as if that should explain everything.

Franco gave a slow nod, and Elise smiled.

"Don't everyone thank me at once," Johnny added as he tapped a command and the next cell clicked open.

Sadly, I didn't expect there'd be a hug waiting for Johnny behind door number two.

"Uh, thank you…" Franco started.

"Johnny," I provided.

"Thank you, Johnny," Franco said.

Johnny gave a wave and pulled open the cell door.

"I see you went ahead with the rest of the plan in our absence," Franco added, gesturing toward the amps still rattling our program.

"Yeah," I said, "not sure how long that part's—"

Amp Therese's voice abruptly cut off, replaced by a squeal of feedback, then a sharp click.

"—gonna last," I finished. "Guess we'll see how much good that did."

In the silence that followed, I heard the distant sounds of fighting above ground.

"Uh, guys?" Johnny said from the doorway of Phineas' cell.

I went to join him and immediately saw the problem.

Phineas' prosthetic limbs were missing. Emphasis on the plural.

I hadn't even realized one of Phineas' legs was a prosthetic, but there he lay on a rough cot with only his right leg and his right arm, which was currently draped over his face, hiding it from sight.

He momentarily peered out from underneath as I walked in.

"Get the others out, kid," he said quietly. "You can't afford to be dragging me along."

"Get up, Phineas," Franco said behind me before I could respond.

He brushed past me and offered his right hand to Phineas. "You know we're going to drag you out of here whether you want us to or not. Just like you would do if it were any one of us."

Phineas regarded the hand for a few long moments, then finally sighed and reached up to clasp it. "Whatever gets you moving, you old fool."

With Phineas' leg hanging over the edge of the cot, Franco bent down, laboriously pulled the larger man over his shoulder, and stood back up.

"Not to rub your nose in it," Franco said, "but you're certainly lighter without the extras."

"Just give me a gun so I can cover your back," Phineas grumbled.

I drew my pulse gun and handed it to Franco as Elise offered her own sidearm to Phineas.

"What are you going to do if we run into trouble?" Franco protested.

Elise hefted her staff pointedly, and I waved my riot gun.

Franco nodded reluctantly, and I fell in by Johnny leading the others back the way we'd come, praying the proper Legion forces were holding their own against Kublich's hybrids out there.

Either way, it was time.

I keyed my earpiece. "We've got the goods, guys. We can be outside in three minutes. Do we have a ride?"

"Do we have a ride?" Johnny half-muttered, half-cackled under his breath. "Alpha be sweet…"

I was too worried at the silence on the comm line to acknowledge his razzing.

Finally, though, as we passed the unconscious form of guard Benny, Carlisle's voice crackled in my earpiece. "Sorry. It's… quite hectic out here. We have a transport. I think it's wise we leave immediately."

I let out a relieved breath and was about to tell the others when a metallic click resounded down the hallway.

"Ah scud biscuits," Johnny said.

And, like that, the flicker of relief kindling in my chest was drowned out by a wash of cold dread. The same dread I'd felt when we'd been caught underground at Vantage.

Only this time, Carlisle wasn't there to pull me out.

At the end of the hall, the one and only door to the stairs hissed open in its tracks.

My breath caught, the dread in my stomach deepening, spilling over first into panic, then to dark rage.

"Well grop me twelve ways to the sun," Johnny mumbled.

There, in the doorway, eyes ablaze with scarlet demon fire, stood High General Adrian Kublich.

For a long moment, no one moved. For others, it might have been the surprise. The fear. For me, it was simply that every muscle in my body was too tightly clenched at the sight of my parents' killer. The sight of the creature who'd ruined my life, who'd started all of this, standing right there. Watching me. Waiting.

Smiling like he'd already won.

I couldn't think. My world shrank to that hallway. I wanted to charge straight in, grab him by the throat, and see how those blazing red eyes of his would handle a knife stab.

"Hal…" Elise whispered, grabbing my arm, pulling me back to reality.

I forced a breath. Tried to think.

"Kublich's here, Carlisle," I muttered quietly. "Get to the rooftop now. I'll make sure the others get out."

Kublich was still a hundred feet away, but I swear he smirked as if he'd heard me. He started toward us with the gait of a predator already savoring the kill he was about to make. And maybe for good reason. Down here, in tight quarters, a raknoth would be beyond deadly.

But I sure as demons' depths wasn't going to let that stop me.

This was exactly the moment I'd been waiting for.

"Howya, High General," Johnny called. "I think you've got something in your eyes, there." He raised his riot gun, taking loose aim. "Maybe you should lie down, sir. You look like demon scud."

Kublich prowled forward, making no sign he'd heard Johnny at all.

"It's over, Kublich," I called. "You can try to take Sanctuary. It won't matter. After tonight, all of Enochia will be coming for you."

The low rumble of his laughter echoed down to us, weighted with horrible certainty.

"Is that what you think, child? That you have accomplished anything but to accelerate our plans? Your father would be disappointed in you, Haldin."

Something snapped inside me.

I almost didn't register Elise's restraining arms around me, her pleading voice in my ear. I wanted to throttle the bastard with my bare hands.

It was the low boom of Johnny's riot gun that snapped me to my senses.

Kublich staggered back a step, a heavy stunner pegged to his chest.

"Always kinda secretly wanted to do that," Johnny muttered beside me.

Kublich peeled the stunner from his chest, regarded it with disdain, and tossed it aside. "Bring the Raish boy to me," he said, his voice deeper than before. "Kill the rest."

I had one moment to wonder who he was talking to. One horrible moment for understanding to set in.

Then the hybrids came.

CHAPTER 37
EXIT PLAN

Think. I needed to think.

A dozen hybrids howling down the hallway toward us. More than that. More streaming in still. And only five of us. Only three in fighting condition.

And then there was Kublich.

There was no way we were fighting our way out of this. And that grinning, demon-eyed bastard knew it.

"We're on our way," Carlisle's voice crackled through the earpiece, followed by the faint sound of gunfire, yells, and the hum of an engine in the background. "Try to keep him talking if you can't get out."

"Plans have changed," I growled.

We needed a way out. And we needed it now.

I clamped a hand on Johnny's shoulder, the bare bones of a shoddy plan whirling in my mind. "Get a cell open. Now."

He only hesitated the length of a questioning glance before he was off, strafing to the cells on our left, firing a stream of stunner at the oncoming hybrids all the way.

I raised my own riot gun and opened up. "Cover him!"

Franco turned so he and Phineas could both fire on the incoming hybrids.

It wasn't enough.

There were too many hybrids, pressing in too ferociously. Too fearlessly.

Elise greeted the first hybrid's skull with her staff and whirled seamlessly into striking another.

I met the third one with the butt of my riot gun. It felt like batting hardwood, but the hybrid went down by way of perturbed balance if not actual pain. I drew my knife, dropped a knee between the hybrid's shoulder blades, and plunged the blade into its neck before it could scramble to its feet.

Even with my thumb braced on the hilt, I wasn't ready for the resistance the blade met. My hand slipped. I felt the edge of my palm slide neatly open, and my own blood oozed down to join the squirming hybrid's.

I adjusted my grip and drove the blade home with both hands. To my relief, the blade sank, and the hybrid went slack.

"Open!" Johnny cried behind me, the roar of his riot gun rejoining the fray.

The air was alive with growls and other unholy sounds.

I clambered to my feet, glancing to the open cell door. "Get to the—"

"Down!" Johnny roared.

I didn't ask questions—just dropped like a sack of stones. Johnny's riot gun roared twice in rapid succession, and two hybrids flopped to the ground by me and Elise, convulsing with the stunners' charges.

Johnny hauled me up by the forearm, and we spun to face the hybrids side by side, riot guns roaring. Elise's staff whirled tirelessly, its wind-whipping song punctuated by the rapid thuds of staff on hide and bone. On my flank, Franco and Phineas dropped target after target with softsteel slugs and careful precision.

The hybrids kept coming, their numbers still growing. I couldn't even see Kublich through the throng anymore. Several of them were sniffing at the air now. Sniffing, I realized, and fixing their pale red gazes on my freely bleeding hand.

"Get to the cell!" I shouted.

Elise spun down from an aerial maneuver to deliver one last bone-shattering blow, then turned and darted for us. Johnny and I shot a few hybrids off her back, shuffling toward the cell ourselves.

"Scud," Johnny growled beside me. "I'm out."

I shot another hybrid down and realized I was out too—just as one of the fallen hybrids pounced to its feet behind Elise.

"No!" I shouted, tearing forward.

Too late.

The thing caught her from behind in some sick parody of a lovers' embrace, gleaming fangs bared to strike at the soft flesh of her throat.

In that moment, my training meant nothing.

There was no cool focus. No plan. I rushed at them like a frightened boy, trying to reach the girl he loved before it was too late—my mind screaming with the flashes of my mom and dad being violently torn from the world.

"Elise!" I screamed, stretching my hand out, desperately lunging—already realizing I was too late.

Except the hybrid had paused, pale eyes fixed hungrily on my outstretched hand. The hand that was still dripping blood.

It was only a moment's hesitation, little more than a hungry glance. But it was enough.

I closed on them and thrust my bloody palm right into the hybrid's hungry red eyes. Relief swelled as the hybrid released Elise. Then it grabbed my arm instead and chomped down.

The pain was immediate and breathtaking, and it tripled when the creature jerked its head, jaws still clamped. I jammed my knife through the hybrid's eye, yelling without hardly realizing it. It went limp with its fangs still buried in my arm, and I staggered with it, trying to pry its jaws open.

To the left, Johnny was on his back, barely fending off a chomping hybrid with his riot gun held cross-body.

"Help him!" I cried at Elise as she bent to help me.

After the briefest hesitation, she whirled away.

There was a loud crack of staff on skull from her direction, followed shortly by Johnny's frenetic, "Yeah, have a bite of *that*, you son of a bitch!"

I pried my arm loose, and then Franco was there, pulling me toward the cell, and Johnny and Elise were scrambling in ahead of us. Phineas was already on the floor inside.

We fell into the cell, Franco yanking the door shut behind us.

A scaly green arm shot in to bar its path. Bones cracked as the door struck it, and there was a terrible screech, but the arm didn't withdraw.

I reached out and flung the hybrid away with telekinesis. Franco slammed the door shut. I turned my mind to locking the bolts manually, then killed the access panel outside with a hastily severed power line. That done, I slumped against the wall, head buzzing.

The first hybrid slammed into the door with a cracking thud. The second impact came with a groan of deforming metal. The door wouldn't hold long.

"Alpha be damned," Johnny growled, "what the grop are those th—"

An enraged bellow filled the room, muffled by the door but still plenty intimidating to make us all jump. A fist-sized dent joined the first one.

"Hal?"

Elise was beside me, gaze flicking between me and my mangled arm, her face drained of blood.

"I'm fine," I grunted.

In truth, the pain wasn't nearly as bad as I would've expected. That's not to say I was actually fine. I was bleeding freely from multiple wounds. I was tired. Hurt. Terrified.

But we needed a way out. So I needed to be fine a little longer.

"Everyone against this wall," I said. "Now."

They didn't argue. There clearly weren't any alternative plans here.

I focused, gathering my will.

"And now?" Johnny asked to my left, closest to the thumping protests of the hardsteel door. "Please tell me there's more to the pla—"

Someone—Elise, I thought—shushed at him.

"What? He's just sitting there! Hal? Hal, what the scud are—"

"Shut your mouth, kid," Phineas rumbled.

Any other day, it would've raised my hackles, hearing Phineas take that tone with Johnny. Then and there, though, it was a boon. A quiet vote of confidence from the bear who didn't do warm and kindly. I drew more energy from the cells in my pack, letting the electric fury course through my veins. Someone might have said something more, but I didn't have the capacity left to process it.

In Johnny's defense, it probably did look like I was just sitting there. In truth, though, I was drinking in more energy than I'd ever thought to channel. My body positively screaming with it. Desperately trying to hold the construct steady in my mind. Leaning on that desperation—the fear, the hatred for Kublich just outside—to force my will into reality.

Then, when I felt myself slipping into darkness, I let it all loose like a detonating bomb.

There was a deep, resounding crack that I felt through the wall and the floor. I think I blacked out for a few seconds. Something crashed at the edge of my awareness. Darkness resolved to Elise's frantic face, and Johnny's stunned one, both of them pulling on me, dragging me to my feet.

"Did it work?" I asked. Or tried to, at least.

It came out more as a slurred groan, the world dipping around me, my head spinning crazily as they hoisted me up. Nevertheless, I saw the thick pile of rubble in the corner of the cell, and the light shining down from above.

We had our way out.

My heart eased at the sight of Franco fixing the grappling module's coiling motor to Phineas' jumpsuit and holding on, both of them beginning the ascent.

"Go," I murmured at Elise. "You next. Go."

I tried to take my own weight back from her and Johnny and nearly brought us all down. My body was stiff, unwieldy. I felt slow and thick in the head, drunk on exhaustion. My arm didn't even hurt. No, it was more than that. I couldn't even feel the arm. Or the leg.

Something was wrong.

Before I had time to wonder about it, though, the cell door gave a horrible moan and wrenched free from its hardsteel frame with a series of sharp cracks.

Johnny spun and opened fire with his sidearm.

I whirled with him and caught a glimpse of Kublich tossing aside the hardsteel cell door like scrap before the room lurched and a plunging sensation informed me that my numb legs had failed to plant themselves under my weight. I watched the cell floor rush up to meet me, powerless to do more than weakly flop an arm out.

Elise caught me as my knees thudded to the floor, at least saving me from a full face-plant. "Hal!"

Franco was yelling something from above.

"Hybrid bite," I croaked as it dawned on me. "Venomous. Can't move."

"No," she whispered, pulling me back toward the opening I'd made. "Please. We have to move, Hal. Please!"

Johnny's steady stream of gunfire ended, his sidearm empty. Ahead, Kublich lowered his arms from his face, red eyes blazing, tendrils of scaly green creeping over his skin.

It was over. I couldn't move.

I was already dead.

So I did the only thing I could. I wrapped Elise and Johnny in a net of my will and pulled.

I didn't get to see their shocked faces, their indignant outrage when they realized what I was doing. I just heard them screaming my name, screaming to stop. Heard the terror and hurt in their voices. It cut me to the core. But I kept lifting until I felt them clear the hole to the ground floor.

Kublich surged forward with a low growl and cuffed me aside. There was no ducking. No moving at all. I hit the cell wall with a jarring thud and barely felt a thing.

"After them!" Kublich's voice roared somewhere far away, more beast than human now.

Bare feet slapped across the cell floor. Hybrids charging for the rubble-strewn corner, a river of scaly green shins and clawed feet rushing past in my limited field of vision. Darkness was clouding my senses now, pulling me down. Exhaustion. Hybrid venom. Whatever it was, it was trying to take me. My window had already closed on even trying to telekinetically lift myself up after the others.

I was dead. About to join my parents by Kublich's hand. The thought made me want to scream. I couldn't. Couldn't move. Couldn't do anything to stop it.

But I could try to take the bastard with me, at least.

I reached out with my senses, found the knife I'd dropped, and focused my will, picking Kublich out of the rushing tide of hybrids, taking aim. It'd have to be a perfect shot. I pulled the energy and—

Something stomped down on my back. Hard. A hybrid, I realized. Just as one of its kin dipped into my line of sight, glistening fangs bared in a hungry snarl. It reached for my throat. Panic tearing through me, I caught its hand with telekinesis, my vision wavering with the effort.

Shouts from above. Sounds of fighting. Elise screaming. I lay there, listening helplessly, waiting for my power to fail, for the hybrid to tear me to pieces. My vision darkening. The venom dragging me down.

At the edge of my sight, Kublich strode up and shoved the two hybrids aside. He didn't need them. I had nothing left. He'd beaten me.

I'd failed.

Failed my parents. Failed my friends, Enochia… It was all I could think as my parents' killer hoisted me up and pinned me against the cell wall like a flimsy plaything, his crimson eyes blazing violent victory.

With my last breath, I reached for Carlisle, unsure he was there at all, more a hopeless prayer than anything else. That he'd get the others out. That he'd finish what we started.

But it was too late.

The world was already fading to black when Kublich's strike fell.

CHAPTER 38

RUDE AWAKENING

The room was dim. Undefined. Like I could feel the walls there in the shadows but couldn't see them. I didn't know how I'd gotten there. Only that I came to it groggily and with a good deal of pain.

Pain. That was good, right? Why was that good?

Because Kublich apparently hadn't killed me, for starters.

But why couldn't I move my arms? And where the scud was I? And—

The others!

I came more alert, taking in my surroundings with bleary eyes, and quickly ran into the answer to one question, at least. I couldn't move my arms because my wrists were shackled and chained to the table I sat at. Had they been that way a moment ago? Of course. They must have been. And that hardly mattered anyhow.

Elise. Carlisle. Johnny. What had happened to them?

"Your friends are dead, Haldin," a voice whispered from the dark edges of the room, surrounding me. Kublich's voice. I was sure of it.

"You're lying."

He had to be. Alpha be sweet, they had to be alive.

I looked around the room, trying to spot him, and almost jumped when I turned back to find him sitting across from me, face fully reptilian, eyes pulsing a menacing crimson.

"Ahh, there we are," he said, eyes burning brighter. It was hard not to shudder at his alien expression, all flaring nose slits and jagged fangs.

"Here we are," I agreed, "but it looks like you forgot your makeup. Your lies are falling apart, Kublich."

He gave a hissing chuckle. "Ever defiant. Even when all hope is lost. You might have made a fine raknoth, had fate smiled upon you."

"I haven't lost hope," I said too quickly, my mind whirling, trying to take stock. Were we still in Sanctuary? Tucked away in some Legion torture chamber? Had Kublich and his hybrids taken the base?

I shifted in my seat, head throbbing, trying to ignore the deep, cutting pain in my shackled wrists. And that's when it dawned on me. I could move again. Another reason why pain was a good sign.

Small victories.

Kublich was watching me with what seemed like glib amusement. I had the uncomfortable feeling he could see straight through to the thoughts unfolding in my head.

"I could never be anything like one of you monsters," I added, mostly to break the silent spell.

His fanged grin only widened. "No? Lacking virtually all relevant details, and yet so righteous in your self-justification." He shook his head. "Such impetuous creatures you humans are."

"So full of scud, and yet so righteous in your own self-justification," I shot back. "Such monstrous creatures you raknoth are. You came here to make supper of our planet. Tell me what relevant details possibly make you the good guys here. You're nothing more than super-charged gropping parasites."

Slowly, carefully, I reached out with my senses to probe the lock of my shackles as I spoke. Or tried to, at least. Something was wrong. Fuzzy. Unfocused.

"Haldin, Haldin..." He hissed the name as if tasting it. His voice grew stern. "You know nothing of my people, child."

The way he said the word, *child*, made me feel like that was exactly what I was. A meddling child, weak and afraid. I did my best to shrug it off. "I know you're okay with destroying my race to make way for your own. I know you're sick, dying. I know..." The words stuck in my throat, tight and trembling. "I know that you killed my parents, you son of a bitch. And I know that, after tonight, if I can't make you pay for it, the rest of Enochia will."

Kublich leaned lazily back in his chair, tapping at the table with scaly knuckles. "Humans... So frail, yet so entitled. So assured of your supremacy. Tell me, do you truly believe your species deserves freedom from my kind's simple survival when you lack the strength to make it so? If so, perhaps you should set to the fields. Release the livestock. Save those poor bovas from the blood hungry tyranny of humans."

I tried again for the lock on my shackles, again to no avail.

"Yeah, Alton Parker said something similar. Right before we threw him off a building."

"We are a pragmatic people."

"You're monsters."

Kublich leaned forward with a feral grin. "Your kind do seem to get the two confused. When you end up at the wrong end of the slaughter, at least."

"You killed my parents," I growled.

"Pragmatically," he said, nodding. "Your father was treading the war path against my kin, whether he knew it or not. Moreover, technically speaking, he committed treason against his beloved Legion. You yourself have willingly watched men hanged for less."

"Grop you. That's bullscud. I—"

"Have been a bit of a nuisance," he said. "I admit, you and your gray-haired friend did push our timetable forward. But after tonight, it won't matter."

"I guess we finally agree on something, then. I don't care how many strings you pull. There's no way you're convincing the entire planet to forget what they saw tonight."

"Haldin..." Even with his reptilian features, I almost thought I saw something like pity in his expression. It chilled my insides.

"Do you truly believe anyone would've believed your message?" he asked. "Do you understand your own people so poorly?"

He was posturing, I told myself. But something about his tone... No. Not just his tone.

What did he mean, *would've*?

Conditional. As if tonight hadn't happened.

"Yes," he said, almost gently. "There, you see it. Your broadcast never made it out of Sanctuary, Haldin. Which means everyone who heard it is either dead or currently on the run from the Legion, dastardly traitors that they are, trying to overthrow Sanctuary from the inside and all."

"You're lying."

"We're past the point of lying, Haldin, I assure you. Mr. Fields and Mr. Hammer won't have any recollection of my probing, of course, but I'm rather offended you and your precious Carlisle imagined I could be so inept as to not only miss your plan, but to leave intact the one network we do not have squarely in our palms."

The room was spinning, closing around me.

"No one's..." My head was spinning with the room now, my breaths coming too fast. "You're lying. And even if you're not, Enochia won't believe what happened at Sanctuary was all just some kind of rebel uprising. They'll figure it out. They'll—"

"They will believe what we tell them to!" Kublich roared, crimson eyes flashing.

The very room shook with his fury, the air shimmering oddly. For a second, I had the strangest impression Kublich might simply vanish into thin air—that all of it would. But then all was calm, and Kublich spoke evenly. "Your kind have always possessed a particular weakness for narrative. There's no limit to the lies you creatures will swallow if it helps you feel good and safe in your own little worlds."

I wanted to tell him to grop himself. I wanted to argue. To do something other than just sit there stupidly. I was just too afraid that he was right—that our best shot had proved worthless.

That I'd failed just like my dad.

And now I was going to die knowing that Enochia would wholeheartedly applaud the news.

"What do you want with me?" I finally asked. I had a pretty good idea, but I asked anyway. "Why am I still alive?"

"You yet draw breath simply because your death will be of more use to us as a sacrifice"—he waved a hand fancifully—"to Alpha. To your precious Sanctum and the blessed illusion of stability it provides. What better time to assure Enochia that we have matters under control? That we will not suffer treason from within our own ranks. The people will never feel safer. They'll redouble their efforts, falling over themselves to hand us the rest of this world on a platter."

I had to keep myself from nodding along. It all made perfect sense.

"You're wrong," I said anyway, out of stubbornness more than any real belief.

Kublich said nothing, seeming distracted by some thought.

What was he playing at? Why tell me any of this? It wasn't like he was going to learn anything of value by my reactions. Which left two options. Either he simply enjoyed toying with me...

Or he was greasing me up to break into my mind.

As I thought it, the air vibrated with another shimmering pulse. Kublich smiled in a way that made my stomach sink. I braced myself. But why even try to break me? What would he gain?

If my friends were still out there—and I had to believe they were—they wouldn't be foolish enough to return anywhere I could find. Not with me in raknoth custody. I didn't know where they'd go, what they'd do next. Kublich couldn't get anything from me. Except…

Except that he could march me in front of a WAN camera like a puppet and make me confess to every crime, admit that my co-conspirators were all cracked in the head, touched by demons—that we'd weaved wild stories, fabricated evidence. He could ensure that, even if the others managed to get the truth out there in the future, it would be preemptively discredited.

I'd be damned if I let that happen.

Kublich laughed as if I'd said something particularly amusing. "I assure you, your cooperation is not necessary."

I went cold.

He'd heard my thoughts. There was no denying this time. Which meant… The world seemed to tilt beneath me, and I was sliding, sliding into cold, clammy darkness. I tried to clear my head. Tried to tighten my mental barriers. But I couldn't feel them.

"All your gifts and training, and you're still just as helpless as the rest of them. Helpless as your sweet mother."

I lunged for his throat only to be jerked to a halt by my chains. He waved a hand dismissively, and I slammed back to the chair, frozen, unable even to draw breath.

"Have you not yet pieced together where we are, Haldin?"

Around us, the shadowy walls began to swirl and crawl. And that's when I knew. I couldn't move. Couldn't breathe. And it didn't matter.

Because none of this was real.

"Oh, I assure you, it's real enough," Kublich said. "But I am nearly finished. My master overestimates the difficulty of sweeping an unconscious human mind. You are no doubt right about your friends, though."

As he spoke, light and color touched the shadowy walls around us, twisting into a vivid image of the temple ruins on a sunny afternoon. I swear I could even smell the dirt and the sun-kissed stone. Because it wasn't just an image.

It was my memory.

"Yes," Kublich said. "But we both know they're too smart to return anywhere you'd know how to find." The walls contorted again, darkening, cooling somehow. Kublich's lips tugged into a satisfied grin. "Just like we both now know the sweetness of a certain raven-haired beauty on a dark, lonely, woodland night."

The swirling images twisted into a silhouette, too dark to identify. But I didn't need to see her face to recognize the feel of Elise's flesh against mine. The sounds of us together in the skimmer.

I felt sick.

"I'm given to understand this is the epitome of the human experience," Kublich said, frowning at our writhing pleasure. "Pathetic as that may—"

"Shut up."

The fire in my voice gave him pause. The air shuddered with it, a ripple passing over Kublich's visage as if he might simply disintegrate. He bared his fangs in challenge. He wasn't smiling anymore.

"I'm going to get out of here."

The walls were alive now, jittering with flashes of a thousand different moments from the past cycles. A thousand moments I'd spent preparing myself for this. For him. Then the flickering reel stabilized, and we were staring at my mom, frail and bloodied in Kublich's arms. Him tossing her broken body aside like refuse. His red-eyed sneer challenging me to stop him.

Something shifted. I don't know how to explain it. But when I looked down, I was no longer chained. I was standing. The table, the chairs, gone. Only me and my parents' killer, snarling at me, the first hints of surprise widening his burning eyes.

I screamed his name and charged.

CHAPTER 39
MASTER

It was like waking up in the middle of a raging ocean. That's the best way I could put it.

For a second, I couldn't remember how I'd ended up in the middle of the thrashing waves. Then I realized I *was* the waves. And so was Kublich. And we were crashing together, churning and mixing and vying for dominance amid the howling winds of our telepathic storms. I didn't have time to ask how or why—to wonder about the cutting pain in my body, somewhere far away.

I threw myself against Kublich's defenses with a single-minded focus born of the fact that I was certain my life depended on it.

He was strong. Stronger than me. Stronger, maybe, than Carlisle. But I was desperate. And, for some reason I didn't have time to wonder at, he was frantic. Out of control. Almost like he was afraid.

I pressed without question. No time to stop, to think. I couldn't. Couldn't give him the chance to regain his footing. I pressed until I felt something give, like breaking through the rough skin of a derja fruit to the soft contents inside.

I pressed on until, with a wild outpouring of eerily alien sensations, I punched into Kublich's mind.

~

HAD I not spent the past few cycles learning to cope with the information overload of my extended senses, Kublich's mind might've broken me. As it was, it nearly did anyway.

Vast. That was the best word for it. His mind was as sprawling as it was alien.

An explosion of memories ripped through me, too rapid to control.

Stars. Planets. Hundreds of them. Thousands.

Landscapes and life forms I couldn't begin to fathom, flashing by too fast to process. Enormous spires of dark glass, and short, jagged bipeds that inexplicably flashed from one point to another in a blink. Forests of neon bright trees, and wriggling, tentacular masses crawling through them.

These and a thousand more flashed through my mind's eye, threatening to completely overwhelm any sense I had left. And through it all, the black emptiness between. The Void, cold and endless, waiting to swallow all that life back whence it came.

I struggled to calm the storm of memories, trying to focus.

Kublich fought me all the way.

No. Not Kublich, I realized through the tumult of impossible sights and of feelings and sounds I didn't even have words for. Al'Kundesha.

That was the true name of this raknoth, who'd lived a hundred lives in a hundred different vessels on a hundred different worlds before coming to this shell that had once been Adrian Kublich.

I couldn't believe it. Any of it. Couldn't grasp the enormity, the vastness of the experiences this ancient creature had lived through. I couldn't wrap my mind around it.

So I clung to that name. The name of my parents' true murderer.

Al'Kundesha.

I used the name like a tether to ground myself, to slow the overwhelming tide of experience crashing down on me.

"No..." he hissed. *"Impossible. Get out, you filthy insect. Out!"*

My mind was reeling too hard to even be intimidated by the rage in his thoughts.

"All those worlds. All those... those things. Creatures. Aliens. What are you? What are you doing here?"

After everything I'd just seen, I barely knew where to start. But I focused on those two questions, just like I'd done with Smirks. Willed them at Al'Kundesha's mind as if trying to trigger my own memories. I was already in. I had the leverage, no matter how powerful this Al'Kundesha might be. I could force the answers.

Or so I thought.

Al'Kundesha was not Smirks. He wasn't human. His mind didn't whip to obey my commands just because I'd made it inside the perimeter. He bucked and kicked against me like a raging bull.

"I am not some petty human to be mindlessly controlled, foolish child!" he roared. *"I will not bow to your softsteel will."*

He surged against me again.

The fighting was quick and ferocious, but, strong as he was, I had the leverage. The effort left me sluggish with fatigue, but I managed to pin him back down.

I brought the questions back to the forefront of my mind... and nearly lost myself in the depths as his resistance gave way without warning.

The memories engulfed me. More planets. More lives. Always coming. Always moving on. All of it moving by in a flash. A few memories, though, lingered as if they bore too much gravity to simply flicker away like the rest.

A line of ten or more bodies, each with sickly lines woven across their exposed skin like black spider webs, each laid out neatly across a garishly patterned rug in the strangest-looking living quarters I'd ever seen.

They were raknoth. Or had been.

"It's getting worse," Al'Kundesha said in the memory, pulling back his sleeve to reveal similar inky lines running down his forearm, only slightly fainter than those on the dead.

"Trust in Zar'Faenor," another replied. "He will make them undo this sorcery."

"Would that the Masters have trusted Zar'Faenor," Al'Kundesha muttered, turning to look out the window at a strange city I'd never seen. "We never should have come to this wretched Urth."

The scene flickered away, falling back to the steady cascade of memories.

Arguments with other raknoth, their eyes all ablaze, their faces and necks all crawling with inky black lines. A frenzied chase through a forest of Urth, so similar to our own wilds. The blonde sorceress who'd conjured their plague straight from the Cursed Void. The moment of helpless fury they'd all shared when she'd ended her own life to escape them.

More arguments.

Another flash, and we were on a strange vessel, leaving the enormous blue planet behind. It was beautiful. A serene orb of ranging oceans, broken by landforms of luscious greens here and barren tans there, all of it overlaid by the wispy swirl of white clouds across the planet.

The scene flashed hurriedly on to a memory I felt instead of saw, like I was experiencing the world through my extended senses. It was how Al'Kundesha saw the world when he was without a host body, I realized.

They were still on the ship, the seven who'd survived the long journey. Al'Kundesha was hiding, his true form—indeed reminiscent of a human brain, if human brains were fleshy green blobs with slithering appendages—lurking silently in the shadows as Adrian Kublich walked by, inspecting the strange craft alongside the response team. Al'Kundesha could taste his blood through the skin. Longed for it.

Zar'Faenor gave the order, and Al'Kundesha reached out to ensnare Kublich's mind for the first time...

But Urth. What had happened on Urth? Why leave it behind? Why come to Enochia?

I tried to focus, to slow it down. But focusing was troublesome.

Something was wrong.

I was slipping. Losing control.

Somewhere in the distance, burning.

Panic touched my thoughts, though I wasn't fully sure why as I pushed the memories away, pulling myself back to the here and now, back to Kublich's senses to find out what was happening.

It was bizarre, seeing the world through eyes that weren't my own—eyes that were so much sharper than any human's. More bizarre, still, to see myself being strangled through those eyes.

He'd been trying to distract me with memories.

Through the raknoth's eyes, I saw myself tinged with red radiance, our foreheads pressed together, my legs hooked around Al'Kundesha's vessel as if to keep him close—which was a curious decision, considering his hand was on my throat.

Not daring to abandon my fading control to return to my own body, I willed his hand to relax its grip—commanded it with all the authority I could muster. Al'Kundesha fought. My awareness dimmed, and, for a second, I thought he'd won. But, slowly, the hand loosened, returning oxygen to my brain and control to my mind.

It was only then I realized I was hanging by shackled wrists, chained to the ceiling, dark blood running down my forearms from where they'd dug too deep.

I could all but taste the metallic tinge of it, mingling with the salty sweat on my brow and the cool, dusty permacrete of the room they were keeping me in. Alpha, did it smell good. Through his ears, I could hear my heart pumping the delectable stuff.

It was disturbing, the way his thoughts seemed to bleed into mine through his senses. Even as I registered the distant but deep pain from my wrists and the strangling pressure still draining from my face, I could also feel the thrill of Al'Kundesha's blood lust.

I turned my attention to the chains holding me, figuring his raknoth hands were equal to the task of liberating me. He didn't make it easy.

"You cannot escape, child. We own Sanctuary. Soon enough, we'll have Haven. Oasis. There's nowhere left for you to run."

"Maybe you should be the one worried about running," I sent, straining to close his hands on the chain. *"I told you I was getting out of here. Do you remember what else I promised to do?"*

"You think to intimidate me, human?" Something shifted in him. I tried to probe at it, but he spoke again, his tone superficially reasonable, subtly urgent. *"Release me now, Haldin, and I will see to it your last hours are at least not spent in torment."*

I heard my incredulous bark of laughter from both my own mouth and Al'Kundesha's. It was creepy.

"Sure. This from the guy who was just trying to strangle me. This from..."

I caught it then. Something familiar at the edge of Al'Kundesha's senses. The source of his sudden change of tone. A scent, I realized. A scent that filled Al'Kundesha with an odd swirling of excitement and dread.

Someone was coming. Someone who frightened even Al'Kundesha.

I could feel them now. Three of them, marching briskly down the hall. Two humans, armed, and one mind that could only be a raknoth. A raknoth whose mental presence dwarfed even Al'Kundesha's. Older. More expansive. It was like staring at the sun.

Zar'Faenor.

I withdrew my extended senses with a curse. It didn't matter who it was. There was nowhere to go. Nowhere to hide. I was stuck right here, barely holding Al'Kundesha from murdering me on the spot. I needed to shut him down, but I had no idea how to go about doing that. Unless...

On a burst of frantic hope, I took control of Al'Kundesha's hands, gripped the chain, and tugged. The link snapped like cheap polymer under his fingers. Distantly, I felt my own bloodied arms falling limply to my sides.

I caught my body with Al'Kundesha's arms. Lowered myself to the floor.

Then I turned Al'Kundesha, ready to command his tremendously strong raknoth body to plunge through the wall at Zar'Faenor and his men approaching outside. It wasn't my best plan, but I was working with what I had.

Except the moment Al'Kundesha took his first step away from my body, it was like my brain had been dunked in a river of liquid fire. I came back to my own body and senses, crying out with pain, clutching at my head. Beside me, Al'Kundesha staggered uncertainly, then turned to face me, baring his fangs in a satisfied sneer.

I tried to scramble to my feet. Tried to reach out in preparation to fight.

Fiery pain poured through my head again.

Before I had time to question how or why, gravity itself seemed to reorient itself, and I was flying through the air toward the wall. Only it couldn't be gravity, my brain dimly noted, because Al'Kundesha was falling the other way.

We thudded to the walls—me hard enough that my vision swam, Al'Kundesha hard enough that the permacrete cracked—and hung there, pinned, facing each other.

Telekinesis.

It was a raknoth and two normal humans out there. I was sure of it. And yet someone was holding us with telekinesis. I didn't understand.

Hesitant to be scorched again, I reached out slowly, carefully. Or tried to, only to find I was no longer in control.

The door swung open and two soldiers in the ivory armor of the Sanctum Guard marched into the room, followed by a third man in a dull gray robe. I took in the wild shock of gray hair and beard. The sharp cheek-bones and lanky figure.

My breath caught.

I'd only ever seen a single image of the man, but there was no mistaking him.

It was Cassius. Carlisle's old master.

Or his body, at least, claimed by Al'Kundesha's master.

He studied me with cold eyes for a long moment.

"Yes," he finally said, "you've figured it out. And yes, you are indeed quite doomed. Now do not struggle unless you desire pain."

His voice was smooth, almost tranquil. It reminded me of Carlisle. It made me feel ill.

I hung helplessly against the wall as he rifled through my memories with lightning speed, surprisingly light-handed, but thorough and effective.

Within a minute, he'd caught up on everything that had transpired between me and Al'Kundesha.

He turned to Al'Kundesha, his expression cold and dispassionate. "You were careless."

"Yes, Master." It was weird, seeing the monster in the High General's uniform pinned to the wall, hanging his head like a guilty tyro. "But the child is strong, my Zar."

The unseen hands let me slide down the wall to the ground. Al'Kundesha remained pinned.

"Young fool," Zar'Faenor said, speaking the two words with finality.

I thought it was directed at me until Al'Kundesha spoke.

"Forgive me, Master."

Al'Kundesha, the creature I'd glimpsed through a hundred different lifetimes, a *young* fool?

"I will not," Zar'Faenor said. "But you will learn." He looked around the room distastefully. "I will turn the child over to the White Tower and have done with it. You will bring Sanctuary under control and await my orders. It is well past time we bring this petty drama to an end."

Al'Kundesha bowed his head. "As you command, Master."

My head was spinning as the Sanctum Guard fixed my shackled wrists together with a new chain. Sanctuary fallen to the hybrids. Zar'Faenor, who seemed to have adopted the abilities of Carlisle's old mentor. Al'Kundesha, and his memories of Urth.

It was all too much to process.

On the bright side, I didn't have to think about doing a thing myself at the moment. Not with Zar'Faenor in my head, forcing me to march like a good puppet. Out the door. Down the hall.

Straight ahead to my own execution.

CHAPTER 40
LONG SHOT

This time, when the voice came to me and I couldn't remember where I was or how I'd gotten there, some corner of my mind at least remembered to be on guard.

"Haldin… Haldin…"

I didn't trust the call. And yet it beckoned to me. It was familiar. A patch of sunlight on a cold, cloudy day. It beckoned, and I wanted to answer. But it was so far. So hard to move toward that strip of warmth through the hazy malaise of—

"Haldin."

I rose from darkness to blue sky and the sound of strong waters rushing over smooth stone.

"Thank the fates," someone breathed.

"Carlisle?" I blinked and looked around.

I was standing on a large, flat boulder that rose a good five feet from the racing river, white water roaring cheerfully along on either side, lush wilds rising from the banks beyond that.

And there, standing across from me on the rock in the warm sun, was Carlisle. Which definitely meant…

"We're not really here, are we?"

His gaze fell to the ground, and he shook his head. "I'm sorry."

I sighed. "It's getting kinda confusing, all this waking up while I'm still sleeping. Not that I'm not happy to see you." I glanced around the vibrant river basin. "This is definitely a lot better than the last time around."

Carlisle's face was plastered with worry. "Kublich?"

I nodded. "Kublich. Al'Kundesha. Whatever you want to call him."

"Are you hurt?"

I couldn't help but chuckle at that, thinking about the state my body was in.

Carlisle was staring at my wrists, and, when I looked down, I saw deep bruises and lacerations where a moment ago there'd been pristine skin.

"I've had better days," I said.

"I'm sorry, Haldin." Carlisle's expression was dire. "If I hadn't taken so long—"

"It's not your fault, Carlisle." It came out more heated than I intended. I tried to force a smile. "Besides, I learned a few things rolling around in Al'Kundesha's head."

It was a rampant understatement, and one that caught Carlisle's sincere attention, but I wasn't really sure where to begin unloading everything I'd seen in Kublich's mind. Aside from starting with the most dangerous point first.

"Which reminds me," I pushed on, "before we say anything else, I need to tell you..."

The words hung in my throat, first out of uncertainty as to how I should drop the news about Zar'Faenor and Cassius' body on him, then as another thought dawned on me.

If this wasn't real, how was I supposed to know this was even Carlisle I was talking to?

"How are you reaching me right now?" I asked.

"I'm asleep in a skimmer, circling a sector out from the White Tower," Carlisle said.

I hesitated, trying to imagine the feasibility of that scenario, and what the raknoth would even stand to gain from tricking me at this point.

Carlisle seemed to understand.

"The first time we met," he said slowly, "you gave my skimmer trunk some... creative modifications."

Tension poured out of my lungs. "Thank Alpha."

I supposed it was possible Al'Kundesha or Zar'Faenor could've gleaned that memory from my mind, but I doubted they'd spent time on such small details. And something about the way he said it...

It was Carlisle. It had to be.

I frowned. "But wait, if you're just hovering around in a skimmer without a cloak…"

He waved away my concern. "Phineas is flying, keeping an eye out. All the same, we should keep this brief. We need to get you out. Right now."

"That's not gonna be easy."

"We have a plan. Franco had a contact."

"Had?"

"Suffice it to say both sides felt this favor, small as their role will be, more than balances whatever debts were owed between them. The important thing is that we have a way in. All I need to know is what floor they're keeping you on."

The beginnings of hope fluttered in my chest. I opened my mouth to answer—I'd been sure to pay attention to every detail on the somber trip over with Zar'Faenor and his Sanctum Guard—but I paused, thinking about Sanctuary. About everything Al'Kundesha had said.

"Is it true our broadcast didn't make it outside of Sanctuary?" I asked.

He grew somber, like he could smell the direction my thoughts were heading. "Hal, we can discuss that once you're safe."

"So it is true."

He studied me for a long moment before giving in and nodding. "It seems Kublich had some manner of kill switch installed in preparation for just such a contingency. Foolish of us not to expect it, but the damage is done."

"You can't pull me out of here," I said before I could second-guess myself.

The words lit a fire in Carlisle's eyes I'd never seen before, frighteningly intense. "I assure you, I can. And I will."

I hesitated, searching for the right words to make him understand.

"Whatever you're thinking," Carlisle said, "we'll find another way."

"No." I shook my head. "No, I don't think we will. This is it, Carlisle. Sanctuary was just the opening act. They're getting ready to mobilize on Haven and Oasis, too. Maybe more from the way they were talking. And my execution is the launch pad that's supposed to win them enough public confidence that no one blinks about any troubling stories they might hear in the next few days."

"All the more reason we should deprive them of that launch pad, clearly."

"Or we let them think they've won and turn it against them right when it'll hurt the most."

To Carlisle's credit, he did seem to consider my words for at least a few seconds before rejecting them. "Hal, it's not worth risking—"

He perked as if some distant point in the sky had drawn his attention.

"Trouble?" I asked.

"Perhaps." He grimaced. "Hard to tell from in here. Phineas will wake me if it's serious." He fixed me with a level stare. "Your floor Haldin. Tell me."

I swallowed, "I met their master, Carlisle."

He watched me cautiously, like I'd just stepped on a trip mine.

"His name's Zar'Faenor. But…"

I clenched my jaw, not wanting to say the words. Not wanting to give Carlisle the pain of knowing.

But he had to find out at some point, didn't he?

"Dammit. He's… Zar'Faenor is using Cassius' body, Carlisle. His abilities too. It's…"

I hesitated. A hundred different things on my tongue, and I didn't want to say a single one of them. I was scared to even look at Carlisle.

But when I did, he was simply standing there, his eyes distant. Vacant, almost.

"I see," he finally said.

"We have to stop him," I said when it became apparent he'd said what he had to say. "He's strong, Carlisle. I think he even knows how to make your runes. They've got my abilities shut down with a pendant sort of like yours."

I absentmindedly fingered the spot where I knew the new little scorcher pendant would be resting on my sleeping chest. Similar as it was to Carlisle's cloaking pendant, I hadn't noticed it until they'd left me alone in my new cell beneath the White Tower. But I'd tested it this way and that before finally collapsing to exhausted sleep, and now I was positive the cursed little device was responsible for the liquid fire that scorched my brain every time I tried to reach out with my senses. Hence my nickname. The scorcher.

When I looked back up, Carlisle was just staring into nothingness.

Finally, he stirred slightly, though his eyes remained distant. "What did you have in mind?"

That was a damn good question. One I'd been furiously trying to work through since the unfortunate idea had planted itself in my head.

"Johnny's still with you guys?"

Carlisle nodded.

"And Franco has connections, right?"

"Severely limited ones at the moment, given our current reputations. But he does know people."

"Right then." I laid a hand on his shoulder, and he finally broke out of his fugue to meet my gaze. "I've got a plan, teacher."

CHAPTER 41

CIVILITY

In the past few cycles, the meaning of the word *hopeless* had begun to take on new depths to me. When we'd been caught at Vantage in an underground death trap. When I'd lain bleeding out in the streets of Divinity. When I'd woken in Sanctuary, shackled and face-to-face with the monster who'd killed my parents. Those had all felt like hopeless situations at the time.

Yet, each time, when it came down to the nails, I'd glimpse it. Some fighting chance. Survival, it seemed, was not a matter of hope, but of willpower and firmly grit teeth. The drive to slog on, no matter what.

So now, though I couldn't move—thought I was alone behind enemy lines, trapped and rendered powerless by that damn little scorcher pendant —I didn't give in to despair.

In just a few hours, when the sun set, I was supposed to die.

I didn't have any plans of satisfying that expectation, of course. Not while the raknoth were still free to run wild on Enochia like the forces of destruction they were.

Of course, no amount of planning and mental fortitude could stop the panic attacks. I was facing execution, after all. All I had for those was the deep breathing. It even helped a little.

The shackles didn't.

They'd done a full-body job on me—arms crossed in the front, shackled at the wrists with a chain that wrapped first around my back and then down to my shackled ankles. Another infuriatingly short chain joined ankle to ankle. Just in case.

At least I wasn't hanging by my wrists anymore. Given the throbbing aches from my wounds, I half-thought my hands might've just popped right off if they'd tried.

And then, tucked safe and secure beneath the robes they'd dressed me in a few hours ago, there was the confounded scorcher pendant. The one thing ensuring I was powerless to escape my bindings. I scowled at the place on my chest where I could feel its cool weight beneath the robe, resisting the urge to try for the hundredth time to rip the thing off with telekinesis.

It wasn't worth the pain. Not yet.

The robe itself was no great comfort, either. A flagrant reminder of my impending demise. The dark garment ran from my neck all the way down to my bare feet, covered in intricate red workings across the shoulders and chest. Had it been of white and gold tones, it would have been quite similar to a cleric's robes, but for one key difference.

Where a cleric's robe bore the triumphant arch of Alpha's sigil, mine portrayed a great red serpent. The sigil of the heretics. The apostates. Deceivers, liars, traitors to the Word of Alpha, and all other manner of unsavory sorts. Above all else, it marked me as someone who was to be ceremonially hanged to death in the Great Hall for all the world to see. Just like Andre Kovaks.

Scud, this might've even been the same robe he'd been wearing.

I couldn't help but think back to the night I'd watched Kovaks' execution on the WAN, sitting between my parents, unaware that in just three cycles —barely a full season—they'd both be dead and I'd be the one whose life and crimes Barbara Sanders was somberly recounting to the watching eyes of Enochia in the final moments.

It didn't seem real.

The faint sound of voices outside drew my attention a second before the door hissed open to reveal my two Sanctum Guard sentinels.

"—alk to my supervisors if you have a problem with it," a woman was saying somewhere behind them, "but for now, what harm's it going to do?"

I recognized the voice even before I saw the woman with the wavy dark hair and the cute little upturned nose that Enochia so loved. It was Barbara Sanders.

My heart beat faster.

She was craning past the guards, her dark brown eyes studying me curiously. I'd always thought she had kind eyes. But maybe that was just part of her appeal. When it came to public figures, who knew? Just look at Alton Parker.

The Sanctum Guard she'd been speaking to glanced back and forth between me and her, then finally shrugged. "You have a visitor, Raish."

I made a show of struggling to sit up only to flop back to the cot with an exasperated sigh. "If only I could sit up to receive her..." I raised my legs and jangled my ankle chains. "Are these really necessary?"

The guards said nothing. Just scowled first at me, then at the back of Barbara's head as she slipped into the holding cell without waiting for any additional permission. Pointedly, they moved into the corners of the cell to stand quiet watch.

"Haldin Raish? I'm Barbara Sanders with the WAN. I wanted to meet you before the ceremony."

I searched her face, looking for any sign of deeper meaning. I saw nothing but professionalism—albeit warm and kind—and my heart sank.

"Yeah, I can see where afterward wouldn't work so well. Pleased to meet you, Lady Sanders."

"Barbara, please."

I inclined my head. "Well I'd offer you my hand, Barbara, but..." I glanced pointedly down at my lack of free limbs.

She forced a polite smile, and I thought I saw empathy in her eyes. Or was it sadness? Or guilt? Probably, I was just reading too much into her every facial tick, hoping against hope I'd see some sign there.

"You're aware we normally record the repentance the day before the ceremonies, yes?"

I nodded. Those slated to be *ceremonialized* by rope and gravity were always afforded the chance to confess their sins the evening before said ceremony took place, as well as to say any final words and farewells.

I glanced at the doorway. "You're not gonna bring your crew in to record this? I'm sure I could find a tear or two close by."

She shook her head, once again striking that balance of distant yet affected. "No, I simply wanted to ask you a few questions while I could. You're also aware your repentance day has been waived for, quote, 'matters of planetwide security?'"

I nodded again.

"Do you happen to know why?" she asked.

Probably because Zar'Faenor and his bloodsucking compatriots wanted to make sure I'd be dead in time for humanity to cheer them on as they went forth to rebuild their race from the ashes of Enochia. Somehow, though, I didn't think Barbara would buy all that, so I went with, "Maybe they were worried the world might fall in love with my good looks and boyish charm."

She didn't laugh. Just fidgeted with her hands, suddenly seeming nervous. "I was thinking it might have something to do with the footage you tried to push through the emergency broadcast system last night."

That caught my attention good and proper. It caught the guards' too, judging by the uncertain look they traded.

I forced myself to breathe. To pretend it was all well, no cause for concern in their eyes. "Rumor has it there was an uprising."

It wasn't an answer, exactly, but I prayed she'd understand what I was trying to tell her.

"So I've heard," she said, studying me. "I've heard a lot of interesting rumors, actually. I want to know what you believe happened."

I glanced at the guards. They were watching me. Closely.

"It doesn't matter what I believe. All that matters is the truth."

"You would have made a fine reporter."

I searched her expression. She seemed genuinely interested in what I had to say—enough that the guards were growing uneasy now. Was that simply her professional curiosity at work? I couldn't be sure. But something about her nature made me want to convince her anyway.

"Let me ask you this," I said slowly. "When's the last time you saw a teenager sentenced to hang by the High Cleric himself just for trying to spin tall tales?"

One of the Sanctum Guard took a half-step forward, clearly debating putting a stop to the whole thing.

Barbara was frowning. "You did break into a Legion base, Mister Raish. A base that's apparently so badly damaged from... well, badly damaged enough that they closed the gates for repairs."

"That wasn't our doing, I can tell you that much."

It was, however, a snippet of news to me. I could only assume Al'Kundesha had closed Sanctuary to hide the fact that the hybrids owned the base and that most of the Legion forces were quite possibly dead.

The real question was how the other Legion bases were responding to the development, and to their High General's insistence that it was all the work of renegades.

Barbara was watching me with a guarded expression. "An ill-timed uprising then. Fine. But that doesn't explain the multiple other counts of terroristic activities on your file. Are you suggesting those claims are inaccurate?"

"Do I seem like a terrorist to you?"

I couldn't keep the heat from my voice.

I'd fought and bled only to be criminalized by the very people I was trying to defend. And now to be sentenced to die by a holy man who'd never even met me, never heard my story… It was too much.

Barbara's expression was troubled. "I…"

"Yeah, yeah," an unfortunate voice drawled from just outside the door. "Work the sob story, kid. See what good it does you."

I tensed as Smirks walked into the cell, scraped up and stepping tenderly, but very much alive.

"Listen," he said to Barbara, "this kid's not some harmless little pup who accidentally scudded the carpet. He's put half a dozen guys I know into the medica. Scud, he threw me out of a damn lev tram and left me to die in an abandoned underway tunnel. He's dangerous, and you should just be glad he's not out there to hurt anyone else."

"Barbara," I said, "allow me to introduce you to Garrett, the human scud-spout who's willing to sell his own kind to—"

Smirks leaned in and gave me a firm cuff to the mouth.

I glared at him, tasting blood.

"Hey!" Barbara cried. "Merciful Alpha, let's be civil here!"

For a moment, I thought about spitting blood at Smirks' stupid face. I decided to take the high road, for civility's sake. And because he was almost certainly out of range.

"That's quite enough, Garrett," someone called into the cell, his voice thin but full of authority.

Sweet Alpha, how many people were lurking out there?

Smirks backed away to stand with the two Sanctum Guard and joined them in bowing their heads toward the door. A second later, Barbara did the same.

But that meant…

Sweet Alpha, indeed.

The High Cleric shuffled slowly into the room, supported by the arm of—

Son of a bitch.

Zar'Faenor.

My mind took off like wild fire.

The High Cleric? I'd accepted that the raknoth probably had strings in high places in the Sanctum. But the gropping High Cleric? Was it possible?

Much as I didn't want to believe it, I couldn't help but wonder the opposite.

Why not?

Now that I saw them there, Zar'Faenor escorting the shuffling High Cleric like a good humble servant—so silent he was barely there at all—I felt foolish for having ever allowed myself to hope that maybe the High Cleric of all people would be beyond their reach.

And if Zar'Faenor had his claws in the High Cleric…

Breathe. Think.

If that was the case, it was just one more obstacle to overcome.

Zar'Faenor betrayed nothing. The raknoth didn't even bother looking at me as the High Cleric paused to allow Barbara to wish him good blessings and kiss the ring of his office. In person, the High Cleric looked older and frailer than he did in the WAN broadcasts. I imagined he was little but skin and bones beneath the voluminous folds of his ornate robes.

"We will speak to the fallen alone," he said to Smirks and the guards.

The three of them left the room without question. Barbara lingered, looking at me with an expression of uncertainty—maybe even concern— then hurried to follow the others when the High Cleric turned his gaze on her.

The door closed behind her, leaving me alone with the leader of the raknoth and the High Cleric of the Sanctum.

I waited for a victorious sneer or something of the sort from Zar'Faenor, but he paid me no mind. The High Cleric studied me with rheumy blue eyes.

Did the old man know what manner of creature stood beside him? If not, I could only assume Zar'Faenor had him so twisted around his clawed finger that any attempt at talking would be pointless. But I didn't have anything else to try.

"Your Holiness," I said, "I don't know what this man has told you, but he is no friend to the Sanctum or to Enochia. He and his ilk would see us enslaved or worse if they had their way."

The High Cleric blinked, a frown forming across his features. Zar'-Faenor was finally looking at me now, his golden-brown eyes impassive.

"You must've seen some sign of what happened at Sanctuary last night," I continued, half-expecting Zar'Faenor to reach out and stop me. "Our people, the loyal servants of the Legion, fought to defend their base and their lives against his army of engineered monstrosities. My team was only four. Do you really believe we could be the cause of so much destruction, or that half the Sanctuary forces would simply turn on their own?"

A shadow of doubt hung over the High Cleric's face.

I fixed him with a desperate stare, hoping the one man who might still turn the tide with a word would somehow see the truth in my eyes. "We're in danger, your Holiness. All of Enochia is."

The High Cleric slowly turned his wary gaze from me to Zar'Faenor, who met his stare calmly.

"I see why the General likes this one," the High Cleric said. The words turned my stomach upside down. Before I could even start to unpack the full implications, though, the High Cleric lowered himself to sit at the edge of my cot, moving with the painstaking effort of old joints and atrophied muscles. "Soon, my child, you will be free of these troubled notions and at rest in the afterlife."

He lightly traced his fingers over Alpha's sigil on his breast, then wrapped his hands behind my head and pulled me gently up to kiss my forehead.

My mind raced. I'd lost him. Probably before he'd ever even entered the room. I looked up to meet his eyes, searching for some glint of hope.

And froze as those pale, rheumy eyes flashed fiery red.

I stiffened. Recoiled. But his grasp was like an iron vise on the back of my head. Then, as quickly as it had appeared, the red fire was gone. His grip softened, and I was once again staring at the faded, cloudy blue eyes of the High Cleric.

"What is it, child?" he asked. "Does my touch startle you so?"

Had I imagined it?

For one awful second, I couldn't help but wonder if maybe I was losing my mind—if maybe I'd been cracked this whole time. But no. That was ridiculous. I knew what I'd seen. I trusted that much.

Which meant the High Cleric of the Sanctum was a raknoth.

"Come," Zar'Faenor said. "You have had your fun. Let us finish our preparations and be done with it."

The High Cleric stood from my cot with a wheezing groan, once again moving as if it cost him a great deal. "Very well," he said. "Very well."

Zar'Faenor was waiting at the door when the High Cleric turned back to say the words that paralyzed my diaphragm as surely as any gut punch

"I look forward to meeting your friends this evening, Haldin." He paused long enough to savor the sight of the blood I could feel draining from my face, then he turned for the door, chuckling to himself. "Such a bright new dawn for Enochia, tomorrow will be."

Zar'Faenor tapped twice on the door, which hissed open immediately. With that, they shuffled out, the raknoth bastard of a High Cleric grasping the crook of Zar'Faenor's arm for support like a kindly old man.

The door hissed shut behind them, leaving me alone with my thundering heart.

CHAPTER 42
GALLOWS

The lonely afternoon hours did not pass kindly. The silence dug at me like a slow, ruthless torturer, reminding me that the people I loved were probably getting ready to fly straight into a trap. Reminding me that it was my fault—that I was the one who'd set them on this course.

Reminding me that, in all likelihood, I really was about to die at the gallows.

Now, the despair came for me. How had I ever convinced myself—and Carlisle, no less—that we had any part of this under control?

How in the name of Alpha had this happened?

I stifled a manic laugh at the thought, imagining that, the way things were going, maybe even Alpha himself would turn out to be a raknoth by the end of the day. The High General of the Legion, the CEO of Enochia's largest biotech giant, Carlisle's old mentor, and now the freaking High Cleric of the Sanctum.

Why not the one true deity, too?

I needed to warn Carlisle. But how? Even if I could somehow sleep long enough to let my mind drift, which in itself sounded impossible right now, what were the chances Carlisle would be hanging right there, doing the same? He and the others had a foolhardy mission to be preparing for.

I kind of doubted he'd listen anyway. He'd gotten a scary glint in his eye just listening to how vulnerable our plan left me. When I'd tried to ask him to tell Elise that I loved her, just in case, he'd refused to hear of it.

"You'll tell her yourself once it's over," he'd said, closer to losing his composure than I'd ever seen. I hadn't pressed the matter.

I wished now that I had. Wished I'd said the words myself when I'd had the chance. Because there was nothing for it. I'd gropped us all with my softsteel-sipping, scud bucket of a plan. And there wasn't a damn thing I could do about it.

I spent the hours trying anyway.

Too soon, the Sanctum Guard came for me. Smirks was with them, looking punchable as ever. The guards hauled me to my feet and prodded me out to the less than uplifting sight of the White Tower subbasements.

"What's a guy gotta do to relieve himself around here?" I asked, in part to stall, but mostly because, whatever happened, I didn't want to be one of the ones who left a mess behind when I went. Not really sure why I cared about *that* little detail when most of the people in attendance would be under the impression that I was some deranged lunatic terrorist, but there it was.

Either way, at least my bowels and bladder were relieved as I went to meet my death.

Smirks rolled his eyes when we returned, but said nothing. We marched down the hall, my chains jangling glumly all the way, and piled into a mag lift. Smirks keyed the top floor. The Great Hall of the High Cleric. The lift hummed to life and greeted my already volatile stomach with the tug of upward acceleration.

I couldn't help but flash through fantasies of escape. If I had any hope of taking down three men with my mobility as severely limited as it was, the lift car was probably the ideal spot. It'd be pointless, of course, with no way to remove the scorcher and, in turn, the chains. I'd be caught within minutes. But I would've enjoyed knocking the smug look off Smirks' face one more time.

Except he didn't look so smug when I glanced back at him. He looked... apprehensive? At least until he caught me watching and shot me a threatening scowl. He held it until I turned back around.

I didn't have long to wonder what was going on in his head. Distance-wise, the ascent was substantial, but the mag lift was fast. Too soon, I felt the lightness of deceleration, and a mild chime informed us we'd arrived. The doors glided quietly open, and I stepped out of the lift car before the guards could prod me along.

The pinnacle of the White Tower was decadent, to say the least, beginning with the grand antechamber—fifty feet high, all regal ivory walls and ceilings and rich white tiles with intricate golden swirls. Our service lift emptied inconspicuously into the corner. I found myself wishing we could've taken one of the primary lifts, which I knew afforded wonderful views of the city throughout the entire ascent, courtesy of their wide duraglass windows.

Next time, I wanted to tell myself.

I swallowed a dry gulp instead.

None of my guards protested as I took the lead, shuffling along in my chains for the dark stone pathway that funneled between two lines of thick columns into the Great Hall beyond.

Under my bare feet, the dark stone was smooth and still pleasantly warm from the myriad squares of sunlight creeping through the duraglass ceiling high above. I closed my eyes for several steps just to focus on the feeling of it. The warmth reminded me of Elise. Which, in turn, only brought the weight of my cataclysmically stupid failure crashing back down.

Why hadn't we just run away together when we'd had the chance? We could've been up in the northern mountains or anywhere else right now, happy and safe in each other's arms.

But it wouldn't have lasted.

That was the only caveat that kept me from braining myself on the nearest stone column. Because there was no happily ever after as long as the raknoth were free on Enochia. I'd been stuck on this path since I'd witnessed Al'Kundesha savaging my mother and father. Since the raknoth had come to Enochia, even. It had always been my path to end up here, standing up to them. And if that path was truly drawing to an end, the least I could do was make damn sure it counted for something, grop-up or no.

The thought made me stand a little straighter as I shuffled into the Great Hall.

The contrast moving from the confined column path to the wide open space made it feel like the Great Hall exploded outward for miles. The duraglass ceiling only added to the effect, rising at an angle from the rear of the hall as if the skies were gradually opening up before you. Even without the trick of design, the hall was enormous. And, I had to admit, beautiful in its own right. Unnecessary and ostentatious, maybe. But majestic and wondrous nonetheless.

The gallows staring me down from across the expanse, though—and the primal bolt of fear it shot through me—dimmed that grandeur.

The archaic wooden structure had been erected on the second of the four great plateau steps that rose from the dark stone floor at the head of the Great Hall. One each for the four facets of life as seen by the Sanctum: mind, body, spirit, and Alpha. The last tier, Alpha, was reserved for the High Cleric alone. The second tier, body, was traditionally where apostates met their worldly ends.

The guards indicated that that was exactly where we were headed. As if maybe I'd forgotten what we'd come here for.

Judging by the position of the sun and the emptiness of the hall, we were still well over half an hour away from show time. I was glad to see Barbara's crew busy setting up. Not because I was eager to have my execution broadcasted—I was starting to think my mom had been all too right about the practice being nothing more than a morbid maneuver to keep the authority of the Sanctum above question. No, I was glad to see them because it reminded me that, death trap or no, we still had a fighting shot at hitting the raknoth where it hurt this evening.

When I saw Barbara, though, my marginal optimism wavered.

She was watching me, her expression worried or maybe nervous, and her face was just a shade too pale. At my gaze, she looked quickly away, refusing to meet my eyes.

An important sign? Or simply a reasonable reaction to the sight of a teenager walking in chains to his own execution?

I tried to focus on what I could control, trusting the others had fulfilled their end of my confounded plan. We reached the steps carved at the side of the larger plateau tiers and began the climb. Steps proved less than shackle-friendly, but I shambled along, goaded by a steady stream of pokes and prods from behind, until I found myself standing at the base of the archaic wooden platform of the gallows.

Aside from me and my escorts, the only other people on the plateau were two guys from Barbara's setup crew and a rotund goodfellow I recognized as the resident Sanctum hangman. Not that the noose he was tying left much to question. But I did remember.

I'd first seen him when my dad had deemed me ready to witness an execution at the ripe age of twelve. The hangman had been portly then, and he'd only grown more round in the several years since. He gave me a practiced once-over as we approached. I suppressed a small shudder as his gaze lingered on my neck, his hands still tying the knot by feel.

"Best you come on up and get situated," he said, his voice thick and his tone matter-of-fact but not unkind. "Folk'll be startin' to drift in soon."

The wooden steps creaked underfoot as I made my last ascent.

"Be seeing ya, kid," came Smirks' voice from behind.

Coming from him, the simple goodbye—and the lack of insult therein—almost seemed sweet. Almost. I only glanced back long enough to confirm he and the two guards were headed back down to the main floor of the hall.

The wood of the gallows had a feel of apathy under my bare feet. It wasn't warm or cool. Wasn't particularly rough or smooth. It simply was.

I stood where the hangman indicated and closed my eyes, trying to calm my swirling thoughts and ignore the labored breathing and occasional wheeze of the hangman as he finished and double checked his noose.

My noose, rather.

A swoop of frightened panic made a bid for my senses, begging me to run.

The voices in the room were multiplying now. I opened my eyes and saw that folks were indeed starting to drift in. All types of them. I made a sort of game of trying to deduce their stories as they filed close enough for me to get a decent look.

Some were clearly devout acolytes and servants of the Sanctum, come to confirm that Alpha's supreme Will was upheld today. Others just as clearly came because they thought it'd be cool to see a man hanged. And then there were the Legion and Sanctum officials, a mixed bag of officers and clerics, attending out of duty or desire.

Soon, the hall was bustling, and I was starting to sweat wondering where Carlisle and the others were, and what they were up to.

We were only fifteen or so minutes away from sunset when I noticed Barbara making her way up to the gallows from the crowd. A tap on my shoulder brought my attention back to the hangman, who hefted the noose, now suspended from the high arm of the gallows.

"Ready, fella?"

I just stared at him, not really sure how to answer that question.

He nodded in perfect understanding and gently slipped the slack loop over my head. "It'll be over real quick, fella. Don't you worry 'bout that."

I let out a deep breath, fighting a strong and sudden urge to cry my eyes out.

To the left, Barbara climbed the gallows steps, headed my way.

She stopped in front of me, chewing her lip and meeting my eyes with an apprehensive, almost frantic look. She didn't look like the fearless, professional reporter I'd seen earlier.

I felt the flicker of hope.

She shot a look at the hangman, who gave her a small nod and shuffled off to give us privacy—as much as we could hope for in the bustling hall, anyway. Barbara just fidgeted with her hands, eyes downward and distant.

"Aren't I supposed to be the one shaking in my boots here?" I asked quietly, frightened I might scare her away.

"You're not wearing any boots."

A shaky laugh escaped me. "Guess that explains it, then."

The sound of my laugh snapped her back from wherever her mind had been drifting. She held my gaze for a long second, then stepped forward and threw her arms around my neck.

I held my breath, waiting. Was this it?

The hug was welcome enough either way, I decided.

Then her hand slipped down the back of my neck, lightly fishing beneath my robe, and I had to stop myself from crying out in relief.

"Back in the cell…" I whispered.

Something clicked against my back.

"I had to meet you," she said, so quietly I almost missed it. "Before I could… I didn't believe any of it. Didn't expect…"

She backed out of the embrace, which was probably for the best. A few people were already starting to stare. I was too relieved to care much, though, as I felt the little tug of something sliding off my chest, over my collarbone. Her hands darted furtively to her pockets as she took a small step back, and I knew.

Barbara Sanders had just saved my life.

I let out a long breath, trying not to look like someone who'd just been freed from the scorcher pendant that had been the only thing keeping me helplessly bound. Barbara looked to be doing much the same.

I checked to make sure the hangman was still far away enough for the din of the crowd to cover us. "Do you understand what's happening here?"

"Not as much as I'd like to," she replied, just as quietly. "But meeting you convinced me to watch what your friends sent me." She shuddered a little. "I couldn't ignore it. Too many things adding up. It's…"

"It's a lot."

She looked at me like that was the first crazy thing I'd said.

"I don't know what your friends are planning. They just told me to be ready to shoot the story of a lifetime and that if you weren't sedated, there'd probably be some kind of pendant masking your, uh, power. I don't understand what in demons' depths that means, but I guess if you're all crazy, what does it matter, right? I… Did this actually help?"

I confirmed I could touch my surroundings with my extended senses and felt some rather unheroic tears welling in my eyes. Maybe it was just the pre-hanging jitters, but it was all a bit overwhelming.

"Help? Barbara, you just saved my life."

Barbara looked less than convinced, but something else drew her eye. The hangman's impatient shuffling. She waved to indicate we were almost done.

"Maybe if you actually make it out of here," she said quietly, "you can thank me by giving me the whole story of what in Alpha's name is going on. Just please, try not to hurt anyone."

The High Cleric's words flashed through my head, bringing the first wave of dread back to my gut.

"Barbara, I don't know what's about to happen here, but it might be bad. Keep an eye out. And be ready to run."

She hesitated, clearly wanting to ask more, but the hangman was shuffling again, and one of her crew members was calling her. She looked at me like she was wondering whether I was a blessing or a ticking bomb, then she left to go check in with her people.

Earlier, I'd thought I liked Barbara Sanders for some intangible reason. She'd easily just earned it ten thousand times over.

Once she'd gone, I closed my eyes and began unlocking my shackles with telekinesis, careful to keep my arms and legs pinned to keep anything from falling off prematurely. Somewhere off to the left, I faintly heard Barbara's voice as she began her broadcast for the WAN. I suppressed the urge to reach out further and check my surroundings. It wouldn't do to accidentally brush up against any of the nearby raknoth or Seekers.

I'd just finished the last shackle lock when the bustling hall began to quiet. The light bleeding through my eyelids had shifted blood orange.

Sunset had come.

I opened my eyes to find the Great Hall alive with a dancing swirl of sunlight—warm hues of reds, yellows, and oranges refracting through the duraglass and coalescing throughout the hall with a cheery yet haunting glow. It was beautiful, even if it did mean my time was up.

At least I had a chance now.

But where were the raknoth?

The key pipes lining the head of the hall cleared their throats and let fly one of the Sanctum's ceremonial tunes, silencing the low din of anxious voices. When I peered over my shoulder, the High Cleric had appeared on the high plateau step from his chambers below.

There was one at least.

He stood calmly at the ledge, looking over the hall as the assembled crowd erupted with cheers and applause. After a minute, the key pipes concluded their soaring song, and the hall fell into reverent silence. I scanned the crowd with an odd swirl of dread and hopefulness. Maybe we had a better shot with just one raknoth anyway. And there was little enemy presence outside of the legionnaires in attendance and the dozen Sanctum Guard lining either side of the hall.

After what the High Cleric had said below, though, I couldn't believe there weren't reinforcements lurking nearby, ready to spring the trap.

They meant to crush us here. I was sure of it.

And there, sliding up to the front ranks right on cue, was Al'Kundesha, watching me from behind Adrian Kublich's dark, stern eyes. Apparently he saw me looking.

"You didn't think I'd miss the occasion?" his voice came to me.

I did my best to ignore him, in part to deprive him of the satisfaction, but mostly to avoid doing anything that might tip him off to my liberated abilities.

"Citizens of Divinity," the High Cleric called, his voice amplified both electronically and by the acoustics of the hall itself. I didn't turn. Just envisioned him in my head, raknoth eyes ablaze and casting a great, long shadow from his precipice.

"I needn't remind you why we gather here today," he continued. "Just as I needn't remind you what is at stake when a demon of the nether manifests itself in this world. We all know the tales of old, of the fiery crowns and the beastly abominations Alpha and his chosen drove into the nether that we might know a good and peaceful existence. But the demon is cunning. Adaptable. It perseveres from the depths, whispering its insidious will to those once pure of flesh and blood. Seducing until they stray, until they find themselves willing vessels to its evil. Vessels like the fallen who was once Haldin Raish, Alpha save him."

"Alpha save him," the crowd echoed.

"Listen to them, Haldin," Al'Kundesha sent.

"Once a vessel has suffered the incursion of a demon, we as servants of the light have but one option available to us. It is our responsibility not only to protect the world from the reach of the demon, but to save the spirit of the vessel as well. What we offer here is not punishment or vengeance. It's absolution. It's the love of Alpha, praise be."

"Praise be."

"Do you see what it is you're about to die for?"

I couldn't listen to any more.

I needed to focus on what I could control—the plan I'd mentally rehearsed a hundred times and yet could hardly seem to recall now. Instead, I was relegated to trying to ignore Al'Kundesha's blather about the waste of it all. I fretted over what he and his ilk were playing at. I worried about the others. Lastly, most painfully, I couldn't help but wonder how my parents would have felt if they'd somehow been alive to see all this.

By the time the hall's hue shift from serene orange to blood red informed me the sun was cresting the horizon, I hadn't managed to think a single helpful thought at all.

"And now," the High Cleric called, "with the end of this blessed day, will come the blessed end of this demon's reign in our city of Divinity!"

"What do you suppose they'll think at the end?" Al'Kundesha sent.

My heart was thundering too hard to worry about what he meant.

The hangman pulled the noose snug around my throat, the feel of the rough rope against the skin of my neck only jostling the plan that much further from my grasp.

I closed my eyes, trying to find my focus.

"Will they make it as far as wondering why you? Why them?"

The plodding thumps of the hangman's footsteps vibrated through the planks against my bare feet as he retreated to the antique lever.

"Or will that be left to the rest of Enochia?"

I wanted to scream at him to shut up.

The hangman gripped the lever.

I couldn't breathe.

Too fast. It was happening too fast.

I stood there, every muscle in my body rigid with anticipation, head spinning in the maddening silence. Perspiration creeping down my brow, down my back.

Then something bit at the edge of my conscious mind, like a boot tread catching dirt after too much ice. Something about Al'Kundesha's words.

Without thinking about it, I threw my senses out wide in every direction. Just for a second. A wide snapshot I could barely process a fraction of. But it was enough. Enough to feel the hybrids beneath the plateau steps and gathering back in the antechamber—so many of them. Enough to feel what I had to assume were my own allies' ships approaching the Great Hall from the rear.

The moment stretched before me, and I felt like I was caught at the eye of an enormous, unfolding storm, the pieces falling into place like hardsteel anvils to the lungs.

This wasn't just a trap to take down a few bothersome rebels.

This was meant to be the spark to the fuel-soaked pyre that was Enochia. An indiscriminate slaughter that would leave the entire planet clamoring and clawing for safety, unsure who or what to trust. Perfectly ripe for conquest.

And we were meant to be the villains in this story.

"Alpha grant you peace, Haldin Raish," called the High Cleric.

I opened my mouth, panic screaming through my veins.

Then the hangman threw the lever, and the floor dropped out beneath me, leaving me free to the will of gravity.

CHAPTER 43
DEMONS

I caught myself with telekinesis before I'd even dropped a foot through the open gallows door, all thoughts of going along with the act—of trying to make it look convincing—forgotten in light of the nightmare I'd just found myself in.

There were more than a few gasps.

Someone screamed.

I ignored them.

"Evacuate this hall, now!" I shouted, loud as I could. "You're all in danger! Go! Run! Please!"

They only gaped. A thousand stupefied stares, certain the only danger they could be in must be from the teenage boy floating in midair before them, defying gravity as surely as he'd just defied his own rightful death.

Another scream from the back of the hall. And another.

Al'Kundesha's eyes glinted red for the briefest instant. But no one noticed. They were too busy turning to see what the screams were about. From my vantage point on the second plateau, I could see all too well.

Hybrids. Dozens of them, charging straight down the dark stone path for the Great Hall.

The crowd went mad.

"Demons!" someone screamed.

"Alpha save us!" cried others. "Alpha save us all!"

"Protect the civilians!" the High Cleric barked from his dais.

The dirty scud-spouting bastard.

"Seize Raish!" he added.

I yanked my wrists and ankles free of the unlocked shackles and thrust my legs out wide to brace on the edges of the trap door while I tugged the noose off. The fit was tight, and the knot hesitant to loosen under my fingers, but I was hardly worried about a little rope burn on my jaw and chin.

Something grabbed my collar just as I freed myself. The hangman. Having followed the High Cleric's order quite literally, he stood there, extended precariously over the opening, unsure what to do next. He had this look in his eye, like he was genuinely confused as to why I'd gone and made a mess of a perfectly good hanging.

I shoved him off, dropped through the trap door, and staggered out from under the gallows. The first thing I saw was Barbara, watching me from where she'd been reporting nearby, her eyes wide, both hands held to her mouth, frozen with shock.

A blood hungry roar snapped her out of it, drawing our attention below. The crowd was in a full on panic now—a writhing stampede of screams and wild eyes, pushing their way everywhere and nowhere at once, some knocking their neighbors to the ground, others falling to their knees in prayer or plain shock.

They had nowhere to run. The only exits were through the antechamber. Through the hybrids.

An explosion rocked the Great Hall from above. Then another, and another.

I could barely look away to register them as, across the hall, the stream of hybrids cleared the pathway of columns and spilled into the Great Hall. In the blink of an eye, a dozen civilians were dead, hungry hybrids drinking them dry, more joining them each second.

I started running their way without thinking.

"Haldin!"

Carlisle's voice.

I looked up in time to see him peering through a neat hole in the dura-glass above the first plateau, Elise and Johnny at his side.

To the left, over the main body of the hall, I spotted multiple Legion transports through the translucent ceiling. Those would be the "rebels" who'd been chased out of Sanctuary last night. The ones who'd lost friends and found themselves with nowhere left to go after Al'Kundesha's treachery. Several of the legionnaires were already heaving more blasted hunks of duraglass aside to clear the way for rappelling lines.

Everything was going according to plan—aside from the army of hybrids ripping their way through a thousand helpless civilians.

Why had I ever thought we could catch the raknoth unprepared? I should've let Carlisle bust me out when I'd had the chance. Too late now.

"We have to get these people out of here," I sent, eyeing the fifteen foot drop to the first plateau then hesitating when I realized Barbara and her cameraman were still frozen in place.

Above, Carlisle gathered Johnny and Elise and jumped through the opening. *"Agreed,"* he sent as he settled them to a smooth landing on the tier below, he and Elise in light battle garb, Johnny positively teeming with guns and spare feeders. *"Where are the raknoth?"*

I couldn't find Al'Kundesha in the crowd. I was half-surprised he hadn't come flying up, red eyes blazing, to tear my head off. Above, the High Cleric was watching me like he was contemplating pouncing from his dais to do just that.

For now, though, they seemed dedicated to this game of theirs—to the extent that the High Cleric said nothing as his Sanctum Guard opened fire on the swarming hybrids, adding man-made thunder to the screams below.

I was about to relay the information to Carlisle when a hybrid launched itself from the crowd to the first tier. Johnny was a second too slow on the draw to keep it from catching one of Barbara's crewmen and sinking its teeth into his throat. Another came for us, leaping from the plateau below straight for us.

Or straight for Barbara, rather.

I caught it with telekinesis and hurled it into the nearest wall—a little too vehemently, judging by the wave of lightheadedness that followed.

Were the raknoth trying to cut out any potential broadcasts before they joined the fray? The hybrid that smashed a camera on the plateau below before Johnny gunned it down made me think yes.

"Come on," I called to Barbara and the cameraman beside her. "Stay close to me."

They numbly shuffled close enough for me to float us all down to the first tier, both of them too shocked to ask questions.

Elise met me with a quick, tight hug and a pack of energy cells. "Just for future reference," she whispered, "if you ever go dying on me, I'm gonna kick your ass."

Johnny shot down another hybrid before turning and handing me one of his three rifles. "Yeah. Whatever she said. Me too."

I numbly accepted the extra feeders Johnny handed me and jammed them into the netting on my pack, too stunned for words by the chaos below. The chaos I'd caused.

Friendly Legion soldiers were rappelling down on both sides of the Great Hall now, dropping thumpers into the thicker clusters of hybrids below. Muffled booms woofed through the hall, joined in short order by more gunfire, those higher on the lines covering those lower as they touched down. Soon enough, we had a couple dozen friendly soldiers on the ground, and twice that still on their way down.

But the hybrids kept coming.

"The raknoth?" Carlisle reminded me, squeezing my shoulder in gentle greeting.

"The High Cleric. He's one of them."

If anyone found that hard to believe, they kept it quiet.

"I'm not sure where the others are," I added, turning to glance back at the fourth tier, "but we need to, oh…"

The ripple of Carlisle's surprise beside me told me he saw it too. Zar'-Faenor had joined the High Cleric up on the ledge of his dais, along with a grim-faced Smirks and a dark-haired woman I'd never seen.

A pair of detonations snapped me back to where some of the legionnaires had blown openings in the duraglass walls on either side of the hall wide enough to make room for the transports to awkwardly cram their tail ends in and start evacuating civilians. James and Phineas rappelled down to join us along with several more legionnaires. Phineas had a fresh pair of prosthetic limbs and had somehow managed to outdress even Johnny for the part of walking arsenal.

Together, we all started for the main floor. All but Carlisle, I realized, pausing.

"These people need us, Carlisle."

He snapped out of his trance, adjusted his cloaking pendant, and, with one long last look at the thing that had taken his old mentor's body, came to join me in running after the others. *"He reached out to test me. He's strong. Stronger than the others."*

"I know." I hesitated. *"Are you going to—"*

"I will do what I must," he sent, that frightening gleam creeping back into his eyes. *"I will not leave Cassius to suffer under that creature's rule."*

There wasn't time to get into it.

We split from Barbara and the rest of the legionnaires streaming down the side stairs to go collect Johnny, James, and Phineas, who'd been covering their descent from the edge of the plateau. I slung my weapon and grabbed Elise around the waist. Carlisle was already doing the same with James and Phineas.

I reached my other arm out to Johnny. "Hop on, buddy."

"So *now* Johnny gets some love," he said, wrapping an arm over my shoulder and allowing me to wrap mine around his ridiculously armed waist. "Where's my kiss, big boy?"

Together, the six of us dropped to the main floor, Carlisle and I pumping our telekinetic brakes. Chaotic as it had been from above, it was worse in the thick of it. Bodies littered the ground. The dark stone floor was already slick with blood in places. My stomach twisted at the sight. But I unslung my rifle and moved into the mess alongside my people.

The fighting came in hectic bursts. The legionnaires were working to drive the civilians to the evac points and open up clear lines of fire down the center of the hall, but there were still far too many innocents trapped in the open—many wounded, some catatonic, others just trying to help. We shot conservatively, sticking close to our Legion support and leaving several of the closer hybrids to Carlisle's daggers and Elise's staff.

Or spear, I saw. She'd upgraded.

I nabbed a knife from Johnny and did what I could to help, but I was so battered and bruised that I was mostly better off with rifle and telekinesis.

We moved through the rampaging horde like a well-oiled machine, but their numbers seemed never ending. Bodies were accumulating far too quickly.

Elise yanked a hybrid off a young boy and cracked its skull so hard I was almost surprised her spear haft didn't shatter. The same probably couldn't be said for the hybrid's skull, but she followed up with a quick underjaw thrust for good measure before helping the boy to his feet.

Carlisle and I broke off to take down a trio of the creatures moving in on a trembling huddle of four. As terrified of us as the wild-eyed survivors clearly were, they didn't argue when Carlisle pulled one of the young men smoothly to his feet and told the rest of them to follow us to the evac line.

The hall was strewn with the dead now. Humans and hybrids alike. Thick pools of blood congealing on the stone—the hybrids apparently too frenzied with the thrill of the chase to focus on feeding.

By the time we got Barbara and the rest of the civilians over to the line at the side of the hall, I felt dead inside. I'd lost count of how many hybrids

I'd taken down, and how many more had nearly gotten the drop on me. I was on the verge of collapse. Phineas was all but carrying James, who'd taken a hybrid bite and was quickly sliding into paralysis, to the nearest transport. At a glance, we'd lost at least a quarter of the legionnaires who'd dropped in from above, and of the couple dozen Sanctum Guard and the legionnaires who'd originally been here for my execution, only a few remained.

At least they were on our side.

They might not fully understand what was happening, but no one here, civilian or otherwise, could believe that I or Carlisle or any of the other so-called rebels fighting to keep the hybrids off the evac lines had had anything to do with bringing the ferocious beasts here today.

Which must've been why the raknoth decided it was time to make their move.

It started with the low rumbling of stone on stone—the door at the base of the plateaus opening. I'd nearly forgotten about the hybrid minds I'd felt beneath the gallows earlier—at least another thirty or forty of them. A fresh wave of hungry roars drew my attention to where another horde of hybrids was erupting into the hall from the direction of the antechamber mag lifts.

I breathed a curse.

"What're we gonna do?" one of the men was stammering further down the line.

In his defense, it was a great question. But also utterly unhelpful. The panic was contagious.

"We're screwed, man," another said. "We're screwed!"

"Cut the chatter and stow the frillies, soldiers!" someone else roared in a tone that sent a jolt of recognition through me. "We have civilians to protect here and exactly zero time for your sad bullscud. You *will* hold the line. Understood?"

I joined the soldiers in shooting a dumbfounded look down the line, though my reason was different than theirs.

"Yes, sir!" the men barked, snapping to the ready.

"Docere Mathis?" I said.

He leaned back from the line long enough to shoot me a dark scowl. "That goes for you too, silver spoon. Eyes on the prize."

Just like I was still a tyro and the rest of it had never happened. I couldn't quite decide in that moment whether Mathis was a wonderful person or a terrible one. Either way, he was right. Had been right from the start.

I'd tried to fill the boots I wasn't ready to fill. Tried to outmaneuver the raknoth just like my dad. I'd failed just like my dad. And now people were dying for it.

I was going to have to face that fact if I made it out of this alive. But for now, I'd be damned if I was going to let another person pay for my mistakes. So I stammered "Yes, sir," and turned back to the line.

Elise arched an eyebrow at me. Johnny just shook his head, muttered something about gropping doceres, and opened fire on the approaching hybrids. I took aim and did the same, as did our allies on the line and across the hall.

Hybrids dropped in swaths.

More came.

I slapped my last feeder home just as a second horde poured out from the direction of the lifts. By the time my weapon clicked empty, a thick wave was closing on us. I dropped the rifle, used telekinesis to take out two more hybrids from afar with my knife, and was stepping forward with Elise to meet the rest when my extended senses trilled in alarm at some rapid shift ahead of us.

Someone was channeling.

No sooner had I registered the fact than the wave of hybrids organically parted as if controlled by a single mind, leaving an opening before us. In the blink of an eye, it was filled with a column of fire, lancing straight for us.

I didn't have time to think. I threw my hands up, fumbling to channel off the heat and pump it elsewhere. Before I could, the flames crashed short of us against some invisible barrier and instead splashed to the sides, straight into the parted walls of hybrids.

Even from a distance, the heat was unpleasant, but it was nothing compared to what the hybrids experienced. Green hides seared charcoal black, coaxing agonized screeches.

Beside me, Carlisle lowered his hand, and I almost joined the legion-naires in their victorious cheers. But I knew what was coming.

When the flames and charred hybrid smoke dissipated, Smirks and his female companion were striding towards us, Zar'Faenor stalking behind them.

The woman was tall and slender, and every inch of her looked mean. She almost could have been Elise's decade-older evil twin, and judging from the utterly frosty glare she skewered Carlisle with, I was guessing she'd been the one to conjure the column of fire.

Frosty the Seeker, then.

I was about to call open fire when the sharp report of Johnny's rifle beat me to it.

The shot was true. Or would have been, had the slug not snapped to a midair halt a foot from Frosty's chest. She gave the slug an indignant glance, then her hands struck out in Johnny's direction like twin vipers. I hit her with a telekinetic blast before she could attack. Gunfire erupted on either side of us. Hybrids roared.

Scud got messy fast.

Legionnaires fired on Smirks and Frosty, but the Seekers were ready, deflecting shots wildly off into the stone walls, or their own hybrids. Behind them, Zar'Faenor sprang at Carlisle with unnerving speed, eyes bursting to a crimson blaze. I hesitated, torn between Zar'Faenor and the Seekers. Then Frosty hit two legionnaires with a lance of flames, and the decision was made.

I charged forward, Elise at my side. Johnny and Phineas fell in on our flanks, Johnny down to his sidearms and Phineas, apparently having depleted his considerable armory, beating down hybrids with the butt of his rifle and the hard composite of his prosthetic fist.

Smirks' eyes locked onto mine, his expression grim. Frosty focused on Elise. I didn't want to know what was going on behind those cold, violent eyes. I didn't love our odds against two Seekers in the middle of this unholy scudstorm, either—especially not beaten and energy depleted as I was. But they had to be stopped. Preferably before the other raknoth joined us.

Frosty licked her lips as we closed, a tiny flame flickering over her hand. Smirks glanced toward Carlisle and Zar'Faenor, uncertain. I was about to hurl my knife at him when a flash of crimson above kicked my reflexes into action. I shoved Elise right and rolled left—just as Al'Kundesha and the High Cleric smashed down side by side, cracking the stone we'd vacated.

Phineas didn't miss a beat. He hit the red-eyed High Cleric with a punch that probably would have broken every bone in a non-prosthetic hand. The High Cleric stumbled backward with a growl. Al'Kundesha moved to retaliate and caught two of Johnny's slugs in the forehead before Carlisle swept in to bowl the raknoth over with telekinesis, Zar'Faenor hot on his heels.

Then I spotted Frosty charging at Elise, who was still pulling herself to her feet after my impromptu shove. I tore forward, forgetting about everything else, only to skid to a halt as Smirks cut me off.

"Wait!" he snapped, hands outstretched.

I'd already let my knife fly, driving it straight for his chest with telekinesis. Something in his voice made me waver, though. Bastard that he was, maybe I even had reservations about running him through.

Either way, the hesitation cost me. The knife jerked to a halt in midair as he caught on with his own telekinesis. I viciously cursed myself for hesitating, painfully aware of the flash of flames from Elise and Frosty's direction.

Then Smirks' gaze darted over my shoulder, his eyes widening, just as my senses screamed a warning on my left flank.

I dipped right and felt the rush of wind from the strike that probably would've knocked my head off. Zar'Faenor. He kept coming, sure and swift. I kicked his planted knee to little effect. Lifted him a few inches with telekinesis to keep his feet off the ground as I backpedaled.

Alpha he was heavy. My head was spinning with the effort.

Then he responded with telekinesis of his own and drove me to my knees with the inexorable weight of a skimmer landing on my shoulders. I lost my grip. He thudded to the dark, bloody stone and stalked toward me with finality, holding me firm in his telekinetic snare.

My mind went oddly blank, watching his murderous approach.

Then I noticed Smirks standing there, my knife in hand, his gaze darting back and forth between us, calculating. A flutter of hope. I didn't trust it. Not until Smirks darted in and jammed my knife into the back of Zar'-Faenor's neck with a snarl.

It was a stupid plan. But, then again, I'm pretty sure Smirks was only just then realizing the full extent of what he was up against. Too late.

The knife jerked to a halt against Zar'Faenor's hide, and the raknoth turned almost casually to backhand Smirks twenty feet through the air before turning back to me, ready to finish it. I reached out to call for Carlisle.

An aggravated shriek split the chaotic hall before I could—the High Cleric's, I realized. Carlisle had the raknoth pinned facedown and was working a dagger laboriously at the back of his skull while Phineas, Johnny, and a few legionnaires harassed Al'Kundesha.

With a frustrated growl, Zar'Faenor leapt to the aid of his distressed underling.

With his telekinetic ocean lifted from my shoulders, I staggered to my feet and whirled for Elise. My stomach plunged at the sight of Frosty hauling her dazed form up by her badly scorched armor skin, cocking a fist to strike.

At the last second, though, Elise snapped to and headbutted the Seeker right in the nose. Frosty stumbled back with a curse, blood already gushing down into her snarling mouth. Elise kicked her spear up to her hand and swung for the Seeker's head. Frosty struck out her hands, cold fury in her eyes, and blasted Elise backward just before her spear haft connected.

I caught Elise with telekinesis and was setting her down when Frosty drew a small gun from her tunic and leveled it at Elise with a feral grin. "Dodge this one, bitch."

I threw my mind at the gun, intending to rip it from Frosty's hand. Once I turned the barrel away from Elise, though, I decided to instead pour energy into the propellant in the bottom round of the gun's feeder.

The gun exploded in Frosty's hand.

Not a large explosion, but enough to leave her right hand in shambles. Before she could do more than cradle her wounded appendage in shock, Elise closed the distance and dealt her a brutal blow to the head.

A scrap of tension bled out of me as Frosty hit the stone floor. One more Seeker down, though I still wasn't sure why Smirks had decided to—

"Hal!" Elise cried, wide eyes directed over my shoulder.

I tried to move, but an inhumanly strong forearm caught me and pulled me tight by the throat just before something plunged into my shoulder. Razor-sharp pain ripped through me. I cried out, thrashing against the iron grip as it pulled me closer.

"Come now," Al'Kundesha growled by my ear. "I did warn you not to struggle."

CHAPTER 44
EQUIVALENT EXCHANGE

Two things occurred to me through the wave of fire ripping through my shoulder.

Firstly, judging by the position of Al'Kundesha's hand on my right shoulder, it wasn't some weapon he'd driven into my upper back, but his own clawed thumb. It was almost as disturbing as it was painful. Almost.

Secondly, and far more importantly, the sneaky bastard must've ridden that pain straight through my mental defenses, because I was no longer in control of my body.

I cursed myself as he settled sharp claws uncomfortably close to my throat. How had I been so careless?

"Don't, girl," came my own flat and empty tone—Al'Kundesha speaking through me, I realized, to chide Elise, who was clearly contemplating trying to liberate me from his grasp. "Drop your stick and behave."

Her face twisted in confusion, then her eyes widened in understanding. The bitter helplessness on her face as she dropped her spear and raised her hands in surrender made me burn with impotent rage.

I cursed myself and Al'Kundesha alike as he turned us to face the others.

Ahead, Carlisle pivoted inside a swipe from the High Cleric and, with a sharp twist and some telekinetic aid, hurled the raknoth into a group of hybrids twenty feet away. Without pause, he tucked just under Zar'Faenor's incoming arms, came to his feet on the raknoth's flank, dagger in hand…

and jolted to a stop mid-thrust, as if a giant, invisible hand had clamped down around him.

Zar'Faenor. It had to be.

They faced each other in motionless silence, locked in some invisible telekinetic struggle. I tried to reach out to help, but Al'Kundesha shut my effort down, wiggling his thumb in my shoulder for a fresh shock of good measure pain.

"Stay," my voice added, my left arm rising to point at Elise, who'd taken a step towards Carlisle.

She froze, jaw tightly clenched.

I watched helplessly, longing to tear Al'Kundesha and the rest of his ilk to pieces. The High Cleric was back on his feet now, stalking toward Carlisle's frozen form.

Panic swelled in my chest.

Then Johnny rose from Phineas' side and leapt onto the High Cleric's back with a wordless cry. He bludgeoned the butt of his sidearm into the raknoth's temple over and over, shouting with each slam.

"Eat. My. Butt. You. Holy. Prick!"

The blows didn't do much serious damage, but Johnny's stunt did distract everyone enough for Carlisle to break free of his mental wrestling match with Zar'Faenor.

He was just bursting into motion when Al'Kundesha, apparently having seen enough, roared loud enough to half-deafen me.

"Enough," he boomed into the hall's resulting silence, using his own voice this time. "Lay down your weapons."

No offer of peace or a quick end. He just dug into my shoulder and let my scream do the convincing.

Zar'Faenor glanced our way in what might have been annoyance. Behind him, the hybrids had fallen still, and what legionnaires remained watched them warily as the last load of civilians piled into the waiting transport. On the other side of the Great Hall, nothing moved.

Johnny slid off the High Cleric's back and dropped his guns in surrender. I was going to be sick. Hundreds lay dead. Civilians. Legionnaires. All lost because of me. And now my friends...

I would have collapsed if Al'Kundesha hadn't been holding me at attention.

The raknoth had won. Again. And I'd failed.

I watched Carlisle, hoping, praying.

"Leave me," I sent desperately. *"Get the others out of here. I know you can.*

You can still rally the Legion. Don't let them die because of me."

He couldn't hear me, of course. Not with Al'Kundesha corralling me.

I could see Carlisle's mind turning, weighing the options, understanding that we weren't all getting out of there alive. Could see his conflict. Then his shoulders eased, and he gave me a look that reached inside and broke something.

It was goodbye.

His daggers fell to the stone with a pair of metallic clangs. I wanted to scream. But I couldn't. I couldn't do a damn thing.

"Kill them all," Zar'Faenor growled.

Time slowed.

Al'Kundesha's hand tightened on my throat, claws breaking the skin. The High Cleric turned with a vicious swipe at Johnny's head. Elise was screaming my name.

Carlisle spun, hands shooting out toward me and Johnny.

Al'Kundesha's hand tugged gratingly away from my throat, resisting every inch. Unseen force plowed the High Cleric away from Johnny mid-strike. Al'Kundesha's second hand was pulled from my shoulder, and the raknoth staggered away from me with a frustrated snarl.

Then Zar'Faenor closed on Carlisle. Carlisle whirled to meet him, graceful as ever, and jerked to a halt as Zar'Faenor's fist tore through his abdomen with a sickening wet *thunk*.

Time stopped. All I could see was Carlisle's face, his mouth agape, face contorted at first with pain and shock but then softening into something else entirely—something I'd never seen from him before. Something I didn't understand.

He looked at peace.

He raised his hands, cupping the face of his old mentor as if greeting a long-lost loved one. As if it were truly Cassius he held, and not a cold-hearted monster wearing his shell. He bowed his head, blood trickling from the corner of his mouth, and pressed his forehead to Zar'Faenor's.

Then something began to happen—the faintest violet light crackling at Carlisle's fingertips. Zar'Faenor's crimson eyes widened. He started to jerk away then froze, eyes dimming. Carlisle's lip twitched upward in the ghost of a smile, then he coughed blood and sagged against Zar'Faenor like he'd just winked out.

I lost control.

Pure, raw emotion screamed out of me, straight at the hardsteel walls of Al'Kundesha's telepathic prison as he approached me from behind. The raknoth caught the rushing tide of my mind, his step faltering. He dug in, and we struggled there, him holding me at bay but not quite pushing me back down.

Then another presence swept in and started ripping at the raknoth, prying his mental grip loose alongside me.

"C'mon, kid!" a voice growled in my mind. *"Fight the bastard!"*

Smirks.

I didn't pause to ask why. I just threw myself at Al'Kundesha all the harder, thrashing and clawing and biting until he had no choice but to give an inch to our combined minds. Then another. Then Elise crashed into Al'Kundesha with a hard boot to the head, and the raknoth's hold broke.

I spun, a hoarse cry tearing out of my throat.

Al'Kundesha was swinging at Elise, but she was ready, dipping, angling her spear to catch his shoulder, planting the haft so that the stone floor did most of the work for her. The spearhead drove home on Al'Kundesha's own momentum, and he growled in pain.

I didn't give him time to recover. I grabbed him with my mind and slammed him to floor, hard enough to crack stones. I raised his head and slammed it again. Lifted his whole body and smashed it into the pulverized stones as hard as I could, over and over.

He roared, fighting me.

I fought harder, barely even noticing when I crumpled to my knees from the exhaustion. I was distantly aware of Smirks' voice spurring me on—of Elise calling my name, fear in her tone. But I couldn't stop. Couldn't let him get away again.

I'd kill him. I'd kill all of them, no matter—

"Haldin."

I gasped, the voice cutting through me like ice water, tugging at me against the maelstrom. Ahead, Al'Kundesha shifted. I reached out, preparing to slam him again.

"Haldin, you have to go. Now."

There was no mistaking it. I felt him all around me now—all around the Great Hall—and it was only then I noticed the peculiar energy in the air. It swirled around us in thick waves, building and building until the air was howling with it, whipping at our hair and clothes.

And at the eye of the bizarre storm sat Carlisle, his head rocked back, a peaceful smile on his face. He still held Zar'Faenor, his fingertips radiant with that violet glow now. The eerie light was spreading across the raknoth's face. Consuming it. The energy building all the while.

"I can't let him live," I sent.

"Let it go, Haldin. Leave him to me."

I could feel the power thrumming around the room, pulsing through him like a giant bomb, ready to explode.

"Kill the Shaper!" Al'Kundesha roared behind me. "Kill him now!"

As one, the hybrids snapped to action.

The wind whipped harder, and it was like Alpha himself had reached down to swat them away across the Great Hall. The few who made it through unscathed, Carlisle took apart one by one, hurling them at the walls, slamming them to the ground hard enough that they wouldn't rise again.

I turned for Al'Kundesha, but Carlisle was already pulling him in, the raknoth punching through stone in futility for a strong enough handhold to stop himself.

"Let it go, Haldin."

Elise pulled me to my feet. Across the hall, what few legionnaires remained were piling into a transport, waving furiously for us to get over there. I watched Al'Kundesha slide closer to Carlisle.

Elise and I traded a look and, by some unspoken agreement, started for Carlisle together.

"No!" his voice poured into my mind. *"Get to the transport. Get the others out."*

"I'm not leaving you. We can still—"

"I'm already dead, Hal," he sent, more softly this time. *"My body is finished. I can't stop what I've started. It's over for me."*

"That's not true. You can... you can..."

But I didn't know how to finish the thought. Because I could feel the truth.

"Cassius is the only thing keeping me from losing control. He's here with me, Hal. I'm ready. But you need to get out. This entire hall is going to go up."

I couldn't look away from him. Couldn't stop seeing my parents, torn away.

"I can't... I can't lose you too."

"I'm sorry, Hal. But you will survive this. You must."

"Hal?" Elise said beside me.

I tore my gaze away from Carlisle and Al'Kundesha. I had to gasp for the breath to speak. "We need to go."

Her eyes widened. "We can't leave him!"

She was right. She was right and it made me want to scream. But there was nothing else to be done. I wished I could turn off the voice inside screaming for survival—that I could have the decency to lay down and die beside him. But I couldn't. The only thing I could do for him now was to make sure he knew his sacrifice wasn't wasted.

I felt like I was suffocating. Maybe Al'Kundesha had punctured my right lung. It didn't matter now.

"He can't stop this," was all I could manage as I took her hand and pulled her with me.

Johnny was laboring to haul Phineas up from the ground when we reached him.

"Leave me, kid," the burly man was mumbling weakly. "Get Elise out."

Johnny ignored him, and so did I. No one else was going to die because of me.

Before I got a hand on Phineas, though, Elise pushed me back and stepped in to help Johnny heave the large man to his feet. "We're not leaving anyone else behind, so get your butt moving, you old bear."

Johnny shot Elise a look that was plain enough. *What about Carlisle?*

She just shook her head, shooting a furtive glance at me.

Tears were streaming down my cheeks. I longed to collapse. To give up. They hauled Phineas off for the waiting transport without a word, refusing to let me. I followed after them, my feet like hunks of softsteel.

"I'm sorry, Carlisle. I'm so sorry."

"I gladly give my life for yours, Hal. You must not blame yourse—"

I felt a kind of mental shudder pass through him, accompanied by a tremendous surge of energy in the air around us. The winds whipped harder than ever.

Ahead, the transport lilted drunkenly.

"Not good," Johnny said, and I noticed his palmlight was flickering erratically in the storm.

"Can't... control this much longer," Carlisle sent. *"Hurry."*

I pulled from the considerable energy of Carlisle's storm to telekinetically float Phineas off Elise and Johnny.

"Come on!" I wheezed, ignoring their surprised looks and breaking into the closest thing to a run my burning lungs and battered body could manage.

It was all I could do not to collapse. Elise and Johnny chased after me, feet pounding heavily on the stone. The legionnaires were shouting out, waving us on.

"Hal... I want you to... want you to kn—"

Another surge of energy crackled through the air, and a gust of wind slapped me off my feet. I hit the stone roughly beside Phineas, who groaned in pain. Somewhere behind me, Johnny swore.

"Raish."

I looked around at Smirks' voice. I'd forgotten about him, but I saw him now, slung limply over the High Cleric's shoulder. Frosty was back on her feet, running beside them for a destroyed section of the duraglass wall not far from the transport.

"I was ready to die like a good boy," Smirks sent, *"but I'd rather not stick with these crazy bastards, if you're feeling charitable."*

I wasn't. I so wasn't. But I faltered anyway, glancing back at Elise and Johnny, who were hauling Phineas up the base of the transport's ramp. Whatever else he'd done, Smirks had tried to help us in the end.

"Carlisle..."

But I didn't have to finish the thought. Carlisle smacked the High Cleric down with the hand of Alpha and began pulling him in, despite the fact that he was already working to keep Al'Kundesha and a dozen hybrids contained.

Smirks spilled out in front of the raknoth and feebly started crawling our way.

Frosty eyed him, then the High Cleric. Then she turned her malicious glare on the waiting transport and waved a hand.

There was a series of loud pops from behind, and the sputtering groan of dying motors. I whirled at the sound of Elise's cry, hurling my senses outward. She hit the side of the building and caught on, the transport lurching out of view behind her, trailing smoke.

It must've been Carlisle who caught Phineas. The big man was floating from the sheer drop back into the hall by the time I was able to help.

"Okay," Johnny said when Elise was safely back inside, "looks like we'd better go see about those lifts."

I turned back to collect Smirks, half-expecting an attack from Frosty.

No such luck.

All I caught was a glimpse of the two disappearing through the destroyed section of wall into the dark evening, slung over the shoulders of the High Cleric, who'd apparently slipped Carlisle's control in the chaos.

"Nice try, kid," Smirks sent.

Then they were gone.

Johnny turned, eyes wide. "Did they just...?" He touched a hand to his earpiece. "Never mind. They're sending another transport back up to—"

The storm flared, whipping into us, and Johnny staggered precariously close to the edge before Elise yanked him back.

"No time for transport," Carlisle sent, the strain evident in his presence. Around us, the wind whipped harder, the air vibrating with energy. *"Jump. Now. Jump!"*

I stepped to the edge, hauling Phineas up with telekinesis, and held my arms out to the others. "I'll catch us."

Elise pressed in beside me without question. Johnny only glanced between me and the nearly two-thousand-foot fall five or six times before tossing his rifle and joining our huddle, pressing Phineas' barely conscious bulk between the three of us.

I clicked their cloaking pendants off. Just in case. Then I teetered, wasting precious seconds for one last look back.

"Go," Carlisle sent. His tone was soft now. At peace in the heart of the torrential storm he was holding fast. *"Go and know that I am proud of you, Haldin. Always."*

It was the last thing I ever heard him say.

It was the moment I knew I'd never forgive myself.

"Thank you, Carlisle." I couldn't breathe under the mountain of guilt on my chest. *"Thank you for everything."*

The last I saw of Carlisle, he was holding Al'Kundesha and an entire company of hybrids pinned to the ground, his forehead resting against his old mentor's, tunic billowing in gale force winds, tiny streaks of violet lightning arcing from his radiant form.

He looked like something out of a legend.

Then we were through the breached wall, falling through the open Divinity air, clinging together like our lives depended on it.

And he was gone.

I wanted to scream.

If I hadn't had the lives of the people I loved literally hanging in my hands, I probably would have. I certainly wouldn't have had the willpower left to stop even a falling pebble, much less four people. But the rushing air and the wide-eyed terror on Johnny's and Elise's faces forced me to hold it together.

I made the requisite links and began channeling energy from the combined falling mass of myself and Johnny to put the telekinetic brakes on Phineas and Elise. The strain was immediate.

Channeling from our own fall instead of an external source effectively halved the workload, but it still left me acting as the conduit for two falling bodies' worth of weight. It was basically the equivalent of lowering a four-hundred-pound weight down the side of a building with a rope.

And given that street level was nearly two thousand feet below—probably a good ten-second drop at free fall and closer to a full minute if we didn't want to die on impact—I was pretty sure I was liable to pass out from the exertion well before we reached a safe falling distance.

Panic clutched my chest, adding to my already considerable difficulty breathing.

I closed my eyes, sinking into the struggle until I almost forgot where I was.

"Hal?" came Elise's concerned voice.

"Hey big guy," Johnny added, "you hang in there now, okay? I don't wanna be a griddlecake... I don't even like griddlecakes, man!"

"You... love... griddlecakes," I grunted between shallow breaths.

"Ah scud, I do," Johnny agreed. "Alpha help me, I do."

"Drop me," Phineas groaned. "You can handle three."

My eyes snapped open at that, a flash of anger spiking me back to alertness.

"Alpha be damned," I growled. "No one else is dying here today, Phineas. So don't even gropping think about—"

By some morbid design of cosmic hilarity, that was the moment Carlisle must have finally let go of whatever he'd been holding back.

One moment, the night sky was calm and dark but for the pale moon low over the city. The next, the world was alive with a blinding flash of violet light.

It receded as quickly as it'd appeared, leaving a greenish-yellow glow burned into my eyes. Then the shockwave rolled over us with an enormous boom, nearly tearing us apart.

The violent gale of air that rushed in on its wake finished the job.

"No!" I screamed, hands and arms slipping, desperately clawing.

The four of us tumbled apart like so much pollen on a Midsummer wind.

I panicked for a precious second, mind whirling with how few I had left to waste, air whipping at my clothes and eyes, laughing away my attempts to think, to focus.

I shut it out. Closed it all down.

I found the street and steadied my wild spin with telekinesis. Found the other three plummeting in my senses—Phineas and Johnny off to the left and right, Elise front and center.

I opened my eyes and saw she'd had the good sense to stick out her arms and legs to slow her descent. She'd also pivoted around to face up toward me, which allowed me a clear view of the wide-eyed terror etched across her face.

"Scud," I muttered, eyeing the far-too-quickly approaching streets.

Six seconds. Maybe.

The tiny shapes of people lined the streets below, pointing emphatically upwards—at us or at the inferno at the top of the White Tower, I didn't know.

I reached out and channeled some of the energy of Elise's fall to push myself toward her. I overdid it. The relative shift in our velocities left me rocketing at Elise. We met with a hard thumping of bodies that took the breath out of both of us. Elise didn't complain. Just hooked her arms and legs around me and held on.

I caught a glimpse of rushing pavement and wide-eyed civilians scattering to clear our imminent landing zone.

No time.

I rolled us around, putting myself between Elise and the pavement. Closed my eyes and reached for the others.

I felt the street no more than a hundred feet below.

No time for intelligent control. No neat give and take. I threw my body down like old tram brakes and tore open the channels.

Energy ripped through me, so sudden and overwhelming I'm surprised I didn't pass out immediately. It roared through my ears. Distorted my vision. Vented explosively out to the air around us without waiting for my permission.

My vision was going dark.

I held on.

In the distance, my friends were screaming. Glass was shattering.

Because of me?

Didn't know. Couldn't think.

I held on.

Impact. Jarring, bone-shaking impact.

I felt Elise shift on top of me. Then I passed out.

CHAPTER 45

PIECES

Flames licked at the dry ashwood pyre, hungrily imploring each bramble and twig abandon its stable existence for one ephemeral moment of brilliant release. And release, they did. The crackles filled the silence that rested too heavily between our somber gathering, inviting someone to step forward and pay their tributes.

No one did.

Not for the first time, I felt Johnny glance my way. Franco was a few seconds later. Elise simply held my hand in silence, though I can't imagine she wasn't thinking similar thoughts. All of them watching me like some wounded pup. Or was it that they were waiting for me to speak first?

As if I had the right.

Carlisle had come to save me. And now he was gone.

The knowledge was a bottomless pit inside me.

Waking up in the medica after our fall hadn't been a pleasant experience. Not one bit. I'd felt exactly like one would expect after having fallen out of a half-mile-high tower. Still did, in fact. But it had been paltry compared to the realization that had followed.

Carlisle was gone. Hundreds had died in the Great Hall. Civilians. Legionnaires. All of them gone because of me—because I'd thought we could beat the raknoth at their own game. And now…

My attention drifted to Franco as he stepped forward, preparing to speak. I felt him watching me again, a silent question in his posture. I kept my eyes on the fire.

"I'd say the lines," Franco finally said, "but something tells me it's not what he would've wanted."

He had that right, at least. When our magnanimous Legion keepers had finally seen fit to allow us to gather in the tiny outpost courtyard, the outpost's cleric had made a point of publicly disavowing himself from any service involving me, the demon previously known as Carlisle, or any who'd associate with us.

Furious as his biting words had made me, though, it was for the best. A Sanctum cleric was the last person Carlisle would've wanted presiding over his pyre.

As it was, it was just the six of us. Me, Johnny, and Elise. Franco, James, and Phineas. If Carlisle had had any family or friends outside of that, we didn't know about them, and I doubted our Legion babysitters would've let us notify them anyway.

"Above all else," Franco continued, "Carlisle was a good man. Determined, yes. Driven. But always kind and good. He lived a hard life. I can't claim to have known him as well as I would've liked. Carlisle was not an easy man to get to know. All I can truly be sure of is that he deserved more than the life he was dealt. But my heart is glad knowing that, at the very least, he wasn't alone in the end."

The way he looked at me as he said that last part... the way the others turned my way... I couldn't bear it. I stared at the ground, a deep, steady ache pulsing through me from my stomach up to my teary eyes.

"I barely knew him for a season," I muttered.

I didn't add that it was my fault he was gone. I knew what they'd say.

"You knew him better than anyone else, Hal," Elise said softly.

I refused to meet their waiting eyes. I kept my gaze on the flickering pyre. Empty.

Carlisle's sacrifice, I'd learned, had atomized the entire Great Hall, and everything in it. There'd been nothing left to burn. Just like with my parents. I wavered on my feet, overwhelmed by it all, the walls starting to crack.

Then their collective attention shifted off me, and I felt some of the pressure bleed away, lowering me mercifully back toward the numb emptiness that'd filled much of the past few days since the White Tower.

"Would anyone else like to say something?" Franco asked.

Silence stretched.

"He… he never made me feel small," James said tentatively. "The things he could do…" He shook his head. "He could've had anything. Probably could've trampled us like insects. But he always looked at me like I mattered, like he saw the best version of who I could be, even if I couldn't. He saved my life, and I won't forget it. I… Thank you, Carlisle."

Everyone voiced their agreement. Everyone but me.

I wanted to say something. Wanted to thank Carlisle for having been exactly the man I'd needed him to be. For showing me what I was truly capable of. I wanted to apologize for having failed him in the end, and to promise to make amends someday. But I couldn't seem to open my mouth. Couldn't seem to do anything but watch the pyre flicker and curl down until the smoldering pile of ash rivaled the one in my gut.

We sat in the courtyard for a while after that, watching the sun set. I listened to the others trade stories about Carlisle. Even added a few of my own, eventually. It wasn't much, and it only deepened the ache in my heart, knowing that this was all Enochia could muster for the man who'd given everything for them. But it was something.

"I don't know what to say, Hal," Franco said when he caught me alone at the edge of the courtyard, staring off at nothing in particular. I didn't know what to say either, so I said nothing as he lay his hand on my shoulder. "I want you to know, Hal, that as long as we're alive, you have family. You're not alone."

On any other day, his words probably would've stirred up a rush of emotions in me. Scud, I might have even had to fight back a tear or two. But I was too tired—too shell-shocked and emotionally raw—to do anything other than reach stiffly up and put my hand over his. He seemed to understand, and after a second, we broke the contact and went back to join the others.

"You okay, buddy?" Johnny asked as I settled down beside him.

I felt Elise's eyes on me, both of them watching me with an intensity that made me want to crawl under a rock. I looked around the courtyard, as if expecting I might find an answer lurking somewhere. "I'm okay."

Had it just been Johnny there, or just Elise, I might have said something else. Maybe. But with both of them staring, and with the others nearby… I wasn't looking to start group therapy time. Not right now.

"What do you need, Hal?" Elise asked, taking my hand. "We're here for you. No matter what."

I honestly wasn't sure how to answer that.

What did I need? It felt like a meaningless question. I was empty. Utterly spent. Numb. Maybe it was denial, or some kind of coping mechanism. Maybe I was just too exhausted to feel a single thing. What I needed right then, I finally decided, was to not think about any of it.

"Are we sure we're safe here?" I asked, directing the question toward Franco. "How are things looking?"

"We're safe," Franco said.

"Ish," Johnny added. "There are still a lot of people asking a lot of questions right now, but we've got enough legionnaires at this outpost who were at the battle for Sanctuary. They have some idea what's going on. And the rest of the Legion is coming around, what with all the witnesses who saw the High General sprout red eyes and try to eat us."

Between the long stints of fitful sleep and the generous armed guard detail they'd had on me at all hours, I hadn't really been able to catch up on much beyond the fact that Enochia was in a tumult and that the raknoth seemed to have gone to ground with the considerable remainder of their hybrid armies. They'd kept me away from the reels. I might have fought it if they hadn't let Elise and Johnny visit, or if they'd tried to keep me any longer. As it was, it hadn't been too hard to convince me to lie there for a few days, letting the hours numbly slide by.

"Are they going to release us?" I asked.

Franco looked less certain about that. "I think we're moving in the right direction, at least. Johnny's right, with all the witness reports of the High General and the High Cleric going red-eyed and murdering civilians, we have a lot less bullscud to cut through this time. We already delivered the footage you tried to broadcast from Sanctuary. It's only a matter of time until all of Legion command is ready to acknowledge the raknoth threat."

"They're still trying to deny it?"

"You know how they are," Johnny said. "Especially when it comes to wild stories about blood-sucking alien invaders. You have to admit, it's a lot to wrap your head around."

"They've got an entire damn conquered Legion fortress for proof," I said.

"An empty base," Franco pointed out.

I scowled at that. Johnny had already filled me in on that much. The hybrids had left Sanctuary a charred, smoking ghost town. Most of the survivors who'd escaped—Johnny's family thankfully among them—had taken up temporary residence in Oasis, Haven, and half a dozen smaller bases.

"But they have hundreds of witnesses," I said. "And the rest of the hybrids can't have just disappeared."

"I've heard rumors that a sizeable force was spotted maneuvering near Haven on the night of the White Tower," Franco said. "Hybrids numbering in the thousands. I haven't been able to confirm it, but if that's truly the case—"

"They were getting ready to launch a full-on assault on Enochia," I said.

"Or at least to knock out the next most secure fortress on the planet while everyone was busy freaking out about an attack on the White Tower," Johnny added.

"But then they lost their commanders," I said, thinking it through. Carlisle kills Zar'Faenor and Al'Kundesha, then the hybrids mysteriously go missing the same night? I doubted it was coincidence.

Franco nodded. "Some might admit that their withdrawal from Sanctuary and everywhere else means the raknoth are redrawing their plans, or possibly restructuring whatever chain of command might exist among them."

"The rest," Elise said, "are probably being none too shy in pointing out that the easiest explanation for the miraculous disappearance of the blood-sucking alien armies is that they never really existed to begin with."

"That's—How can they..." But I couldn't even finish my thought for the weight of the answer slapping me in the face. People believed what they wanted to believe, usually right up until the proof became so undeniably vast that they were forced to sink or swim.

"They're going to see reason, Hal," Franco said. "Some may just need a few days to gather reports and process."

"They'll get there," Johnny agreed. "I've even heard some of the legionnaires around here starting to admit that maybe you guys weren't really terrorists after all. Except for the whole Demon of Divin-nnnever mind," he said, cutting off midsentence at a sharp look from Elise.

I glanced between them. "Demon of what?"

Elise glared at Johnny, then sighed. "Demon of Divinity."

"What's the Demon of Divinity?" I asked, pretty sure I already knew the answer.

Johnny's face scrunched in apology as he slowly raised a finger to point at me.

"It's been all over the reels," Elise started slowly. "The whole planet's talking about what happened at the White Tower. And there are plenty of eye witnesses trying to explain how things really happened, of course. But, you know, things got hazy when the fighting started and the cameras started going down. The one thing pretty much everyone saw, though, was you floating on thin air when they tried to… you know."

"Demon of Divinity," I repeated.

"Just don't think about it," Elise said.

"Or think of it like being a celebrity," Johnny said.

"For being a gropping demon?" I growled.

"Well…" Johnny raised a finger, as if a wise point were imminent, then dropped it back down. "That part's a little shaky right now, I guess. What?" he added, spreading his hands at the glare Elise shot him. "They'll come around." He waved a hand at me. "Look at that face. Who could hate that face?"

"Half this damn outpost, apparently," I muttered, suddenly understanding all the strange, frightened, and sometimes outright violent looks I'd been getting these past few days. Sweet Alpha, one of the techs had nearly jumped out of her skin when I roused from sleep to find her changing one of my IV bags.

Demon.

Alpha-damn this planet.

I'd lost everything, then I'd picked myself up just to lose it again. And it still wasn't enough. I stood, unable to cope with it anymore, needing to be alone. My armed guard bristled at my approach, but I strode past them without a word, headed straight back for my bed in the medica.

No one tried to stop me.

THE FOLLOWING days were not happy ones.

Whether by Franco's doing or simply by the merit of pulling their own heads out of the dirt, Legion command finally deigned it acceptable to grant me limited freedom within the outpost. It hardly made things better. Everywhere I went, people stared. Some stopped what they were doing and openly reached for weapons. Some just looked angry or scared. Others curious. A few even looked sympathetic, but none spoke. Well, aside from the few who called me Demon under their breaths.

I was half-surprised one of the more brazen packs hadn't tried to jump me yet.

Of course, it probably helped that I was rarely alone. Elise and Johnny barely left my side, inundating me with a steady stream of concerned affection and updates they gleaned from the reels when I wasn't paying attention. I suppose I could've turned to the reels myself, but I wasn't ready to hear the things they were saying about me and Carlisle. Elise tried to show me a few pieces from the survivors who wanted to thank us, but I couldn't bring myself to watch those either.

Enochia was reeling in the power vacuums left behind by the simultaneous death and disappearance of the High General and the High Cleric. Replacements vied for position like a pack of wild hounds, some with purer intentions than others. And meanwhile, by my count, there were still at least five raknoth and at least one or two turned Seekers out there, doing Alpha knew what with their hybrid army.

No one seemed to know where Alton Parker had vanished off to, but I could only assume he was intimately involved. The missing High Cleric aside, that left three more nameless, faceless raknoth who could feasibly be anyone, anywhere. It occurred to me that what remained of the Seeker core could be invaluable in tracking our enemies down, but it wasn't like anyone here was going to listen to me.

That became abundantly clear on the day that a new High Cleric was chosen. Not that the Sanctum said it outright. But when the stories about me and Carlisle—good or bad—began vanishing from the reels without a trace, somehow, it didn't strike me as a good sign.

I couldn't help wondering how long it would be before an assassin might show up in the night to quietly rid the world of my problematic existence. At least if that happened, I'd be with my parents again.

I thought about them every day. About the kind of man my dad had been to stand up to the High General of the Legion. About my mom's eternal warmth, and the way she'd always managed to remain her own person, to balance the belief and the doubt.

I thought about Carlisle. What he'd gone through in the twelve years since losing Cassius. Everything he'd done for me in our short time together. As well as I'd come to know him, it was strange to realize how little I knew about where he'd come from, or the person he'd been before I'd met him. The thought saddened me. But maybe it didn't really matter who he'd been in the past.

The more I thought about Carlisle, the more I wished I could have talked to him about the things I'd seen in Al'Kundesha's memories. Visions of Urth haunted my dreams, and I couldn't help but wonder what had happened to those strange distant people who'd somehow touched the raknoth with the sickness that had apparently driven them here.

Could Urth still be out there, turning happily along, holding some answer to the raknoth threat?

I cautiously talked to Franco about it. I didn't want to be the one to suggest we go looking for the alien spaceship that must still be hidden somewhere on Enochia. I definitely didn't want to be the one to propose the possibility of one day finding Urth ourselves. But luckily, Franco was Franco. Once the seed was planted, he needed to know too. He couldn't help but start digging.

In the meantime, I tried to convince myself the entire thing was nothing more than an idle musing. More of a daydream fantasy than a real intention. After all, there was certainly no shortage of messes to be cleaned up on Enochia before we worried about Urth.

I just wasn't sure where my place was in all of it.

Johnny didn't hesitate to return to Legion duty, convinced as he was that it was the best way he could help. I was less than certain, but maybe my view had been skewed by my stint as a hunted man. Either way, I refrained from making any plans for official Legion reinstatement. I kind of doubted they would've taken me even if I did.

I couldn't deny that I longed for vengeance, but with Al'Kundesha and Zar'Faenor dead, I wasn't entirely sure where I should expect to find it. The raknoth were still out there, recovering and doing Alpha knew what else. I needed to know they'd face justice for what they'd done. But right then, I also needed time. Time to recover. Time to train Elise to use her new abilities.

So when the day came that Johnny was set to ship off to his new position at Haven, I offered my hand and tried to sound believable as I told him I'd be right behind him when the time came.

He frowned down at my hand, then slapped it aside and wrapped me in a bear hug. "Broto," he said, still hugging me, "when the scud hits, I'll never doubt again that you're the one standing firm behind me."

I smiled a little despite myself. "You want a redo on that one?"

I felt him shaking his head as he gave me a few pats on the back. "Nah. That came out perfect." He finally stepped back, his grin sobering as he studied my face. "You take care of yourself, okay buddy?"

I nodded.

"Who knows," he added. "With a little luck, maybe I can even see to it they don't call you a terrorist next time we need your help."

I smiled. "Crazier things have happened, I guess."

"No kidding. Secret powers. Alien invasions. You scoring a girlfriend before me." He shook his head. "Boggles the mind, it does." He glanced at his waiting transport, which was nearly loaded now. "Anyway…"

I clapped him on the shoulder. "Don't let them give you any scud at Haven, okay?"

"Of course not. I've got a whole plan figured out."

I smiled. "Oh yeah? Just gonna tell them to grop off and regale them with your record as a war hero?"

He grinned, shaking his head. "Nah. I think I'll probably just tell 'em I'm best friends with the Demon of Divinity."

END BOOK ONE

AUTHOR'S NOTE
(UPDATED SEPTEMBER 7TH, 2020)

Let me ask you something, Dear Reader: Do you remember the worst nightmare you've ever had?

It's probably a rhetorical question here, given that it's kinda hard to reply via book back matter. But, if you're like me, you probably have a few (thousand) you'll never forget.

Truth be told, when I was a wee little lad, it was actually a rare occasion I *didn't* jolt awake at least once to go running and crying to dear ol' Mom about the nightmare flavor of the night. It was pretty bad.

There were the running-from-monsters dreams (*legs like Jello in quicksand*). There were the random falling dreams (*I never woke up in time to avoid impact*). There were the midnight murder castle sagas (*embarrassingly gratuitous for the mind of a five-year-old child*).

There was even a gang of persistent mobsters who'd often chase me from one shifting dreamscape to the next, beating me bloody whenever they caught me (*my guidance counselor recommended I try sprouting wings and flying away from them—those cheeky pricks sprouted handguns and shot me down*).

(In hindsight, it's *possible* I was wound a bit tight for a child.)

Through it all, though, there was one nightmare that I'll always remember above all the rest. The one that struck me straight to the core.

See, by that point, the nightmares had become so frequent and multilayered (a nightmare within a nightmare, Inception-style) that I could never really trust that I was *actually* safe until I'd made it to dear ol' Ma's arms.

Expanding on the Inception metaphor, she was basically the totem *(bless her friggin' heart)* that anchored me back to the real world and convinced me that I was actually awake and everything was okay. (For real this time.)

Then came that fateful night.

That night, I was running from the red-eyed lizard people at the carnival *(you know, THAT old chestnut).* Running straight to dear ol' Ma, in that particular dream.

I still remember the way she reached for me in that yellow pajama dress of hers, beckoning me into the safety of her embrace.

And I'll never forget the stomach-clenching horror I felt as she morphed into one of the monsters right before my eyes.

(We're talking full-on green, scaly Mama-monster in a friggin' yellow nightgown. Which, admittedly, sounds kinda comical nowadays. But back then…)

Imagine, little Momma's Boy waking from yet another terrible nightmare only to find, for the first time ever, that he had no one to run to. That he was in fact suddenly TERRIFIED of the one person who was always supposed to be there, no matter what.

That night, for the first time ever, I felt what it was like to lose my trusted totem. Reality was broken. Nowhere was safe.

Of course, I got over it in the light of day. But that feeling? It stuck with me. I'll never forget it. I'm pretty sure it was the first time I'd ever felt truly unsafe—my first naive little inkling that the world, for all its bubbly "rightness," could also be a dangerous place, and that even the people we trust the most can sometimes fail us without warning, sometimes for reasons beyond their control.

Momma couldn't protect me from everything, after all.

(How's *that* for a sobering tale of five-year-old disillusionment?!)

And while I'd totally be lying if I said I ever suspected back then that this experience had planted the seeds of what would eventually grow into an epic dystopian alien invasion trilogy...

Well, I guess it doesn't matter what I suspected. Because that's totally what happened. (Or so I tell myself now, looking back through narrative-colored glasses.)

It's often said that most writers' first novels end up being highly autobiographical, whether they like it or not (and even if that "autobiographical" nature ends up hidden beneath several layers of otherworldly magic powers and alien incursions and whatnot).

To that end, you probably won't be all that surprised to hear that this story—that of a young man finding his once-unshakeable world suddenly overturned by insidious alien invasion—was actually the first full-length novel I ever wrote.

(It probably also doesn't come as a surprise that the red-eyed lizard people made their triumphant return as the culprits of this shadowy planetary heist.)

What you might NOT have guessed (unless you happen to be quite the shrewd psychoanalyst) is that I also lost my father to pancreatic cancer in the middle of writing this book.

And while that's not something I just toss casually into discussion most days, in this case it seems particularly pertinent.

See, it's probably no coincidence that this story begins and ends with Hal losing father figures. I still remember the first night I sat down and started writing. I'd just gotten home from grad school to visit my father as he began chemo in the wake of his diagnosis.

Interestingly enough, the very first draft actually didn't even show Hal's life in Sanctuary before Kublich's attack. It opened (perhaps cringe-worthily) directly with Hal hearing his mother scream and racing out of the sim room to find a red-eyed monster laying into his parents.

That same draft made it about as far as Hal's trial at the White Tower before I finally realized the rather obvious fact that I had no clue how to finish the story.

It was only months after my father had passed that I finally came back to the manuscript and saw Carlisle's sacrifice sitting there clear as day, just waiting to be written. Once that was done, I returned to the opening chapter to add an *actual* opening and properly explore what it was Hal had had before that red-eyed monster came bursting in to take it all away.

The reader needed to better understand what Hal had lost, I told myself. Which was probably true. But in hindsight, I can't help but think now that the same thing was probably doubly true of myself.

The funniest part in all of this is that it took me well over a year to look back and realize what I'd actually done—how the pieces had fallen in such neat, predictable synchronicity with the events of my own life.

And if you're currently wondering why in the name of Alpha I'm telling you ANY of this overly personal mumbo jumbo... well, amongst other things, I guess it's because there's the stuff that we bumbling pen monkeys *mean* to say with our stories... and then there's the stuff that falls out of us whether we intend to let it or not.

In my limited experience, it's that latter bit that tends to scratch at the good stuff.

All of which to say, I sure hope you've found something of value in these pages—even if it was just a compelling read. This story has meant a lot to me for a lot of different reasons, and I truly do appreciate you coming along for the ride.

In fact, now that we're proper old chums, I'd love to give you something more than a simple *thank you*.

I'd love to give you the rest of the story.

See, the more I realized how much of me was tied up in this book, the more I was pulled to circle back and revisit the events surrounding Hal's journey in *Shadows of Divinity*.

I ended up writing two additional stories. (In addition to the next two books of the main trilogy, that is.)

The first was a kind of eulogy for Carlisle, written in the format of a short story called *Eye of the Storm*.

The second was a full-length novel called *Fallen*, which explored the events both leading up to and throughout *Shadows of Divinity* through the eyes of none other than Garrett (AKA Smirks) the Seeker.

I was pleasantly surprised by what I found in writing them both. And today, I'd like to share them with you, free of charge. All you have to do is tell me where to send them.

Interested?

Just go to: *lukermitchell.com/shadows-of-divinity-signup*

There, you'll be able to join my mailing list and download your free copies of *Fallen* and *Eye of the Storm*.

Plus, in addition to occasional behind-the-scenes notes like the one above (which was actually adapted from a few of my Sunday newsletters), as a member of the list, you'll *also* get access to free books from all of my other fictional worlds—as well as discounts and short stories you won't find anywhere else. (Carlisle's *Eye of the Storm* story, for instance, is only available in the box set or to my mailing list readers.)

All you have to do is visit the link above to join the party and grab both Enochian War stories free today!

'Nuff said? Got it.

If newsletters and email shenanigans aren't your bag, no worries. You can also just go to *lukermitchell.com/books* to find the full list of my published works—including *Demons of Divinity* (Enochian War Book Two). Whichever way you go, I sure do hope you enjoy your next adventure!

Thanks so much for reading.

We'll see you on the other side.

Cheers,
Luke Mitchell

ABOUT THE AUTHOR

Not a llama. Mostly human.

Luke is a storyteller whose dreams include learning the ways of the Force, becoming a sentient robot, and maybe even one day growing up. Also, lots of zombies… Don't ask.

Oh, and that "growing up" bit? That was a lie.

After studying engineering science at Penn State and neuroengineering at Drexel, Luke finally decided to throw in the towel on building a working Iron Man suit and opted instead to simply make things up and write them down. Boy, is he having more fun now.

When he's not holed up in his writing cave trying to string words together, he can often be found powerlifting, video-gaming, reading, and/or drinking the darkest, most roasty beers he can get his mitts on. Sometimes all at once.

But you know what? That's enough about Luke. He's really not that interesting. Still, if you'd like to say hi to him for whatever reason, he'd probably be glad to hear from you!

Go to **lukermitchell.com/shadows-of-divinity-signup** to join the mailing list and grab your free copies of *Fallen* and the list-exclusive, *Eye of the Storm*, today!

~

Additionally (as you wish)…

Follow me on BookBub for new release alerts
bookbub.com/authors/luke-r-mitchell

Browse the rest of my published titles
lukermitchell.com/books

Join the Patreon team for digital copies of ALL of my work (past, present, and future) — and much more!
patreon.com/lukermitchell

Thank you for reading!